GREEK
BUYING HIS BRIDE

GREEK BACHELORS
COLLECTION

January 2018

February 2018

March 2018

April 2018

May 2018

June 2018

GREEK BACHELORS: BUYING HIS BRIDE

SARAH MORGAN

CAITLIN CREWS

JULIA JAMES

Published in Great Britain 2017
By Mills & Boon, an imprint of HarperCollins*Publishers*
1 London Bridge Street, London, SE1 9GF

GREEK BACHELORS: BUYING HIS BRIDE © 2017 Harlequin Books S.A.

Bought: The Greek's Innocent Virgin © Sarah Morgan 2008
His for a Price © Caitlin Crews 2014
Securing the Greek's Legacy © Julia James 2014

ISBN: 978-0-263-93564-6

09-0518

MIX
Paper from
responsible sources
FSC™ C007454

This book is produced from independently certified FSC™ paper to ensure responsible forest management.

For more information visit: www.harpercollins.co.uk/green

Printed and bound in Spain
by CPI, Barcelona

BOUGHT: THE GREEK'S INNOCENT VIRGIN

SARAH MORGAN

USA Today bestselling author **Sarah Morgan** writes lively, sexy stories for both the Mills & Boon Modern and Medical Romance lines. As a child, Sarah dreamed of being a writer and, although she took a few interesting detours on the way, she is now living that dream. With her writing career, she has successfully combined business with pleasure and she firmly believes that reading romance is one of the most satisfying and fat-free escapist pleasures available.

CHAPTER ONE

'I'VE FOUND HER, Angelos. And she's a goddess.'

Hearing the sound of his father's voice, Angelos Zouvelekis interrupted his conversation with the Greek ambassador to France and turned. 'Found who?' The fact that his father had made an effort to come tonight was a good sign. A few months ago he had been a broken man, unwilling to leave his isolated villa after his second painful divorce in six years.

'The perfect woman for you.' His father shook his head in disbelief, but the corners of his eyes crinkled as he smiled. 'Sometimes I wonder if you're really my son. This place is full of gorgeous, beautiful women and what do you do? You talk to boring men in suits. Where did I go wrong with you?'

Seeing the surprise in the ambassador's eyes, Angelos smoothly excused himself and drew his father to one side. 'For me, tonight is about business. I hold this ball every year. The purpose is to part the rich and famous from their money.'

'Business, business, business.' Visibly exasperated, his father raised his hands in despair. 'Does business keep you warm at night? Does it cook you dinner? Does it raise your children? *Always* with you it is business, Angelos, and already you are a billionaire! You have enough money! You don't need any more money! *What you need is a good woman!*'

Several heads turned in their direction, but Angelos simply

laughed. 'Tonight I'm not making money. I'm giving it away. And you're shocking everyone. Behave yourself,' he said mildly, 'or I'll tell Security to remove you from the building.' But it had been such a long time since his father had summoned sufficient energy to nag him about marriage that he felt nothing but relief. 'And I don't need you to find me a woman.'

'Why? Do you find one on your own? No, you don't. Not a proper one. You spend your time with women who would not make suitable wives.'

'That's why I pick them,' Angelos murmured, but his father frowned his disapproval, dismissing his comment with another wave of his hand.

'I know who you pick! The whole world knows who you pick, Angelos, because the stories are in every newspaper. One week it is a Savannah, the next it is a Gisella—never the same woman for more than a few weeks, and always they are thin, thin, thin.' His Greek accent thickening his words, Costas Zouvelekis made a disparaging noise. 'How can you be happy with a woman who doesn't enjoy her food? Does a woman like that cook for you? No. Does she enjoy life? No, of course not. How can a woman enjoy life when she is starving hungry? The women you pick have the legs and the hair, and they are like athletes in the bedroom, but would they care for your children? No. Would they—?'

'I don't need a woman to cook. I have staff for that purpose.' Angelos wondered briefly whether inviting his father to this particular function might have been a mistake after all. 'And I don't have any children for a woman to care for.'

His father gave a snort of exasperation. 'I know you don't, and I *want* you to have children. That is the point I am making! You are thirty-four years old and how many times have you been married? None. I am sixty-three and how many times have I been married? Three. It is time you started catching up, Angelos. Make me a grandfather!'

'Ariadne has already made you a grandfather twice.'

'That's different. She's my daughter and you are my son. I want to hold the sons of my son in my arms.'

'I'll get married when I find the right woman, not before.' Angelos drew his father onto the balcony that circled the ballroom and refrained from pointing out that his father's last two attempts at marriage had created emotional and financial devastation.

There was no way he was making that mistake.

'You won't find the right woman by dating the wrong ones! And what are we doing in Paris? Why can't you hold this ball in Athens? *What is wrong with Athens?*'

'The world is bigger than Greece.' Angelos suppressed a yawn as the conversation shifted onto another familiar topic. 'I conduct business all over the globe.'

'And I never understand why! Did I have to leave Greece to make my first million? No!' Costas peered into the ballroom. 'Where has she gone? I can't see her.'

Angelos raised his eyebrows in question. 'Who are you looking for?'

'The goddess with the body. She was perfect. And now she has disappeared. She was all eyes and curves and soft-looking. Now, *that* girl would make a good mother. I can imagine her with your children snuggled on her lap and a moussaka cooling on your table.'

Angelos glanced at his father with amusement. 'I suggest you don't tell her that. These days it is heresy to make that sort of comment to a woman. They invariably have rather different aspirations.'

'The women *you* pick have different aspirations.' His father's voice was fierce as he searched the room with his eyes. 'Believe me, this one was built to be a mother. If you don't want her, then I might be interested myself.'

All trace of amusement left him, and Angelos inhaled sharply.

'Not again!' *Didn't his father ever learn?* 'Promise me that this time you'll just take her to bed. *Don't* marry her,' he advised, taking a glass of orange juice from a passing waiter and swapping it for the glass of champagne in his father's hand.

'You only think about bed and sex, but I have more respect for women than that.'

'You need to develop a more cynical approach to the opposite sex,' Angelos advised. 'What respect did Tara show you when she left you after six months, taking with her enough money to keep her going for life?'

His father's knuckles whitened as he gripped the stem of the glass. 'We both made a mistake.'

Mistake? Angelos ground his teeth. He was sure that as far as Tara was concerned the marriage had been a resounding success. She was now an extremely rich young woman.

His father deflated before his eyes, his vulnerability exposed. 'She was very mixed up. She didn't know what she wanted.'

'She knew *exactly* what she wanted—' Angelos broke off, trapped between the option of upsetting his father still further by highlighting the ruthless efficiency of Tara's campaign, or of letting the subject drop and risking the possibility that, even after two such divorces, his trusting father *still* hadn't learned the lessons that needed to be learned.

Costas sighed. 'A relationship should be about love and caring.'

Angelos winced at this sentimental and dangerous observation and made a mental note to instruct his security team to screen all women showing the slightest interest in his father in order to protect him from further unscrupulous individuals. 'Didn't your last two marriages teach you anything about women?'

'Yes. They taught me that you can't trust a thin one.' Costas regained some of his spirit. 'They want to be size zero—but why is it called that? Because they are zero use to anyone! They are too thin and hungry to live the life a woman is supposed to live. Next time I marry she will be a proper shape.'

'After everything that has happened over the past six years, you *still* believe that love exists?'

His father's face fell. 'I was in love with your mother for forty years. Of course I believe that love exists.'

Cursing himself for his lack of tact, Angelos put a hand on his father's shoulder. 'You should stop trying to replace her,' he said roughly. 'What you had was rare.' So rare that he'd given up hope of finding it himself. And he wasn't willing to risk settling for anything less.

'I will find it again.'

Not before it had cost the family a fortune in divorce settlements and mental anguish.

Frustrated by his father's misguided optimism about the female sex, Angelos ran a hand over the back of his neck. 'Stay single. It's less complicated.'

'I'm not staying single. I hate being single. It isn't natural for a man to be single. And you shouldn't be single, either.'

Seeing that his father was about to launch into another lecture in favour of the curvaceous woman, Angelos decided that the conversation had gone on long enough. 'You don't need to worry about me. I'm seeing a woman.' It wasn't the relationship that his father was hoping for, but he didn't need to know that.

His father scowled at him suspiciously. 'Is she a proper shape?'

'She is a perfect shape,' Angelos drawled, thinking of the A list Hollywood actress who had spent two *extremely* exciting nights in his bed the week before. Would he be seeing her again? Possibly. She had the legs and the hair and she was definitely an athlete in the bedroom. Was he interested in marrying her? Absolutely not. They would bore each other to death within a month, let alone a lifetime.

But hope was already lighting his father's eyes. 'And when will I meet her? You never introduce me to your girlfriends.'

With good reason. Introducing a woman to his father would deliver the exact message he was so careful never to send. 'When a woman is important to me, you will meet her,' Angelos said smoothly. 'And now I want to introduce you to Nicole. She's my Director of Public Affairs here in Paris, and she definitely loves food. I know you'll have plenty to say to one another.' He guided his father towards the reliable Nicole, made the necessary introductions, and then turned back to the ballroom to continue networking.

And stopped dead, his attention caught by the woman directly in front of him.

She walked as though she owned the place, with a gentle swing of her hips and a faint smile on her glossy mouth, as if something or someone had amused her. Her blonde hair was piled on her head and her vivid red dress provided a dazzling splash of colour amidst the predictable boring black. *She looked like an exotic rainforest bird let loose among a flock of crows.*

Instantly forgetting the Hollywood actress, Angelos watched her for a moment and then gave a slow, satisfied smile of his own. His father would be pleased on two counts, he thought, as he moved purposefully towards the unknown woman. Firstly because he was about to stop thinking about business and turn his attentions to the pursuit of pleasure, and secondly because the source of that pleasure definitely, very definitely, had curves.

Not that he required her to perform the various domestic functions that his father had listed. Despite his father's obvious concerns for him, he wasn't interested in a woman's capacity to cook, clean or raise his children. At this point in his life all he expected from a woman was entertainment, and she looked as though she'd been designed for exactly that purpose.

* * *

Smile, walk, smile, don't panic—

It was like being back in the school playground, with the bullies circling like gladiators while the malevolent crowd of girls pressed in, watching with sadistic fascination. Waiting for the kill.

The memory was so disturbingly vivid that feelings of terror and humiliation stirred to life, catching her unawares. No matter how many years passed, her past was always there, lurking inside her like dark, filthy slime.

She struggled to throw off all her old insecurities.

It was ridiculous to think of that here, now, when that part of her life had ended long ago.

This wasn't the playground, and she'd moved beyond that. The bullies might still be out there, but they couldn't see her any more. Her disguise was perfect.

Or was it?

She shouldn't have worn red. Red made her stand out like a beacon. And if she didn't eat something soon she was going to pass out.

Didn't anyone eat at these functions?

Wasn't anyone else starving hungry?

No wonder they were thin.

Wishing she'd never decided to test herself in this way, Chantal attempted to stroll casually across the room. *Confidence is everything*, she reminded herself. *Chin high, eyes up. Red is fine. They're only people. Don't let them intimidate you. They know nothing about you. From the outside you more or less look like them, and they can't see who you are on the inside.*

To distract herself, she played her usual game of make-believe. The game she'd invented as a means to survive in the lawless, ruthless environment she'd inhabited as a child. Her life had followed a pattern. A new playground, a new set of lies. A new layer of protection.

Who was she going to be this evening?

An heiress, maybe? Or possibly an actress?

A model?

No. Not a model. She would never be able to convince anyone that she was a model. She wasn't tall enough or thin enough.

She paused, still pondering her options. Nothing too complicated. Not that she was worried about being found out, because she would never see any of these people again.

Just for tonight, she could be anyone she wanted to be.

A penniless Italian *contessa* with lots of breeding and no money?

No. This was a charity ball. It wouldn't do to admit to having no money.

An heiress would be best.

An heiress wishing to remain incognito to avoid fortune hunters.

Yes. That was a good one.

Her excuse for not spending the money she didn't have would be that she didn't want to draw attention to herself.

The ballroom was amazing, with its high ceilings and glittering chandeliers. She had to remind herself not to stare at the paintings or the statues, and to adopt an expression of casual indifference—as though this was her world and such an exhibition of art and culture surrounded her on a daily basis.

As if—

'Champagne?' The question came from behind her and she turned swiftly, her eyes widening as she was confronted by a man so devilishly good-looking that every woman in the room was watching him longingly.

Her limbs weakened.

Arrogant, was the first word that came to mind.

Devastating, was the second.

His eyes glittered dark and he studied her with a disturbing degree of interest as he handed her a glass.

What was it about dinner jackets, she mused, that turned men into gods? Not that this man needed the assistance of well cut clothes to look good. He would have looked good in anything—or nothing. He was also the sort of man who wouldn't have looked twice at her in normal circumstances.

Chantal felt a sudden explosion of awareness engulf her body, and a deadly sexual warmth spread across her pelvis and down her limbs. He hadn't touched her. He hadn't even shaken her hand. And yet—

Dangerous was the word that finally caused her to take a defensive step backwards.

'I thought I knew everyone on the invitation list, but obviously I was wrong.' He spoke with the easy confidence that was the natural inheritance of the rich and powerful, his voice smooth and seductive, one dark eyebrow raised in anticipation of an introduction.

Still struggling to understand the reaction of her body, Chantal ignored the question in his eyes. She wasn't about to introduce herself—not least because she wasn't on the invitation list. Nor was she ever likely to be on the invitation list for an event like this.

She studied him for a moment, taking in the lean perfection of his bone structure and the lazy amusement in his eyes. He was looking at her in the way a man looked at a woman he was interested in taking to bed, and for a moment Chantal forgot to breathe.

Definitely dangerous.

The chemistry between them was so intense and so inexplicable that she felt flustered and hot.

Common sense told her that this was the time to make an elegant excuse and move on. She couldn't afford to indulge in a flirtation with anyone, because to draw that much attention to herself was to risk being exposed. 'Obviously you're a man who likes to be in control of his environment.'

'Am I?'

'If you're expecting to know everyone on the invitation list, then yes. That suggests a need to be in control, don't you think?'

'Or perhaps I'm just selective about who I spend time with.'

'Which means that you prefer the predictable to the possible. Knowing everyone surely limits the opportunity for surprises?'

His dark eyes gleamed with appreciation. 'I'm not easy to surprise. In my experience, the possible almost always turns out to be the probable. People are boringly predictable.' His mouth was a sensuous curve and she knew—*she just knew*—that this man would know everything there was to know about kissing a woman.

For a moment the mental image of his handsome dark head bending towards hers was so vivid that she couldn't formulate a reply, and his eyes drifted to her mouth, as if he were enjoying a similar fantasy.

'What? No argument? No desire to prove me wrong?' His gaze slid to the curved neckline of her dress and rested for a moment on her narrow waist. 'Tell me something about yourself that's likely to surprise me.'

Just about anything about her would have surprised him.

Her background.

Her true identity.

The fact that she wasn't supposed to be here.

'I'm starving,' she said truthfully, and he laughed with genuine amusement.

The sound turned heads in their direction, but he didn't seem to care. 'That's you at your most surprising?'

She glanced around her, her eyes resting on the impossibly slender frame of the nearest woman. 'It's pretty surprising to admit to liking food in this sort of company. I don't see a single woman here who is likely to be battling an addiction to chocolate truffles.'

'You don't see a single *real* woman. If you're hungry, then you must eat.' He lifted a hand and attracted the attention of a waiter with the natural confidence of someone used to being in control. She watched enviously, wishing she possessed even a fraction of his poise.

'I assumed the canapés were just for show.'

'You think their purpose is to test the self control of the guests?'

'If so, then I'm about to fail that test.' Smiling at the waiter, Chantal handed him her empty glass and piled several morsels on her napkin, resisting the temptation to snatch the entire trayful and put them in her handbag for later. 'Thank you. These look delicious.' The waiter bowed and moved away.

'So why are you hungry?' The man's eyes lingered on her hair. 'You haven't eaten all day because you were at the hairdresser's?'

She hadn't eaten all day because she'd worked a double shift serving food to other people. And because there was no point in wasting money on food when you knew a free meal was coming.

'Something like that.' Sliding a morsel of warm pastry into her mouth, Chantal struggled not to moan with delight as the texture and flavour exploded on her palate. 'These *are* delicious. Aren't you going to try one?'

His eyes were on her lips, and that simple connection was enough to stoke the flames that were licking around her pelvis.

They were in a crowded ballroom. So why did it feel as though it was just the two of them?

Flustered, she realised that she really, really needed to leave— but at that moment he helped himself to a canapé from her napkin, and the gesture was strangely intimate. Chantal was wondering how eating could be intimate when he smiled at her, and that smile was so irresistibly sexy that she couldn't do anything except smile back.

'You're right, they *are* delicious.' He lifted his hand and gently brushed a crumb from the corner of her mouth. 'So far all I know about you is that you like food and that you don't spend all day obsessing about your figure. Are you going to give me any more clues about yourself?'

'Why?'

'I'd like an introduction.'

She felt her heart skip and jump. 'If I tell you my name then you'll have to tell me *your* name, and it's much more fun if we remain strangers.'

He was silent for a moment. 'You don't know my name?'

'Of course not.'

The faint gleam in his eyes told her that this wasn't the answer he'd expected. 'All right,' he drawled softly, 'no names. So, how would you describe yourself?'

A liar, a cheat and a fraud?

'A person's perception of themselves is almost always at odds with how others perceive them,' Chantal murmured, choosing to be intentionally vague. 'But I like to think of myself as—adaptable.'

'You're not going to tell me who you really are?'

She didn't want to think about who she really was. Suppressing a shudder, Chantal gave what she hoped was a mysterious smile. 'Does it matter? Perhaps I'm a princess? Or maybe I'm the CEO of a corporation? Or an heiress determined to hide her identity?'

'All of those people were included on the invitation list. So which are you? Princess, heiress or CEO?' His tone was dry, but his eyes were sharp and assessing and Chantal knew that she ought to end the conversation and move on immediately. This man's intelligence was not in dispute, and it wouldn't take him long to work out that there was something about her that didn't ring true.

It didn't matter how much she struggled to bury it, the darkness of her past was always there—a constant reminder that all this was all a pretence.

'I'm a woman. The sort of woman who prefers not to be

stereotyped. I like to think that our horizons can be as broad as we want them to be.'

'You think I stereotype women?'

'I'm sure you do it all the time. Everyone does.' Trying to look as though she belonged in this environment, Chantal pretended to smile a greeting at someone across the room. Unfortunately for her, the man in question chose that moment to look at her and smile back. Flustered, she turned away. *It was definitely time to leave.* 'I don't like labels. I prefer to be just—me.'

Now that they'd finished the canapés, the man lifted two more glasses of champagne from the tray of a passing waiter and handed her one. 'The mere fact that you are here tells me a great deal about you.'

'Really?' Engulfed by a wave of horror at the thought of him knowing even the slightest bit about her, Chantal took a large mouthful of champagne.

'Yes.' His eyes narrowed thoughtfully as they rested on her face. 'Tickets to this event are highly sought after and difficult to obtain. In order to have been among the lucky few, you have to be seriously wealthy.'

Chantal thought of the dingy room she'd left a few hours earlier. The landlord had increased the rent, and in two weeks' time she'd be homeless.

The only jobs that paid decently she wasn't prepared to do.

'The concept of wealth means different things to different people,' she murmured, curling her fingers around the stem of the glass. 'Is it money or is it good health? Or perhaps a warm, loving family? To consider wealth to be the exclusive privilege of those with money is to risk missing out on a full life, don't you agree?'

There was a cynical tone to his laugh. 'If you truly believe that, then you're an unusual woman. Most members of your sex think that money is the *only* route to a full life.'

People were openly staring at them and Chantal felt a flicker of panic. Could they see through the red dress and the make-up? She felt as though she had the word 'impostor' stamped on her forehead in large letters. Her hand shaking, she took another mouthful of champagne. 'There you go again—stereotyping. Clearly you regard women as a homogonous breed, endowed with identical characteristics.'

'Most of the women I meet *are* a homogonous breed,' he said dryly, and for a moment she forgot about the people watching them and looked at him curiously, wondering what events in his life had triggered that remark.

He was handsome, yes, but there was also a hardness to him. An outer shell that she guessed wouldn't be easily penetrated. Perhaps she recognised it because she'd developed the same shell herself.

'Maybe you're moving in the wrong circles. Or perhaps there's something about you that attracts a particular type of woman.'

'That would be my wallet.' His smile was impossibly sexy, and Chantal was captivated by the unexpected glimpse of humour that lay beneath his sophisticated exterior.

In fact she was enjoying the conversation so much that she just couldn't quite bring herself to end it, even though she knew she should. Talking to him had restored her much needed confidence. He made her feel beautiful, and the attraction between them was something she'd never encountered before. *Powerful, intoxicating....*

'So I assume that's why people are staring at us,' she said lightly. 'They're wondering whether I'm about to put my hand in your pocket and rob you.'

Without warning he lifted a hand and gently trailed ran his finger over the curve of his jaw, a thoughtful look in his eyes. 'The men are staring because you're the most beautiful woman in the room.'

The unexpected compliment took her breath away. 'Really?'

She struggled to keep her tone light. 'So why aren't they all queuing up to drag me onto the dance floor?'

'Because you're with me.' His tone was casual, but there was a steely undertone that instantly dismissed the competition.

Possessive, she thought to herself, trying desperately to ignore the thrill of excitement that buzzed through her body like an electric current.

He was the most confident, self assured man she'd ever met, and he was way out of her league. She was playing a dangerous, dangerous game by lingering, and she knew that she ought to walk away before the situation grew more complicated.

Before her lies exploded in her face.

But Chantal couldn't move. She felt more alive then she'd ever felt before. 'That doesn't explain why the women are glaring at me.'

The gleam in his eyes suggested that he considered her question ridiculously naive. 'The women are glaring because they're nervous about their men. You are *serious* competition. And they're trying to work out which designer is responsible for your incredible dress.'

Chantal wasn't sure whether it was his words or the seductive stroke of his fingers that caused the sudden rush of heat through her body.

'My dress is a one off, designed specifically for me,' she said truthfully. 'And I have a feeling that the women are glaring at me because I'm talking to you.' And she couldn't blame them for that. He was a man who would incite jealousy wherever he went.

He was breathtakingly gorgeous and she wondered briefly about his nationality. He wasn't French and didn't look English. But his English was perfect. The product of a first-class education.

At that unsettling thought, her insecurities sprang to life again and she reminded herself that for now, at least, he was with *her*.

Yes, they were surrounded by stick-thin, stunning model types, but *she* was the one he was smiling at.

And she didn't even bother trying to subdue the little flicker of triumph that accompanied *that* realisation.

Perhaps it had been worth coming after all, just to experience this one perfect moment.

In a room full of the very cream of society, he'd singled her out.

Knowing that, wasn't it time she left her insecurities in the past?

'They're not looking at me.' His hand fell to his side and there was a cynical gleam in his eyes. 'Or if they are then they're not seeing me. They're seeing my wallet. When it comes to dress size they want to see one zero, but when it comes to a man's wallet they're rather more ambitious.'

Chantal laughed, and refrained from pointing out that he could be penniless and women would still stare. 'If you're so rich that women can't see past your wallet, then there's an obvious solution.' Her eyes twinkling, she stood on tiptoe and spoke softly in his ear, 'Give away all your money.'

His head turned fractionally, so that his lips almost brushed her cheek. 'You think I should do that?'

He smelt amazing, Chantal thought dizzily, resting a hand on his shoulder to steady herself. 'It would stop women stereotyping you as a rich, available man.'

'How do you know I'm available?'

Feeling distinctly light-headed, Chantal stepped away slightly, deciding regretfully that it really was time to move on from this conversation and this man. *Before she forgot who she really was.* 'Because if you weren't, some extremely jealous woman would have stabbed me in the back with her cutlery by now.'

His eyes were on her mouth. 'So your advice is to give away my money?'

'Absolutely. Only then can you be sure of a woman's motives.'

The musicians started to play the seductive, powerful notes of a tango, and Chantal closed her eyes for a moment, wishing they hadn't chosen that particular moment to perform that number.

It reminded her of Buenos Aires.

She'd spent two months travelling around Argentina, and she loved South American music.

The rhythm was so familiar that her body swayed instinctively, and the next moment the glass was removed from her hand and she felt her mysterious companion slide a hand around her back and pull her close. So close that, had the dance not been a tango, their contact would have drawn comment.

Her eyes opened. 'What are you doing?'

'Dancing. With you.'

'You didn't ask me.'

'I never ask a question when I already know the answer. It wastes time.'

'Arrogant,' she murmured, and he gave a slow smile.

'Self-aware.'

'Over-confident.' Laughing, she tilted her head to look at him. 'I might have said no.' She could feel the warmth of his hand on the bare skin at the base of her spine and the contact sent spirals of heat coursing through her body.

'You wouldn't have said no.'

And he was absolutely right.

There was no way she would have been able to say no to this man.

The throbbing, sexy music coiled itself around them and Chantal was breathlessly conscious of the strength and power of his body pressed against hers.

He clasped her hand in his and drew her nearer still, until it felt as though there wasn't a single part of her that wasn't touching him. The music washed over them and he moved in response to that intoxicating rhythm, using subtle changes in pressure to lead her around the dance floor.

She was so aware of him that she couldn't breathe. He was in her personal space and she felt suffocated and seduced at the same time, intoxicated and drugged by the powerful chemistry that had erupted between them from the first moment they'd met.

What they were doing ceased to feel like dancing. It was—

An exploration of sexuality?

Her body slid over his, his leg following her leg, his hands on her hips. He moved with a confidence and innate sensuality that left her in no doubt that this man would be an incredible lover.

For some lucky woman.

And that woman would never be someone like her.

But for now—just for now—he was hers. And she was going to make the most of the moment.

They danced chest to chest, eyes locked, breath mingling, the heat and their chemistry turning the dance into something close to a primal mating ritual.

Chantal ceased to register the other people on the dance floor and suddenly there was just the two of them, their bodies moving together in perfect understanding as they executed something far deeper and more complex than a few dance steps. It was erotic, passionate and deeply intimate. They'd never met before this evening, and yet instinctively she knew what he wanted from her and moved in response to his demands.

Her senses were heightened and she was lost in the music and the moment as they danced with fluency and sensuality. One moment they were chest to chest and she could feel the steady thump of his heartbeat against hers, and then he would turn her and she could feel the seductive slide of his hands over her hips as he moved her body in a dance that only just bordered on the socially acceptable. The movement of his leg drew the silk of her dress up her own leg, and the warmth of his breath against her neck made her shiver. How was it possible to be hot and cold at the same time?

How was it possible to feel this way about a man she'd never met before and wouldn't ever meet again?

Perhaps that was why, she mused, gasping slightly as he tipped her slightly off balance, forcing her to lean into his body. Because she would never see him again, she could let go and enjoy herself.

For tonight, she was this man's dance partner.

And dancing with him was shameful, sinful and like nothing she'd ever experienced before.

Her mind and body moved into a different place altogether and when the music finally shifted to a different rhythm it took her a moment to register her surroundings and return to reality.

They stared at each other for an endless moment, and then he released her and stepped away from her.

There was a strange light in his dark eyes as he studied her.

'I'll fetch us both a drink.' His tone was noticeably cooler than it had been before they'd danced.

He strode off and she blinked several times, disorientated by the sudden change in his attitude. A moment ago they'd been in another world, just the two of them, and now—

She took a few deep breaths, trying to settle the intense reaction of her body. He seemed angry—but why would he be angry?

It had been his choice to dance, not hers.

And she hadn't trodden on his toes or fallen on the floor.

Wondering what she'd done to bring about such a change in him, she was about to melt into the background when a woman approached her.

'I'm Marianna Killington-Forbes.' She spoke in a lazy English upper-class accent, and the smile that touched her mouth went nowhere near her eyes. 'You look very familiar. Have we met?'

Oh, yes, they'd met.

Chantal's legs started to shake as her disguise fell away. She felt naked and exposed, her past no longer safely concealed but rising in front of her like some vile, malevolent demon. She was going to die of embarrassment and humiliation. Right now. Right here. 'I—'

'She doesn't speak much English, Marianna. I told her to stay with me and not wander off, but we were separated in the crowd.' The heavily accented voice came from directly behind her, and Chantal turned to find a man by her side. She guessed him to be in his seventies, but he was still ridiculously handsome and his eyes were kind as he smiled down at her. He said something to her in a language that she didn't understand and then took her freezing cold hand in his, tucking it firmly into the bend of his arm as he drew her close. 'Marianna?' His eyes lost some of their warmth as he looked at her tormentor. 'Is there something that you wish to say? I can try and translate, if you would like?'

The woman's mouth tightened. 'She didn't seem to be having any problems communicating with Angelos.'

The man smiled. 'As you no doubt noticed, they use an entirely different method of communication.'

Jealousy flashed in the other woman's eyes and she turned her attention back to Chantal. 'Well, I wish you luck with your relationship. The ability not to converse could stand you in good stead, given that Angelos never expects conversation from his women anyway.'

Still frozen with horror that Marianna had recognised her face, Chantal watched with relief as the other woman stalked away, apparently unable to recall her name or exactly how she knew her.

'You're shaking.' The man's voice was soft, and Chantal clung to his arm, struggling to pull herself together. Desperately hoping that her dance partner wasn't going to choose that moment to reappear, she took several deep breaths.

'Do you think—could you just stay with me for a minute?' Her voice cracked. 'I don't want to be left on my own just now.'

'You are not on your own.' His hand covered hers, and she felt the warmth of his fingers thaw the chill in her bones.

'Thank you,' she whispered, so pathetically grateful for his intervention that she almost hugged him on the spot. 'I don't know why you did that, but I'll never forget it. You've been so, so kind. How did you know I needed rescuing?'

'When she walked up to you, your face turned white. I thought you were going to faint. You don't like her, no?'

'Well, I—'

'Don't be embarrassed. I don't like her either,' the man said firmly. 'I never could stand that woman. I wonder why she was invited.'

Chantal thought back to the misery of her schooldays. 'Her daddy is very rich.'

'Really? He clearly didn't spend his money feeding his family.' The man made a disparaging noise. 'To look at her you'd think she was starved from birth. Her bones should be classified as a lethal weapon. If you bumped into her, you'd be bruised all over.'

Despite her insecurities, Chantal couldn't help laughing. He was not only kind, he was also funny. She glanced at him curiously, thinking that he reminded her of someone. 'I'd better leave—' She started to move, but he tightened his grip on her arm.

'If you leave,' he said softly, 'then they'll think they've won. Is that what you want?'

She stilled, wondering how he knew what she was feeling. 'Everyone is staring at me—'

'So smile,' the man instructed calmly. 'Lift your chin and smile. You have as much right to be here as the rest of them.' Without giving her the chance to argue, he led her to two vacant chairs. 'Sit for a moment and keep a lonely old man company. I hate these things. I always feel out of place.'

'That can't possibly be true. You look as confident as anyone here.'

'But appearances can be deceptive, can't they?' His gentle comment made it clear that he was aware of how uncomfortable and insecure she felt.

His unusual insight probably should have worried her, but it didn't. All she felt was the most profound gratitude. Not only had he rescued her from a potentially embarrassing situation, he was now pretending that her fears and insecurities were nothing out of the ordinary.

'Why are you being so kind to me?'

'I'm not being kind. I hate these events. You can't blame me for enjoying myself with the best-looking woman in the room.'

She wished her hands would stop shaking. 'If you hate them, why did you come?'

'To please my son. He is worried that I haven't been getting out enough lately.'

'In that case he won't want to see you wasting your time with me.' And she should be leaving. Before Marianna remembered who she was.

'That dance—' The man glanced towards her, the corners of his eyes crinkling. 'It was like watching one person. The rhythm was perfect, the chemistry between the two of you— Only lovers can dance the Argentine tango like that.'

Lovers?

Chantal opened her mouth to tell him that they hadn't even exchanged names, but then decided that it would be embarrassing to admit that she'd danced like that with a total stranger.

What had Marianne called him? Angelos?

So she'd been right about one thing; *he definitely wasn't English.*

What would it be like, she mused dreamily, *to be loved by a man like that?*

'And even now you can't stop thinking about him, can you?' The man sounded pleased. 'You share something deep. He cares. I can see with my own eyes. The way he looked at you. The way you looked at him. The way you moved together, as if there was no one else in the room. The body says more than words. I can see from watching you that your relationship is serious.'

His observation shocked her out of her dreams. 'Oh. Well, no, it isn't exactly—'

'You don't have to be secretive with me. I may be old enough to be your father, but that doesn't mean I've forgotten what it's like to be in love. I want to know how you felt the first time you saw him. Tell me!'

Chantal hesitated and then smiled, drawn by the kindness in his eyes. It was strange, she mused. She didn't make friends easily, and yet after only five minutes in his company she would have died for this man. 'I thought he was amazing,' she said honestly. 'He was charming, clever and surprisingly easy to talk to.'

'And sexy?'

'Oh, yes. Incredible.' She lowered her voice, afraid that the people around them might overhear. 'I've never been so attracted to anyone in my life before.'

The man nodded with satisfaction. 'I knew it. And you're crazy about him, aren't you?'

'Well—' Chantal gave a helpless shrug. 'Yes. But we haven't exactly known each other for—'

'It's either right or it's wrong! All these long engagements—all nonsense. If a man and woman are right together, they're right straight away—not in six months or six years.'

Slightly disturbed by that comment, Chantal thought for a moment. *Right together?* Hardly. If he was as rich as she suspected, then she couldn't think of two people less suited.

She would never be comfortable in his world. And he wouldn't want her in his.

If he knew who she was then he'd join the crowd at the edge of the playground.

Dismissing that thought, she glanced at the man next to her. He really did remind her of someone. 'So, if you're such an expert on body language, why do you think he looked so angry?' She wondered why she was asking the advice of a total stranger. But he didn't feel like a stranger, and talking to him seemed like the most natural thing in the world.

'That's easy enough to answer. A man never likes to admit that he's well and truly fallen for a woman. I was the same when I met my wife. I struggled for weeks. Loving a woman makes a man vulnerable, and a strong man doesn't like to be vulnerable. I resisted her.'

'So what did your wife do to win you over?'

'She did what women always do when they want something. Talk, talk, talk until a man's resistance is ground into the dust.'

Chantal laughed. 'Are you still together?'

'We had forty years.' The man's smile faded. 'She died fifteen years ago and I've never met anyone else to touch her. But I haven't given up trying. And I can still remember how it feels to move around a dance floor.'

Moved by the emotion in his voice, Chantal stood up impulsively and held out her hands. 'Show me.' She angled her head and listened to the music. 'It's a waltz. Do you waltz?'

He laughed with delight. 'You want me to waltz with you?'

'Why is that funny?'

'I'm seventy three.'

'There's no man in the room I'd rather dance with.'

'Then you are a brave woman, because Angelos is an extremely possessive man. He would *not* be amused if I took you onto the dance floor. But I can see now why you've succeeded where so many have failed. I'm sure it's that wonderful spirit of yours that has made you different from all the others.'

'All the others?' Chantal frowned. 'All what others?'

'All the other women who have aspired to be where you are tonight. By his side. In his heart.' The man's eyes misted and Chantal felt her stomach lurch.

'You know him well?' Who exactly was this man? Desperately she tried to rerun the conversation. *Exactly what had she said?* 'You didn't mention that you knew him well.'

'If I'd done that you might not have talked so freely, and that would have been a pity. It was a most illuminating conversation.' The older man was still smiling, and at that moment Chantal saw her dance partner approach, the expression on his handsome face dark and forbidding.

He stopped in front of them, broad shouldered and powerful, an ominous frown touching his dark brows as he saw their clasped hands.

Chantal instantly withdrew her hands, her heart starting to thud. *Why was he looking at her like that?* The man she was sitting with was clearly a man of mature years. What possible reason was there for the shimmering anger she saw in the eyes of her handsome dance partner?

He couldn't possibly be jealous. That would be too ridiculous for words.

She didn't know what to say, so she just sat holding her breath, waiting for him to speak.

An expression of grim disapproval settled on his face as he glanced between the two of them and finally, after what seemed like an age, straightened his shoulders and spoke.

'I see you've met my father.'

CHAPTER TWO

CHANTAL served the group of tourists seated at the table and then sank into a chair at an adjacent table, staring blankly at an empty coffee cup.

It didn't matter how much time passed, she still felt horribly, miserably embarrassed. And sad. Really, really sad. As if she'd lost something special that she'd never be able to get back.

What was the matter with her?

Two weeks had passed since the ball. *Two weeks since she'd gate-crashed the most prestigious social event of the year—*

Why couldn't she just forget it and move on?

Why couldn't she just forget *him*?

Without thinking, she slipped a hand into the pocket of her skirt and touched the piece of torn newspaper she'd been carrying around for the past two weeks. She'd touched and stared at the picture so many times that it was crumpled and thin, and in immediate danger of falling apart. Now she wished that she'd bought a hundred copies of the newspaper and stored them safely, so that when she was old and grey she could remind herself of that one perfect night.

That one perfect man.

The memory of that dance still made her nerve-endings tingle. The chemistry that had sizzled between them had been the most exciting, astonishing experience of her life. Even now, as she remembered the seductive, intoxicating feel of his body against hers, her heart-rate increased.

But it hadn't just been the chemistry that had kept her by his side long after she should have made her escape. She'd *liked* him. She'd liked his sharp observations, his intelligence and his dry sense of humour.

Angelos Zouvelekis.

Thanks to the article in her pocket, she now knew exactly who he was.

Billionaire and philanthropist. *Greek* billionaire and philanthropist.

Of course. Greek. The clues had all been there, if she'd only looked for them. His hair was the deep, glossy black of a Kalamata olive and his bronzed skin hinted at a life spent bathed in the warmth of the Mediterranean sun.

She'd fallen for a Greek billionaire as well known for his bachelor status as for his phenomenal business success.

And, for her, the fairy tale ended there—because she couldn't have picked a more unsuitable man if she'd tried.

Tears stung her eyes and she blinked rapidly. *Ironic, really,* she thought to herself. Every other woman would have considered Angelos Zouvelekis to be the most suitable man on the planet. Every other woman would have known immediately who he was.

Not her. She hadn't had a clue. If she had, maybe she would have walked away sooner.

Found a different man to fall in love with.

Oh, for goodness' sake! She sucked in a breath, impatient with herself for thinking that way. No one fell in love that easily! It just didn't happen. What she was feeling wasn't love. It was just—just—

Rubbing a hand over her face, she struggled to pull herself together.

She didn't actually understand what it was that she was

feeling, but she wished it would stop because it was pulling her down. And anyway, what she felt about him was irrelevant, because he'd made it perfectly clear what he'd thought of her.

He'd been so, so angry.

Somehow—and she'd never actually found out how—he'd obviously discovered that she hadn't been invited to the ball.

Chantal covered her face with her hands and shook her head, trying to erase the hideously embarrassing memory. Just remembering his hard, icy tone made her want to sink through the floor.

What had he called her? Greedy, unscrupulous and dishonest.

And perhaps she'd deserved it. After all, it *had* been dishonest to use a ticket that wasn't hers.

To call her greedy and unscrupulous was a bit over the top, but, given the outrageous price of the tickets, she could see how he might have thought that about her.

And to make matters worse there had been that incredibly sticky moment when his father had expressed his undiluted joy that his son was finally in a loving relationship.

Remembering the look of thunderous incredulity that had transformed Angelos's features from handsome to intimidating, Chantal slid lower in her seat.

That had been the biggest mistake of all: voicing her dreams and fantasies to the elderly man who had helped her so much. But she'd adored him on sight, and he'd been so kind to her. So approachable and sympathetic. Almost a father figure, although she didn't really know what one of those looked like. As far as she was concerned, the species was extinct.

Perhaps that was why she'd been so drawn to him.

Angelos's father.

She gave a whimper of disbelief and regret. Of all the men in the room, why had she chosen *him* as a sounding board for her fantasies?

Telling herself firmly that it was in the past, and she needed to forget it, Chantal straightened her shoulders and tried to think positively about the future.

Obviously she couldn't stay in Paris. She needed to travel to somewhere remote. A place where there was absolutely no chance of bumping into one very angry Greek male. The Amazon, maybe? Or the Himalayas? Even a man with a global business wasn't likely to have an office in Nepal, was he?

She sat for a moment, trying to stir up some enthusiasm for her next step.

It was exciting to be able to travel anywhere and be anyone. She was lucky to be free to make the decisions she wanted to make. How many other people had absolutely no ties? Most people had jobs to restrict their movements, or families to think of. She had no such restrictions.

She had no family to answer to. No one who cared what she did. She could move continents tomorrow without having to ask anyone's permission, and she could be anyone she wanted to be.

Chantal waited for the usual buzz of excitement that came from the prospect of reinventing herself yet again, but nothing happened. Instead of the thrill of adventure, her mood was totally flat.

She felt as though she'd lost something and she didn't understand why she would feel that way.

What had she lost?

'Chantal!' The café owner's voice cut through the embarrassing memories like a sharp knife. 'I am not paying you to rest! We have customers. Get on your feet and serve them! This is your last warning.'

Chantal sprang to her feet, realising with another spurt of embarrassment that she'd sat down at the table she was supposed to be cleaning.

Her cheeks pink, she quickly gathered up the empty cup and two glasses and hurried into the kitchen.

'More time working and less time dreaming, or I'll be looking for a new waitress.' The small, rotund little Frenchman gave an unpleasant smile, openly staring at the thrust of her breasts under her white blouse. 'Unless you want to apply for a different role.'

Chantal lifted her eyes to his, his comment triggering a response so violent that it shocked her. It took her a moment to find her voice. 'Look for a new waitress,' she said hoarsely. 'I resign.' And, just to reinforce that decision, she removed the ridiculous little apron that she'd been forced to wear over the vestigial black skirt and white blouse.

The café owner thought that it attracted customers. And it did. But they were almost always the type of customer she would have chosen to avoid.

Vile self-loathing curled inside her and she thrust the apron into his hands, not even bothering to ask for the money he owed her.

She didn't care about the money.

She just wanted to get away. The truth was that Chantal, waitress, had never really worked for her. Neither had Chantal, chambermaid, or Chantal, barmaid.

The darkness of her past pressed in on her and she hurried towards the door, desperately needing to be outside in the warm Paris sunshine.

The café owner was subjecting her to a tirade of fluent French, but Chantal ignored him and virtually ran out of the door.

She'd move on. Travel somewhere exotic where she knew no one.

Maybe Egypt would be exciting. She could see the pyramids and swim in the Red Sea—

Calming down slightly, she left the café without glancing back and started to walk along the wide boulevard that led towards the Eiffel Tower. The trees were in full leaf, and the fountains bubbled and gushed, the sound soothing and cooling in the warm air.

It was lunchtime, and tourists mingled with elegantly dressed

Parisian mothers taking their toddlers for a stroll. A little blonde girl tripped and fell, and instantly her mother was by her side, gathering her into her arms for a hug.

Just for an instant Chantal watched, and then she put her head down and hurried on, ignoring the faint stab of envy that tore at her insides.

She was twenty-four; far too old to be envying a child her mother.

She quickened her pace, dodging a group of teenagers who were gliding in circles on rollerblades. They mocked each other and laughed, their effortless camaraderie making her feel even more wistful.

None of them looked displaced or insecure.

They all belonged.

Above her the Eiffel Tower rose high, but Chantal didn't spare it a glance. In the two months she'd spent in Paris she hadn't once joined the throngs who jostled with each other in long queues for a chance to reach the top. She'd avoided the standard tourist traps and opted instead to discover the hidden Paris.

But now it was time to move on.

Not thinking or caring about her destination, she just walked, determined to enjoy her last moments in a city she'd grown to love.

Eventually she reached the river Seine, and she paused for a moment on the embankment, watching the way the sun glinted on the water. Behind her cars roared past, weaving in and out of lanes in an alarmingly random fashion. Horns blared, and drivers shook their fists and yelled abuse at each other through open windows.

It was a typical day in Paris.

She crossed the river and made her way up to the Rue du Faubourg Saint-Honoré with its designer shops. This area was the heart of Paris design and fashion; Chanel, Lanvin, Yves St Laurent, Versace—they were all here. She paused outside a window, her attention caught by a dress on display, her brain automatically memorising the cut and the line.

Why were people prepared to pay such an indecent sum of money for something so simple? she mused. A length of fabric and a reel of cotton thread could produce the same for a fraction of the amount.

The dress she'd made for the ball had been a huge success, and no one had seemed to recognise it as an old piece of discarded curtain lining.

The low growl of a powerful engine broke her concentration, and she glanced behind her as a shiny black Lamborghini jerked to a halt in the road.

Chantal felt her heart skitter, and slowly the world around her faded into the background. She was oblivious to the fact that several other women had turned to stare and equally oblivious to the cacophony of car horns as other drivers registered their protest.

She knew that car.

She'd seen it two weeks before—at the ball she hadn't been invited to.

It belonged to the man that she hadn't been supposed to dance with.

The son of the man she wished she'd never talked to.

His attention caught by the gleaming blonde hair and long, long legs of the woman staring into the shop window, Angelos Zouvelekis slammed his foot on the brake and brought the car to an abrupt halt.

Ignoring the sudden swivel of heads that followed his action, he stared hard at the woman.

Was it her?

Had he finally found her, or was it wishful thinking on his part?

She looked different. Wondering if he'd made a mistake,

Angelos narrowed his eyes and imagined this woman with her hair piled on top of her head and her arms and shoulders revealed by the clever cut of her couture dress.

And then her eyes met his, and all doubt faded. Even from this distance he caught a flash of sapphire-blue—the same unusual colour that had caught his attention that fateful night at the ball.

Her eyes were unforgettable.

Finally he'd found her. And where else but shopping in one of the most expensive districts of Paris?

It should have been the first place he'd instructed his security team to look, Angelos thought cynically, wondering which deluded fool had provided the money she was clearly about to spend.

The fact that he'd been compelled to search for her at all made the anger explode inside him and he switched off the engine and sprang from the car, as indifferent to the 'No Parking' signs as he was to the gaping audience of admiring women who were now watching his movements with lustful interest.

At that precise moment he wasn't interested in any woman except the one who was staring at him, and he almost laughed as he saw the shock in her eyes.

It didn't surprise him that she was shocked to see him, given the way they'd parted company.

He was shocked, too. In normal circumstances he went out of his way to avoid women like her. If anyone had told him a month ago that he would have used all his contacts to track down someone whose behaviour appalled and disgusted him, he would have laughed.

But here he was, about to make her day. Thanks to a twist of fate, he was about to give her all she'd dreamed of and more.

As he walked purposefully towards her he consoled himself with the knowledge that although she had won the first round, the second, third and fourth were going to be his.

She was also about to discover the truth behind that famous saying *Be careful what you wish for...*

This woman had made her wishes perfectly clear, but he was absolutely sure that by the time he'd finished with her she would be wishing she'd targeted a man less able to defend himself.

Angelos ground his teeth, furious and frustrated at the position he now found himself in. She was obviously the sort of woman who devoted her life to leeching from those better off than her. A woman with no scruples and no morals. She was the lowest of the low, and the knowledge that he'd been well and truly manipulated for the first time in his life did nothing for his temper.

If there was one word he would never have applied to himself, it was *gullible*.

He looked straight at her, and was instantly gripped by a spasm of lust so powerful that his brain momentarily ceased to function.

She was all woman.

From the tumbling blonde hair to the generous swell of her breasts and the soft curve of her narrow waist, she was entirely and uncontrovertibly feminine.

Over the past two weeks he'd been so furiously angry with her that he'd forgotten how incredibly beautiful she was. Her assets would not have been valued by any of the glossy magazines—her shape was too feminine for that—but she was a woman that any red-blooded male would fantasise about taking to bed.

Appalled at himself, Angelos dragged his gaze away from her and tried to refocus his mind.

It had been a long two weeks, he reminded himself as he searched for a logical explanation for his unwelcome and wholly inappropriate reaction to her. An extremely long two weeks.

Back in control, he risked another glance at her. This time he thought he saw guilt in her eyes and had to remind himself that guilt was connected to conscience, and this woman wasn't familiar with either word.

'Isabelle.' He was unable to keep the contempt out of his voice and for a moment she just stared at him, wide eyed, her expression faintly puzzled.

Then she spoke, and her voice was husky and feminine. 'Who is Isabelle?'

The denial on her part was entirely predictable, but all the same temper exploded inside him. 'We are no longer playing "Guess the Identity".'

'But I'm not—'

'Don't!' Driven to the limits of his self control, he growled the warning and she backed away a few steps.

As well she might, Angelos thought grimly, *after the stunt she'd pulled.*

'Get in the car.' He was too angry to bother with pleasantries, and he saw a flicker of panic in her eyes.

'You've obviously mistaken me for someone else.'

He reached into his pocket and removed the evidence. 'There's no mistake. Next time you're trying to remain incognito, *don't* drop your ticket.'

She stared at the ticket in his hand, and it was clear that she didn't know what to say.

'Now I understand why you were so reluctant to introduce yourself.' He watched the various emotions flicker across her eyes. Consternation, confusion—*fear*? 'So now we've cleared up the sticky subject of your identity, let's go.'

She was still looking at the ticket. 'Go where?'

'With me. This is your lucky day.' He wondered whether it was possible for words to actually choke a man. 'You've hit the jackpot.'

Her gaze shifted from the ticket to his face. 'I honestly don't know what you're talking about.'

So, not only had she won this round, but she intended to make him suffer by rubbing it in.

He was so livid that had he been a lion he would have savaged her on the spot and left her body for the hyenas.

As it was, the desire to walk away was so powerful that he actually stepped back from her. Then a vision of his father flew into his head and he reminded himself of the reason he was standing here now.

Cursing softly, he ran a hand over the back of his neck, wondering if there had been any change in his father's condition.

Reminding himself that the sooner this was sorted, the sooner he could return to Greece and monitor his father's progress in person, Angelos stood his ground. 'Amazing though it seems, I'm about to further the acquaintance that you saw fit to initiate.' Furious at finding himself manipulated by a set of circumstances that were now far beyond his control, he tightened his jaw. 'Get in the car.'

'I really need to tell you something—' she sounded young, and just a little bit desperate, but he was too angry to feel sympathy.

He knew from personal experience that youth and greed existed happily together. Thanks in part to the numerous glossy magazines that made their profit from fuelling envy, there were plenty of people who wanted maximum lifestyle for minimum effort.

'I'm not interested in anything you have to say. This time *I'm* doing the talking, and I don't want an audience.'

She didn't move, and the crowd of people behind her seemed to have grown larger. 'I don't see what there is to talk about.'

'You'll find out soon enough. Unlike you, I prefer to keep my personal business personal. Let's go.' *Before someone recognised him and took a photograph that would appear in tomorrow's newspapers.* 'My hotel isn't far from here.'

'Your *hotel*?' Her expression grew suddenly frosty, as if he'd delivered the worst insult possible. 'Pick another girl, Mr Zouvelekis. I'm not the sort of woman who likes to become intimately acquainted with the inside of a man's hotel room— even less so when that man is a stranger.'

Her prim, dignified rejection was so at odds with what he already knew about her character that he didn't know whether to laugh or punch something.

'A stranger?' He failed to keep the disdain out of his voice. 'I'm the same stranger that you danced with, and we both know where that dance would have led. If you hadn't shown your true colours so early in the evening, we would have ended the night naked in my hotel room.'

Her lips parted in murmured denial, but although her mouth was trying to form the right words, the chemistry between them was still sizzling.

Even while struggling against a shockingly powerful urge to wring her neck, Angelos found himself being distracted by the smooth, creamy perfection of her skin and the way her full breasts pressed against her white shirt.

No wonder he hadn't been concentrating the night of the ball. *She was spectacular.*

Exasperated with himself, he forced his attention back to her eyes. 'Even if I wasn't already aware of your reputation, Isabelle, your performance at the ball would have been more than enough to convince me that, quite apart from being that "sort of woman", in fact your *specialist subject* is the inside of men's hotel rooms.'

'My reputation?' She sounded astonished, as though it were news to her that she *had* a reputation, and he gave her a warning glance.

'Now I know who you are, I can understand why you went to such extraordinary lengths not to introduce yourself. Next time you want to trap a billionaire, change your name.'

Her eyes widened, and suddenly he forgot everything that he'd been intending to say.

She had the most amazing eyes he'd ever seen. Standing this close, and with the benefit of the spring sunshine to light her face, he could see that the sapphire was broken by flecks of green— as if an adoring artist had been determined to do everything possible to increase the impact of those eyes on a woefully poorly prepared male race. And as for her body—

He gritted his teeth, aware that it had been her body that had contributed to the situation they now found themselves in. His libido had smothered the sound of alarm bells ringing in his head.

His comment silenced her for a moment and she watched him, her chest rising and falling under the white lace blouse.

Aware that the audience around them was listening intently to the entire conversation, Angelos reached out and slid an arm round her waist, jerking her against him.

'I'll give you some more free advice,' he murmured softly, his lips close to her ear. His actions were those of a lover, but his words were those of an aggressor, and he felt the sudden tension in her body, 'if you want a man to believe in your virtue, don't wear a skirt that reveals your chosen brand of underwear. Not that I'm complaining, you understand. If we have to do this, we might as well both enjoy it. In fact, I'm wondering what extras come with the waitress costume? Whipped cream? Melted chocolate?'

'Do what? What are you talking about?'

He felt her try to pull away and pressed his hand into the hollow of her back, distracted by how small her waist was. *How could anyone manage to be curvy and slender at the same time?*

'I'm talking about our new relationship, *agape mou.* The one you wanted so badly.'

'You're being ridiculous. Let me go.'

'Believe me, there's nothing I'd like more. But unfortunately I can't. Thanks to you, we're both in a situation that can't be easily solved. You're coming with me now, so that we can analyse our extremely limited options.' They were still locked together, the softness of her body pressed against the unyielding hardness of his, and he was finding it harder and harder to focus on what needed to be done. What had started as a means of ensuring that their conversation remained private had swiftly turned into something much, much more intimate.

It was like being back on the dance floor.

The scent of her skin and hair invaded his senses and he felt the immediate reaction of his body. Sexual awareness erupted and she obviously felt it too because she gave a moan of denial.

'Why would you want me to come with you? I seem to remember you telling me that you would rather be celibate than spend the rest of your life with a woman like me.'

He tensed. He'd flung those words at her on the night of the ball, and having them thrown back at him now was a harsh reminder of the realities of the current situation.

'I have no intention of spending the rest of my life with you. Just a few weeks. I'm sure that will be more than enough for both of us.'

'A few weeks?' She gave a brief shake of her head. 'I still have no idea what you're talking about, and my answer is still no.'

'So far I haven't asked you a question that needed an answer. Either you get in the car, or I'll lift you into it myself.'

'We have an audience who can see quite clearly that you are bullying me. Do you really think you can kidnap me in broad daylight?'

'No. I plan to be a great deal more subtle than that.' He brought his mouth down on hers and directed all the anger and frustration he was feeling into his kiss. But the moment her soft lips melded with his, his mind blanked and all control vanished. Her mouth was like a wicked, forbidden drug and even as he lost himself in the kiss he knew that the taste of her lips was going to stay with him for ever. Sweet, seductive, dangerously sinful—

Abruptly he lifted his head, astounded by his own ferocious hunger.

As he frowned down at her beautiful face, he noticed that her eyes were dazed and her cheeks were flushed. Her fingers were locked into the fabric of his shirt, as if for support.

Aware that he was fast approaching the point where he'd be prepared to risk a conviction for committing an indecent act in a public place, Angelos released her. 'No Parisian will intervene in a lovers' quarrel, *agape mou*. They know that the path of true love rarely runs smoothly, and by now they are all longing to see me ride roughshod over your objections and go for the happy ending.'

Without waiting for her response, he took her arm, controlling her easily with one hand while he used the other to open the car door.

As he propelled her into the passenger seat, a woman watching gave an envious sigh and turned to her friend.

'*L'amour*,' she said, and Angelos gave a grim smile as he slid into the driver's seat and started the engine.

Not *l'amour*, he thought viciously as he trod hard on the accelerator and made for the hotel.

Not *l'amour* at all.

What he had in mind had a much less romantic description attached to it.

CHAPTER THREE

WHAT did he want with her?

The living room of his penthouse suite was bigger than her entire flat, and looked out over the whole of Paris. It was a view that only the privileged few ever enjoyed, and at any other time Chantal would have been enchanted. But not now.

Her body was still in a state of helpless excitement following that one devastating kiss.

If dancing with him had been erotic, then kissing him had been—

She couldn't find a word for it.

Her legs still trembling, she looked around for somewhere solid to prop herself. She needed the support just in case he kissed her again.

But that wasn't going to happen, was it?

He wasn't even looking at her. Instead he was staring in brooding silence down into the streets below.

Her tongue sneaked out and touched her lower lip, still slightly swollen from the bruising force of his kiss. She was well aware that he'd used the kiss as a means of distracting their audience, but that knowledge in no way diminished the chemistry that had exploded between them.

Was the chemistry responsible for the anger she sensed in him?

The truth was, she no longer understood what was going on.

She'd attributed his anger on the night of the ball to the fact that he'd somehow discovered that she was an uninvited guest. When he'd first waved the crumpled ticket at her, she'd assumed that he was displaying the evidence.

And then he'd called her 'Isabelle', and she'd realised that he believed her to be the owner of the ticket. And the crazy thing was she didn't even *know* 'Isabelle'.

Obviously he didn't yet know that she'd gatecrashed the party.

Deeply regretting the impulse that had made her use a ticket that wasn't hers, Chantal glanced around furtively, half expecting someone in uniform to put a hand on her shoulder and arrest her.

Could you be arrested for something like that?

Did it count as identity theft if the transgression had only been for one short evening? Did it count as identity theft if the victim was none the wiser and the thief almost immediately gave the identity back? It wasn't really theft, was it? More a case of—borrowing. She'd borrowed someone else's name for a short time, just to see whether time and maturity had given her the confidence to mingle with people who'd used to make her feel insignificant.

Trying to ignore the shimmer of insecurity that had started to take hold, Chantal stood there awkwardly.

Now what?

Since he'd picked up her from the street, Angelos hadn't spoken a word. He'd strapped her with restrained violence into the passenger seat and proceeded to drive skilfully through the fast Paris traffic before finally pulling up outside the most expensive hotel in the city.

Only then had he finally glanced in her direction. His tone icy cold, he'd uttered just one word. 'Out.'

The simmer of anger in his dark eyes had made her insides quake, but remembering the few weeks she'd spent working in the hotel when she'd first arrived in Paris, she hadn't wanted to draw attention to herself by arguing with him on the pavement. So Chantal had simply lowered her head and followed him meekly into the lift that led directly to the penthouse suite, hoping that none of the staff would recognise her.

As soon as the door had closed behind them, she'd regretted following him and now she was finally alone with him she felt a flutter of nerves in her stomach.

She tried to look relaxed. *As if his kiss hadn't turned her insides into a mass of squirming, helpless longing.* 'All right. I'm here. What did you want to say to me?' *Why didn't he speak?* She just wished he'd say *something*. Anything—instead of just standing there with his back to her, his broad shoulders stiff with tension. 'Perhaps I should just leave—'

He turned, the angular lines of his handsome face set and hard. 'If you leave, I'll just bring you back.' He was autocratic and intimidating and she stood frozen to the spot, confused by the conflict she sensed in him.

He'd kissed her, but it was obvious that he wasn't happy about it.

'Let's just get one thing straight from the outset,' she muttered, deciding that she might as well make her position clear. 'I *won't* have sex with you, so if that's what this is all about, you might as well just let me go now.'

A protracted silence followed her impulsive declaration. The only indication that he'd even heard her was a slight narrowing of his dark eyes.

The silence unnerved her and she tried again. 'I'm just saying that although I'm sure every other woman you meet is desperate to—I mean, you're a good-looking guy, but…' Her voice trailed off, her chattiness extinguished by his total lack of response.

Finally, after what felt like a lifetime, he spoke.

'Do I look like the sort of man who picks up a woman from the street when he wants sex?'

Chantal could have told him that those men came in all shapes and sizes, but she chose to keep her thoughts to herself. 'I have no idea what sort of man you are. And I don't want to find out.'

'Really?' One dark eyebrow lifted in mockery. 'You expect me to believe that after the virtuoso performance you gave on the night of the ball?'

Remembering the erotic dance they'd shared, Chantal felt her heart-rate double. 'It was just a dance…' her voice trailed off again as his eyes locked on hers.

And suddenly there it was again.

The same silent connection that had drawn them together the night of the ball.

Something flickered in the depths of his eyes, something dark and dangerous, and she knew that his mind was in the same place as hers: *the exquisite agony of anticipation as their bodies had moved and slid together, the heat, the restrained passion, the delicious intimacy—*

They stared at each other until the tension in the room was wound so tightly that it came close to snapping.

This time he was the one to break the silence. 'Tell me something—' his voice was lethally soft '—is that how you trap all your men? You dance with them first? Is it your idea of a free trial? Try before you buy?'

His cynicism clashed with the image of him that her mind had greedily stored away. She'd remembered a gentleness, but there was nothing gentle about his man. He was all hard angles and sharp anger. 'I'm not for sale, Mr Zouvelekis.'

'I think the people who watched you dance might have trouble believing that.'

And the amazing thing was she hadn't been aware of anything or anyone but him. She'd been so absorbed by the rhythm of the music and the movement of his body that she'd been lost in her own world. The dance had been special. Something astonishing that they'd created together.

But that was ridiculous, of course. A prime example of her imagination running away yet again. For him, it hadn't been special. It had been a prelude to sex.

Not only was he turning the dance into something sleazy, he was judging her.

And although she didn't know anything about this Isabelle woman, she knew all about being judged.

Chantal straightened her shoulders. 'I danced because you insisted on it. *You* hauled me onto the dance floor like some possessive herd bull. But on that dance floor we were equally matched.' For a brief moment she'd experienced the bliss of having a man completely in tune with her. 'If I gave, then it's because you demanded. Whatever I did, you were there before me.'

'You manipulated the entire scenario. With a different man your plan might have worked.'

'I didn't have a plan. And *you* approached *me*.'

'You paraded yourself in front of me in a dress designed specifically to capture a man's attention.'

She decided that this wasn't the time to feel pride that her work on a length of material that had begun life dressing windows had been so successful and convincing. 'I didn't exactly *parade*.'

'Let me give you a few hints,' he purred, his lashes lowering to conceal the expression in his eyes. 'I'm Greek. I'm Greek all the way through. And when it comes to women we're still very traditional. Greek men like to do the choosing *and* the chasing.'

Chantal frowned, thinking about the article she'd read about him the day after the ball. 'I thought you were supposed to be very forward thinking. You have more women in executive positions than most companies.'

'That's business. In my personal life I'm very traditional,' he drawled. 'And it doesn't matter whether it's the boardroom or the bedroom, the important thing is to find the right woman for the job. As far as wife material goes, you don't fit my ideal profile. Next time spend more hours on your research.'

'Research?' Chantal shook her head in confusion. 'Did you think you were some sort of *project*, or something?'

Contempt flickered across his features. 'Do you really think that I haven't heard about you?'

So obviously Isabelle had a reputation as a gold-digger.

Floored by that piece of news, Chantal stood still, her brain a hopeless tangle of indecision. It was obvious that she needed to try once again to tell him that she wasn't this Isabelle person, but doing that would mean admitting to an even worse crime. She was a thief, and strictly speaking she'd impersonated someone else. Could that be classed as fraud if the ticket had been in the bin? Possibly. Could she go to gaol? Possibly. She didn't really know, but she did know that he was angry enough to make trouble.

Trouble that she didn't need.

Better a gold-digger than a thief.

Deciding that for the time being the less she revealed the better, Chantal licked her lips. 'You're wrong about me.'

'Not wrong. It's obvious that you went to the ball with the intention of targeting me.'

Astonished by his interpretation of the facts, Chantal shook her head. 'I didn't even know who you were until I picked up a newspaper the next day.'

'Do you think I'm stupid?'

'Not stupid. Arrogant.'

'Realistic,' he shot back. 'And justifiably cautious. Clearly you have no idea how many women have trodden that same path before you. So I'll tell you once again that I could never be attracted to anyone as manipulative as you. Dishonesty is not a trait I've ever admired in a woman.'

Chantal froze, doubly relieved that she hadn't told him the truth.

He wouldn't understand, would he?

She cringed at the thought of the reaction that such a confession would invoke. This was a man with the world at his fingertips. What would someone like him know about her life? How could he even begin to understand what had driven her to do something like that?

A dark memory of the last time someone had discovered the truth about her rose, and she felt a flicker of the old panic. And then she reminded herself that her past was all safely hidden. It was buried so deep that no one would ever discover the truth about her. That part of her was gone for ever, and she was perfectly safe.

She was whoever she wanted to be.

And at the moment that might as well be Isabelle.

Trapped by a situation entirely of her own making, Chantal wiped her damp palms over the limited fabric of her skirt, wishing there was more of it. She felt horribly exposed—even more so as his gaze travelled slowly down the length of her legs.

She felt the same tingling feeling she'd felt the night of the ball and she lifted her chin, reminding herself that so far every second she'd spent with this man had been a disaster. '*Stop* looking at me.'

'If you don't want a man to look at you,' he bit out, 'try wearing a skirt that covers your bottom. If outfits could talk, then yours is saying "take me". You're a walking advert for sex. I'm surprised you haven't been arrested, walking the streets dressed in that. Or perhaps *un*dressed would be a better description.'

This was the point where she should tell him that she had until a few hours ago been working as a waitress. But she had no intention of doing that. And anyway, when had she ever allowed herself to be defined by her job? 'How I dress is my choice.'

'I agree absolutely,' he drawled, a cynical gleam in his dark eyes. 'But, having made that choice, you cannot then object when a man responds in a predictable way. We're not very advanced when it comes to matters as basic as sex. You chose to dress like that, and therefore it follows that you wanted to invoke a certain reaction in the male sex. And that is entirely in keeping with your reputation.'

Chantal felt a flicker of unease. What exactly had Isabelle been up to?

It would have been helpful to know.

Apart from the obvious deduction that she was the sort of woman willing to carelessly drop a coveted ticket in a hotel dustbin, Chantal knew nothing about her. But her curious, inventive mind had already started filling in the gaps. What had made a woman discard a ticket to an event to which only a select few were allowed access?

Who was she?

Judging from the derisive curl of Angelos's mouth, no one she ever wanted to meet.

Chantal chewed her lip, trying not to reflect on the irony of the fact that she'd obviously borrowed the identity of a woman whose life was every bit as complex as her own.

Now what?

What should she do? Her whole life had been a web of lies since childhood, but her lies were only self-protection, and they'd never actually harmed anyone, had they? This was the first time that any of her stories had caught up with her and she felt a flutter of nerves in her stomach.

After their one explosive encounter she'd been left with the impression that he wouldn't ever want to cross her path again. Even now she didn't understand why he'd brought her here. At first she'd assumed it was for sex, but there was nothing lover like about the way he was glaring at her.

'So what do you want from me?' He came from a different world, and that world still had the ability to shrink her back to a terrified schoolgirl.

Victim.

The word flew into her head and she pushed it away immediately, straightening her shoulders.

She wasn't going to be anyone's victim. Never again.

Visibly tense, he tugged impatiently at the knot of his tie and undid the top button of his shirt, clearly finding it constricting. 'You are going to continue the charade that you began the night of the ball.'

'Sorry?'

Anger flashed in his dark eyes and his hand sliced through the air in a furious gesture. 'Do *not* pretend that you don't know what I'm talking about,' he breathed, 'when we *both* know that you used the ball as a means to meet me.'

'I've already told you that I didn't. I—'

'You virtually threw yourself across my path. And from the moment we met you couldn't stop looking at me.'

'Well, in order to have noticed you must have been looking at me too,' Chantal offered logically, and he inhaled sharply.

'You danced as though we were already horizontal in the bedroom.'

'You danced too.'

Her comment did nothing to alleviate his temper. He muttered something in Greek that she just *knew* would be better off not translated.

'I ought to congratulate you.' He switched back to English, his derisive tone suggesting that congratulations were the last thing on his mind. 'I thought I'd been on the receiving end of every possible trick, but you took the whole thing to an entirely new level.'

'You're obviously very angry, but—'

'You're right, I'm angry. Over the years various women have gone to enormous lengths to attract my attention. They pose as businesswomen, they apply for a job with me, they book tables in restaurants where I am dining, they hover outside my house in the hope of bumping into me. Sometimes they just turn up in my office wearing next to nothing, in the hope that they'll attract my attention.'

'Really?' Astonished that some women had the confidence to go to those lengths to meet someone, Chantal gaped at him. 'Gosh. That's amazing.'

'It is *not* amazing. It is intrusive and unacceptable.'

'It must be one of the drawbacks of being a billionaire, I suppose. Can't you laugh about it?'

He threw her an incredulous glance and sucked in a breath. 'It is not amusing. Particularly when a woman stoops so low as to target *my father* in order to gain my attention.'

'Ah.' Finally sensing the direction of the conversation, Chantal gave an awkward shrug. 'Actually, that wasn't exactly what happened.'

The expression on his handsome face was grim as he surveyed her. 'That is *exactly* what happened. Having danced with me, you then targeted him—like the greedy, unscrupulous, predatory woman you so clearly are.'

'I didn't know he was your father until you arrived with the drinks. And *he* approached *me*.'

'Of course he did. My father's fatal weakness is beautiful women—a fact of which you were well aware.'

'I knew nothing about your father until that night.' *Until he'd rescued her.* 'I really liked him.'

Angelos shot her a look so fierce it would have stopped a riot. 'I'm sure you did. He's rich. And you have a taste for rich men— don't you, Isabelle?'

'Do I?'

'Obviously. Given that you have already fleeced two in divorce settlements—one of them older than my father. For a woman of twenty six, you've been extremely busy.'

Chantal gasped. This Isabelle woman had married two men? One of them considerably older than her?

Perhaps continuing to let him believe that she was Isabelle hadn't been such a sensible idea, after all.

The situation was going from bad to worse, and it was obvious that she just needed to walk away from it and try and put the whole thing behind her.

'I'm obviously not your favourite person right now,' she ventured cautiously, 'so why am I here? Why did you come looking for me?'

'Because of the lies you told my father.'

'Lies?' Shrinking at the memory of that particular conversation, Chantal stood there helplessly. She couldn't explain without revealing things about herself that she'd spent her life concealing.

'You told him that we were in love—that you fell in love with me the first moment you saw me. Is it coming back to you yet, or do you need me to carry on?'

'Well—I didn't exactly—it was more that he assumed—'

A muscle flickered in his lean jaw. 'And did you correct him?'

Chantal breathed in and out. 'No.'

'Of course you didn't.' His tone was silky smooth. 'Presumably because your plan was all coming together nicely.'

'How does talking to your father bring me closer to marrying you?' Chantal wondered briefly what had made him so suspicious of women.

'You saw his face. You saw how delighted he was when he thought we were together.'

'He's obviously very keen to see you married,' Chantal said, her expression softening at the thought of his father. 'But I'm sure when you explained that it was all a misunderstanding he understood.'

Angelos tensed and turned away from her, his broad shoulders rigid with tension. 'Unfortunately I wasn't able to do that.'

'Why not?'

He turned back to face her and a muscle flickered in his lean jaw. 'My father had a heart attack that night. He was in hospital here in Paris for a week and then I had him flown back to Greece.'

'No!' Genuinely distressed by that piece of news, Chantal lifted her hand to her mouth and shook her head. 'Please tell me that isn't true—'

His eyes darkened ominously. 'You think I would joke about such a thing?'

'No! I just—' She felt as though something was crumbling inside her and she rubbed her fingers across her forehead, trying desperately to pull herself together. What was the matter with her? He wasn't *her* father. It was ridiculous to feel this way. 'I'm sorry. It's just that—is he going to be all right?'

'Why would you care?'

'Because I liked him so much. Is he recovering?'

'According to the doctors, his recovery so far has been nothing short of miraculous. Apparently he has been clinging to life, determined to live long enough to witness my marriage to the wonderful woman he saw me with that night at the ball.' His tone was acid. 'It seems that our "relationship" has given him a reason to live.'

'I'm glad he's going to be all right, but—' Chantal stared at him in growing dismay as his words sunk in '—you didn't—you haven't told him the truth, then?'

'What do you think?'

That he was a man who loved his father. Greek. Family mattered to Greeks. 'Obviously you didn't want to as he was poorly, and no one would blame you for that.' Feeling awkward, she cleared her throat. 'So that means he still thinks that we— that we're—'

'In love,' Angelos slotted in helpfully. 'Crazy about each other. All the things you told him that night. When he finally regained consciousness he distracted himself from the stresses of hospital by lying in bed naming his grandchildren.'

'Oh—' Chantal breathed out heavily and thought quickly.

'So obviously you're waiting to find the right time to explain that there was a misunderstanding?'

'And when do you think he'd like to hear that piece of unwelcome news?' His tone was biting. 'Before or after his next heart attack—which, according to the specialists, is a distinct possibility.'

Chantal was horrified. 'I seriously hope they're wrong about that.'

'So,' he said grimly, 'do I.'

'I hope he's resting.'

'He is currently staying on my island in Greece.'

'Your island?' *He had an island?* It was just as well she hadn't known who he was, Chantal thought weakly, because she never would have had the courage to talk to him in the first place. 'He's on his own on an island? Is that the best place for him?'

'He has a team of nurses and doctors attending to him and I intend to join him shortly.'

'Well, in that case—' she licked her lips '—I'm sure once you're there you'll find the right time to tell him that we're not exactly—together.'

'I don't intend to tell him. Not until he's well. On the contrary, the doctors have instructed that he should be kept as relaxed as possible over the coming weeks. No stresses. No worries. He should be surrounded by people he loves and trusts.'

'Right. Well, that sounds sensible.' Chantal stared at him. 'So—what does this have to do with me?'

His mouth tightened. 'Unfortunately for both of us you played your game rather well the night of the ball. My father enjoyed your company enormously. He is looking forward to your arrival on the island so that he can get to know his future daughter-in-law.'

CHAPTER FOUR

SHE LOOKED the picture of innocence, Angelos thought savagely. There was a gentleness in her eyes and a softness to her face that was totally at odds with her reputation as a man-eater. Not just a man-eater, he reminded himself grimly. Her tastes were more refined than that. She was a clever, manipulative, rich-man-eater.

'He thinks we're getting married?' Her eyes were wide and shocked, and Angelos fought back his distaste.

He couldn't believe he'd actually allowed himself to be manipulated in this way. Only once in his life before had he ever been taken in by a woman, and on that occasion he'd had inexperience as his excuse. He'd been just eighteen years of age, and dizzy with lust. Lust—love—how easily those two became intertwined. His mouth tightened at the thought.

He was no longer eighteen.

So what was his excuse this time?

He resisted the temptation to turn the full force of his anger onto the woman standing in front of him. 'You told him that you were crazy about me. That we were madly in love.' Angelos struggled to keep his voice level. 'As far as my father is concerned, the next step is marriage.'

Her gaze softened. 'He is *such* a lovely man. I thought that at the time.'

I'll just bet you did. Angelos made a mental note not to leave her alone with his father for too long. Despite her protests, he had no doubt that once she discovered her 'relationship' with him had no long-term prospects she would have no compunction about turning her attentions to his more vulnerable father. 'Before you start congratulating yourself on your success, remember that this is *me* you're dealing with—not my father.'

'You want me to go to Greece with you? That's what you've brought me here to ask me?'

'I don't *want* you to go to Greece with me. But that is what is going to happen.'

Obviously the two men she'd duped hadn't been able to see past those sapphire eyes, he thought grimly. And this time she'd obviously decided to go for the jackpot. The sheer audacity of her plan amazed even him. His views on marriage were well known, as were his views on his father's two very public and very expensive divorces. The fact that she'd believed that she might be successful said a great deal about her ego.

'I don't understand why you would think it's a good idea. Your father would never believe that we were together!'

'Thanks to your convincing display at the ball, he *already* believes that we are together,' Angelos told her. 'Your role is simply to produce more of the same. It shouldn't be too hard. I'll be working for most of the day. You will get to sit by a pool with a drink in your hand and a view of the Aegean Sea, singing my praises. From what I can gather, you're in between men at the moment. Think of it as a free holiday—which isn't quite on the same level as a meal ticket for life, but given the stunt you pulled you're lucky even to get that from me.'

She watched him, and he could almost see her brain working as she thought about what he'd said.

'No.'

'Don't try and negotiate with me,' he warned softly. 'There won't be a better offer.'

'I'm not hoping for a "better offer".'

'Then why refuse?'

'Because it wouldn't be fair on your father. I don't understand why you think it's a good idea.' She frowned slightly. 'When he finds out that you're lying, he'll be devastated.'

The same uncomfortable truth had occurred to Angelos, but he'd been unable to find any other solution. 'It is a shame this conscience of yours didn't emerge a little sooner. Thanks to you, I don't have a choice. When my father is stronger, I'll tell him that we weren't as compatible as we thought.'

'It would never work.'

'Why not?'

'If you glare at me the way you're glaring at me now, he's never going to be convinced that our relationship is real.'

'The mere fact that I am bringing you to the island will be enough to convince him.'

'Why?'

Angelos tensed. 'I don't take women there.'

Her eyebrows rose. 'Never?'

'It is a place for family.'

'And none of your previous women have earned that distinction?'

'You are not family either, Isabelle,' Angelos warned her softly. 'Do not forget that. You're merely a necessary part of my father's convalescence.'

She frowned. 'I'm not sure—'

'I don't understand why you're hesitating. I'm offering you an all-expenses-paid luxury holiday.'

She looked at him, her gaze disturbingly direct. 'That's why I'm hesitating.'

He thought he could buy her.

But she didn't accept gifts from men, or hospitality. Ever. She lived her life by that principle.

Chantal gave a shiver, acknowledging the irony of her situation. She'd taken the ticket of a woman who clearly didn't share her scruples.

'I can't do it,' she said hoarsely and his eyes narrowed.

'You *will* do it—if I have to drag you there myself.'

'No. My answer has to be no.' Something dark and ugly uncurled inside her and she gave a little shake of her head. 'You don't understand.'

'I understand perfectly. And that's what frightens you, isn't it? For once you're dealing with a man who *does* understand you. All your declarations about liking my father have proved to be as meaningless and empty as I believed them to be.'

'That isn't true.'

'If it were true then you would be doing everything possible to aid his recovery.'

Chantal turned away, remembering just how kind his father had been to her that night of the ball. She remembered the warmth of his hand on hers and how he'd stood next to her, protecting her.

She owed him her help. She *wanted* to help. But how could she when helping meant accepting Angelos's hospitality?

The obvious solution would be to pay for herself, but given the pathetic state of her finances that wouldn't be possible. She might be able to scrape together enough to cover the cost of her flight ticket, but there was no way she'd have anything left over to cover her living costs.

'The fact that you are even hesitating shows me that you are every bit as cold-hearted as your reputation suggests.' His tone was harsh. 'I have explained that your presence would help my father, but as usual all you are thinking of is yourself.'

Stung by the injustice of that accusation, Chantal turned. 'That is not true.' She lifted her fingers to her forehead, trying to think the situation through.

Would it be so very wrong to say yes?

It wasn't as if she and Angelos were having an affair. Despite the chemistry between them, it wasn't that sort of relationship. All they'd ever shared was one dance and a lot of cross words. She would be living in the villa as a favour to him. To help his father.

That was quite different from—

Pushing aside her reservations, she gave a swift nod. 'I'll do it. But I insist on paying for my flight ticket.'

A stunned expression crossed his handsome face and then he gave a humourless laugh. 'It's a little late to try and impress me,' he drawled, 'and anyway, I don't issue tickets when I fly by private jet.'

The colour poured into her cheeks and she felt a rush of humiliation. Private jet. Of course. How could she have been so stupid? She should have known that this man wouldn't exactly fly budget airlines.

'Wait—what I mean is, I don't want you paying for me,' she stammered, and he raised an eyebrow.

'I could probably calculate your share if you wanted me to. But it would have several noughts attached to it. If you're trying to persuade me that you're not interested in my wealth, then you're wasting your time. The evidence is stacked against you.'

Chantal bit her lip. She didn't have the money to reimburse him for the flight, so she couldn't push the point, but she felt deeply uncomfortable.

'If I come with you—' she lifted her chin and looked him in the eye '—it's just because of your father. Not for any other reason.'

'What other reason would there be? I'm not like the other men you've met, Isabelle. It takes more than a little hot chemistry to cloud my judgement.'

Uncomfortably aware of his scrutiny, she blushed and walked across to the window, turning her back to him.

He was so different from his father. Hard where his father had been soft. Intimidating where his father had been approachable.

Remembering just how much she'd liked the older man, she felt something tug deep inside her and felt a sudden pang of regret that he was now so poorly.

She remembered how delighted he'd seemed that his son was 'in love' and her expression softened. Clearly the son hadn't inherited his knife-sharp cynicism from his father.

From her vantage point on the balcony, Chantal stared down at the streets of Paris. She could see the Seine, winding through the city, and the bold jut of the Eiffel Tower, its structure glinting in the warm sunshine.

And across the city, in the dirtiest, cheapest, most forgotten part of Paris, was the room that she'd vacated that morning. The price had become prohibitive. Too much for a waitress. It was time to move on.

Why not to Greece? She had no other place to go. Nowhere else she needed to be.

Wouldn't that solve all her problems in the short term as well as helping out a man she genuinely cared about?

If her presence helped his recovery, then wasn't that reason enough to go?

She could stay as long as she was needed, and then use Greece as a base for her next adventure. The only drawback was being in the company of Angelos Zouvelekis. He unsettled her more than any man she'd ever met.

But he'd be working, wouldn't he? *Adding more noughts to his billions?*

All she had to do during the day was lie by the pool and chat to his father.

'You'll have to tell him the truth at some point.'

'Obviously. But not until he is stronger and has something else to focus on. Having had such a close brush with death, it seems that the only thing on his mind is the fact that I haven't yet given him grandchildren. When he is properly recovered he will find something else to occupy him.'

She turned. 'You don't intend to give him grandchildren?'

'At some point. But only when I find a woman whose genes I would be proud for my children to inherit.' His tone left her in no doubt that he wouldn't be allowing *her* genes anywhere near his offspring.

And that was an attitude she was more than familiar with.

She'd never fitted in, had she?

All her life she'd felt displaced.

As a child she'd lived her life around the edges of a world to which she didn't belong. And rarely had anyone shown her kindness.

His father had shown her kindness.

'I'll do it,' she said firmly. 'If you think it will help.'

'It never occurred to me that you wouldn't,' he drawled, contempt flickering in his eyes. 'From what I've heard, you never spend your money if you can spend someone else's.'

She tensed. 'I'm doing this for your father.'

'Of course you are. Your generosity is legendary.'

Chantal was almost relieved that she wasn't Isabelle. 'No matter what you think,' she said quietly, 'I'm not interested in your money.'

It had been something else entirely that had drawn her to him. A powerful connection that she couldn't explain. A chemistry that taunted both of them, because it was something that neither wanted to pursue.

The Aegean Sea stretched beneath them, the changing light producing more shades of blue than an artist's palette.

'It's beautiful,' she murmured, but she was talking to herself—because Angelos had been on the phone since his private jet had lifted off from Paris. And he was still on the phone. He lounged on a sofa opposite her, his eyes fixed on a computer screen, the table in front of him strewn with papers. Occasionally he broke the conversation for long enough to scan a set of figures, then he was talking again, in rapid Greek.

He'd paid her no attention whatsoever.

And perhaps that was just as well, she reflected, because her astonishment and awe when she'd seen the inside of his private jet had bordered on the gauche.

She had no idea how Isabelle would have reacted, but her mouth had dropped open in disbelief as she'd taken in the sumptuous cream leather sofas and the soft carpeting.

If it hadn't been for the uniformed cabin attendant's instruction to fasten her seat belt, she would have believed that it was all a mistake and she was actually in a high-class apartment. She'd been afraid to eat or drink in case she dropped something and her one trip to the bathroom had left her wishing she'd had time to design herself a new wardrobe.

By contrast, Angelos had merely divested himself of the jacket of his suit, loosened his tie, and ordered a black coffee.

Greek coffee, she assumed, staring at the thick black grounds that remained in the bottom of his cup.

Her most anxious moment had occurred when he'd asked for her passport. But she needn't have worried because he'd simply handed it straight to one of his staff—a woman who clearly had no idea which name was supposed to be inside the document.

Since then he hadn't looked at her. Hadn't once asked after her comfort. Hadn't even hurled an insult in her direction or given her one of his looks.

It was almost as if he preferred to think she didn't exist.

Which had made her journey more comfortable, but didn't bode well for the roles they were supposed to play.

His last few moments of freedom, she mused, wondering how he was ever going to manage to maintain this charade once they arrived at his island.

She waited until he'd terminated his latest phone call and then spoke. 'Are we pretending to be lovers who have had a row?'

He glanced up from the figures he was scanning, his thick dark lashes drawing attention to his eyes. 'A row?'

'We are supposed to be adding to your father's relaxation. I don't think being with two people who react to each other in stony silence is going to do much for his peace of mind. If we *were* already married, then I think divorce would be looming.'

His eyes narrowed, and he dropped the paper onto the table. 'When I need to talk to you, I'll talk.'

'Fine. But there are a few things I need to know if I'm going to stand any chance of being convincing.'

'Such as?'

'Details. Facts. The sort of things that would have come up in conversation. Does anyone else live on the island, or is it just you?'

He leaned back in his chair. 'Stop pretending you're not already in possession of a full list of my assets.'

Chantal sighed. Clearly a woman like Isabelle would have known the answer to that question. 'Has it ever occurred to you that you might have misjudged me?'

'No. Why would it?' He tucked his pen back into his pocket. 'Don't even *think* about playing any of your usual games.'

'Don't worry.' Having no idea what Isabelle's usual games were, Chantal kept her answer suitably vague. 'I'm just going to lie by the pool and chat to your father.'

'And don't get any ideas on that score, either.'

'What?' She felt a flicker of exasperation. 'I thought that was what you wanted me to do?'

'Your role is to convince my father that we are a happy couple. I'm well aware that your taste can run to older men if the price is right. In this case, don't even think about it.'

It took her a moment to grasp his meaning. 'Are you suggesting that I'm interested in your *father*?'

'You seemed interested enough the night of the ball. You were all over him. Flirting.'

'*Talking.*'

'Laughing. Asking him to dance.'

'I liked him. He was kind to me.' *And so few people in her life had ever been kind to her.*

'My father is kind to everyone.'

'And you disapprove of that quality?'

'When it comes to glamorous women it's a weakness, not a quality.'

'If everyone was kinder to each other the world would be a better place.'

He gave a cynical laugh. 'And we both know what form you'd want that kindness to take. As you already know, my father is a rich man. Not quite as rich as I am, but I've no doubt you were happy to consider him good enough for back-up.'

Appalled and fascinated by the thought of what might drive a woman to such desperation, Chantal studied him for a moment. Her response was cautious. 'That's what you think I'd do?'

'Given that your last husband was seventy-five—yes.'

Seventy five? Chantal almost gasped aloud. Isabelle had married a man of *seventy-five*? She wondered briefly whether she should have told the truth about who she was. No. If he was shocked by Isabelle, how much more shocked would he be to learn the truth about *her* life?

'I'm just warning you not to try any tricks, because I'll be watching.'

'Tricks? What tricks are you expecting?'

'You've failed with me. Don't even think about targeting my father. A man who has made two mistakes in marriage will not be allowed to make a third!'

'Mistake?' She blinked at him. 'He told me that he was married to your mother for forty years. It didn't sound like a mistake to me. He was totally in love.' She watched as shock flared in his eyes.

'You asked him about my *mother*?'

'No! He—' Thrown by his anger, she broke off, struggling to remember exactly how the conversation had evolved. 'We were talking about love. He told me that she died. I—I'm very sorry.'

He didn't respond, but she saw that his knuckles were white. 'He *never* talks about my mother.'

'Well, he talked to *me*. Maybe it was because I was a stranger. Or because we just seemed to click. I don't know. I *liked* him—' She gave a helpless shrug. 'Why do you dissect every conversation? Who made you so cynical?'

'Women like you. I know who you are, Isabelle.'

He had no idea who she was.

And she had no intention of telling him. Perhaps one day he'd find out, when he bumped into the real Isabelle on the party circuit. But by then she'd be long gone.

She sank back against her seat. He intimidated her, but at the same time he intrigued her, and suddenly she really wanted to understand what drove his deep-rooted cynicism. Something in his past, obviously. She, better than anyone, knew that even when you tried to move on the past had a way of winding itself around your ankles like seaweed—taking hold, *dragging you back to the place you were trying to escape from.*

'So—' she changed the subject to a topic less inflammatory '—what do you do with a whole island to yourself?'

'It has been in my family for five generations. My ancestors grew olives and made wine. I rebuilt the villa five years ago. It is the one place where we can guarantee a level of privacy, away from media intrusion.'

'Five generations?' Chantal felt a flash of envy. What must it be like to have family you could trace back for generations? What was it like to be part of a group of people who cared about each other?

'They led a simple life,' he told her, stretching his legs out in front of him, 'and that is what the island is for. So if you're hoping for a glamorous holiday, then you'll be disappointed. The only thing that glitters is the sea when the sun hits it. You can leave your silk and diamonds at home. We don't dress for dinner. It's basic. I prefer it that way.'

So did she.

Chantal relaxed slightly. The dress code had been one of her major concerns about this trip. Given the deficiencies of her wardrobe, the thought of 'dressing for dinner' had filled her with dismay. And as for leaving her silk or diamonds at home—not only did she not possess any silk and diamonds, she didn't have a permanent home in which to leave them.

'It sounds perfect.'

'Don't be ridiculous. We both know you're going to hate it. I think we're about to discover just how "adaptable" you are, Isabelle.'

Probably a great deal more adaptable than he thought.

She braced herself as the plane came into land. 'Is this it?'

'No.' He unfastened his seat belt and rose to his feet. 'There is no landing strip on the island; it's too mountainous and craggy. We take a boat from here. So if you've any thoughts of running away, you're going to be disappointed. Unless you develop fins and a tail, once you're on the island you're stuck there.'

Angelos felt the spray on his face and increased the power, revelling in the sudden surge that had the luxury speedboat bouncing over the water, leaving a line of foam in its wake.

This stretch of sea was notoriously rough, but he didn't slacken the pace. Instead he steered the boat bows-on to the dancing waves.

Would the woman be seasick?

For a moment he almost relished what lay ahead.

Someone like her, who preyed on vulnerable men, would be frustrated and out of her depth on the island. There would be no one to seduce.

And not only that she'd been forced to leave all her seduction tools behind, he thought, smiling to himself as he contemplated what the mixture of seaspray and wind must be doing to her hair.

With a certain sadistic pleasure, he glanced over his shoulder—and felt a flash of surprise. Her hair was blowing wildly in the wind, but instead of clutching at it, as he'd expected, she was resting her head back against the safety rail of the boat and her eyes were closed.

She looked strangely content. Which made no sense at all.

He glanced towards the one small bag she'd brought aboard the flight from Paris. Her lack of luggage was a clear indication that she expected to be taken on some serious shopping trips—which meant that she was going to be severely disappointed. They weren't going anywhere, and she would be forced to wear whatever items she'd brought with her. And wear them again. And again. And launder them herself.

Angelos smiled as he thought about the role that she was going to be expected to play as his prospective wife.

Knowing his father, the first thing he'd want to see would be her prowess in the kitchen.

Can she cook, Angelos?

Undoubtedly not. In fact, he was willing to bet she'd never been near a hot stove in her life, let alone slaved over one. Why would she, when the men she'd married had given her a lifestyle beyond her wildest dreams?

If she'd had any sense she would have taken the money from her last divorce and settled in the Caribbean, instead of moving on to her next victim.

As they drew closer to the island Angelos slowed the boat and pulled in alongside the jetty. He cut the engine, and the air was filled with the insistent rasp of cicadas.

Above them he glimpsed the whitewashed walls of the villa. Hot pink bougainvillaea tumbled joyfully over the walls, basking in the hot Greek sunshine, and the path that led up from the jetty was thickly bordered with blue agapanthus.

'Home.'

It was only when she looked at him that he realised he'd spoken the word aloud.

'Is it home? I thought you lived in Athens?'

'My business requires that I travel a lot and I have a home in Athens because my headquarters is based there. But I have offices in almost all the major cities in the world. It's a necessity.'

'You don't like the city?'

'Sometimes. But the villa feels more like home than any other property I own. It is the place we spend time as a family.' He didn't know which surprised him more. His own confession or her nod of immediate understanding.

'I can see why you love it. It's beautiful.'

It seemed such an unlikely response from a woman with a love of the bright lights that he felt a flicker of irritation and suddenly regretted that circumstances had forced him to bring her with him. The island was usually a place to escape from the stresses and demands of his life. This time he'd been forced to bring the stress along with him.

He was about to make a sharp comment when he caught sight of the expression on her face. Her eyes sparkled with excitement and she was staring at the white-pebbled beach as though she couldn't wait to slip her shoes off and take a walk.

Surprised by her reaction, Angelos frowned. Pretty though it was, the island was a long way from the mainland. There were no trendy cafes, no boutique hotels or designer shops. No men and no nightclubs. In fact, nothing to entertain a woman like Isabelle. Just beaches, olives groves and dusty tracks winding their way over the headland.

He'd expected to see boredom or impatience on her face. Certainly not excitement. Suddenly she seemed vivid and alive and his eyes were drawn to the thrust of her breasts under the thin white top. Her body was lush and feminine, her mouth full and tempting, and her eyes were shining with almost child-like enthusiasm.

Angelos tightened his jaw, not knowing whether to be amused or irritated by the powerful and predictable response of his body.

Was he really that shallow?

Obviously the answer to that question was yes.

With a cynical laugh at his own expense, he turned away and secured the boat to the jetty with the rope.

It was ironic, he reflected, that the woman he'd finally brought home to this island was probably the last person on earth he'd contemplate marrying.

But, just as long as he kept that fact from his father, there shouldn't be a problem.

Feeling the heat of the sun on the back of her neck, Chantal followed Angelos up the path that led from the jetty to the villa. The garden seemed to tumble down the hillside, a joyful haven so breathtakingly beautiful that she paused for a moment just to enjoy the scent and colour. Orange and magnolia trees bordered the path, and the sea sparkled turquoise in the dazzling sunlight.

Aware that Angelos was glaring at her impatiently, she hurried towards him, followed him round a bend in the path and had her first proper view of the villa.

It had obviously been built to give the owners the benefit of what must surely be the best views in Greece, and her first impression left her speechless with wonder.

Between the villa and the sea lay a series of terraces, shaded by vines and linked by narrow paths. And on the same level as the villa itself was a large curved pool which followed the shape of the hillside and which appeared to merge with the ocean beyond.

Despite its obvious size, the villa itself was a vision of Mediterranean charm. Bougainvillaea tumbled from balconies, down over whitewashed walls to the scented gardens below. On the ground floor an arched entrance offered a tantalising view of a shaded stone courtyard with a central fountain. Doors opened from the main living area to the pool and inside the spacious room she could see rich-coloured textiles set against cool white walls.

'*Kalispera!*' A nurse appeared, wearing a crisp white uniform and a stern expression on her face.

Angelos walked towards her. 'How is my father today?'

'Determined to do himself as much damage as possible!' The nurse set her mouth in a disapproving line, and Angelos lifted an eyebrow.

'His tests are not good?'

'His tests are excellent, but he refuses to make any changes to his lifestyle.' Clearly exasperated with her patient, the nurse glanced at Chantal. 'Perhaps you will be able to influence him. He's been very excited about your arrival. Hopefully now you are here he will join you for dinner. I couldn't persuade him to eat lunch.'

Angelos frowned. 'He isn't eating?'

'He doesn't have much of an appetite.' Her tone sharp, the nurse flipped through her notebook, checking her facts. 'Black coffee for breakfast, nothing for lunch, and now he's asking for a drink.'

'Presumably not water?' Angelos said wearily. 'All right. I'll talk to him.'

'I'd appreciate that.' The nurse gave a brief nod and slipped the book back into her pocket. 'I'll go and talk to the kitchen about his diet. See if there's anything we can make that might tempt him.'

Angelos took Chantal's arm and steered her towards the pool. It was set high enough up to give a breathtaking view of the bay and several small islands in the distance, and for a moment she just stood there, wondering if there was a place more peaceful or beautiful anywhere on earth. She'd travelled, and seen many sights, but there was something about this place that made her catch her breath.

'It's stunning.'

Angelos turned towards her and smiled and that smile was so intimate and sexy that her stomach flipped. For a moment she was blinded. The world around her shrank and there was nothing but him. No view, no villa, no other person. She just gazed back at him, the words in her mouth melting away unspoken.

She was just reminding herself of the need to breathe when he leaned towards her, a smile in his eyes as his lips brushed against her cheek.

'Don't get too comfortable. I'm watching you,' he murmured softly in her ear, and she realised then that the smile and the sudden softening in his eyes had been for the benefit of his father, who was beaming with delight as he watched them.

And she took a step backwards, confused and disorientated because for one deeply humiliating moment she'd actually believed that the smile was for her.

And then she remembered. *Men like him didn't smile at women like her.*

Reminding herself of the dangers of slipping into fantasy land, she stepped away from him and walked to his father, automatically gravitating towards a friendly face. 'It's good to see you again, Mr Zouvelekis.'

'Call me Costas. After all, we're virtually family.' The older man struggled to his feet. Then he took her hands and squeezed, and the pressure of his fingers and the warmth in his eyes made the breath catch in her throat.

To be shown affection was such a rare and surprising gift that she clung to his fingers, unwilling to end a contact that felt so good.

Virtually family.

Never in her most extravagant fantasies would she have allowed herself to imagine a father as amazing as him. 'How are you?' Looking at him now, she could see that he'd lost weight and that his face had a greyish tinge.

'Better now I have something beautiful to look at. The nurses Angelos found—' He peered around him to check that the nurse was out of earshot and then pulled a face. 'He might as well have employed men.'

'Believe me, I tried,' Angelos said sternly. 'You're not supposed to be looking at the nurses.'

'I'm not.' Costas sounded gloomy. 'What is there to look at? That woman has the appeal of a wrestler. If she gets bored with nursing she could be a prison governor. Why did you employ her?'

'I employed her because her credentials are excellent. She tells me you haven't been eating.'

'She is a spy,' Costas grumbled, still holding Chantal's hands. 'Yesterday I tipped my medicine into a plant, and she immediately delivered another dose. *Obviously* she was watching from the bushes.'

Chantal chuckled. 'So that's why the garden is looking so good.'

Costas laughed too. Only Angleos wasn't amused.

'I'm paying her to make sure you make a full recovery.'

'If life is going to be this tedious I'm not sure that I want to. Still—' Costas lifted both Chantal's hands to his lips and kissed them gallantly. 'You're here now, and that changes everything.'

'Take your hands *off* my woman,' Angelos drawled, his expression faintly exasperated as he firmly removed Chantal's hands from his father's and enclosed them in a cool, hard grip. 'It isn't good for your blood pressure.'

'You have nothing to fear from me, Angelos.' His father looked suddenly tired, but the smile lingered in his eyes. 'The way she was looking at you a moment ago—no one else existed. That is how love should be. A woman in love can be in a crowd of handsome men, but she sees only one of them.'

Realising that it was true, Chantal felt suddenly vulnerable. She'd looked at Angelos. And he'd looked at her. The difference was that Angelos had been acting a part, whereas her reaction had been genuine. For a moment she'd forgotten that none of this was real. Staring into his eyes, she'd been taken straight back to those endless minutes on the dance floor, where their connection had been disturbingly intense and entirely genuine. The attraction between them had been primal and instinctive, undiluted by the complications of identity.

Costas sank into the nearest chair, as if standing was just too much. 'We haven't even been officially introduced.'

'I'm Chantal,' she said, and then caught the sardonic lift of Angelos's brows and knew instantly what he was thinking. *That she was embarrassed to admit her true identity.*

And the irony of the situation wasn't lost on her. She'd spent her life trying to be someone different, but now that she'd been offered a genuine alias she didn't want to take it.

She didn't want to be a woman who took money from a man.

It wasn't that she aspired to be perfect. Far from it. But that was the one sin she wasn't prepared to commit.

Maybe if Isabelle had been someone different she would have sat comfortably in her shoes for a few days, but as it was she was beginning to wonder whether her failure to confess her identity had been a mistake.

Costas sat for a moment, his weathered hand clutching the edge of the table.

Angelos stepped closer, a frown in his eyes. 'Are you unwell?' There was no missing the sharp anxiety in his voice, and Chantal found herself experiencing the same anxiety.

Costas Zouvelekis looked drained and exhausted, as if almost all of the life had been drained from him. She remembered him as an energetic, good-humoured man, and was shocked that his illness could have wrought such changes in such a short time.

'I'm fine. Don't fuss.' He glared at Angelos, and there was

pride in his eyes. Then he said something in Greek, and Chantal knew from the sudden tension in Angelos's powerful frame that Costas had been talking about her.

'I'm sure you have family matters you want to discuss, so I'll just—'

'You are family.' Costas gestured to the chair opposite. 'Sit down, and Maria will fetch you a drink to celebrate the occasion. The day my son finally brings a girl to his real home. Until I saw you in the boat I still couldn't believe it would happen. You have made me a very, *very* happy man.'

The nurse stepped out onto the terrace. 'You should take a nap before dinner, Mr Zouvelekis.'

Costas scowled. 'Nap? What am I? A baby?' But he rose to his feet swiftly, as if relieved that someone had suggested it. His gaze softened as he looked at Chantal. 'I would feel guilty leaving you when you've only just arrived, but I'm sure Angelos will find a way of entertaining you in the meantime.' His saucy wink implied that he knew exactly what form that entertainment was likely to take, but Angelos simply smiled as he strolled forward and helped his father to his feet.

Chantal watched the two of them, envy closing her throat. So it hadn't been her imagination. Angelos *was* capable of gentleness. It was there in his eyes when he talked to his father, and it stayed there until his father was safely in the villa and out of sight.

Only then did he turn to her, and the sudden chill in his eyes was a blunt reminder that she was only here because of his love for her father.

'*Chantal?*' His voice heavy with emphasis, Angelos sat back in his chair and contemplated her with ill-concealed mockery in his eyes. 'Changing the name doesn't change the person, *agape mou*. Remember that.'

'Chantal is my name.'

He smiled and reached for the jug of iced fruit juice that

Maria had placed on the table in front of them. 'I should imagine that it's useful to have more than one name.'

His contempt for her stung, and she rose to her feet. 'I think I'll go and shower and change.'

'Sit down.' His voice was so soft that it barely reached her ears, but there was no missing the authority in his tone and she sat in automatic response.

Only afterwards did she wonder why she'd responded without question.

'Do you expect everyone to obey you?'

'No. In fact I enjoy being challenged. There is no point in winning if there is no one else in the race.'

It was the sort of remark she'd come to expect of him. He was so confident about everything. *So sure of himself.* There was no doubt in her mind that this man had never felt out of place in his life. 'If you're bored, then please feel free to go and find something more interesting to do,' she muttered. 'Don't feel you have to entertain me. I'll be perfectly fine on my own.'

In fact she wished he *would* leave her on her own, because then she could talk some sense into herself. She found him incredibly, impossibly distracting and it was ridiculous to feel this way when he clearly considered the chemistry between them to be nothing short of an inconvenience.

Looking at his dark, luxuriant lashes and his wide, sensuous mouth, she felt the strength ooze from her body. *She just wanted him to kiss her.*

Those dark eyes locked on hers and the strength of the connection between them was so powerful that it shook her. 'My father likes you.'

'And I like him.' Her mouth was dry and her heart was thumping. 'He's an extremely nice man.'

They were talking about his father, but she knew, *she just knew*, that he was as distracted as she was. The chemistry between them was a living thing, a wild and dangerous force, curling itself around them like a million invisible threads.

Did he want to kiss her, too?

Was he thinking what she was thinking?

As if in answer to her question, Angelos dropped his gaze to her mouth and his eyes darkened. ' "Nice" is a non-descriptive word that should almost always be substituted with something more specific. What are you trying to say? That's he's rich? Quite handsome for his age?'

They were talking, and yet an entirely different conversation was going on between them—one that didn't involve words. The air vibrated with the force of it, and Chantal's nerves were strained tight. She didn't understand what was happening. It wasn't as if they were flirting. In fact, the words they were exchanging were barely civil.

'I'm trying to say that he's kind and approachable.' The heat around them rose to stifling proportions and her heart thumped uncomfortably. The atmosphere made her feel so jumpy that she was about to stand up in an attempt to disturb the tension when Maria walked onto the terrace and quietly informed Angelos that he was needed on the phone.

Her words shattered the explosive atmosphere and achieved what neither of them had managed to achieve by themselves.

With a sharply indrawn breath, Angelos rose to his feet. 'It will be the Athens office.' He looked at Chantal, but his glance was brief, as if he didn't trust himself to look for longer. 'This is going to take a while. Maria will show you to your room.'

CHAPTER FIVE

CHANTAL watched as he walked away from her, hating herself for feeling regret at his departure. What was it about him that was so irresistibly attractive? He was breathtakingly handsome, of course, but it couldn't be just that, could it? Perhaps it was his strength—that aura of power that clung to him—or perhaps it was something else entirely.

It didn't really matter. All that mattered was that she was helplessly, hopelessly attracted to him and it didn't make any difference that their relationship had been doomed from the start.

Their mutual desire was awkward, she admitted silently, finally turning her head and studying the still, glass-like surface of the pool. Confusing. He didn't want to feel it because Isabelle clearly wasn't the sort of woman who drew his admiration. She didn't want to feel it because he wasn't the sort of man she could ever get involved with.

Suddenly aware that Maria was waiting patiently to escort her into the villa, Chantal rose quickly and followed her down a different path and into a fabulous bedroom suite that opened directly onto the pool terrace. It was light and airy, decorated entirely in white, and brightened by touches of deep blue. Colourful oil paintings adorned the walls and a large rug softened the floor. It was tasteful and understated, and as she glanced through an open door into a spacious, marble bathroom Chantal tried not to look over-awed.

If this was a guest bedroom, she couldn't begin to imagine what the master suite was like—and if Angelos Zouvelekis thought this was living 'simply' then she could only feel relieved that she wouldn't be exposed to any of the other aspects of his life.

But she already knew that their lives were as different as it was possible to be. He had wealth and he had family. She had neither. And as for possessions—

She turned and glanced at her one small case, which now stood in the middle of the room. It was a forlorn reminder of the fundamental differences in their lives.

What was she doing here?

Maria was watching her, her expression sympathetic, as if she sensed Chantal's growing misery.

'I will help you unpack,' she volunteered, but Chantal shook her head vigorously, her face burning with embarrassment at the thought of this woman seeing her lack of belongings.

She waited for Maria to leave, then opened the case herself and stared at the few outfits she'd brought with her.

Two dresses, a skirt, a pair of shorts, a few cheap tops and a swimming costume.

That was it. Nothing glamorous. Nothing that suited a few hedonistic weeks with a billionaire.

She didn't belong here.

What arrogance had made her think her presence would have any effect on his father's recovery? It was inevitable that Costas Zouvelekis would discover that their relationship wasn't real and once he discovered the truth everything would be worse.

She should never have come.

And she should never have used that ticket to the ball.

Pretending was one thing; actually trying to live a life that wasn't hers was dangerous and delusional.

But what could she do? For the time being, at least, she was trapped here and she had to make the best of it.

She fingered one of the dresses, wondering whether she could adapt it in some way. Or perhaps she didn't need to. Angelos had said that there was no dressing up on the island, so hopefully what she'd brought with her would be fine. She just had a sinking feeling that her idea of simple and his weren't going to coincide.

Hot and uncomfortable after her journey, she was just contemplating a shower when a faint breeze blew through the window. Walking across to the open doors, Chantal stared at the pool glistening in the afternoon sunlight. The water looked cool and inviting, and she couldn't think of a reason why she shouldn't swim.

Angelos was working and Costas was resting, so no one would be watching her. And by the time Angelos returned from making his next million she would be back in her room.

In fact, if she was very clever, it might be possible to avoid him for the entire fortnight. If Angelos worked during the day then their paths would only cross at mealtimes.

Angelos completed the last of his phone calls and ran a hand over his face in mounting frustration.

It was clear that his presence was needed in Athens. Ordinarily he would have taken a helicopter back to the city for a few days, but he didn't feel comfortable leaving until he was satisfied that his father was making a good recovery. Nor did he want to leave the older man with a woman less than half his age—especially when the woman in question fulfilled his father's definition of female perfection and was known to favour older men.

Just thinking about her made his stress levels soar to dangerous heights and he rose to his feet with a soft curse, rolling his shoulders to relieve the tension that had been mounting since he'd picked her up from the streets of Paris.

His body was humming with unfulfilled desire and he suppressed it ruthlessly.

What he needed was exercise: a hard, demanding physical workout that would use up some of his excess energy and take his mind off his ravenous libido. A hundred laps of the pool would be nowhere near as mentally and physically invigorating as truly satisfying sex, but it was the only thing on offer so it would have to do.

He flicked off the computer, found a pair of swimming shorts and strolled out onto the terrace, flexing the muscles of his shoulders in readiness.

So focused was he on his own needs that he felt a flare of irritation when he heard a soft splash coming from the pool and realised that someone else had shared his idea.

It couldn't be his father, because he was resting, which meant that it could only be the one person he'd been hoping to avoid.

His first reaction was to acknowledge that she was a remarkably good swimmer. Accustomed to women who preferred to pose by the edge of the pool rather than actually expose themselves to the realities of getting wet, he watched for a moment, surprised by her skill. She slid through the water with the fluid grace of a sea creature and Angelos was gripped by an attack of lust so powerful that it shocked him.

Also accustomed to being with women whose choice of swimwear could only be described as minimal, he couldn't immediately understand why a plain black swimming costume, clearly designed for sport rather than seduction, could have had such a powerful effect on him. A few minutes of studied concentration gave him the answer. His reaction had nothing to do with the swimming costume itself and everything to do with the woman wearing it.

The costume moulded to her shapely body, emphasising her long, slender legs, the tempting curve of her hips and her astonishingly small waist. Her body was incredible, and a rush of red-hot lust engulfed him. His reaction to her was so absolutely primitive that he took a step backwards, seriously disconcerted by the almost overpowering response of his body. He was *not* a man who indulged in thoughtless, mindless sex. Not since his teenage years had impulse played any part in his relationships.

It was true that beautiful women played an extremely important part in his life, but he was fiercely exacting in his choice and he was *always* the one in control. He made the rules. Relationships began and ended when he decided they should begin and end.

Understanding the true meaning of the word *temptation* for the first time in his life, Angelos inhaled deeply and attempted to obliterate thoughts that were as inappropriate as they were unwelcome. But his head was filled with a disturbingly clear image of her lush breasts trapped against his body and those long, long legs wrapped around his waist.

After the stress of the past two weeks, all he wanted to do was drag her out of the pool, strip her naked, and slake his lust in a vigorous session of mindless sex designed to leave them both numb and exhausted. At that precise moment he didn't actually *care* that she represented everything he despised in a woman. He'd even stopped caring that she'd ripped off two vulnerable men. How could that possibly affect him? *Vulnerable* wasn't a word that appeared in his vocabulary, so he wasn't in the least bit worried for himself. He was as tough and uncompromising as she was and all that interested him was a thorough exploration of the physical connection that drew them together.

Trapped in a vortex of sexual hunger, he suddenly acknowledged a more immediate problem.

Once she finished the lap and saw him, she'd also see the very visible outwards signs of his reaction to her.

Solving the problem with his customary decisiveness, Angelos strode to the edge of the pool and executed a perfect dive, plunging head-first into the deep end and allowing the cool water to close around his thoroughly overheated body.

He rose to the surface and then powered through the water in a perfect crawl, reaching the side just as she turned.

He saw from the shock in her eyes that she hadn't been aware of his presence until that moment.

'I didn't know anyone was—I thought you were working—' The water clung to her cheeks and her upper lip, and her dark eyelashes were fused into spikes. Far from attempting to keep her hair dry and away from the vicious attack of the pool chemicals, she'd obviously swum under the water and it now lay sleek and smooth against her head. Wet, it was darker than its usual shade, but her eyes still sparkled the same miraculous blue.

Disconcerted by the feeling that this whole situation was slowly spiralling out of control, Angelos dragged his eyes away from the tempting fullness of her mouth. *The cold water was supposed to have helped.*

'I needed some exercise.' Suddenly he wished he'd chosen a run on the beach as an alternative to the swim. It would have been hot, but he doubted that it was possible to be any hotter than he was at the moment. His entire body felt as though someone had lit a furnace inside it.

How was it possible to feel hot in cold water?

'Did you finish your business?' It was an innocent enough question, but sufficient to remind him of the stress he'd been trying to put out of his mind.

'For now.' Deciding that lingering next to her was putting unacceptable pressure on his self-control, Angelos terminated the conversation by plunging forward and swimming twenty lengths in rapid succession, pushing his body to the limits as he chose athletic endeavour as a means to work off some of his mounting tension.

He finished yet another length, and turned, but this time his body collided with something soft and yielding.

She gave a soft gasp and swallowed a mouthful of water as she sank below the surface of the pool.

'*Theos mou*—' Angelos immediately hauled her back to the surface, his hands sliding round her waist to support her as she choked and coughed. In the water she was slippery and lithe, and she rested her hands on his shoulders as she regained her breath. His fingers felt the smoothness of her skin and the surprising delicacy of her frame. He'd just decided that touching her had been a mistake of monumental proportions, when she looked at him. The light in her eyes changed from a sparkle of blue to a deeper shade and Angelos suddenly wanted her more than he'd ever wanted anyone in his life before.

Without thinking, he lowered his head and kissed her. Instantly her mouth opened in response to the demands of his. He probed with his tongue and the hot, sweet flavour of her mouth sent fire spurting through his veins. His fingers tightened on her waist and he pulled her hard against him, feeling her lithe, sinuous body twine itself around the hard length of his like a delicate flower seeking support and strength. She pressed herself against him, clearly as hungry for him as he was for her, and the last desperate flicker of self-restraint died inside him.

He was immersed in her—the scent of her, the feel of her, the race of her heart against his seeking hands—and his physical arousal was so powerful that it obliterated all other thought.

The water of the pool lapped quietly around them, and his kiss changed from exploratory to hard and savagely urgent. Fantasy merged with reality as her legs wound themselves around his waist and he felt her feminine mound press against him. He slid her costume from her shoulders. Her nipples were hard against his chest, physical evidence that her degree of desperation was no less than his. His hands swift and skilled, he tugged her costume down her legs. She unwound herself from him for long enough to free herself of the wet cloth, and then she was pressing against him again, and this time it was her hands that were doing the exploring.

Angelos felt her seeking fingers close around him. Light exploded in his head and a desperate urgency consumed him. The entire focus of his world became this one moment. *This one woman.*

Pumped up, and more aroused than he'd ever been in his life before, he closed his hands over the top of her thighs, driven by an almost primal need for satisfaction. In the water she was weightless, and she writhed and moved against him as she searched instinctively for the ultimate connection. Taking control, Angelos dug his fingers into her soft flesh and angled himself slightly until the tip of his erection finally met the burning heat of her damp core. The contact drew a gasp from her lips, and for a moment they remained poised on the very edge of the final intimacy. Then Angelos could wait no more. He entered her with a smooth, expert thrust and drove himself full length into her soft, quivering body.

She was exquisitely, maddeningly tight, and as her moist feminine heat closed around him his world imploded. Dimly he registered the sudden tension in her body, and felt a sharp pain in his shoulders as she dug her nails into hard muscle. His brain tried desperately to decipher the signals, but she was hot, so un-bearably, deliciously hot after the cold of the water, that it took him a moment to clear his head sufficiently and register that something wasn't as he'd expected. He tried to control his own reaction, but at that moment her vice-like grip on his shoulders eased and she slid her arms round his neck, drawing closer to him as she moved her hips and pressed herself to him, urging him on.

Her soft moans of excitement drove him over the edge and his mind emptied. Blind to everything except the lure of imme-diate pleasure, Angelos surged into her again and again, losing himself in her soft heat, his usual self-control entirely absent, obliterated by a degree of sensation so overwhelming that it fell outside even his experience.

He felt her sudden gasp of disbelief, felt her body tremble against his, and then she shot into a climax so intense that the aftershocks ripped through his failing control. His own excitement amplified by her abandoned, extravagant response, he ground into her one more time before his body erupted and agonising pleasure transported him into a different stratosphere.

Angelos recovered first and, despite the unusually slow workings of his brain, realised that he had to do something with the limp, satiated woman who was currently clinging to him, her arms around his neck, her head buried in his shoulder.

Although they were shielded to some extent by the lush foliage that crowded and coloured the terrace, it was still an extremely public place.

What the hell had they both been thinking?

And then he realised that neither of them had been thinking at all. If he *had* been thinking then he wouldn't have chosen the swimming pool as a venue for an erotic encounter with a woman. The concept of sex as a spectator sport had never interested him and, given that sex was clearly an experience that was entirely new to her, he could only assume that she hadn't been thinking, either.

And that, of course, raised any number of questions.

But none of them could be voiced at this particular moment.

His stunned reaction to the realisation that she had been a virgin was eclipsed by the more immediate need to return her exquisite body to the swimming costume before someone walked onto the terrace and saw her naked.

Discovering that his skills at dressing a woman were by no means as well developed as his skills at *undressing*, Angelos slid a hand down her leg and attempted to ease her back into the costume. Despite marshalling all his powers of concentration, her full, creamy breasts were temptingly close and his movements were hindered by the fact that she flopped limp and unresisting in his arms.

'We *have* to get you dressed,' he breathed with exasperation, finally sliding the costume as far as her waist and then lifting her away from him in order to tackle the arms.

She was as limp as a rag doll, and when her eyes finally lifted to his she appeared to have difficulty focusing. With a soft curse he yanked at the straps of her costume and slid them over her arms until her body was finally covered.

Having achieved that first objective, Angelos lifted one of her hands and placed it on the side of the pool, so that she could support herself in the water. Then he stepped back from her, consciously placing distance between them. '*Talk* to me.'

His sharp command was met by dazed silence. She was looking at him as though he was from another planet, and he knew the feeling because he'd never felt so disconnected from reality in his life. Finally her lips moved, but no sound emerged. She appeared to be having difficulty forming words.

Against his will, his eyes were drawn to the softness of her mouth and he felt his body stir again. Perplexed and infuriated by the effect she was having on him, he stepped forward again, put his hands on her waist and lifted her bodily out of the water. It was clear to him that if there was any hope of a conversation it wouldn't be with both of them half naked in the pool—and anyway, the cold water was proving to be a remarkably ineffective libido-dampener.

Having lifted her clear of the water, Angelos placed his hands on the side and the muscles bunched in his shoulders as he levered himself upwards and sprang from the pool.

Water streaming off his body, he prowled over to the nearest sun lounger and reached for a towel. Securing it firmly around his waist, he took several deep breaths. Only then, when he was confident that he was back in control, did he turn to face her.

She hadn't moved.

She was still seated on the side of the pool, where he'd left her, like a doll whose body wasn't capable of independent movement.

With a soft curse he strode over to her, hauled her to her feet and wrapped a towel around her shivering frame with business-like efficiency. Then he pushed her into the nearest chair, his mind returning to its usual state of focus now that she was covered. 'Start talking.'

Talking?

He wanted her to speak about what had just happened?

Feeling dazed, and slightly removed from what was happening around her, Chantal stared at him blankly.

She had no idea what she was supposed to say. For her it had been—

She gave up trying to find the words. What exactly did he want to hear? That she was now a different person from the one she'd been yesterday? That it had surpassed her wildest dreams? *That she could have happily stayed in that pool with him for the rest of her life?*

Her gaze slid to his, but the contact was too much, *too intimate*, and she looked away immediately. But not before a disturbing image of him half naked had been imprinted on her brain. He was a vision of masculine power, with water glistening on his powerful torso, his eyes disturbingly intent as they rested on her face.

And *still* she couldn't speak—because the words were all jammed together in her head and she had no idea how to articulate the fact that *everything* felt different now.

Why didn't *he* say something? Or was he pretending that it hadn't happened?

She was just contemplating that disturbing possibility when she saw his mouth tighten.

How did he manage to look businesslike and intimidating, wearing just a towel?

'*Speak* to me,' he demanded, and his sharp tone finally roused her from her semi-conscious state.

'It was amazing,' she said faintly. 'You're very good.'

Shock flared in his dark eyes and he muttered something in Greek under his breath. 'That is *not* what I was asking you,' he breathed, faint colour highlighting the perfection of his bone structure. 'Let's do this another way. I'll ask the questions. You answer. Obviously you're *not* Isabelle Ducat.'

Realising that she'd just embarrassed herself, Chantal coloured deeply and shrank deeper inside the towel.

She'd just *assumed* that he'd wanted to talk about the sex because, for her, no other issues existed. What they'd just shared had driven everything else from her head. But obviously he wasn't similarly afflicted. For him there were issues much, much more important than talking about the sex. *Like her identity*.

Buying herself a little more time, she cleared her throat and tried avoidance tactics. 'What makes you think I'm not Isabelle Ducat?'

'Because the list of Isabelle's previous lovers reads like a telephone directory,' Angelos informed her helpfully. 'Whereas I now know that your list contains only one name. Mine.'

His blunt reminder of the intimacy they'd just shared caused the colour in her cheeks to deepen still further. Wriggling like a fish on a hook, she breathed deeply and told herself that he couldn't absolutely *know*. Could he? 'I don't see how you—'

'Don't even go there,' he warned in a soft voice. 'Unless you want me to treble your blushes by describing in meticulous detail exactly *how* I know.'

She breathed in and out and concentrated on a point between his feet and his knees. 'Oh.'

'Look at me,' he demanded, and she shrank slightly lower in her seat.

She couldn't look at him. It was just too, *too* embarrassing.

He sighed heavily. '*Please* will you look at me?' This time his voice was slightly less autocratic, as if he knew that he wasn't going to achieve his objective by sheer force alone.

Reluctantly, she looked. 'What do you want to know?'

'Start with who you really are.'

Who was she?

She wasn't sure she knew any more. She certainly didn't feel anything like the person she'd been half an hour previously.

Would her body ever feel the same again? 'I'm not Isabelle.'

'I *know* that.' His wide, sensuous mouth compressed as he struggled to contain his volatile nature. 'What I *don't* know is who you are and why you took her identity.'

'I didn't take her identity. Not really. You were the one who thought I was Isabelle.'

'You were in possession of her ticket.'

'Which just goes to show that external appearances can be deceptive.'

'The only deception around here was *yours.*'

Sensing a dangerous tension in him, Chantal felt her heart bump against her chest. 'It's true that I used the ticket, but I didn't pose as her. I didn't once use her name, and you weren't supposed to see the ticket.'

'This conversation is going round in circles and you are making *no* sense. How did you obtain the ticket in the first place?'

It was like being on the witness stand, being cross-examined by a very unsympathetic prosecutor.

What would he say, she wondered, when he discovered that the truth was even worse than the lie? 'It's a long story.'

'Give me the short version,' he ordered in a tense voice. 'I'm a guy who likes to get straight to the point, and we've already taken the long route. Let's try it from a different direction. How do you know Isabelle?'

'I *don't* know her. I met her in the hotel where she was staying.' Unable to look at him, Chantal examined each strand of the soft fluffy towel that now enveloped her. 'I was—' *oh hell* '—I was cleaning her room.'

There.

She'd said it.

Bracing herself for his reaction to her shocking confession, she sat there waiting, her fingers coiled in the damp folds of the towel.

Angelos said nothing.

Clearly he was so appalled that he'd flown a *cleaner* out to his island on his private jet that he couldn't even find the words to express his disgust. She gave a tiny shrug and tried to ignore the pain that tore at her insides.

'It's all right.' She tried to sound dismissive. Casual. 'Go ahead and say what's on your mind.' After all, she was used to it. *Used to being judged and instantly dismissed*. Struggling to close her armour around her. She lifted her eyes to his and she found him watching her from beneath thick dark lashes that concealed his expression.

'I'm still waiting for you to explain how you came to have the ticket.' He spoke with exaggerated patience. 'I'm assuming that if I wait long enough you will get to the point in the end.'

'I've reached the point.'

He rubbed his fingers over his forehead, as if to ease the tension. 'Chantal—that is your name, isn't it?' He spoke slowly and softly, as if he were hanging onto control by a thread. 'I'm not a very patient man. If a member of my staff had taken as long to tell me something as you have, I would have fired them by now.'

She stiffened defensively. 'I just told you I was working as a cleaner.'

'I heard you. At the moment I'm not interested in your career choice. What I'm still waiting to hear is how you came by the ticket.'

'But—'

'I'm *not* good with long, involved stories,' he informed her, his tone exasperated. 'Get to the point, *please,* before we both age any further.'

Chantal opened her mouth to say that she'd thought that the fact she was actually a cleaner *was* the point, but the burning impatience in his eyes made her think twice. Obviously he wanted more. 'I was cleaning her room. She was having a complete tantrum about what she should wear—flinging clothes all over the place and expecting me to pick them up. I thought she needed help, so I told her which dress I thought suited her best, and she just exploded in a rage. What did someone like *me* know about how to dress for an event like that? What did *I* know about attracting a rich man? I suffered fifteen minutes of verbal abuse, and then she decided that she wasn't going at all. So she flung her ticket in the bin and checked out of the hotel. I think she left Paris that same afternoon.'

'So you took the ticket out of her bin?' He condensed her lengthy confession into a few very blunt words.

'It sounds bad, I know. But—'

'—But you wanted to prove her wrong about not being able to attract a rich man?'

Affronted, Chantal glared at him. 'Of course not! It was nothing to do with attracting a rich man. It was a confidence thing.' She subsided in her seat. 'She made me feel *so* small— as if I were a completely different species to her.' She could have told him the rest of her story, of course, but there was no way she was doing that, when she'd already told him far, far too much about herself. As far as she was concerned she'd given him everything he was having. The rest was staying locked inside. She straightened her shoulders. 'And that's why I took the ticket. It wasn't about meeting men. I needed to prove to myself that she was wrong about me. Just for one night I wanted to dress up and be in her world.'

'You borrowed one of her dresses?'

'Don't be ridiculous. I would never have fitted into one of her dresses—and anyway, I wouldn't have done something like that. I made my own dress.'

'In the space of a few hours?'

Stung by his disbelieving tone, Chantal frowned at him. 'I'm good at sewing.' She'd had to be. It was the only way she could afford to dress the way she wanted to dress.

'So you turned up at the ball, like Cinderella, just to prove to her that she was wrong?'

'It wasn't about her at all. It was about me. I was proving it to myself. She made me feel—' The confession sat like a leaden lump in her mouth. 'She made me feel worthless. *Less* than her. I wanted to prove to myself that the people at the ball were just people. That I could mix and mingle in that world.' It wasn't the whole truth, but it was all he was getting from her.

'So that explains the bizarre conversation we had on the night of the ball when you wouldn't tell me who you were,' he muttered. '*Finally* I understand all that rambling about stereotypes and people not judging other people.'

'That's what they do,' Chantal said simply. 'People judge all the time, based on a number of superficial factors and their judgements are almost always wrong.'

'I don't suppose it occurred to you to tell me the truth?'

'You're joking! Of course not. You would have had me thrown out. And anyway, you were *furious* when you saw I'd been talking to your father.'

'Not because you were talking to him, but because you gave him the impression that we were seriously in love. The fact that you are here today is purely a result of the lies you told that night.'

She stared at him numbly. The warmth and passion they'd shared only moments ago had gone. 'I sat next to your father because he was the only friendly face in the place. I didn't know who he was. I didn't know who *you* were. And then he and I started to talk and—'

'And?'

She was silent for a moment, unwilling to confess that her imagination had run away with her. She didn't want him to know the impact he'd had on her at their first meeting. 'It was just a misunderstanding,' she said lamely, and he muttered something in Greek under his breath.

'You let me carry on believing that you were Isabelle, despite having had ample opportunity to tell me the truth. And I suppose the reason for that is all too obvious.' His tone was suddenly cool. 'I was offering you an all-expenses-paid holiday on a Greek Island. No wonder you stayed silent.'

It was the worst thing he could have said to her.

'You think I came here for a free holiday? That's *not* what happened!' Deeply offended by his interpretation, she leaped out of her chair, clutching the towel like a shield. '*You* were the one who insisted that I came.'

'And you didn't resist.'

Her heart was pounding. 'I came because you led me to believe that it would make a difference to your father, and I care about him. He was very kind to me.'

'So you made this enormous sacrifice for a guy you'd met once?' He lifted an eyebrow. 'You were doing me a *favour* by agreeing to fly by private jet to a secluded island for a few weeks of relaxation?' He was tying her in knots and he knew it.

'I don't care what you believe. It's the truth. But you're obviously so cynical and suspicious of women's motives that you think there's only one possible interpretation. Maybe you should give all your money away. Then you'd know, wouldn't you?' Still smarting with indignation, she blinked rapidly to clear the tears that had sprung into her eyes. He wasn't worth crying over. No

man was worth that. All she could do now was pick up the pieces
and start again. And learn from her mistakes.

But first she needed to get out of here.

After what they'd just done she could no longer stay as his
guest. It wasn't possible.

Before she could move, Maria appeared on the terrace, an
apologetic look on her face. She said something in Greek to
Angelos and he gave a low growl, almost vibrating with impatience at the interruption.

'*Theos mou*, not now—' He raked his fingers through his
glossy hair and then cast a look at Chantal. 'I have been waiting
for this phone call—the timing isn't good, but I have to take it.
We'll finish this conversation later.'

Not if she had anything to do with it.

Still bruised by his total lack of sensitivity, she didn't respond.
What was there to finish?

He'd made his feelings perfectly clear, and she really didn't
want to listen to any more.

He thought she was some sort of cold-blooded gold-digger.

Wrung out with the emotion of it all, Chantal watched in
silence as he strode across the terrace. He was as cool and in
control as ever. There was no evidence to suggest that he was a
man caught up in the middle of an emotional crisis. *Which was
yet another fundamental difference between them,* she thought
numbly, her eyes clinging hungrily to his broad, muscular shoulders until they disappeared from view along with the rest of him.

She still wasn't sure how the whole thing had happened, or
why it had happened. All she knew was that she felt like a balloon
that had been popped before the party started.

Apart from acknowledging her utter lack of experience,
Angelos apparently hadn't given a second thought to what had
happened in the pool.

And yet *she'd* been unable to think of anything else. Every time he'd fired a question at her, she'd just wanted to say, *'But what about the sex?'*

It had been the most shocking, exhilarating, explosive experience of her life, and having suddenly discovered the depth of her sexuality she could now barely focus on anything else. The memory of their encounter was so clear that it dominated her mind in full, glorious Technicolor and her body ached in a way that was deliciously unfamiliar.

All the way through their conversation she'd just wanted him to stop talking, take her in his arms and do it all over again. Because she'd truly believed that what they'd shared had been unique and infinitely special.

And that was why she'd done it, of course. Because it had felt absolutely right. For the first time in her life she hadn't even stopped to question what she was doing.

But it hadn't been special for him, had it?

It hadn't even been worthy of comment. To him it had just been sex. And not just sex, but sex that obviously wasn't even worth remarking on. Disappointing sex. In fact, judging from his reaction, the whole episode had obviously been an entirely forgettable experience—nothing more than an exercise session for him—while the verbal exchange that had followed had possessed all the warmth and intimacy of a business meeting.

She cringed as she forced herself to face the truth.

He hadn't been able to get her out of the pool fast enough, had he?

She'd been ready to wind her arms round his neck and start it all again, but he'd lifted her out and plonked her on the side, clearly *not* sharing her desire for a repeat performance.

Obviously, as a woman, you couldn't win, she thought gloomily. Too much experience, like Isabelle, made you a slut. Too little made you boring.

Alone on the terrace, she released her death grip on the towel and allowed it to slide to the floor. Her costume had almost dried in the heat, and she ran a finger over her thigh, wondering if her body felt different on the outside—because it certainly felt different on the inside.

For the first time in her life she'd discovered what it was like to completely lose control, and the feeling was exciting and terrifying at the same time.

Uncomfortable thoughts from her childhood drifted into her head but she pushed them away again instantly, just not able to go there at this moment.

One thing she *did* know was that the sex had changed everything. She'd agreed to accept his hospitality only because he'd convinced her that his father's recovery depended on her presence. She'd been comfortable with it because there had been nothing personal in the invitation.

But now everything had changed.

And it was perfectly obvious what she had to do.

CHAPTER SIX

SERIOUSLY distracted, Angelos took his business call, snapped the head off the person on the other end of the phone and then instructed his PA in Athens not to put through any more calls.

At that moment he wasn't interested in talking to his senior management team. Nor was he interested in talking to any of the businessmen who clamoured for his attention on an almost hourly basis.

There were urgent matters demanding his attention. But for the first time in his life he didn't even care.

He should have been thinking about work, but all he could think about was sex.

Sex with Chantal.

Cursing softly in Greek, he paced the length of his office. His entire body was burning and unfulfilled and all he wanted to do was stride back onto the terrace, drag her somewhere extremely private and indulge in a repeat performance—complete with several encores.

Never in his life had he been so hot for a woman, and he didn't understand it because she possessed none of the qualities that he admired.

True, she was beautiful, but she was also dishonest—and she'd admitted as such. All right, so she wasn't Isabelle Ducat. She'd hadn't chosen to make a living out of divorce. But she *had* taken a ticket that wasn't hers, and she hadn't corrected him when he'd assumed her to be the owner of the ticket.

She'd posed as someone else, apparently more than comfortable to perpetrate that particular untruth. That fact alone should have been the sexual equivalent of sitting in a bath of ice cubes, because he *hated* deception.

He might have felt more kindly towards her had she just admitted that a few weeks in Greece with a billionaire had sounded like fun. Instead of which she'd insisted that she'd agreed to accompany him out of concern for his father.

So why, knowing all that, was his libido raging madly out of control?

Why did he feel like a teenager whose hormones were well and truly in control?

With a humourless laugh he forced himself to accept the obvious.

Because the sex had been nothing short of stupendous. That was why.

Deceitful she might be, but she'd also been a virgin, and the fact that he was her first lover had given him an incredible buzz.

Which meant that clearly he wasn't as modern in his attitudes as he liked to think.

He narrowed his eyes and ran through the facts logically.

All right, so she hadn't told him the truth. But she was right that he was the one who had insisted that she come. And, had she told him the truth about her identity, would it have changed anything?

No. He still would have wanted her to come for the sake of his father.

So what difference did any of it make?

She was here now, wasn't she?

The chemistry between them was amazing.

What was the problem?

She was here for a free holiday with a billionaire, so why not give her that holiday? And if it cost him a few dresses and the odd diamond necklace, so what?

They'd share incredible sex during the night, and during the day he'd arrange for her to spend as much time shopping as she could handle. She was using him for money, so why shouldn't he use her for sex?

Unable to concentrate, and deciding to abandon all further thoughts of work for the day, he strode into the suite of rooms that his father occupied when he was staying in the villa. 'How are you feeling?'

'Better by the hour.' Costas Zouvelekis was already dressed, ready for dinner. 'What did you do with your afternoon?'

Angelos stilled as erotic images flew into his brain. What had he done with his afternoon? *He'd had the most incredible sex of his life.*

In a public place.

He ran a hand over the back of his neck, seriously discomforted by the thought of what his father might have seen if he'd woken early from his rest and decided to relax by the pool. 'I worked.'

'Did you? Well, I hope you didn't leave Chantal on her own for too long. She's a woman worth guarding.'

'From whom? There is no one else here.'

'From boredom,' Costas said dryly, as he adjusted his shirt. 'When women become bored, they stray.'

Stray?

Angelos reflected silently on the fact that the last time he'd seen Chantal she'd been so shattered after his lovemaking that she hadn't seemed capable of moving her lips, let alone her legs.

'She isn't going to stray.' Why would she? He was in a position to give her the fantasy, and he had enough experience of her sex to know what she'd want. Jewels, dresses, handbags with strange names that were only available for a price, an unreasonable number of shoes, probably still more shoes—

He gave a faint smile. As long as he didn't have to be part of the selection process, he was more than happy to fund a seriously extravagant shopping spree.

Clearly she wasn't used to a life of luxury.

It would be fun to spoil her.

Never, ever become involved with a gorgeous Greek billionaire.

Having made herself sign off on that promise, Chantal snapped the suitcase shut and placed it on the floor. In the spacious, elegant room it looked laughably out of place.

Determined not to brood, she gave a little shrug and told herself that it didn't matter. The one good thing about having very few belongings was that it didn't take long to pack.

She was just about to reach for the phone and see if she could arrange for a car to take her to Athens when the bedroom door opened and Angelos strode into the room.

Clearly fresh from the shower, he'd changed into a pair of lightweight linen trousers and a shirt that emphasised his athletic physique. Tall and broad-shouldered, he emanated power and sexuality.

Her body leapt to life and she turned away, mortified that she was so susceptible to him. *Well, tough.* She was going to do what he was obviously doing and just not think about the sex. 'I was trying to arrange for a car. Now you're here, perhaps you could do it for me?'

'To go where, precisely?'

'Athens. I'll arrange a flight home from there.'

There was a tense silence. *'Home?'*

'Yes.' Summoning up as much dignity as she could, she reached into her bag and removed the roll of cash she'd counted out carefully a few minutes earlier. 'This is for you.' She thrust it into his hand and he stared at it in astonishment.

'What is this?'

'Money. You should know, since it obviously plays such an

important part in your life.' It was all the money she had, minus the amount she was going to need for her flight home. 'You can put that towards what I've cost you so far. Whatever you may think, I *don't* want a free holiday. I never should have come. I see that now. It's inevitable that a man like you would think that my reasons for coming here have something to do with money. In the circumstances, I don't even blame you for thinking that.' Some of her pride salvaged, she stepped forward and picked up the case, avoiding eye contact. It was terribly, terribly important that she didn't look at him. If she looked, she was lost.

'I don't want your money.' He dropped the money unceremoniously onto the nearest hard surface and Chantal tried not to flinch as she remembered just how long it had taken her to earn that amount.

'Well, I want you to have it. In fact, I insist.'

He glanced at the roll of notes and then back at her. 'Obviously my comments upset you,' he breathed. 'But you have to admit that I had cause.'

'Of course. Why else would someone like me be with someone like you?'

His body tensed. 'You pretended to be Isabelle Ducat, and she is the queen of gold-diggers.'

'Maybe. But even when you knew that I wasn't Isabelle your assumption was that I'd just come along for a free holiday.' Still suffering from a serious assault on her pride, Chantal clutched her case. 'It's obvious that you've discovered the sort of person I really am, so there's no point in me staying. Please arrange for me to leave the island. Is there a water taxi you can call?'

'I have no intention of calling you a taxi.' His tone had a raw edge to it. 'Put the case down.'

'No.'

He inhaled deeply. 'I can see that I've *seriously* upset you—'

'What makes you think that?' Her tone flippant, she walked

towards the door. 'We gold diggers have very thick skins. It's part of the job description.'

With incredibly quick reflexes, he crossed the room and grabbed her. 'Tell me why you accepted my invitation.' He hauled her hard against him, and she gasped as the contact ignited a flash of excitement deep inside her.

'You already know why.' Desperately she tried to shut down her response. 'It seemed a perfect way to enjoy a free holiday in the sun.'

'So, if that is the case, then why are you leaving now?'

'Because what we did makes it impossible for me to stay.'

'You are saying that because your feelings are hurt.' His mouth was dangerously close to hers and the heat between them was mounting. 'I am willing to admit that I owe you an apology.'

'No, you don't. I don't blame you for what you thought. It was a perfectly reasonable assumption in the circumstances.' Desperate to get away before she made a fool of herself yet again, Chantal tried to wriggle out of his grasp. 'Why else would someone like me have accompanied you?'

He held her firm. 'Why did you?'

Swamped by an almost agonising sexual tension, her anger subsided. 'Because of your father,' she muttered. 'You persuaded me that I could make a difference to his recovery. He was so kind to me that night at the ball. No one has ever been that kind to me before. I was feeling really vulnerable and horribly out of place. Which just goes to show that Isabelle was right all along. I didn't fit in.'

'Why would you want to?' He looked genuinely perplexed. 'Individuality is to be celebrated.'

Spoken like a billionaire who didn't follow any of life's rules, she thought weakly, wishing she possessed just a fraction of his self belief. 'You need masses of confidence to be different. I stood out. I felt as though everyone was staring.'

'They *were* staring. Because of your dress.'

'Yes, the dress was a huge mistake.'

'The dress was amazing. Where did you find it?'

She concentrated on one of the buttons of his shirt. 'They were refurbishing one of the hotel rooms and I found some red lining material that they'd thrown away. I thought it would look perfect.'

A stunned silence followed her frank confession. 'Are you telling me that your red dress started life on the inside of a *curtain*?'

'A very expensive curtain.' She shrugged. 'Why are you looking so shocked? You just said that individuality is to be celebrated.'

His handsome face was a mask of incredulous disbelief and he released her. 'That night—' His voice not quite steady, he rubbed his fingers over the bridge of his nose. 'You really *didn't* have a clue who I was, did you?'

She tried not to feel disappointed that he'd let her go. 'Of course I didn't know who you were. Why would I?'

It took him a moment to answer. 'Women usually do.'

'The women *you* mix with do. But I'm not one of those. And I wouldn't want to be,' she said firmly. She knew far too much about that type of woman. 'I only spoke to you because you spoke to me first. I'd been standing there, wishing I'd never decided to go to the ball, and then there you were.' She swallowed as she remembered the sharp intensity of that moment. 'And you were—there was—something—'

Their eyes met for a moment and he frowned. 'If all that is true, and you genuinely came to the villa because of concern for my father's health, then why are you leaving now?'

Because she had to.

Her fingers tightened on the case and she looked away from him so that she wouldn't be tempted. 'Because everything has changed. You know I'm not Isabelle, and our relationship has become—' She broke off and searched for the right word. 'Become personal. It goes against my principles.'

'Our relationship is now *exactly* the way my father always wanted it to be so to leave now makes no sense. We've merely dropped the pretence. It actually makes the situation simpler, not more complicated.'

'Not to me. We had—' She broke off again and cleared her throat, trying not to mind that he was quite prepared to pretend that the sex had never happened. 'What we did changes things.'

'I don't see how.'

'You think I'm just leeching from you.'

He glanced briefly towards the roll of notes he'd so carelessly discarded. 'Is that why you gave me the money?'

'I'm giving you the money because I don't want you to pay for me. I've never taken money from a man in my life.'

'I haven't offered you money.'

'You're paying for me to be here. That amounts to the same thing. You think I'm a gold-digger.'

Amusement flickered in his dark eyes. 'Gold-diggers generally aren't innocent virgins, *agape mou*. You're obviously not quite as familiar with the job description as you think you are.'

She couldn't think of a suitable reply, so she stayed silent.

He sighed. 'You're *not* leaving.'

She wished she could put the whole episode behind her as easily as he clearly had. 'I have to.' For so many reasons. Preserving her sanity was one, but so was maintaining her self respect.

'Chantal.' There was a decisive tone to his voice, like a judge who was summing up. 'You claim that you came here because of my father—'

'I did.'

'Then why would you leave? My father's needs are as great as they ever were. Greater, in fact. Since you arrived he has talked of nothing else. He is looking forward to joining us at dinner tonight. Nothing has changed.'

Chantal chewed her lip.

For him, nothing had changed. She wished she felt similarly indifferent. 'Everything has changed.' Her eyes moved to his and then skidded away. 'We—'

'Yes,' he said softly, 'we did. And given that you were a virgin I'm assuming that you aren't protected by any form of contraception?'

Her heart stumbled.

Pregnant? It hadn't even occurred to her that she might become pregnant. For a moment she forgot he was standing there as she considered that possibility. After her own childhood she'd never thought that she'd—

'I'll take your silence as a no,' he drawled softly, and she was silent for a moment as she did some rapid calculations in her head.

'It will be fine,' she muttered finally, her cheeks blossoming with colour because this was one topic she wasn't used to discussing with a man. 'So you don't need to think what you're thinking.'

'What am I thinking?'

'That I've set the ultimate honey trap.' She looked him in the eye, her expression fierce. 'Even if I *were* pregnant, I wouldn't take money from you.'

'Let's not argue about an issue which might never arise. The more pressing concern is what we do in the short term.'

'You're going to let me leave the island.'

His exasperated glance suggested that he wasn't used to people defying him. 'Whatever you may think of me, I'm not in the habit of indulging in careless sex regardless of the consequences.'

'So why did you with me?'

His dark eyes fastened on hers. 'I have been asking myself that same question for the past few hours. I'm sure the answer will come to me in time.'

She shrank as she imagined how much he must now be regretting his uncharacteristic lack of control. It was all too easy to imagine him calculating what that one awkward lapse was going to cost him in terms of money and adverse publicity. 'Well, anyway, it doesn't change the facts. I need to leave.'

'My father was kind to you.'

'Yes.'

'Then you must stay. You owe him this favour.'

She stared at him helplessly. 'That's not fair—'

'I don't play fair, Chantal,' he said softly. 'I play to win.'

She closed her eyes and tried to find the steely streak she needed to refuse. 'I can't—'

'His health is fragile. You have the ability to make him happy. Can you deprive him of that?'

She opened her eyes. 'You're totally ruthless, aren't you?'

'Focused.'

She turned her head away, feeling as though she were a leaf caught in a hurricane. The force of his personality was too powerful to resist.

'I don't see how my presence will really help him…' But she was wavering and he sensed it, moving in for the kill like a lion spotting a wonded antelope.

'Your presence could make all the difference to his recovery.'

She wanted to say no, but she couldn't forget the kindness his father had shown her.

'All right.' The words were dragged from her lips. 'I'll stay—'

'Of course you will.' Clearly supremely confident of his own negotiation skills, he didn't look surprised by her decision.

'—But only if you let me pay you.'

'I don't understand your desire to be independent.'

'It isn't about independence—' She broke off, realising that if she stuck by that claim then she'd have to explain herself. *And she had no intention of doing that.* He already knew far too much about her.

His dark eyes narrowed. 'I don't want your money.'

'*Take it*,' she said fiercely. 'Or I'm going home right now.'

He studied her in silence, his expression unreadable. 'All right. If it makes you happy.' With economy of movement he reached for the roll of notes and slipped it into his pocket. 'So, now that problem is solved you can unpack your suitcase. My father is waiting for us on the terrace. Why don't you change and then join us?'

It was only after he'd strode from the room that Chantal realised they *still* hadn't discussed what had happened in the pool.

'I'm not that hungry,' Costas protested as Chantal spooned a small helping of roasted peppers onto his plate.

'They're delicious,' she enthused. 'You just have to try them. Just a mouthful.'

'Women.' Costas sighed and picked up his fork. 'They never let a man rest.'

'You can rest later.' She helped herself to a different dish, examining the contents closely. 'What's this?'

'*Fasoláda*—kidney beans baked in the oven with vegetables, herbs and olive oil. It's delicious. Try it.'

'Only if you try some, too.' Her smile engaging, she spooned a small amount onto his plate and watched while he ate. 'Well?'

'It's good.'

Feeling like a spare part, Angelos watched as she cleverly coaxed his father to eat, selecting small quantities of healthy food for him to try.

Only when she was satisfied that he'd eaten something did she turn her attentions to her own plate. After several mouthfuls she smiled at his father. 'You're right, it *is* delicious. I'd swim through a shark-infested pond to eat this again.'

His father laughed with delight and reached for another dish. 'If you think that's good, then you should try this one—'

The two of them were like excited children and Angelos watched as his father flirted outrageously with Chantal.

Now that he knew she wasn't Isabelle Ducat, he was noticing things he should have noticed before. Like the fact that she didn't actually flirt. No simpering, no hair tossing, no lowered lashes. Nothing, in fact, that could be described as flirtatious. She just had an open, friendly attitude.

He remembered that night of the ball, and recalled that one of the things about her he'd found so attractive was that she'd been so different from everyone around her.

She'd shown a cheeky sense of humour, a playfulness that was quite different from flirting.

It was no wonder his father had *liked her.*

And no wonder that she was having such a powerful effect on him.

He'd never been so aware of a woman. The curve of her mouth when she smiled; the slight dimple at the corner of her mouth, the light that appeared in her eyes when she laughed.

And then there was her body… At that point he found his descriptive powers severely challenged. All he knew was that she appeared to have been designed specifically to distract a man from whatever path he was taking.

Suddenly he couldn't wait for dinner to end so that he could finish what they'd started in the pool.

Trying not to dwell on the fact that Angelos had barely spoken to her over dinner, Chantal stepped into the shower. In the end she'd left him on the terrace with his father, both of them engrossed in an unintelligible conversation about the Far Eastern money markets.

And now she stood under the sharp jets of water, satisfied that Costas had at least eaten something. She just needed to make sure that he did that at every mealtime.

Reaching for one of the fluffy towels that were piled in uniform rows, Chantal walked out of the shower and into the bedroom.

Angelos was sprawled on the bed, talking in rapid Greek into his mobile phone.

Shocked to see him there, she was about to retreat into the bathroom when he noticed her and ended the call with a decisive stab of one long finger. 'You were so long I was about to join you in the shower.'

'What are you doing in my bedroom?'

'*Our* bedroom, *agape mou*,' he drawled softly, extending a hand in her direction. 'Come to bed.'

She clutched the towel. 'What for?'

His eyes shimmered with amusement. 'I understand that you're inexperienced, but surely not *that* inexperienced.'

Chantal didn't move. 'You're suggesting that we share a bed?'

'Generally that's what happens.' Dark lashes veiled his expression and she felt her tummy jump like a grasshopper.

'But you—I—' She broke off. 'It was a one off.'

'I don't do "one-offs". I've already told you, casual affairs are not my style.'

'But that's ridiculous—we hardly know each other.'

'On the contrary. We *know* each other in the most literal and intimate sense of the word,' he drawled, and she felt the colour flood into her cheeks.

'That's different. Neither of us was thinking.'

'Sex doesn't generally require a great deal of intellectual input.'

Her heart was pounding against her chest. 'But you didn't even enjoy it,' she blurted out impulsively. 'You were really bored.'

'*Bored?*' Incredulous dark eyes swept her flushed cheeks. 'At what point, precisely, did I appear to be bored?'

'Afterwards—when you didn't once mention it.'

'I've always considered sex to be more of a practical than an academic subject. More about doing than talking.' His voice was deep and impossibly sexy. 'And at the time we had rather more pressing topics to discuss—such as your identity. Call me old-fashioned, but my preference is always to at least know the name of the person with whom I've been intimate.' He sprang off the bed and strolled towards her, a look of intent on his handsome face.

As his hand slid decisively around her wrist, her bones melted away like chocolate over a flame. 'Angelos—'

'I like the way you say my name,' he purred, sliding his other hand behind her neck and drawing her towards him. 'And for the next few hours that's the only word I want to hear from you. I'm tired of talking.'

She opened her mouth to give him all the reasons why she had no intention of doing this, but he was standing so close that a helpless rush of excitement engulfed her. It was like being in the path of a red-hot lava flow.

Her body was trembling with delicious anticipation and she gave a moan and swayed towards him. He brought his mouth down on hers and his powerful body urged her back towards the bed, his hand divesting her of the towel just seconds before she tumbled back onto the mattress.

He came down on top of her with single-minded intent, his heated gaze devouring every detail of her trembling naked body.

A frantic mixture of desperation and embarrassment, Chantal squirmed under his frank appraisal. *What if he didn't like what he saw?* 'Angelos—'

Clearly suffering none of the inhibitions she suffered, his eyes drifted back to hers and he lowered his head once again. 'You really are *incredibly* beautiful,' he groaned, and this time when he kissed her it was like dropping a burning match into a barrel of gunpowder. Her insides exploded in a shower of agonising sensation and she dug her nails into the firm muscle of his shoulders, so unbelievably aroused that she couldn't really grasp what was happening to her.

He controlled her utterly, completely sure of himself as he turned his attention to her breasts, using his fingers and his mouth with such erotic expertise that the heat inside her grew to hazardous levels.

She was burning. Every single inch of her body was sizzling and smouldering. She lifted her hips in frantic demand and expectation.

His fingers slid lower, skimming her abdomen and resting just short of this ultimate destination. The fact that he was still capable of control when she had none might have been humiliating, but she no longer cared. She was just too desperate to care.

'Am I the first man to touch you?' His husky demand penetrated her dazed brain.

'Yes, yes—' But he hadn't touched her yet, had he? And if he didn't do it soon she thought she might explode, because it wasn't possible to be any more aroused than she was at that moment. 'Angelos—please—'

He gave a satisfied smile and stripped off his boxer shorts. 'I have never wanted a woman as much as I want you. You're mine. Exclusively.' It was an unashamed statement of possession but she didn't even care.

Confronted by the breathtaking vision of Angelos naked, she felt her mouth dry and her excitement levels shoot higher still.

He was magnificent: his shoulders broad, his abdomen flat and as for the rest of him—

Reminding herself that they'd already done it once, and everything had fitted, Chantal gasped as she felt his hair-roughened thigh brush against her.

Why didn't he touch her?

What was he waiting for?

The ache inside her was almost painful and she arched against him, unconsciously begging for his touch, aware that he was torturing her on purpose.

At last his fingers moved, brushing through the soft curls that protected her soft, damp core. And then finally he touched her where she was longing to be touched, and his fingers were so impossibly sure and skilful that she immediately shot into an orgasm so intense that she couldn't breathe. Consumed by sensation, she sobbed his name—and then whimpered in disbelief as he pulled her beneath him and surged into her with propulsive force, taking her with long, hard strokes that launched her into the outer reaches of ecstasy.

Out of her mind with excitement, Chantal clutched at his shoulders, his primal possession starting up a chain reaction that was outside her control. Without having time to breathe or recover she was plunged straight into another orgasm, her body tightening around his, driving him to his own peak. The sudden increase in masculine thrust sent her over the edge yet again, so that this time they exploded together, both of them consumed by the same fire.

In the aftermath she lay shocked and stunned and he smoothed her hair away from her face with a surprisingly gentle hand. 'You are amazing—'

She was just about to point out that *he* was the one who had made it all happen when his fingers began another extremely intimate exploration.

With a moan of excitement and disbelief, she gazed at him in a state of helpless abandon. 'You can't mean to do it again—'

'You're *so* innocent. I love the fact that this is all new to you. You have much to learn, *agape mou*,' he said huskily, 'and I am delighted to be the one to teach you.'

CHAPTER SEVEN

CHANTAL woke to find the bed empty and no sign of Angelos.

Even without glancing at her watch she knew it was late.

Hot sun shone through the open bedroom doors, illuminating the room like a stage set, and from outside by the pool she could hear the low hum of male voices.

Obviously the physical demands of the night and the complete absence of sleep hadn't affected him at all.

Memories flooded back into her head with embarrassing clarity.

It had been like being caught in the focus of an earthquake, watching helplessly as everything familiar had crumbled around her. She'd had no control over her reactions. *She hadn't recognised herself.*

Covering her face with her hands, she gave a groan of disbelief as she forced herself to face the uncomfortable truth.

She had made love with a man she barely knew. Again and again. And then again.

And not just any man. A man with more wealth than she could possibly imagine. A billionaire. Which made the situation a hundred times worse as far as she was concerned.

Hadn't she always promised herself that she would *never* have that sort of relationship? Not when she, of all people, knew what such a relationship meant.

She'd come here on her own terms, living by her own rules. And now everything had changed. Sex had shifted the balance. Instead of being a guest, she was—she was—

What was she? His mistress? His lover?

It didn't really matter what she called herself, because the reality was that technically she was now a kept woman. She was on *his* territory, living by *his* rules. *He was paying for her.* She was staying in his villa, eating his food, swimming in his pool, luxuriating in his bathroom—

Her breathing suddenly increased and she sat upright in bed, faintly panicky as the reality of her situation sank in.

She'd let a man buy her.

All right, he hadn't actually given her *cash,* but she was using his hospitality, which amounted to the same thing, and she couldn't allow that to carry on. Not for one moment did she fool herself into believing that the money she'd given him anywhere near covered their expenses so far.

Which meant that she *had* to leave.

How could she stay when staying went against everything she believed in? He wanted sex from her, that was all. Sex.

She became conscious of every delicious ache and tingle in her body and she glanced at the rumpled sheets, admitting to herself that her reluctance to leave wasn't all to do with his father.

She was crazy about Angelos.

What woman wouldn't be?

But it wasn't an equal relationship, was it? And she'd always promised herself that this wasn't going to happen to her.

Angelos had drained his third cup of coffee and was trying to concentrate on what his father was saying when Chantal stepped hesitantly onto the terrace.

No one looking at her could have been in any doubt as to how she'd spent the previous night. Her eyes were adorably sleepy, her mouth was soft and bruised, and the haphazard way that her blonde hair had been pinned to the top of her head suggested that her hands hadn't been quite steady at the time.

The simple pair of shorts she'd elected to wear simply accentuated her ridiculously narrow waist and the generous curve of her hips. She somehow managed to ooze sexuality and innocence at the same time, and the combination was intoxicating.

His mind suddenly wiped of all coherent thought, Angelos endeavoured to recall exactly *why* he'd opted to join his father for breakfast when there had been such a good reason for staying in bed. Looking at her now, he cursed his generosity in allowing her to sleep, wishing instead that he'd woken her up and continued his exploration of her exquisite body with the benefit of full daylight.

Clearly her mind was running along the same lines as his because she met his gaze and her cheeks immediately turned a deep shade of rose. Her eyes slid longingly to his mouth and then she looked away again.

'I'm sorry I'm so late,' she mumbled, and Angelos watched with growing amusement, wondering whether she was aware that she'd as good as announced their level of intimacy to anyone watching.

He loved the fact that she couldn't hide her feelings.

At least his father would need no convincing as to the exact nature of their relationship, he thought with wry humour as he stood up and pulled out a chair for her.

She blushed more than any woman he'd ever met and he found it incredibly appealing.

'*Kalimera.*' His hand brushed against hers and he heard her softly indrawn breath. Then she sat quickly in the chair and the sudden flash of lush, creamy flesh and the glorious scent of her hair sent an explosion of lust tearing through his body. The desire to remove her clothing and rediscover her amazing and addictive curves was so powerful that Angelos inhaled sharply and stepped backwards.

Costas chuckled and put down his coffee cup. 'It's time I left the two of you alone.'

Realising that his reaction to her had clearly been as transparent as hers had been to him, Angelos frowned. 'Don't be ridiculous.'

What was the matter with him?

Discretion and discipline were just two of the rules he stringently applied to his love life, but so far both had been notably absent in his dealings with Chantal.

When he remembered the passionate interlude in the swimming pool, he felt as though he were reviewing the actions of a stranger.

His father's smile widened. 'You should congratulate yourself, Chantal,' he said cheerfully, reaching for another piece of fruit. 'You've achieved what other women have only dreamed of achieving. You've distracted my son from the share price. This is the first meal I've shared with him when he hasn't bored me to death on the subject of the money markets. In fact, he hasn't noticed me since he sat down at the table. Clearly he has something far more absorbing on his mind.'

Wishing he'd encouraged his father to leave them alone, Angelos ignored the growing sexual hunger inside him and instead applied cold, hard logic to the situation. What would he normally be doing after a night of incredible sex?

The answer was that *he* would be working, having left the woman in his life to occupy herself in whatever way she found most amusing. In his experience, that usually involved shops.

And that, of course, was exactly what he should do in this case. Send her shopping. It would remove the distraction caused by having her around, enable him to get some work done, and it would please her. And he *wanted* to please her.

Satisfied with that solution, Angelos lounged in his chair, a faint smile touching his sensuous mouth as he anticipated being on the receiving end of her gratitude that coming night.

'Contrary to my father's expectations, I do have to work today,' he said smoothly. 'You're welcome to occupy yourself around the villa, or Jannis can take you by boat to the mainland. We keep a car there, so if you fancy a trip of some sort. Shopping, perhaps?' He waited for her face to brighten with the appropriate display of enthusiasm, but she merely stared at him.

'Shopping for what? I don't need anything.'

'Then feel free to buy something you *don't* need,' Angelos drawled, extremely amused by her naïve response. He decided that he liked her more and more. She was original, and entirely different from the women he usually dated. 'The female desire to shop usually stems more from want than need.'

'There's nothing I want, either.'

Never before having found himself in the position of having to encourage a female to spend money, Angelos was momentarily at a loss as to how to respond. Then it occurred to him that she might be assuming that he was expecting her to pay for herself. 'I'm offering you my credit card, *agape mou.*'

Her narrow shoulders tensed. 'I don't want your credit card. I don't want anything from you.'

His father laughed with delight. 'A woman who doesn't want anything from you, Angelos. Take my advice and hold onto her.'

Angelos frowned. Was she playing a game? Was this all to do with his remark about gold-diggers? *Was she trying to impress him?* 'If you change you mind just speak to Jannis,' he said smoothly. 'He can take you anywhere you want to go.' But he was starting to wonder whether that should be the bedroom. If it weren't for the numerous business calls that were demanding his attention, he would drag her there right now, without even giving her time for breakfast.

Early night, he promised himself, his body tightening as he remembered how responsive she'd been the night before. 'Coffee?'

'Please.' She reached forward and lifted the pot, not waiting for Maria to serve her. Then she smiled at his father. 'How are you feeling?'

'Like a spring lamb. After breakfast I am starting some exercises with the physiotherapist.' He glanced at Angelos. 'You chose her. Is she better-looking than the nurses?'

'She's a grandmother,' Angelos said dryly as he lifted an orange from the bowl. 'And the purpose of her visit is to assist in your recovery, not liven up your love life.'

'I have no problems with a mature woman, but *is she thin*?'

Intercepting Chantal's surprised look, Angelos smiled. 'My father is very wary of thin women.' Deftly he peeled the orange and placed the segments on her plate. 'Try this. It's straight from the tree and absolutely delicious.'

His father waved a finger. 'It isn't natural for a woman to be thin. A thin woman—'

'—has her priorities all wrong,' Angelos finished, watching transfixed as Chantal licked her fingers of the last of the juice. Her lips were soft and pink, and as they closed round her fingers he felt the immediate and predictable response of his body. 'My father thinks a woman should enjoy her food.'

'When it tastes as good as this, it would be hard not to.' She reached for another segment of orange and then met his gaze. Her hand stilled.

Aware of the effect he'd had on her, Angelos smiled.

The anticipation was burning him up inside and clearly she felt the same way.

Driven by the demands of his libido, he was tempted once again to ignore the mounting pressures of his business—but then he reminded himself that the wait would be good for both of them. It would make the conclusion all the more satisfying.

By the time the sun set, both of them would be so desperate that the night ahead would prove to be doubly satisfying.

It was the perfect solution.

Why hadn't she thought of it immediately he'd suggested that she might like to go shopping?

As the boat sped across the bay, Chantal kept a close eye on the coastline.

When they arrived at the harbour, she leaned forward and spoke to Jannis. 'This is perfect. Can we stop here?'

He moored the boat. 'There are no expensive shops here. I will drive you to Athens.'

'I don't want expensive shops.' She stepped out of the boat and scanned the restaurants that were strung along the beach. 'This will do fine.'

'You wish to spend half an hour here?'

'No, I want to spend the day here.' Grabbing her bag, she smiled at him. 'Thank you so much for the lift. Is there a water taxi or anything that would take me back to the island?'

Jannis looked startled. 'No taxi—' He cleared his throat. 'If you give me a time, I would be honoured to collect you.'

Chantal wrinkled her nose and thought for a moment. She didn't really want him to collect her, but what alternative did she have? 'All right. If you're sure. Shall we say five o'clock?'

That should give her plenty of time to do what needed to be done.

Never had Angelos found so little in his working day to interest him.

After just one phone call he found himself staring at the door of his office, wondering what Chantal was doing.

Was she lying in the sun? Swimming?

The memory of her body outlined by a tight swimming costume sent the heat surging through his body and he ran a hand over the back of his neck, struggling against the impulse to go outside and check that she had everything she needed.

Concentration eluded him, and by the time Maria came to tell him that lunch was served on the terrace he'd already decided to take the rest of the day off and take Chantal back to bed. So it came as a shock to discover that she wasn't there.

'Jannis took her in the boat to the mainland,' Maria told him as she placed several dishes on the table. 'He's picking her up at five o'clock.'

She was planning to be out all day?

Angelos's expression didn't alter. *So much for her protests about not wanting or needing anything.*

Obviously that had all been for his benefit, he thought cynically as he picked an olive out of a bowl and silently examined its dark, glossy skin. As soon as he was out of the way she'd vanished on a shopping trip.

Which wasn't surprising.

What was surprising was how disappointed he felt.

Why should he be disappointed when she was simply doing what her sex was programmed to do?

Exhausted after a night without sleep and a day spent on her feet in the heat, Chantal lay on the sun lounger, sipping an iced drink and listening as Costas Zouvelekis entertained her with stories of Angelos as a child.

'—and he was so competitive. *Always* he had to win.' Costas gave a wry smile at the memory. 'If he found something difficult, then he just set his jaw and tried again until he succeeded.'

'I hope you're not showing her baby pictures.' A deep, dark drawl came from behind them, and Chantal turned and saw Angelos standing there, a sardonic expression in his eyes as he watched them.

He looked so sleek and handsome that her stomach dropped like an express elevator with a major technical fault.

Watching her reaction with an approving smile, Costas stood up. 'I'm going to have a short rest before dinner.'

Angelos watched him walk across the terrace and into the villa and then his gaze swivelled back to Chantal. 'I missed you today.' His eyes dropped to her mouth, and for a moment she couldn't breathe. Her body heated in an instantaneous response that shocked her. The attraction between them was so powerful that it obliterated everything else. And it didn't matter how much she tried to control it, she just wanted him *now*.

'You missed me?'

'Did you doubt it?' His voice was low and seductive and he sat down on the edge of her lounger. The width of his shoulders blocked out the sun, and for a moment she was in the shade unable to think of anything except the differences between them. *Her* legs were creamy and smooth. In contrast his thighs were strong and well muscled, shadowed by dark hairs that simply emphasised his masculinity. Male and female—the contrast between them increased the sexual heat still further.

'Did you work today?' She shifted her gaze from his legs to his face and then wished she hadn't because the dark stubble that hazed his jaw was just another indication of his virility.

'I tried to, but I confess my concentration was a little lacking.' His eyes were hooded, the sudden curve of his mouth slow and seductive. 'Are you tired?'

'Tired?'

'You had a long day—' with his customary assurance he ran a long, bronzed finger over her trembling thigh and lingered at the curve of her knee '—and you didn't have much sleep last night.'

'Last night?'

'You are supposed to answer me, *agape mou*,' he drawled softly, 'not just repeat everything I say like a parrot.' But the amusement in his eyes made it clear that he was well aware of the effect he was having on her, and the fact that he knew simply increased her embarrassment.

No wonder he had a healthy ego, Chantal thought faintly, *if all women were as useless at hiding their feelings as she was.*

She tried to think of something cool and dismissive to say, but he was just too close for her to concentrate on speech. The density of his eyelashes made his eyes seem even darker and for a moment she just gazed at him, enraptured by the lean perfection of his bone structure and his firm, sensuous mouth. He was extravagantly, impossibly handsome and it was impossible not to stare.

With a soft laugh he leaned forward, but stopped just short of kissing her, his mouth tantalisingly close to hers. 'If you won't talk,' he murmured softly, the words brushing her lips in a sensuous promise, 'then we will have to find some other way of communicating.'

Her excitement levels soaring through the roof, Chantal gave a low moan of desperation, the anticipation of his kiss so acute that it was like a physical pain. When he finally ended the torture and captured her mouth with his, the heat erupted between them in a violent explosion of sexual chemistry.

The passion threatened to soar out of control, but this time Angelo pulled back. '*Not* here.' His usually faultless accent was a long way short of perfect and his voice was hoarse. 'We will go inside.'

'No.' Seriously disturbed by how out of control she felt when he touched her, Chantal slid away from him.

'No?' It was his turn to repeat her words, and he did so in such a disbelieving tone that at any other time she would have smiled. But she was a long way from smiling. Her insides were suffering from a serious case of turbulence.

'No. We can't. Not until we've sorted something out. It's important.'

'Ah—' His gaze softened with understanding. 'You are talking about contraception, but you needn't worry. This time I promise to take very good care of you—as I did last night.'

'I'm not talking about contraception.' The fact that it hadn't even occurred to her was yet another indication of just how dangerously he affected her.

His gaze was indulgent. 'You want to show me your purchases?'

'What purchases?' Concentrating was impossible when everything about him made a woman want to touch: his glossy hair, his bronzed skin, the sheer masculinity of his athletic physique.

'You spent the day shopping,' he reminded her, his eyes amused. 'I'll tell Maria to make dinner an extra-special occasion, so that you can have an excuse to wear whatever it is that you bought.'

'I didn't buy anything.'

He lifted a brow in sardonic appraisal. 'You spent an entire day shopping and you didn't buy anything? How is that possible?'

'I wasn't shopping.' Deciding that the sooner they sorted everything out the sooner her principles would be satisfied, and they could do what they were both longing to do, Chantal dug her hand into her bag and pulled out an envelope. 'Here. This is for you.' She pushed it into his hand and he looked at her quizzically, before flipping open the envelope with a lean finger and examining the contents.

'Not again!' A flash of exasperation in his eyes, he fingered the notes and looked at her with a total lack of comprehension. 'Why are you giving me money this time?'

'It's for my food, expenses—w-whatever you want to call it,' Chantal stammered. 'And please don't argue, because I *really* want you to take it. Actually, I insist on it. I mean, when I was here because of your father it didn't matter so much because I was here for a reason. But now that we've had—now that our relationship has changed—and it's—I can't have sex without paying you…' Aware that her words were spilling out in the wrong order, she let her voice trail off. She waited for him to give a nod of understanding, but his only response was a long, incredulous silence.

Finally, after what seemed like ages, he spoke. 'You're *paying* me for sex?'

'No!' Flustered, she shook her head. 'Of *course* not.'

'You said that you can't have sex without paying me.'

'I didn't mean it the way it sounded.'

'But you're giving me money?'

'Because I don't want you subsidising me.'

'You are making *no* sense whatsoever.'

That was probably true. It was almost impossible to make sense or sound even vaguely coherent when he was sitting so close to her and the dark hairs on his thigh were brushing against the sensitive skin of her leg. He was everything male and all she could think of was— 'After what happened yesterday—last night—I have to pay you something towards my food.'

He dropped the envelope onto her lap. 'When you said that there was something important that we needed to talk about, I assumed you meant contraception.'

'This *is* important. If you don't take the money then I'll feel as though you're keeping me, and I don't want that.'

He stared at her. 'That's what most women dream about. Finding a rich man to indulge them.'

'Well, it isn't what *I* dream about. It isn't what I want and as far as I'm concerned the only way we can continue this relationship is if you let me pay for my keep.'

'Forget it.' His tone was clipped and the heated atmosphere cooled considerably. 'I don't want your money.'

'Why not?' Genuinely astonished by his reaction, it was her turn to stare. 'You *hate* it when women are only interested in you for your money.'

'But you're not interested in me for my money, are you?' He

rose to his feet with the effortless grace of a panther. 'You didn't even know who I was when we first met.'

'I know who you are now.'

'But any benefit you've derived from my wealth has been a by-product of our relationship, not the cause of it. There's a subtle distinction.'

'Is there? Well, it's too subtle for me to understand,' she mumbled. 'As far as I'm concerned I want to make a financial contribution. I *have* to. Why should you pay for what I'm eating? I don't understand your problem. It should make you feel good, knowing that I'm with you because I *want* to be with you, not because of the money or the lifestyle.' And it was necessary for her. *Dark feelings tangled with her newfound happiness.*

'Taking money from you would *not* make me feel good. If you want to know what will make me feel good then come with me now and I'll show you.' He reached out a hand and hauled her to her feet. As his arms came round her waist she turned her head away, using every drop of will power at her disposal.

'I can't do that.' The temptation to just turn her head and kiss him was agonising. 'Not if you won't let me pay anything towards the cost of staying here.' She could feel the warmth of his breath against her cheek and the friction of his body against hers: *hard muscle and rough male skin against her own soft flesh.*

'You're saying no? You're refusing me? You're pretending you don't want this?' His voice was a soft, masculine purr and she gave a low moan of denial as she felt the warm pressure of his hand against the bare flesh of her back. His lips brushed the corner of her mouth and her head swam and her eyes drifted shut.

'I'm saying no,' she whispered, 'unless you take the money. *Take* the money, Angelos.'

He muttered something in Greek and released her, tension visible in every muscle of his powerful frame. 'I will *not* let you pay.'

'If I don't pay,' she muttered, battling against a powerful desire to throw herself back into his arms and abandon her principles, 'then I'll have to go home.'

'You didn't seem to have a problem with the concept of accepting my hospitality when we were in Paris.'

'That was different. You wanted me to help your father. I was doing you a favour.'

'And I want you to do me several more favours,' he breathed, the exasperation in his eyes suddenly replaced by something much, much more dangerous. 'Come to bed and I will show you.'

'*Don't* tease me.'

'Why not? I love it when you blush.' He slid a finger under her chin, forcing her to look at him. 'I want you, and I want you *now*. And you want me, too. You are aching for me—aren't you?' His fingers moved purposefully down her body, his touch skilled and sure as he transformed her into a quivering wreck with just the stroke of his hand.

'You're not playing fair, Angelos—'

'*You* are the one who is not playing fair.' His hand lingered on the curve of her hip in a deliberately intimate caress. 'Imposing all these ridiculous rules on our relationship.'

'Just one rule,' she gasped, trying to ignore the seductive stroke of his fingers.

'You can stop this foolishness, *agape mou*. I'm suitably impressed. And none of that matters any more. All day I have been thinking about last night.'

'Impressed? What do you mean?'

'I'm impressed by your determination *not* to take my money. It's very refreshing. But there's no need to go over the top.'

'I'm not saying it to impress you,' she moaned, pushing against his chest. 'And you're not listening to me.'

'I'm listening. I just don't like what I'm hearing.'

'Do you always ignore things you don't like?'

'No.' He gave a casual shrug. 'I just turn them into things I do like. And *I* don't understand *your* problem. We are in a relationship and I am spoiling you. What's wrong with that?'

'Everything, if the spoiling is financial.' Desire sizzled between them and her struggle to ignore it seemed impossible.

He was clearly fighting the same battle. His gaze dropped to her mouth and lingered there. 'And what if I took you out to dinner? Would you insist on paying?'

'Of course I would.'

Incredulous dark eyes lifted to hers. 'You'd be pushing a pile of used euros into my hand at the end of the meal? Is that what you're saying?'

'Maybe. Gold credit cards aren't the only way to pay, you know.' She looked away from him and reminded herself why she was doing this. 'If I let you pay, it would mean that you were buying me.'

'If I pay, it means I'm spoiling you.'

'But you only want to spoil me because we had sex.'

'I want to spoil you because that is what people do in a relationship. That is normal behaviour, Chantal!' Driven to the point of explosion by the conversation, he ran his fingers through her hair. 'This conversation is going round and round in circles, and I don't even want to be talking.'

'I don't want to talk, either,' she whispered, her heart pounding as his bronzed fingers slid over her shoulder and toyed with the narrow strap of her costume. 'Take the money and the conversation ends.'

He bent his head and touched her shoulder with his mouth. 'I will *not* take the money.' His mouth was hot against her flesh and her eyes drifted shut.

'Yesterday you thought I was a gold-digger and you weren't very pleased about it. Now I'm trying to pay and you're not very pleased about that, either. That's very contradictory behaviour.'

He lifted his head and inhaled deeply, clearly at the limits of his patience. 'All right. If it makes you more comfortable, I will take the money.' He lifted the roll of cash and tucked it into his pocket with an exaggerated flourish. 'Satisfied?'

'Yes.' Her heart bumped hard against her chest. 'I'm glad you agree with me.'

'At this precise moment I'm prepared to agree to just about anything. Anything you want, the answer is yes. *Now* can we stop talking?'

She gave a tremulous smile and slid her arms round his neck. 'You understand what I'm saying?'

'No, but I'm willing to do anything you say,' he growled, his tongue probing gently as he yanked her hard against him. 'Let's go to bed. Now. Before you think up some other crazy rule.'

CHAPTER EIGHT

THREE days later, Angelos lounged in his glass-fronted office in the villa, trying to concentrate on the page of figures in front of him, his normally razor-sharp mind as blunt as a spoon.

It was only three hours since he'd left Chantal lying in bed and all he wanted to do was return there and pick up where they'd left off. It didn't matter how long he spent with her, he just wanted more. In fact his hunger had grown to the point where all he could think of was sex.

It was the first time in his life that he'd found a woman to be more absorbing than work. In fact, right at this moment, work seemed like nothing more than an irritating necessity—something to do while Chantal slept off the physical excesses of the night.

Witnessing her stunned reaction to her own sexuality had proved to be indescribably erotic. He'd discovered that there was something infinitely exciting about a passionate woman with absolutely no knowledge of the powers of her own body.

And that was the key to his current problem. She'd been a virgin, which made the whole experience a novelty, and she just adored sex, which doubled the excitement.

In the circumstances, it was hardly surprising that his mind wasn't on his work.

Staring at the complex spreadsheet on the screen in front of him, he wondered whether to abandon the pretence of working and just indulge in a two week long marathon sex session, designed to cure his obsession with her.

Why not?

He didn't believe in micro-management. He employed the very best and expected them to get on with the jobs they were being paid to do. Theoretically he should be able to take a break, if that was what he wanted.

And it was.

Given the choice, he would have been hauling her back to bed at every conceivable opportunity during the day. At coffee-time, at lunchtime, after every frustrating phone call—

But that wasn't an option because she was never around during the day.

On the few occasions he'd prowled onto the terrace, intending to surprise her, he'd discovered that she'd left after breakfast and had no intention of returning until teatime. He felt vaguely irritated by the length of time she spent away from the villa each day. For a woman who claimed not to enjoy shopping, she spent a great deal of time—well, shopping. Or was she sightseeing?

Whichever—she certainly wasn't lying by the pool dreaming of him and hoping for a midday rendezvous.

He frowned. Perhaps she thought she was doing him a favour by not distracting him from his work. Or possibly she was lonely. It was true that when his father wasn't resting he was kept busy all day with physiotherapists, nurses and doctors.

Or was she playing a more complicated game altogether?

While it was true that she was very inexperienced, it was also true that she was a woman, with a woman's instincts. Did she think that by staying out all day she would make him all the more desperate for her?

If so, then her plan was succeeding beyond her wildest dreams.

He was so desperate he was climbing the walls.

Remembering the erotic activities of the night before, Angelos decided that there was nothing going on in his working day that couldn't be put off until tomorrow. He'd join her shopping or sightseeing or whatever it was she was doing, make it clear that by staying out all day she was *not* doing him a favour and then he'd bring her back to the villa for a relaxing swim and a siesta.

Chantal delivered a large lunch order to the group of English tourists who were sitting at the best table in the taverna. 'Two moussaka, one souvlaki, one meatballs—'

It was impossibly hot, her feet ached, and she was exhausted after yet another night without sleep. She would have given anything to have spent the day sleeping by the pool.

Anything except her pride.

'Large Greek salad.' As she placed the plate in the centre of the table she heard the deep, throaty growl of a high performance sports car from somewhere behind her.

One of the men glanced towards the sound. 'That's my dream car,' he muttered enviously, reaching for his beer. 'When I have my mid-life crisis, I'm ditching my sensible family car and buying that piece of premium engineering.'

'Hummus and taramasalata—' Feeling as though she was going to melt in the heat, Chantal deposited the last of the dishes on the table. 'Can I get you anything else?'

Her question received no response. The men were listing every component of the car and the women were apparently similarly entranced.

One leaned towards the other. 'Incredible body,' she breathed, and her friend gave a feline smile.

'Devastating. Monumental sex appeal.'

It took a moment for Chantal to realise that the women were talking about the driver, not the car. The nerves on the back of her neck prickled and she turned.

Angelos slammed the car door and then strode into the restaurant as if he owned it, his hair glinting blue black in the glare of the sun. His gaze cool and confident, he scanned the tables, apparently unaware of the level of interest his arrival had created.

Then he saw her, and the flash of sexual hunger in his eyes was immediate and unmistakable.

Chantal felt her knees weaken and the look they shared held such intimacy that they might have been back in the bedroom.

'Obviously he's taken,' the woman behind her murmured regretfully, but Chantal barely heard her because her heart was bumping against her chest and now she felt as though her body was melting on the inside as well as the outside.

She gave him a faltering smile and walked over to him.

'Hello. This is a surprise. Can I get you a drink?'

'*What* do you think you're doing?' His voice was dangerously soft and out of the corner of her eye Chantal saw the owner of the taverna approach.

'Working. And I can't really talk to you now. It's lunchtime and we're very busy.' She started to move away, but strong fingers clamped around her wrist like a vice.

'You're *working*?' His voice rang with disbelief. 'What do you mean, *working*?'

'Well—' She cleared her throat, unsure how to answer. 'I do a job and get paid for it. It's a fairly standard formula. And I really need to go now, because this is our busiest time and—'

'*Why?*'

'You're asking an awful lot of obvious questions.' Casting an apologetic smile at the taverna owner, she tried once again to free herself. 'I'm working for the same reason everyone else works. Because I need the money.'

His eyes narrowed. 'Before this moment I never considered myself to be stupid, but I honestly cannot think of a reason why you would need money. I gave you my credit card.'

'I need my *own* money.'

'You are entitled to treat my credit card as your own.'

She looked at him in exasperation. 'I need proper money.'

'This is the twenty first century. A credit card *is* proper money,' he drawled, a sardonic gleam in his eyes. 'What do you need this "proper money" for?'

'All the normal things. But mostly to pay *you*. So using your credit card wouldn't have helped. I can hardly use your own money to pay you, can I? It rather defeats the object.'

There was an ominous silence. 'You are working so that you can pay me? That's where the money you gave me the other afternoon came from?' He glanced around the restaurant. 'You have been spending the last three days working here?'

'Yes.' Seeing the shock in his eyes, she felt suddenly defensive. 'What's wrong with that? Your father is busy during the day, and you're working. We don't all have a Swiss bank account full of hidden billions. I've already used up all the money I brought with me.' Aware that virtually everyone in the restaurant was following their exchange, she tried again to move away, but his grip tightened.

'We need to talk.'

'Maybe. But not now and not here.' Mortified, she glanced around her. 'Everyone is staring, Angelos.'

He frowned slightly and turned his head, taking in the gaping diners in a glance. Two streaks of colour highlighted his impressive cheekbones and he drew in a slow, deep breath. 'We need to leave this place.'

'*You* leave. I'm not going anywhere. You may not think much of this job but it's the only one I have. And if you don't let me go, so that I can serve those people over there, then I won't have it for long.'

'It doesn't matter. Because you won't be coming back here again.' Treating the customers to a full-on display of Greek volatility, Angelos fired several incomprehensible sentences in the direction of the taverna-owner, who nodded vigorously.

'My apologies.' He waved his hands towards Chantal, dismissing her hastily. 'I didn't know who you were.'

'What's that supposed to mean?' As the taverna-owner backed away and started clearing tables himself, Chantal looked at Angelos. 'Who does he think I am?'

'Mine,' Angelos said silkily, pulling her towards him with a purposeful movement that was unmistakably possessive. 'And now we are *both* leaving.' Without waiting to hear her response he walked towards the car, his firm grip on her wrist giving her no choice but to follow.

'Angelos, wait!' She took two strides to his one, jogging to keep up with him. 'This is my job.'

'Not any more. He is going to find someone else to serve his customers.'

'You can't do that! I don't want you to do that.' Chantal dug her heels in, jerked her arm and freed herself. 'I need to work.'

'Not if the purpose of working is to give me money that I don't want.' He swung her off her feet and deposited her in the passenger seat. 'We'll continue this conversation somewhere more private. I *hate* public scenes.'

'Then stop giving people something to stare at! For crying out loud, Angelos—'

'I *don't* want you working,' he growled, springing into the car with the athletic grace of a jungle cat. 'You don't need to work.'

'Yes, I do. If you won't let me pay, then I'll feel as though I'm your—'

'You're my *what*?' Simmering with anger, he trod hard on the accelerator and the car sped away from the waterfront with a throaty roar. 'What are you, Chantal? How do you see yourself?' His anger simmered like a pot of boiling oil and instead of responding she cast a desperate glance over her shoulder.

The restaurant was already fading into the distance. 'Angelos, take me back! *Please*.'

'You are *not* working in that place.'

She sighed and slumped in her seat. 'Have you any idea how hard it was to persuade him to give me that job?'

'I don't want to think about it.'

'I don't understand why you're so angry.'

'Don't you?' He changed gears viciously. 'Seeing my woman serving drinks in a bar doesn't generally do much for my mood.'

His woman?

'You sound like a caveman.' The phrase was possessive, and yet it sent a thrill through her body. No matter how much she tried to remind herself that expecting anything from this man was asking for heartbreak, she couldn't help the feeling of happiness that bathed her entire being.

'Fine. So I sound like a caveman.' His harsh tone held not one hint of regret. 'Get used to it. That's the man I am.'

'What about equality?'

'You're forgetting.' At the last minute he braked and took a sharp bend with consummate skill. 'I celebrate individuality. Men and women are different. They're supposed to be different.'

She didn't need him to point out their differences when they were right in front of her nose. Swamped by a feeling of helpless longing, it was a struggle for her to remember her principles. 'It isn't all about you, Angelos. I'm here, too.'

'It is you who I am thinking about!' His usually flawless English faltered slightly. 'Are you seriously telling me that you'd rather stand on your feet all day slogging your guts out for a minimum wage than lie by my pool being pampered?'

'Actually, yes. Because we're having an—' she stumbled over the terminology '—intimate relationship—I can't let you pay for me.'

'If we *weren't* having an intimate relationship then I wouldn't be paying for you.' Visibly exasperated, he muttered something in Greek under his breath. 'I admire your principles, but you are taking this too far. It ends now.'

'You still think I'm just doing it to impress you?' It occurred to her that they were driving away from the harbour, up into the hills, and now he was negotiating a series of terrifying hairpin bends, his eyes fixed on the road, his knuckles white as he gripped the wheel.

'Yes, but I blame myself for that. My comments on Isabelle Ducat and also on my father's ex-wives were hardly flattering. But they were *not* aimed at you. I have *never* applied those comments to you. You are different.'

'Yes, I'm different.' She clutched her seat, wishing he'd slow down. 'I don't want to be a kept woman. I need to pay my own way. I need to be useful.'

'I can think of a million ways in which you can be useful and none of them involve you balancing plates in a busy restaurant. I want no more talk about working and no more talk about paying me.'

'This isn't about you, Angelos.' Her hair blew across her face and she anchored it with her hand. 'It's about me. Even if you hadn't mentioned those other women, I still would have insisted on paying.'

'Why?'

'Because it's necessary. To not pay would make me feel like a—' She broke off, realising that she'd led the conversation up a dark, dangerous road that she didn't want to travel ever again. But it was too late.

With a smooth movement he swung the wheel and stopped the car by the side of the road in a shower of dust. Then he turned towards them, his eyes dangerously stormy. 'How would it make you feel? Tell me. I want to know.'

Her heart was thumping. 'Well—'

'*Say it!*'

'As though you're paying me to have sex.'

'You are saying that I make you feel like a prostitute?'

The word made her shrink inside. 'No! I'm not saying that—'

'Have I *ever* offered you money in exchange for sex?' His

voice was harsh and she shook her head, struggling with the feeling of nausea that threatened to overtake her.

'No, but—'

'There is no but. The answer is just *no*.' His mouth tightened. 'Do you think I brought you to Greece with the intention of seducing you?'

'No, but this is just normal behaviour for you, and you're angry because I'm not conforming. You have relationships all the time and I'm willing to bet there's a standard pattern. You sleep with a woman, you shower her with jewels until you become bored and then you move onto the next one.' *Why, oh why, had she ever started this conversation?*

'Normal behaviour?' He watched her for a moment, a tiny muscle working in his lean jaw. 'Let me remind you how "normal" my behaviour has been so far, *agape mou*. Four days ago I made love to you in my swimming pool, which just happens to be situated on the terrace in full view of most of the villa—'

Her cheeks warmed. 'You're a very sexual man.'

'I'm also a very private man,' he gritted. 'With an extraordinarily short attention span and an antisocial work habit. All those traits seem to have vanished since you arrived in Greece.'

'You've worked every day since we arrived.'

'Since we arrived I have spent approximately eighteen minutes at my computer, and most of that was spent unravelling a problem I caused by *not* concentrating.'

As the significance of his words slowly dawned on her, she wondered whether the anger in his tone was directed at himself or her. 'You're having trouble concentrating?'

He was silent for a moment, his fingers drumming an impatient rhythm on the steering wheel. '*Never* have I spent so much time achieving so little.' It was as if the confession had been dragged from him and she was silent while she tried to work out why that piece of information should make her feel light-headed.

'*I'm* the reason your concentration is affected?'

'Yes.'

'Well—' Discovering that her mouth was dry, Chantal ran her tongue over her lower lip and tried not to allow herself to read too much into it. 'I suppose that's pretty normal in a new relationship.'

'It isn't normal for me.' He spoke the words with almost violent emphasis. 'Neither is arguing in a public place, forgetting contraception, or taking the wrong road when I'm driving. None of those things constitute my normal behaviour.'

Chantal glanced over her shoulder, her heart bumping so hard she could hardly breathe. 'This is the wrong road?'

Exasperation lighting his dark eyes, he gestured impatiently to the olive groves that clung to the mountain side. 'Do you see a harbour?'

'I assumed you'd come this way on purpose.'

'I was so blind with anger to find you serving food to a lot of rude, ungrateful tourists that I turned left instead of right.' He glared at her. '*Why* is that funny?'

The darkness inside her had melted away and she couldn't stop smiling. 'Can't you see the funny side?'

'There *is* no funny side,' he said angrily. 'I hate feeling like this.'

'Out of control…' She placed a hand on his thigh, feeling the hard muscle flex beneath her fingers. 'You're not a man who likes to be out of control.'

With a driven sigh, he rubbed the tips of his fingers across his forehead. 'Jannis is probably organising a search party as we speak.' His reluctant confession was oddly endearing and Chantal felt happiness burst to life inside her.

She couldn't help it. Even though she knew it was foolish and risky to dream, the fact that she was having such an effect on him made her feel good.

'Poor Jannis… So—' her eyes were drawn to the dark hairs on his arms '—if your behaviour isn't normal, what are we going to do?'

'For a start, I'm taking you back to the villa so that I don't have to waste part of my working day tracking you down,' he growled, sliding a hand behind her head and drawing her towards him. 'From now on I want to know where you are every minute of the day. I want you where I can find you.'

His mouth was so close to hers that she could hardly breathe. 'I have to check in and out?'

'No, because you won't be going anywhere. From now on your world revolves around the bedroom and the pool.' He breathed the words against her mouth and her head swam and her eyes drifted shut.

She knew she ought to make some sort of protest, but she was desperate for him to kiss her and she didn't want to delay that activity by speaking. Instead she leaned towards him, closing the distance, unable to resist the passion that drew them together.

He kissed her with devastating expertise, his mouth hungry and demanding, but as her body was consumed by ferocious excitement she made a final, desperate attempt to protect her principles. 'I *need* to work.'

'You'll be too busy to work,' he vowed thickly, his hand stroking her ribcage and resting just short of her breast. 'You're going to forget this nonsense about working.'

The blood was pounding in her veins and she felt drugged and desperate. She just couldn't concentrate on anything when he was this close.

Resolving to find a different way to satisfy her principles, she gave up on the idea of returning to the taverna. Her body was on fire and all she wanted to do was go back to the villa. 'Do you think you can find your way back to the harbour? If you don't like public displays then I think we should go back really quickly, before we embarrass ourselves more than we already have.'

Casting a searing look in her direction, he started the engine and turned the car.

* * *

Later that evening, Angelos strolled onto the terrace for dinner, replete and re-energized after an *extremely* satisfying afternoon. A marathon session of explosive, steamy sex had been followed by a profitable work session, his concentration sharpened by the knowledge that Chantal was now safely confined to the villa. He'd left her sated and deliciously sleepy, but already he was looking forward to the night ahead.

She was the most responsive woman he'd ever known.

His father was already seated at the table, a glass of iced lemonade in one hand, the newspaper in the other. 'Have you seen the share price?'

'No.' His mind a long way from the share price, Angelos pulled out the chair opposite and was just wondering where Chantal was when she appeared in the doorway that led from the kitchen.

She was balancing several dishes, the tip of her tongue caught between her teeth as she tried not to drop them.

Remembering the last time he'd seen her cheeks that flushed, Angelos gave a lazy smile and sat back in his chair. 'Why are you serving food? Has Maria had an accident?'

'No, she's busy talking to the dietician.' Carefully she placed a dish of grilled fish and lemon slices in front of Costas, and then put a dish in front of Angelos. 'Try it,' she urged, her eyes sparkling with pride. 'I want to know what you think.'

Captivated by the triumph in her expression, it took Angelos a moment to drag his eyes from her face to the food in front of him. 'You want my opinion on moussaka?'

'On this moussaka, yes. Because I made it. And I did something special with the aubergines.' Breathless with anticipation, she watched his face anxiously. 'Does it look all right? Maria said it was good, but I think she was just being kind.'

Unable to hide his astonishment, Angelos stared at her. 'You cooked? When?' Noticing the satisfied smile on his father's face, he realised just how much his question had revealed about their afternoon activity.

'Maria taught me. We made *dolmades*, too. Pretty fiddly, but I did OK, I think.' Beaming with pride, Chantal slid into the seat next to him and waited expectantly. 'Are you going to try it?'

Angelos was still adjusting to the fact that she'd surprised him yet again.

She hadn't been lying in bed, recovering. She'd been slaving in the kitchen, in the heat, cooking him dinner. 'Why?'

'Because you need to eat.'

'No.' His tone was impatient as he searched for an answer to his question. 'I mean why are you cooking for me when I employ Maria for that task? You should have been relaxing.'

'Maria is very busy shopping and preparing your father's special diet, and she has the whole of the villa to look after. If I can cook, then I can help her.'

'You don't need to help her.' His words drew her gaze, and suddenly there was a stubborn tilt to her chin that he hadn't seen before.

'You won't let me earn money, so this will be my contribution.'

'I don't *want* your contribution.' He saw the hurt in her eyes and cursed himself for being tactless. 'I don't mean that I don't want the food. I just mean that you don't need to cook.'

'Yes, I do.' She reached forward and served herself a generous helping. 'You're very old-fashioned—do you know that?'

Angelos drew a deep breath. 'I am certainly *not* old-fashioned.'

'You are. You don't want a woman to work. You're not comfortable with the whole concept of equality.' She dissected the food on her plate with a fork, examining each layer with the delight of a child opening a present. 'You think a woman should spend her life on a sun lounger, ready for you whenever you want to take a break from your pressing work schedule.'

'That is *not* true.'

'Then why did you make me give up my job?'

Costas looked interested. 'Job? What job?'

'I found myself a job in a taverna.' Chantal smiled at his father. 'But Angelos didn't want me working there.'

Costas chuckled. 'I'm starting to understand why he has been so bad-tempered during the day.'

'I have *not* been bad-tempered.' Angelos lifted his wine. 'And it is ridiculous to suggest that I don't want women to work. A large proportion of my senior executives are women.'

'But I'm ready to bet that they're not women you have relationships with,' Chantal said mildly. 'I'm sure you neatly separate your work and social life. Which makes you hypocritical as well as old-fashioned. You're happy for a woman to work, just not *your* woman. From that I assume you usually date heiresses.'

It occurred to him that he'd never felt so out of control of a conversation. 'Why would you assume that?'

'Because you don't want women to take your money, but you don't want them to make their own money, either. That rules out a large chunk of the population and really only leaves heiresses.'

Aware that his father was following the exchange with delight, Angelos gritted his teeth. 'This conversation is pointless.'

'You're just saying that because you're losing the argument.' She looked at his plate. 'Aren't you at least going to try the moussaka? I think it's very good. I'm proud of it.'

'Most women would be delighted that a man is prepared to support them,' Angelos growled as he picked up his fork. 'Just because I don't happen to think a woman should pay when she's in a relationship with me, it doesn't make me old-fashioned or hypocritical.'

'But you're very wary that a woman might only be interested in your money. Which makes it all rather contradictory, doesn't it? It makes the whole thing very confusing for you, and even more confusing for me.'

Costas started to laugh, and once he started he couldn't stop, the spasms shaking his body. 'That has to be the first time a woman has ever beaten you in an argument. Come to think of it, she's probably the first woman you've ever spent time with who can string a sentence together. She's perfect, Angelos.' He reached for a napkin and mopped his eyes, trying to get himself under control. 'An original, just like your mother. That woman always tied me in knots. Manipulated me into saying all sorts of things I didn't mean.'

'Was she an heiress?' Chantal asked the question with interest, and Angelos watched as his father's gaze misted again.

'She was just a girl,' Costas said gruffly. 'A girl that I loved. And I would have loved her the same way whether she'd been rich or poor. And she could cook. That is where I went wrong with the other two. They couldn't cook.'

'Why would they need to? They didn't eat,' Angelos pointed out dryly, and his father shuddered.

'Do *not* remind me.' He looked longingly across the table. 'Perhaps I should try the moussaka?'

'The doctor wanted you to eat the fish,' Chantal said firmly, 'and it's delicious. Maria and I baked it in lemon and Greek herbs. Try it. I want to know if you like it. If not, I'll strike it off our list. We're trying something different every day.' She watched expectantly, a sparkle in her eyes, and Costas obediently picked up his fork and ate.

'So you went and found yourself a job?'

'That's right.' She heaped his plate with salad. 'Obviously there's limited opportunity for employment around here, but I needed the money.'

Costas sampled the fish. 'It's delicious.'

'You like it? Really?' Delighted, Chantal smiled, and Angelos found himself staring hungrily at her mouth. It didn't matter whether she was smiling, talking or kissing—her mouth was incredible.

Costas was devouring his food with enthusiasm. 'Don't listen to Angelos. You can cook for me again tomorrow. If it tastes like this, you can cook for me every day.'

'I'll bring the menus to you and you can tell me what you like best. We can adapt them together.' Chantal reached across the table and took the salt from his hand. '*Don't* add salt,' she scolded gently. 'It isn't good for you.'

'I like salt.'

'The herbs should give you all the seasoning you need.'

Angelos lounged in his chair, watching the spirited interchange in amused silence. It had been years since he'd seen his father so relaxed and content.

Not since his mother was alive.

And there was no doubt who was responsible for the change in him.

Chantal.

She sampled the food on her own plate tentatively, chewing slowly. Then she gave a low, appreciative murmur, the sound so sensual and evocative that his body hardened in an instantaneous response.

Watching her across the table, he decided that his father was correct about one thing—there was something indescribably erotic about a woman who enjoyed her food.

She glanced at him and paused with the fork halfway to her mouth. 'You're not eating. Is something wrong?'

Angelos glanced at his plate and realised that he'd forgotten to eat. 'It's too hot.'

'No, it's not. Maria told me you prefer it served slightly cooler, so that's what I did. Don't you like it?'

'It's delicious.'

'Then what's the matter?' She put her fork down, her gaze self conscious. 'You're staring at me.'

She was the matter. She had a volcanic effect on his libido.

Suddenly he couldn't wait for the meal to end so that he could take her back to bed.

'He is not used to being with a woman who eats,' Costas said cheerfully. 'The sight is as rare as a snow leopard in the middle of Athens.'

Aware that the faster he ate, the sooner the evening would end, Angelos swiftly finished the food on his plate and then served himself an extra helping just to please her.

He ate quickly, but was forced to wait until his father and Chantal had finished discussing the relative merits of different forms of exercise.

Finally his father yawned and excused himself. Immediately Angelos rose and led Chantal back into the bedroom.

'Don't you want coffee?' She gave a gasp as he pulled her hard against him.

'No,' he growled, his mouth sliding down the inviting curve of her neck. 'I don't want coffee. Nor do I want fruit or conversation. In fact, *agape mou*, the only thing I want is you. Naked. Right now.'

Her head tilted back and her eyes drifted shut. 'Don't do that. I can't think when you do that—'

'I don't want you to think.'

'Angelos…' She gave a low whimper. 'We only got out of bed a few hours ago.'

'*That* was a mistake. We should never have left the bed.' He stroked a hand over the curve of her bottom and it was his turn to groan. 'I can't decide whether this is your best feature. I need you naked so that I can assess all your qualities together.'

Her fingers dug into his shoulder. 'My bottom is too big.'

'Your bottom is perfect. *You* are perfect. Even my father adores you,' he said as he bent his head and kissed her neck. 'You are playing an important part in his recovery and I'm grateful for that. Don't think I don't know that you are the reason he's eating properly, and has swapped his wine for juice and water.'

'I adore him.' She pulled away slightly and gave a faltering smile. 'In fact, I envy you.'

'You do?' His eyes narrowed. It was the first time she'd shown any interest in his financial status.

'Yes, you're incredibly lucky. I'd do anything to have a father like yours.'

It wasn't the comment he'd been expecting, and it took a moment for her words to register. 'You envy me my *father*?'

'Yes.' She looked into his eyes and then frowned slightly. 'Why? What did you think I was going to say?'

Deciding that this was one of those occasions when it was best not to be honest, Angelos stayed silent, but she breathed in sharply and stepped away from him. 'You assumed I envied you your wealth.' She watched him for a moment and then gave a little laugh. 'You still don't know me at all, do you?'

'It was a natural assumption. No one has envied me my father before.'

'I'm sure they have. He's lovely.' There was something in her wistful tone that caught his attention.

'Is your own father alive?'

He saw her sudden tension, and then she pulled away from him. 'He and my mother didn't—' She stopped. 'They didn't stay in touch. I have no idea where he is now.'

'You've never tried to trace him?'

She stilled, her back to him. 'No.'

'Is he the source of your insecurities?' Angelos put his hands on her shoulders and turned her to face him. 'Is he the reason you have a low opinion of yourself?'

For a moment she didn't answer, and then she raised herself on tiptoe and brushed her mouth against his. 'Just kiss me, Angelos,' she murmured huskily. 'Stop talking and kiss me.'

He realised just how little he knew about her life, but the blood was pounding in his head and the touch of her mouth against his drove all rational thought from his head. Since when had it become a challenge to concentrate on anything?

All he wanted to do was rip her clothes off and explore her lush, spectacular body in minute detail.

Driven by the thunderous force of his libido, Angelos tumbled her back onto the bed and brought his mouth down on hers, his hands swiftly removing her clothes from her deliciously squirming body.

'*Angelos*, please—' Her soft whimper of desperation removed every last scrap of his self-control and the need to satisfy his sexual hunger took precedence over everything else.

With something close to desperation he came down on top of her and immediately she parted her legs, her silky-soft thighs brushing against his as she arched expectantly.

Responding to an urge so powerful that it went far beyond anything he had experienced before, he thrust into her soft, damp core, her immediate moan of pleasure adding still more fuel to his passion. She was hot and tight and he was so overwhelmed by how good she felt that he drove deep in his need to satisfy the almost agonising attack of lust that gripped him.

Her nails dug into his shoulders and she gasped his name one more time and then he felt the orgasm ripple through her body, drawing him over the edge.

His world exploded and he thrust hard, swallowing her whimpers of ecstasy with the demands of his mouth as he emptied his body into hers.

In the aftermath, neither of them spoke. *Neither of them was able to speak.*

After what seemed like an age, Angelos rolled back against the pillows and gathered her against him, unwilling to let her go even for a moment. 'Tell me why you were working as a cleaner.'

She didn't answer immediately. 'It was the only job I could find when I arrived in Paris.'

'Where were you before Paris?'

'Buenos Aires. I worked with horses for a while.'

'Presumably that's where you learned to tango?' He suddenly discovered that he wanted to know everything about her. He wasn't comfortable with the knowledge that he knew so little of her life. 'And before that?'

'I travelled in Peru. And before that I was in India, Australia and New Zealand…'

Listening to the endless list of countries that she'd visited, he found himself more and more intrigued. 'Obviously you're not one for putting down roots.' He rolled onto his side so that he could look at her, but immediately her eyes slid from his.

'I'm not really a roots sort of person. I just wanted to travel.'

'Did you go to university?' Even though he was looking at her profile he saw something alter in her expression.

'No.' Her tone was flat. 'I didn't.'

'But you're obviously very bright—'

'I didn't do that well at school. I didn't like school. Can we talk about something else?' She sat up sharply, as if something had upset her. 'What about you? Tell me how you came to make your billions.'

Judging from her tense expression that it was best to allow her the change of subject, Angelos tugged her back down into his arms. 'I didn't like school, either. I found it very restricting. I wanted to do things my way.'

The tension in her body eased and she relaxed against him. 'I expect you had to be first in everything?'

'Of course.'

A bubble of laughter escaped her lips. 'You haven't changed much, have you?'

'No.' Pleased to see her back to her good natured self, Angelos continued to talk. 'My father was a very successful man. He wanted me to join his business.'

'But you didn't.'

'Of course not. Where would be the challenge in that? I had

no desire to be a caretaker for a business that someone else had developed.'

'So you did your own thing.' She slid her arm around him. 'It's nice to know that you're vulnerable, like everyone else.'

Vulnerable?

Startled by her interpretation of his motives, Angelos frowned up at the ceiling. '*How* am I vulnerable?'

'You obviously wanted to prove something to your father.'

Considering that possibility for the first time in his life, Angelos gave a surprised laugh. 'You're probably right—but don't tell my competitors. If they hear a rumour that I'm vulnerable, my working life will become far more challenging and I will have less time to spend in bed with you.'

'I expect your father is very proud of you.' There was a wistful note in her voice that caught his attention.

'What about you?' Deciding that he'd backed off enough, he gently eased the subject back to her own childhood. 'If your father wasn't around, then presumably it was your mother who brought you up? Where did you live?'

'We moved around a lot when I was young, and then later I was at boarding school. That's enough talking for now. I'm tired, Angelos. Goodnight.' She rolled over so that her back was facing him and tugged the silk sheet up over her shoulders, the gesture clearly declaring that the subject was closed.

Angelos stared in silence at her tense body, his mind working overtime.

It was obvious that she found any mention of her mother, her childhood or her schooldays extraordinarily stressful. Obviously it hadn't been a good time for her, and yet it was equally obvious that she was bright and intelligent and should have excelled.

He wanted to continue the conversation—*he wanted to understand her*—and that thought troubled him, because he'd never before had the slightest inclination to understand a woman.

Deciding that he would achieve more by continuing the conversation when she was more relaxed, he lay down and pulled her into his arms.

He didn't mind her sleeping with her back to him, but there was no way he was allowing her to shut herself off.

CHAPTER NINE

'PACK a bag,' Angelos instructed as he emerged from the shower with droplets of water still clinging to his bronzed skin. A towel was looped casually around his hips, leaving his torso bare.

He would have made a Greek god sob with envy, Chantal thought as she stared at the smooth, well-defined muscles of his shoulders. Secretly she was hoping that he might decide to come back to bed.

'Why do I need to pack a bag? I don't want to leave here.' She knew she sounded desperate, but she couldn't help it.

She'd been so incredibly happy. Happier than she'd ever been in her life before.

And she didn't want it to end.

She still couldn't believe that two weeks had passed already.

'We're not leaving.' Reaching for his watch, he cast her an amused glance. 'I'm glad you like it here.'

'I love it.' She loved *him*. It didn't matter how many times she reminded herself that this relationship wasn't going anywhere, she still couldn't control her feelings.

She loved him, she loved his father, and she loved the island. They were protected from the outside world and at times it felt as though real life would never intrude again.

He raked strands of damp hair out of his eyes. 'Then you will be pleased to hear that we're not leaving yet. But we have to go to Athens for two days.'

'Athens?' Dragging her eyes from the tantalising line of hair that disappeared below the towel, Chantal sat up, the sheet clutched to her chest. 'Why?'

'Unfortunately my lengthy absence from work has created a few problems which require my personal attention.' Without elaborating, he vanished into the dressing room and emerged with a crisp white shirt in his hand.

'You go,' she said quickly. 'I'll stay here.'

'No way. I've already learned that I can't concentrate on my work unless you are around. Where I go, you go. That's the deal.' He released the towel and she had a brief glimpse of his magnificent torso before he slipped his arms into the shirt. Her stomach plummeted and she wished for the millionth time that she wasn't so receptive to him. It was as if her body had been created to respond to his.

'I don't want to go to Athens.' Swamped by a feeling of foreboding, she wrapped her arms around her knees and searched for plausible excuses. 'We can't leave your father on his own.'

'He has a doctor, two nurses and a dietician.' Angelos finished dressing swiftly. 'Not to mention Maria. And it is just for one night. I'll spend this afternoon in the office, then we will attend the function, stay the night in my house in Athens, and then return.'

'Function?'

He reached for a tie. 'Another fundraising occasion. Unfortunately my presence is mandatory.'

Wondering if she would ever become indifferent to his body, Chantal watched as he fastened the button at his bronzed throat. 'If you're spending the evening at a function, then I might as well wait for you here. It's not as if I'll get to spend time with you.'

'I'm not leaving you here.'

'I don't want to go.' Defensive as a child, she watched him

warily. 'I'll be totally out of place at something like that. You know I will.'

'Why would you be out of place?'

'Because I'm not like the people in your world.'

'This is my world,' he said smoothly, prowling over to the bed and bending down to kiss her once again, 'and you are in it.'

But she was only in it because he was enjoying the sex. There was nothing more to it than that. *Not even at her most deluded had she ever pretended she was part of his world.* 'Being here is different from going out to that sort of event. I don't fit.'

He stroked her hair away from her face. 'You went to the ball in Paris.'

'And that was a mistake.'

'A mistake, *agape mou*?' He gave a slow, sexy smile. 'I don't think so.'

'All right—meeting you wasn't a mistake. But the ball itself was a mistake. I felt totally out of place. And this time I won't have your father to save me.'

'*Save* you?' His dark brows met in a sudden frown. 'Who will you need saving from?'

She looked away from him, feeling the darkness closing in. *He had no idea what her life had been like.* 'It just isn't me, Angelos. Forget it.'

'*Don't* look away from me.' He slid a hand over her cheek and turned her head towards him. 'And don't try and hide what you're thinking. I want to know everything about you.'

But she didn't *want* him to know everything. He already knew far more than most people.

She forced herself to smile. 'Then you should know that I feel out of place at glittering functions. You go to Athens. But come back quickly.'

'I can't believe you don't want to go.' A trace of exasperation in his expression, he studied her face. 'You are the only woman

I've ever met who isn't always looking for an excuse to dress up and party.'

'If that's what you want, then go and find a woman who enjoys parties.'

'I'm with the woman I want to be with. You have no reason to feel insecure.'

'I'm not insecure,' she lied, and then blushed as he lifted an eyebrow in silent challenge. 'Oh, all right—maybe I am a little insecure. But only in certain situations.'

'You have no reason to be insecure in *any* situation.'

'I just feel—' she hesitated '—different.'

'You *are* different.' He rose to his feet with his usual athletic grace. 'Which is why I am with you. You are generous, and beautiful, and you care about the things that matter.'

'*I don't fit.*' She tried to reason with him. 'At that ball in Paris, everyone was staring at me.'

'Because you are beautiful,' he said dryly. 'You were more beautiful than any other woman in the room that night in Paris. And a million times more genuine. You have no reason to have such a low opinion of yourself.'

'It's just that I'm not comfortable going to events like that.'

'How many have you attended?'

Chantal coloured. 'Just the one.'

'And you were gatecrashing, rather than arriving as an invited guest,' he drawled softly, 'so it was hardly surprising that you were on tenterhooks for the whole evening. Come with me tonight. You will have fun.'

'I won't know anyone—'

'You will know me.' Supremely confident that his presence would be more than enough for anyone, he strolled across the room and picked up his jacket. 'Don't argue with me.'

He just didn't understand.

She tried a different approach. 'I don't have anything suitable to wear.'

'Now you are talking like a woman.' He smiled. 'We will find you something to wear that will give you confidence.'

But she knew only too well that confidence came from the inside, not the outside. And what was inside her was so foul that it tarnished the baby shoots of her confidence like some malevolent pest. 'I don't want to go, Angelos.'

'Pack,' he ordered, his tone firm. 'You have nothing to worry about. I will be there with you. If you need saving, then I will save you.'

But he didn't understand what threatened her, did he?

What did he know about insecurity or lack of confidence? He was super-bright, highly educated and immensely successful. And his home-life had clearly been both loving and supportive.

She stared at him helplessly, swamped by a feeling of foreboding that couldn't be ignored.

It didn't matter how firmly she told herself that she was wrong, she just knew that the idyll was over.

Their fabulous two weeks was about to end with a bang.

This was the other side of his life, Chantal thought as the private helicopter swooped over the Greek mainland towards Athens. Closeted on his secluded island, she'd barely thought of his billionaire status. They'd been a man and a woman, nothing more. 'I didn't know the island had a helipad.'

'I rarely use it. When I go to the island, I go to relax and unwind.' Dressed in a light grey suit that emphasised his sleek, dark looks, Angelos looked every inch the successful business tycoon, and his phone just didn't stop ringing.

Watching him snap into work mode to answer yet another call, Chantal studied his profile as he talked. *Why was she suddenly finding him intimidating?*

Was it the fact that he was dressed more formally than he'd been at the villa?

Reminding herself that he was the same man she'd woken up

next to that morning, she took a deep breath and tried to calm herself. But she couldn't subdue the feeling of unease that dulled the edge of the happiness she'd discovered over the past two weeks.

Angelos finished his call and glanced at her. 'As I have said I have to spend a few hours in the office this afternoon. But first I will take you shopping for something to wear this evening.'

Chantal thought about the small amount of money in her bag. 'Just don't take me anywhere ridiculously pricey.'

'I will enjoy spoiling you.'

'I don't want your money.'

'I'm not offering you money,' he drawled, leaning across and releasing the catch on her seat belt. 'I'm buying you a gift. Now stop talking about it. We've arrived.'

A plush, air-conditioned car whisked them from the airport into the centre of Athens and as they weaved through the heavy traffic. Chantal found herself intrigued by the busy, bustling city.

It was nice to see places in comfort and style, she conceded as she watched people wilting in the heat outside.

To her right she noticed a colourful market and craned her neck to get a closer look, wishing that they had time to stop and explore.

But Angelos clearly had something different in mind, and a few minutes later the driver turned into a wide road and stopped outside a glass-fronted designer boutique.

Angelos switched off his phone and urged her out onto the pavement.

The clothes in the window were frighteningly elegant and chic, but one dress in particular caught her eye. She studied it for a moment, automatically noting the cut and style and deciding how she'd adapt it if she were making it.

Angelos urged her into the shop and immediately a gaggle of sales staff converged on them, drawn by his unmistakable air of authority. He had 'billionaire' written all over him, and she could see them glancing at her simple dress and wondering what a man like him was doing with a girl like her.

Having sex, she thought gloomily. *That's what he's doing*.

Ignoring them, he glanced impatiently at his watch and turned towards her. 'Choose something.'

Just like that.

He was a man who didn't know how it felt to be intimidated by one's surroundings.

She glanced around at all the chrome and glass, wondering if she was supposed to wash her hands before she touched any of the clothes.

Ignoring the hovering sales assistants, because she knew that if she looked at them they'd destroy her fragile confidence, Chantal walked tentatively towards the dress that she'd seen in the window.

The design was ridiculously simple. It was the quality of the fabric that turned it into something special.

'It would look wonderful on you. It's cut to conceal that extra bit of weight,' an assistant murmured, and Angelos frowned.

'Then it won't suit her,' he said smoothly, 'because she doesn't have any extra weight.'

Ridiculously grateful that he'd countered the bitchy comment, Chantal stared at the dress. It was cut on the bias and she could see that it would hang well on a woman with curves.

'How much is it?'

Her question was met by appalled silence, and the assistants glanced at each other and then at Angelos, who responded with a cool stare.

'You're running a business. Surely you know the answer to that question?'

After a brief hesitation, one of the assistants cleared her throat. 'It's—' She breathed in, as though she'd never been asked that question before '—forty thousand euros.'

Chantal stepped away from the dress, feeling suddenly faint. 'That's outrageous.'

'Is it?' Angelos frowned. 'If you like it, at least try it.'

She turned towards him, her jaw set at a stubborn angle. 'At *forty thousand euros*? I don't think so.'

'The price isn't relevant.'

'Of course it's relevant. I can't afford it.'

'But I can.'

His casual statement merely reminded her of the enormous gulf between their circumstances and she shook her head, taking another step back from the dress.

'No.' Aware that the assistant was gaping at her as if she'd lost her mind, Chantal backed towards the door. 'Can we talk for a moment?'

Anglos let out an exasperated sigh and followed her out into the stifling heat of the street. 'What is going on? Stop dithering. You need something to wear this evening. You have to buy a dress. That one will do fine.'

'Why did you bring me here?' Feeling raw inside, she wrapped her arms around her body. 'Were you trying to make me look stupid or something?'

His dark eyes were suddenly wary, as if he sensed a trap. 'I brought you here to buy you a dress.'

'But that dress is *forty thousand euros*.' She almost choked on the words. 'I can't afford that.'

'Obviously I was *not* intending *you* to pay.'

Her breathing grew more rapid. 'Haven't you learned a single thing about me in the time we've been together? *I don't want your money.*'

'I wasn't offering you money,' he replied, his tone suddenly guarded. 'I was buying you a dress. A gift.'

He just didn't get it.

'I don't want a forty-thousand-euro gift. What does that say about our relationship?'

'That I care about you enough to be generous?'

'I don't want that sort of generosity. *That isn't how I want our relationship to be.*' Discovering that her eyes were swimming with tears, she blinked rapidly. 'Anyway, anyone who spends that much on a dress that someone else could be wearing too has got to be stupid.'

He drew in a long breath. 'You are very difficult to please.'

'No, I'm not. I'm easy to please. When you peel my orange for breakfast, you please me. When you rub my shoulders before I go to sleep, that pleases me. When you defend me from a nasty comment, that pleases me. *I'm easy to please, Angelos.*' Her heart was pounding. 'Just don't try and buy me.'

'I am *not* trying to buy you.' This time his tone was exasperated. 'I'm trying to spoil you. And I did not bring you here to make you look stupid. I brought you here because this is the place where every other woman of my acquaintance begs to be brought. I understood it to be retail Nirvana.'

'Not for me.'

'Obviously not. You are very complicated. Keeping pace with you requires a degree in psychology. So—' he gestured towards the row of expensive shops '—if this isn't the place for you, where do you want to go?'

'Somewhere I can afford.' On impulse she grabbed his hand and dragged him down the street towards the market they'd passed in the car.

'Where are we going?'

'To find a dress.'

'There are no boutiques in this direction. And it's forty degrees in the shade,' Angelos muttered as he strode along next to her. 'No one walks at this time of day in Athens.'

'Billionaires don't walk, but normal people *do* walk, Angelos. Just for five minutes, try living like a normal person.' She crossed the road, dodging between the frantic traffic, and found the market. 'I want to look here.'

Angelos scanned the crowded market in speechless amazement, and then jerked her against him. 'You are going to a ball. The cream of Athens society will be there. And you want to wear a dress that you have purchased from the stall of a market trader?'

'Not a dress, no—' Ignoring him, she tugged herself free from his grip and walked up and down the rows of stalls until she found what she wanted. A stall selling brightly coloured hand-printed silk. She stopped, her eyes scanning the rolls until something caught her eye. It was a deep sea-green, flecked with bright blue. 'That one, please.' Reaching into her bag, she pulled out a notebook and pencil and drew a quick sketch. Then she did some fast calculations.

'You are buying fabric?' Angelos glanced at his watch, not even bothering to conceal his irritation. 'Even with all the money at my disposal, I will not be able to find someone in Athens who will be able to make a dress for you at this late stage.'

'I'm making it myself.' Using the figures in her notebook, she ordered the fabric she needed and was delighted to find that she had enough money for the purchase.

Angelos muttered something in Greek and then switched to English. 'I was happy to buy you that dress in the shop.'

'But I wouldn't have been happy to wear it. Not unless I'd paid for it myself. Relax, Angelos. I'm happy.' She handed the money over to the man with a smile, and tucked the fabric into her bag. Then she moved onto the next stall and bought some thread, and to another, where she bought a plain hairslide and a selection of tiny shells.

Angelos watched in disbelief. 'I don't have a sewing machine in my house.'

'I sew by hand.' She made her last purchase. A tube of glue. 'I just need a couple of hours to myself, that's all. You won't miss me. You'll be on the phone. You always are.' She smiled at him. 'I don't know why you're so cross. I've saved you a fortune. And I'm happy because I paid for it myself.'

'You're *ridiculously* independent,' he breathed. 'I *wanted* to spoil you.'

Her insides melted and she stood on tiptoe to kiss him. 'Spoil me in other ways,' she said softly. 'I like being with you. It's enough.'

He stared down at her and the look in his eyes was blatantly sexual. 'Let's go home.'

Angelos glanced at his watch. If they didn't hurry up they'd be late. Not that he minded for himself. In fact, arriving late would have been his preference, but he was worried about Chantal. She was already nervous enough. He didn't want her to make a late entrance, especially when she was wearing a dress that she'd made herself from a scrap of fabric she'd bought in a market.

Didn't she realise that she was going to be exposing herself to the sort of scrutiny that she hated?

Cursing fluently, he ran a hand over the back of his neck and wished he'd just purchased the other dress and demolished her objections.

'Angelos?'

Hearing her voice, he turned. And caught his breath.

The unexceptional piece of fabric from the market had been transformed into an elegant dress. It fell from two shoestring straps, skimmed the feminine curves of her body and pooled on the floor, the hemline shimmering with tiny shells. Her sleek hair spilled like warm sunshine over her bare shoulders and a delicate bracelet of shells encircled one slender wrist. In one hand she carried a matching fabric evening bag.

She looked spectacular. And impossibly sexy. Like a mermaid allowed one night of earthly pleasure.

Lust slammed through his body with predictable force and his mouth dried.

Clearly apprehensive, she took a few steps towards him and then hesitated. 'Say something—' Her tone was light, but her expression was anxious as she watched his reaction. 'And make sure it's something nice.'

Driven by the demands of his libido, Angelos strode across to her and pulled her into his arms, anchoring her against the almost painful throb of his erection. Then he bent his head and captured her glossy mouth with his, kissing her until he felt the hard tips of her breasts press through the thin cotton of his shirt.

She sank against him for a few seconds and then dragged her mouth from his. 'You just removed *all* my lipstick,' she protested breathlessly, and Angelos wondered whether it would be risky to admit that her lipstick wasn't the only thing he wanted to remove at that moment.

'You look amazing.'

Her face brightened. 'Really? I'm not going to embarrass you?'

'No, but I might well embarrass myself if you go out looking like that.' He ran a hand over her bare shoulder. 'You look like a very, very sexy mermaid. I can't look at you without wanting to take you to bed. I can't believe you made that dress. How did you learn to sew?'

'I taught myself. You like it?' She sounded delighted, and he realised with a stab of surprise just how much he wanted her to be happy.

She still hadn't said much about her childhood, but he sensed that she'd had an *extremely* hard life and he hated the fact that she had so little confidence.

Vowing to change all that, he admired the shells on the dress. He'd never been remotely interested in women's fashions, but even he could see that what she'd produced was nothing short of spectacular.

'You should be really proud of yourself.'

Her amazing blue eyes widened. 'Should I?'

'You have an incredible talent.'

She frowned slightly, as if it hadn't occurred to her, and he felt a flash of frustration that her astonishing ability had clearly gone unrecognised for so long.

Never one to allow raw talent to go to waste, Angelos promised himself that he was going to change that.

Perhaps, if she spent enough time with him, some of his confidence would rub off on her. 'I hate to say this—' he slid his hand over the tempting curve of her bottom '—but we need to leave.'

Her smile faltered. 'We could just stay in—'

'I want to show you off.' And it was true. Not only was she stunningly beautiful, she was also bright, funny and incredibly warm-natured. 'And you have no reason to be under-confident. You will outshine every woman in the room. And they will all want to know where you bought your dress, so you'd better have some answers ready.'

The dinner was an elegant affair, attended by the cream of Athens society. They welcomed her graciously, but Chantal couldn't help but be aware of the curiosity in their eyes as they watched her and wondered.

'They're staring,' she murmured to Angelos as he placed a tall flute of champagne in her hand.

'Of course they're staring. Your dress is every bit as amazing as the one you wore in Paris.'

'I wish I'd worn something different.' Hideously self-conscious, she felt as though she were standing naked. 'They're gossiping and wondering.'

'Are they?' He slid an arm round her waist and drew her against him. 'Then we'd better give them something decent to gossip about.' He lowered his mouth to hers and kissed her gently, undoubtedly aware that the affectionate gesture was unlikely to have been missed by a single person in the room. Leisurely and unhurried, he finally lifted his head and she gave a soft gasp of disbelief.

'I thought you weren't into public displays.'

'I'm not,' he drawled, angling his head and eyeing those around him with cool disdain. 'Which just goes to prove how much you've changed me. If people wish to gossip, *agape mou*, then let them gossip. It doesn't affect us. And now I'm going to introduce you to some people who matter to me.'

His arm possessive as it rested on her waist, he drew her into the sophisticated crowd and immediately people surged forward.

He moved among them, speaking briefly to some, at greater length to others, always with authority and a natural air of command. People pressed in on them, all desperate to be associated with him in some way.

'Why does everyone want to talk to you?' Chantal touched his arm. 'Are you a genius or is it just because you're rich?'

He threw back his head and laughed and several people glanced towards them in astonishment, clearly wondering who or what had amused him so much. 'Both.' His eyes teased her gently. 'I'm a genius, and that's why I'm rich. The two invariably go together.'

'And you're arrogant. Don't forget that bit.' Laughing at him, she glanced around her. 'I just can't believe these people are all genuine.'

'They're not.' He took her hand and led her onto the terrace. Beneath them lay the city, glittering like jewelled cloth. 'I'm glad you came tonight.'

'You didn't give me any choice.' She placed a hand on his chest, keeping him slightly at a distance. *It was the only way she could concentrate.* 'We have things we need to talk about, Angelos…'

'Yes.' His voice soft, he moved slightly so that his powerful shoulders shielded her from curious guests. 'So, let's talk.'

'Here?' Surprised, she tilted her head back to look at him. 'You don't want to wait until we're home?'

'When we're home, we won't be talking.' His powerful thigh brushed suggestively against hers and she gave a stifled gasp.

'Oh—' Invisible sensuous threads were pulling them together in the semi-darkness.

'What do you want to say, Chantal?'

She could tell from his voice that he was as tightly wound as she was and she took a deep breath, trying to subdue the throbbing passion that threatened to consume both of them. 'It's time to tell your father the truth.' *He seems so much better now.*

'I agree. We'll do it tomorrow.'

'I don't want him hurt.'

'He won't be hurt. He'll be thrilled.'

'Thrilled that you lied to him?'

'When have I lied to him?' His tone was smooth and he lifted a hand and stroked a strand of hair away from her eyes. 'He believed that we were together.'

'But—'

'And we are together.'

What exactly did he mean by that? Confused, it took her a moment to speak. 'What are you saying?'

'That it doesn't end here. Did you really think I'd let you go?' He was so close now that she could feel the heat from his body, and desire curled low in her pelvis.

Her heartbeat was suddenly uneven. 'What are you suggesting?'

'Isn't it obvious? When we leave the island, you will come with me.'

His words were so unexpected that her heart stopped altogether. 'Where to?'

'Wherever I go.' Supremely confident of her response, he looked at her expectantly and her breath caught.

Why not?

He wanted her. And she wanted him. For a moment excitement flared inside her, but it was almost immediately doused. She couldn't accept, could she? *How could she possibly accept?* 'Would I be able to work?'

Astonishment shimmered in his eyes. 'Why would you want to?'

'I've already made that clear.'

'I travel a great deal. Naturally you would travel with me. So the answer is no, you would not be able to work.'

She stilled, a feeling of numbness growing inside her. 'So I'd be your kept woman?'

His eyes narrowed. 'You would be my lover. My companion. You can chose the title yourself.'

'I can't afford to be with you,' she said simply. 'Your lifestyle is too expensive. It's all private jets and fast cars and top restaurants. What I earn in a week wouldn't even cover your phone bill.'

'I am not expecting you to pay for anything. I don't *want* you to pay for anything. I will provide everything you need.'

'So what will that make me? A prostitute with one employer?'

A stunned silence followed her outburst and then he grabbed her wrist in a vice-like grip and propelled her across the balcony, through the crowded ballroom and out again into the street.

As usual everyone seemed to anticipate his wishes before he'd even expressed himself, and moments later his car purred to a halt in front of them.

For a moment Angelos just stood there, and Chantal glanced at his rigid profile.

He was angry. *So angry.* Every inch of his powerful frame vibrated with emotion and she sighed.

'Angelos—'

'Get in,' he ground out finally. 'Get in or so help me I'll put you in the car myself—and then you'll know the meaning of gossip.'

She glanced over her shoulder and realised that their rapid exit had drawn attention.

'We really—'

'Don't say another word.' He sprang into the car and flattened the accelerator to the floor, driving like an Athenian born and bred.

Anyone who thought driving in Paris was a nightmare should try Athens, Chantal though faintly, choosing to close her eyes rather than watch as Angelos zigzagged the car through the heavy traffic.

Finally he pulled in, ignoring the cars that zoomed past them at an alarming rate. 'Where are we?'

'Somewhere anonymous.' He turned to face her, his expression grim.

'I don't know why you're so angry.'

'You accuse me of treating you like a prostitute and *you don't know why I'm angry*?'

'Actually, I didn't accuse you of treating me like a prostitute. I just said that if you paid for everything it would make me feel like a prostitute. That isn't the same thing.'

'Have you any idea how many women have wanted to hear me say the words I just said to you?'

'I'm sure lots of women would have been very flattered,' she mumbled, and he inhaled sharply.

'But you're not one of them?'

'No.' She swallowed. 'Unfortunately not.'

He ran a hand over his face, visibly struggling with his temper. 'What do I have to do? *What is it you want from me?* Tell me, because I'm damned if I know.'

'Nothing.' She almost choked on the word. 'That's the point. Our circumstances are just too far apart. I can't afford to live with you as your equal and I won't let you keep me.'

'Chantal—' His voice was tense. 'All around the world there are couples living together whose financial situation is not equal. Men go out to work, women raise children. In some families that situation is reversed, but one thing is sure—they don't all have financial equality.'

'Maybe not.'

'I can't believe you're saying no to me.'

She swallowed and looked out of the window. 'That's just because no one has ever said no to you before. You'll get over it. It will probably be character building.'

'My character is fully formed,' he muttered thickly. 'What I don't understand is *why* is this issue is so important to you.'

She stilled. 'It just is.'

'No.' He turned to face her, his tone was an angry growl. 'That isn't good enough. If I'm supposed to let you go, Chantal, then at least do me the courtesy of explaining *why*.'

She stayed silent, aware that he was almost boiling with impatience in the seat next to her.

'Chantal.' His tone was dark and threatening. 'I'm not letting you go unless—'

'My mother was a prostitute.'

She heard his sharply indrawn breath and turned to look at him. 'That's right.' She was surprised by how calm she sounded. 'That's who I am, Angelos. The daughter of a prostitute. Obviously getting pregnant with me was a career-limiting move, but she managed to get round that.'

'Chantal—'

She turned her head, unable to look at him. Humiliation threatened to crush her, but she forced herself to give him the details he needed to hear. 'You wanted the truth, and I'm telling you the truth just this once. After this don't ever ask me to talk about it again.' Why had she bothered saying that, when she knew that after this he wouldn't want to go anywhere near her? She knew full well that this was going to be the last conversation they ever had. 'At first we moved around a lot. I started a new school every term.'

'Look at me, Chantal.' He reached out and touched her arm, but she shrank away from him, her eyes still fixed in the middle distance.

'I found it hard to settle in.'

After a moment, he let his hand drop. 'I'm sure you did. I understand now why you found school difficult and couldn't wait to leave. Did they know about your mother?'

'Oh, yes.' She kept her tone light. 'No matter how hard I tried to keep it a secret, somehow someone always found out what my mother did. Obviously no one was allowed to be friends with me—no one wanted to be. And when I was on my own in the playground, or being tormented, I used to just escape in my head and pretend I was someone else. If I hated the situation I was in, I just imagined something different.'

There was a tense silence. 'You don't have to talk about this,' he breathed and she turned then and allowed herself to look at him. *For the last time.*

'I do have to talk about it. It's important that you understand who I am.'

His dark brows met in a sharp frown. 'This isn't about who you are.'

'Yes, it is. It's what shaped me. It's what made me who I am.'

And having to reveal herself to this man was the lowest point of her life. Hot tears of humiliation stung her eyes and for a moment she wondered whether she had what it took to carry on. And then she remembered how they'd reached this point. He thought he had feelings for her. *But he didn't know who she really was, did he?*

She blinked rapidly. 'When I was ten, my mother met a very rich man. He introduced her to another rich man, and pretty soon her entire clientele had changed. We went up in the world. I suppose you could call it a promotion. I was sent to a very elite boarding school, with my fees paid by one of her regulars.'

'The girls at the boarding school—'

'Did they know what my mother did? Oh, yes—' She gave a humourless laugh. 'Several of them had fathers who were my mother's clients—although I don't think any of them actually realised that.'

He rubbed his fingers over his forehead and muttered something in Greek. 'Now I understand why your schooldays were difficult.'

'Those girls stripped away what little confidence I had—' She swallowed. 'And I let them, because I suppose deep down I hated myself as much as they hated me. I was the daughter of a prostitute. Hardly something to boast about, was it? That's why I travelled. I always hoped I could leave it behind, but it never worked that way because it's part of who I am.' *And it always would be.*

'Do you still see your mother?'

Chantal shook her head. 'She was never interested in me. She only put me in that school because one of her clients thought she wasn't paying me enough attention. Anyway, I left at sixteen—' She gave a tiny shrug. 'I had no wish to stay there any longer than I had to.'

'Did the school do nothing about the fact you were bullied?'

'The school was horrified by the effect that having me as a pupil had on their reputation. They were delighted when I decided to leave.'

He was silent for a moment, his powerful body still. 'And that's why you're so determined never to take money from a man. Now I understand why you keep thrusting money at me.'

'I promised myself that I would never let a man keep me.' She looked at him, hanging onto her composure with difficulty. 'So now you understand. Will you explain to your father? And tell him why? I'd hate him to think less of me.' The tears were building, and this time she knew she wasn't going to be able to hold them back. In order to prove to him that their relationship would never work she'd lifted her protective shield and allowed him to see who she really was.

'Chantal—'

'Thanks, Angelos.' Choked by humiliation, she couldn't bear to hear what he had to say and so reached down and picked up her bag. 'You may be filthy rich and arrogant, but you never once made me feel small or insignificant. You're a pretty decent guy, really, but I promise not to ruin your reputation by telling anyone.' Without giving him time to reply, she opened the car door and stepped into the crazy Athens traffic.

Her vision was so severely blurred by tears that she narrowly missed being run over twice as she darted across the road. Horns blared, drivers shouted abuse in Greek, but she just kept running, banking on the fact that he wouldn't be able to follow her quickly.

She reached the other side and lost herself in a maze of side streets and then, finally, she stopped running and leaned against a wall.

She could hear shouts and the crashing of plates and cutlery from a nearby kitchen, a man yelling abuse from an apartment high up above her and the constant noise of traffic. And nearby she heard the sound of someone crying: muffled, heart-wrenching sobs, so pitiful and desolate that a few people paused and glanced with concern.

Only when she saw that they were looking at her did she realise that *she* was the one who was crying. And she sank to the ground and gave way to the emotion that had been building inside her.

CHAPTER TEN

IT WAS the last half-hour of her shift.

Chantal placed the drinks on the table and took out her notepad. 'Are you ready to order?'

'Can we have five minutes?' The group of American tourists were still huddled over the menu, arguing about the translation.

Chantal smiled at them and glanced around the café, checking that no one else was trying to attract her attention. Unable to help herself, her eyes slid to the road—but there was no sports car, no Greek billionaire—no one.

She tried to lift her flagging spirits.

What had she expected?

That he'd come after her?

How ridiculous was that? Why would he come after her when she'd spent so much time carefully explaining why she couldn't stay with him? And anyway he didn't know where she was.

He wouldn't know that she'd chosen to come back to Paris, would he? He'd assume that she'd moved on somewhere new, as she always had in the past. And she probably should have done exactly that.

But she just hadn't been able to bring herself to do it.

Paris was something that she'd shared with him. It was as if by being here she was holding on to a tiny part of him.

She didn't understand why there was some comfort in

knowing that he'd walked these streets and breathed this air, but there was.

Not that it made any difference. Even if he did know where she was, he wouldn't care.

He knew who she was now. No more hiding. No more pretending.

Trying to ignore the dull feeling of misery that had sat in her insides for every moment of the last month, Chantal walked briskly back to the American party and helped them with their menu.

Her shift came to an end, and she made her way back to the old house in which she rented a room. As usual the key refused to turn in the lock, and it took a further five minutes of determined coaxing before she was able to gain access to her property.

As she climbed the five flights of stairs to her tiny room, she wondered what Angelos was doing.

Dining with a room full of diplomats?

Negotiating some mega-deal in New York?

Or lying by the pool discussing the money markets with his father?

Infuriated by the lump in her throat, she pushed open the door of her room and stopped dead.

The subject of her thoughts was sprawled on her sofa—six foot two of powerful Greek male dominating the tiny room.

She blinked several times, wondering whether her vision was playing tricks on her. Was the power of wishful thinking really that strong?

'What are you—? How did you get in?'

'Your landlady let me in.' He glanced around him. 'I don't know what she's charging you, but whatever it is you've been robbed. This place isn't fit for human habitation.'

Stunned that he was there, and not understanding what could possibly have brought him all this way, Chantal pushed the door shut. 'What are you doing here?'

'Claiming what's mine.' His glance was unmistakably possessive and she felt her legs tremble.

'Angelos—'

'Start packing. I gave your landlady notice. You're going to
need something bigger than this.'

She dropped her bag on the floor. 'I can't afford anything
bigger.'

'Yes, you can.'

She closed her eyes. *Hadn't he listened to a word she'd said?*
Or had he just been stubborn? 'I've already told you I don't want
your money—'

'I'm not offering you my money.' His voice a soft drawl, he
rose to his feet. 'Sit down, Chantal.'

Her legs were shaking so badly that she plopped down onto
the nearest chair without argument, staring at the neat file he
dropped into her lap. 'What's this?'

'It's your business plan. Some of the figures may be a little
on the conservative side, but I've factored in reduced working
hours.'

She glanced up at him. 'Reduced working hours? I don't
know what you're talking about.'

He gave her a confident smile that was unashamedly masculine. 'You won't be designing clothes when we're in bed and
since we're going to be spending a significant proportion of our
time there the figures have been adjusted to give you a relatively
short working day. But the profit margins are incredible.'

'I *still* don't know what you're talking about.'

'I want us to be together, and since you won't agree to that
unless you're financially independent then the obvious solution
is to make you financially independent. Read the business plan.'

Dazed and confused, she opened the file on her lap and started
to read. *'Zouvelekis Couture?'*

'You already have at least twenty desperate customers waiting
for you to dress them for various important occasions, so read

fast,' he advised, a satisfied gleam in his eyes as he registered her astonishment. 'As I said, you can't work from this room.'

'You're suggesting I make dresses?'

'Don't misunderstand me,' he drawled. 'I don't care what you choose to do in life as long as it delivers an income which will allow you to transcend that major hang-up of yours.'

She flipped through the file. 'I couldn't possibly charge that much—'

'I knew you would say that, and I have already appointed someone qualified to deal with pricing issues.' He removed the file from her hand and pulled her to her feet. 'You can either take a salary and pay me in rolls of used notes at the end of every month, or alternatively your company can become part of Zouvelekis Industries. Whichever makes you feel more comfortable.'

She stood up. 'Angelos, I can't just—'

'*Don't* give me any more objections,' he warned. 'Because I have already spent hours crunching the numbers on this one and researching your potential market. As far as I'm concerned the problem is solved.'

It was difficult to breathe. 'You've spent hours on it?'

'Yes.'

'You did that for me?'

'No. I did it for *me*,' he murmured dryly. 'So that you can come and live with me.'

'You still want me to live with you?'

'It's hard to sustain a marriage when the two people aren't together.'

Her knees gave way and she plopped back down onto the chair. 'What did you just say?'

'What is the matter with you?' He looked at her with unconcealed impatience. 'You are repeating everything I say, not listening.'

'I'm just—I don't know what to say.'

'Then I'll do that talking. You owe me three euros.'

Her head was spinning. 'What for? Angelos, did you just say—?' But the words stuck in her mouth, because he was drawing something out of his pocket, something glittery and polished and— 'It's a ring.'

He dragged her back to her feet and hauled her against him. 'In between writing your business plan and researching the market for couture clothes, I found a ring. I bought you a rare pink diamond, originally purchased by a rich sheikh for his youngest wife. It was of unsurpassed beauty and great historical significance.'

She stared doubtfully at the cheap plastic ring that he still held in his hand. 'I think they saw you coming.'

He glanced down at the ring, as if he'd forgotten he was holding it. 'This isn't that ring. I suddenly realised that if I presented you with a rare pink diamond of unsurpassed beauty and great historical significance you'd only agree to accept it if I let you pay.'

'Oh.' Her heart performed several tiny jumps. 'You're starting to know me quite well—'

'So I bought you this instead.' He took her hand and slipped the ring on her finger. 'It's plastic and it cost three euros. If you want to reimburse me for it, that's fine. I don't care, as long as you agree to marry me.'

Her stomach dropped and her mouth fell open with disbelief. 'You want to marry me?'

'Why does that surprise you?'

'Well, because—' she licked her lips '—because I'm—'

'Good, kind, beautiful, generous, independent, modest, impossibly sexy—'

'Stop!' She cut him off with a bubble of nervous laughter. 'Angelos, *you can't marry me*!'

He pulled a face. 'Never say *can't* to me,' he advised silkily, running a gentle finger over her cheek. 'It's the one word guaranteed to send me into achievement overdrive.'

'*My mother was a prostitute.*'

'I don't care if your mother was a hippopotamus,' he drawled. 'I'm not proposing to your mother. I'm proposing to you.'

She made a sound that was somewhere between a sob and a laugh. 'You can't do this. You're making the wrong decision—'

'*Wrong* is another word you should never say to me. My ego is far too fragile to accept it.' His eyes teased her but she was too shaken to respond.

'You'll regret it—I'll embarrass you—'

'You could never embarrass me. On the contrary, I'm immensely proud of you.'

'Your father—'

'My father insists on it.' He took her face in his hands, his eyes holding hers. 'You are an essential addition to the family. But there is something I want to know. That night of the ball, why did you tell my father that we were a couple?'

'Because it was what I wanted,' she said shyly. 'I was pretending.'

'Just like you used to pretend in the playground.' He gave a slow, satisfied nod, as if she'd given the answer he'd wanted and expected. 'It was only after you left that I worked that out and realised that you loved me.'

The fact that he knew how she felt left her feeling horribly vulnerable. She tried to pull away from him, but his hands held her firmly.

'You're not running away from me this time. You won't take anything material, and I understand that.' His voice was hoarse. 'That's why I'm not giving you an expensive ring. I won't give you a reason to refuse me.'

'Angelos—'

'Do you have any idea how I felt that night when you told me all those things about your mother and then just ran into the middle of the road? I thought you were going to be killed!'

'I felt so terrible—'

'I know you felt terrible, and I wanted to follow you and tell you that none of it mattered. But by the time I crossed the road you had vanished.'

'You abandoned your car in the middle of all that traffic?'

'Yes—and that required some fast talking with the police when I eventually returned to it. *Where were you?* When I realized you must have had your passport on you, I had a team of people at the airports and the ferry, but no one could find you.'

'Yes, well, I've always kept my passport with me at all times—I've travelled around so much it became an automatic habit,' she explained. 'I worked in Athens for a few weeks until I'd made enough money to come here.'

'Why Paris?'

'Because—' She broke off, and he breathed out slowly and gently rubbed her cheek with his thumb.

'Because this is where we first met? That is why I chose to look here.' He slid his arms around her and dragged her hard against him. 'Promise me that you will never, *ever* run from me again.'

'We can't be together—' Her face was muffled against his chest. 'Our circumstances are just too different.'

'Money is not the issue here. I'm not offering you money. I'm offering you the things that money can't buy—the things you've never had before—like emotional support and my protection.' His hold on her tightened. 'If someone so much as *looks* at you the wrong way, or makes you feel inferior or awkward, I'll knock them flat.'

Unbelievably touched, she gave a stifled laugh. 'I've always thought you had a dodgy temper.'

'I'm offering you my family, Chantal,' he said softly, relaxing his hold so that he could look at her. 'My father's divorces ripped us all apart—I think you know that. If I was harsh with you when we met, it's because I was determined not to let another woman trample over my family. But that was before I fell in love with you.'

It took her a moment to find her voice. 'You *love* me?'

'Yes. And until I met you I'd given up on ever loving a woman the way my father loved my mother.'

'Love?' She still couldn't believe she was hearing him correctly. 'You're offering me love?'

'What did you think? Why do you think I want us to be together?'

She blushed awkwardly. 'I suppose—sex?'

'You think a man would only ever be interested in you for sex? You are clearly unaware of the many qualities you possess,' he said softly, and then smiled. 'The fact that you're an incredibly exciting woman is a bonus.'

She was so overwhelmed she could hardly speak. 'Qualities? *Many* qualities? No one has ever said anything like that to me before.'

'Well, get used to it, because I'll be saying it all the time,' he drawled. 'I want a great deal more than sex from you, *agape mou*. I am a very ambitious man. I want *everything*. And I want to give you everything in return. In time I'm even hoping that you'll let me spoil you in a material way, but if your business takes off the way I know it will, you will be able to spoil yourself under my direction.'

'I can't believe you're saying this. I love you too,' she mumbled, burying her face in his chest. 'I really do. I think I loved you from the first moment I saw you.'

'I know you did.' He shrugged. 'How could you not?'

Half-laughing, half-crying, she tilted her head to look at him. 'Arrogant.'

'Confident.' Supremely sure of himself, he smiled down at her. 'So? Will you make my father a happy man and marry me?'

She gave a choked laugh of disbelief. 'You thought I was a gold-digger.'

'It was a natural assumption for a man in my position. You have to understand that my father's last two wives both fitted that description…' He hesitated. 'And I once had a similar experience myself.'

'You did?'

'I was just eighteen and I thought she cared about me.' He shrugged. 'Fortunately for me I discovered the truth about her before too much damage was done, but it was a lesson that I didn't forget.'

'You were hurt?'

'Honestly?' He gave a wry smile. 'My ego was more bruised than my heart, because I was forced to acknowledge that I wasn't all things to all women. But it did teach me to be wary.'

'I understand that. And I don't blame you for thinking that about me.'

'I did not think it for long. And my father *never* thought it. He loved you from that first moment.'

'At that ball in Paris—someone recognised me from my old boarding school. She came over, and I was so horrified that I couldn't speak. Your father rescued me and sent her packing. I couldn't believe he would do that for a stranger. I fell in love with him on sight. No one had ever done something like that for me before.' She smiled up at him. 'What do you think he will say when you tell him?'

'He will be delighted.' His arms tightened around her. 'It's just as well I saw you first, or I think he might have made you his fourth wife.'

'I love him.' Her smiled faded as she gazed into his breath-takingly handsome face. 'I kidded myself that I was only staying for your father's sake, but it wasn't true. I was staying because I couldn't bear to leave you.'

'And you're not going to leave me ever again.' He lowered his head and kissed her gently. 'I love you.'

'I can't believe you don't care who I am—'

'I *love* who you are. You are gentle and good and soon you will also be confident.'

She pulled a face. 'I can't imagine ever being confident.'

'With me loving you, how could you not be? We will work on it together.'

'*Zouvelekis Couture…*' She tilted her head to one side. 'You want my business to have your name?'

'Soon it will be *your* name too, and everyone will know that you are my wife.'

'Are you sure you want people to know?' She caught his look of exasperation and blushed. 'Sorry, sorry. It's just that I can't become confident overnight. You'll have to teach me how—just as you've taught me everything you know about sex.'

'Ah…' He gave a wicked smile and lowered his head to hers, his lips teasing the corner of her mouth. 'I haven't taught you *everything* I know about sex. There are definitely a few more things you need to learn.'

'Is that right?' Chantal wound her arms around his neck and smiled up at him. 'In that case, what are we waiting for?'

HIS FOR A PRICE

CAITLIN CREWS

*To Megan Haslam, my wonderful editor, for
twenty great books together!
Here's to twenty more!*

USA TODAY bestselling and RITA® Award–
nominated author **Caitlin Crews** loves writing
romance. She teaches her favourite romance novels
in creative writing classes at places like UCLA
Extension's prestigious Writers' Programme,
where she finally gets to utilise the MA and
PhD in English Literature she received from the
University of York in England. She currently lives
in California, with her very own hero and too
many pets. Visit her at caitlincrews.com.

CHAPTER ONE

IF SHE STOOD very still—if she held her breath and kept herself from so much as blinking—Mattie Whitaker was sure she could make the words that her older brother Chase had just said to her disappear. Rewind them then erase them entirely.

Outside the rambling old mansion high above the Hudson River some two hours north of Manhattan, the cold rain came down in sheets. Stark, weather-stripped trees slapped back against the October wind all the way down the battered brown lawn toward the sullen river, and the estate had shrunk to blurred gray clouds, solemn green pines and the solid shape of the old brick house called Greenleigh, despite the lack of much remaining green. Behind her, at the desk that she would always think of as her father's no matter how many months he'd been gone now, Chase was silent.

There would be no rewinding. No erasing. No escaping what she knew was coming. But then, if she was honest, she'd always known this day would arrive. Sooner or later.

"I didn't hear you correctly," Mattie said. Eventually.

"We both know you did."

It should have made her feel better that he sounded as torn as she felt, which was better than that polite distance with which he usually treated her. It didn't.

"Say it again, then." She pressed her fingers against the frigid windowpane before her and let the cold soak into her skin. No use crying over the inevitable, her father would have said in that bleakly matter-of-fact way he'd said everything after they'd lost their mother.

Save your tears for things you can change, Mattie.

Chase sighed, and Mattie knew that if she turned to look at him, he'd be a pale shell of the grinning, always-in-on-the-joke British tabloid staple he'd been throughout his widely celebrated bachelorhood in London, where he'd lived as some kind of tribute to their long-dead British mother. It had been a long, hard four months since their father had dropped dead unexpectedly. Harder on Chase, she expected, who had all their father's corporate genius to live up to, but she didn't feel like being generous just now. About anything.

Mattie still didn't turn around. That might make this real.

Not that hiding from things has ever worked, either, whispered a wry voice inside her that remembered all the things she wanted to forget—the smell of the leather seats in that doomed car, the screech of the tires, her own voice singing them straight into hell—

Mattie shut that down. Fast and hard. But her hands were shaking.

"You promised me we'd do this together," Chase said quietly instead of repeating himself. Which was true. She'd said exactly that at their father's funeral, sick with loss and grief, and not really considering the implications. "It's you and me now, Mats."

He hadn't called her that in a very long time, since they'd been trapped in that car together, in fact, and she hated that he was doing it now, for this ugly purpose. She steeled herself against it. Against him.

"You and me and the brand-new husband you're selling me off to like some kind of fatted cow, you mean," Mattie corrected him, her voice cool, which was much better than bitter. Or panicked. Or terrified. "I didn't realize we were living in the Dark Ages."

"Dad was nothing if not clear that smart, carefully chosen marriages lead to better business practices." Chase's voice was sardonic then, or maybe that was bitterness, and Mattie turned, at last, to find him watching her with that hollow look in his dark blue eyes and his arms crossed over his chest. "I'm in the same boat. Amos Elliott has been gunning for me since the day of the funeral but he's made it known that if I take one of his daughters off his hands, I'll find my dealings with the Board of Directors that much more pleasant. Welcome to the Dark Ages, Mattie."

She laughed, but it was an empty sound. "Should that make me feel better? Because it doesn't. It's nothing but a little more misery to spread around."

"We need money and support—serious money and very concrete support—or we lose the company," Chase said, his voice flat and low. So unlike him, really, if Mattie wanted to consider that. She didn't. "There's no prettying that up. The shareholders are mutinous. Amos Elliott and the Board of Directors are plotting my downfall as we speak. This is our legacy and we're on the brink of losing it."

And what's left of them—of us. He didn't say that last part, but he might as well have. It echoed inside of Mattie as if he'd shouted it through a bullhorn, and she heard the rest of it, too. The part where he reminded her who was to blame for losing their mother—but then, he didn't have to remind her. He'd never had to remind her and he never had. There was no point. There was scarcely a moment in her entire life when she didn't remind herself.

Still. "This is a major sacrifice, to put it mildly," she pointed out, because the thoughtless, careless, giddily reckless creature she played in the tabloids would. "I could view this as an opportunity to walk away, instead. Start my life over without having to worry about parental disapproval or the stuffy, disapproving Whitaker Industries shareholders." She studied her brother's hard, closed-off expression as if she was a stranger to him, and she blamed herself for that, too. "You could do the same."

"Yes," Chase agreed, his voice cool. "But then we'd be the useless creatures Dad already thought we were. I can't live with that. I don't think you can, either. And I imagine you knew we had no other options but this before you came here today."

"You mean before I answered your summons?" Mattie clenched her shaking hands into fists. It was better than tears. Anything was better than tears. Particularly because Chase was right. She couldn't live with what she'd done twenty years ago; she certainly wouldn't be able to live with the fallout if she walked away from the ruins of her family now. This was all her fault, in the end. The least she could do was her part to help fix it. "You've been back from London for how long?"

Her brother looked wary then. "A week."

"But you only called when you needed me to sell myself. I'm touched, really."

"Fine," Chase said roughly, shoving a hand through his dark hair. "Make me the enemy. It doesn't change anything."

"Yes," she agreed then, feeling ashamed of herself for kicking at him, yet unable to stop. "I knew it before I came here. But that doesn't mean I'm happy to go gentle into the deep, dark night that is Nicodemus Stathis."

Chase's mouth moved in what might have been a smile,

had these been happier times. Had either one of them had any choice in this. Had he done much smiling in her direction in the past twenty years. "Make sure you tell him that yourself. I'm sure he'll find that entertaining."

"Nicodemus has always found me wildly entertaining," Mattie said, and it felt better to square her shoulders, to lengthen her spine, as she told that whopper of a lie. It felt better to make her voice brisk and to smooth her palms down the front of the deliberately very black dress she'd worn, to send the message she wished she could, too. "I'm sure if you asked him he'd list that in the top five reasons he's always insisted he wanted to marry me. That and his fantasy of merging our two corporate kingdoms like some feudal wet dream in which he gets to play lord of the castle with the biggest, longest, thickest—"

She remembered, belatedly, that she was talking to her older brother, who might not be as close to her as she'd like but was nonetheless *her older brother,* and smiled faintly.

"Share," she amended. "Of the company. The biggest *share*."

"Of course that's precisely what you meant," Chase replied drily, but Mattie heard something like an apology in his voice, a kind of sorrow, right underneath what nearly passed for laughter.

Because his hands were tied. Big Bart Whitaker had been an institution unto himself. No one had expected him to simply drop dead four months ago—least of all Bart. There had been no time to prepare. No time to ease Chase from his flashy London VP position into his new role as President and CEO of Whitaker Industries, as had always been Bart's ultimate intention. No time to allay the fears of the board and the major shareholders, who only knew Chase from what they read about him in all those smirking British tabloids. No time to grieve when there were too many challenges, too many risks, too many enemies.

Their father had loved the company his own grandfather had built from little more than innate Whitaker stubbornness and a desire to best the likes of Andrew Carnegie. And Mattie thought both she and Chase had always loved their father in their own complicated ways, especially after they'd lost their mother and Big Bart was all they'd had left.

Which meant they would each do what they had to do. There was no escaping this, and if she was honest, Mattie had known that long before her father died. It was as inevitable as the preview of the upstate New York winter coming down hard outside, and there was no use pretending otherwise.

Mattie would make the best of it. She would ignore that deep, dark, aching place inside her that simply *hurt*. That was scared, so very scared, of how Nicodemus Stathis made her feel. And how easy it would be to lose herself in him, until there was nothing left of her at all.

But you owe this to them, she reminded herself sternly. *All of them.*

"He's here already, isn't he?" she asked after a moment, when there was no putting it off any longer. She could stand here all day and it wouldn't change anything. It would only make the dread in her belly feel more like a brick.

Chase's gaze met hers, which she supposed was a point in his favor, though she wasn't feeling particularly charitable at the moment. "He said he'd wait for you in the library."

She didn't look at her brother again. She looked at the polished cherry desk, instead, and missed their father with a rush that nearly left her lightheaded. She would have done anything, in that moment, to see his craggy face again. To hear that rumbling voice of his, even if he'd only ordered her to do this exact thing, as he'd threatened to do many times over the past ten years.

Now everything was precarious and dangerous, Bart was gone, and they were the only Whitakers left. Chase and Mattie against the world. Even if Chase and Mattie's togetherness had been defined as more of a polite distance in the long years since their aristocratic mother's death— separate boarding schools in the English countryside, universities in different countries and adult lives on opposite sides of the Atlantic Ocean. But Mattie knew that all of that, too, was her fault.

She was the guilty party. She would accept her sentence, though perhaps not as gracefully as she should.

"Well," she said brightly as she turned toward the door. "I hope we'll see you at the wedding, Chase. I'll be the one dragged up the aisle in chains, possibly literally. It will be like sacrificing the local virgin to appease the ravenous dragon. I'll try not to scream too loudly while being burned alive, etcetera."

Chase sighed. "If I could change any of this, I would. You know that's true."

But he could have been talking about so many things, and Mattie knew that the truth was that she'd save her tears because they were useless. And maybe she'd save the family business, too, while she was at it. It was, truly, the least she could do.

Nicodemus Stathis might have been the bane of her existence for as long as she could remember, but she could handle him. She'd *been* handling him for years.

She could do this.

So she held her head up high—almost as if she believed that—and she marched off to assuage her guilt and do her duty, at last, however much it felt like she was walking straight toward her own doom.

* * *

The worst thing about Nicodemus Stathis was that he was gorgeous, Mattie thought moments later in that mix of unwanted desire and sheer, unreasonable panic that he always brought out in her. So gorgeous it was tempting to overlook all the rest of the things he was, like profoundly dangerous to her. So gorgeous it had a way of confusing the issue, tangling her up into knots and making her despair of herself.

So absurdly gorgeous, in fact, that it was nothing but unfair.

He stood by the French doors on the far side of the library, his strong back to the warmth and the light of the book-laden room, his attention somewhere out in all that gray and rattling wet. He stood quietly, but that did nothing to disguise the fact that he was the most ruthless, wholly relentless man she'd ever known. It was obvious at a glance. The thick, jet-black hair, the graceful way he held his obviously dangerous form so still, the harsh beguilement of the mouth she could only see in the reflection of the glass. The menace in him that his smooth, sleek clothes couldn't begin to conceal. He didn't turn to look at her as she made her way toward him, but she knew perfectly well he knew she was there.

He'd have known the moment she descended the stairs in the great hall outside the library. He always knew. She'd often thought he was half cat. She didn't like to speculate about the other half, but she was fairly certain it, too, had fangs.

"I hope you're not gloating, Nicodemus," she said briskly, because she thought simply waiting for him to turn around and fix those unholy dark eyes of his on her might make her dizzy—and she felt vulnerable enough as it was. She thought she could smell the smug male satisfaction heavy in the air, choking the oxygen from the room as surely as if one of the fireplaces had backed up. It put her teeth on edge. "It's so unattractive."

"At this point the hole you have dug for yourself rivals a swimming pool or two," Nicodemus replied, in that voice of his that reverberated in her the way it always had, low and dangerous with that hint of his Greek childhood still clinging to his words and wrapping tight around the center of her. "But by all means, Mattie. Keep digging."

"Here I am," she said brightly. "Sacrificial lamb to the slaughter, as ordered. What a happy day this must be for you."

Nicodemus turned then. Slowly, so slowly, like that might take the edge off the swift, hard *punch* of seeing him full on. It didn't, of course. Nothing ever did. Mattie ordered herself to breathe—and not to keel over. He was as absurdly gorgeous as ever, damn him. No disfiguring accidents had turned him into a troll since she'd seen him at her father's funeral.

He was as smoothly muscled as he'd been when he was in his twenties and honed to steel-like perfection by the construction work he'd somehow catapulted into a multi-million-dollar corporation by the time he was twenty-six. The fine, hard lines of his face were nearly elegant while his corded strength was as apparent in the line of his pugilistic jaw as in that impossibly chiseled chest of his that he'd concealed very poorly today behind a tight, black, obviously wildly expensive T-shirt that made no concession whatsoever to the weather. He was too elemental. He'd always made the hair at the back of her neck stand on end, her nipples pull painfully taut and her stomach draw tight, and today was no different.

Today was worse. And on top of that, Nicodemus was smiling.

I am lost already, she thought.

Nicodemus was a sheer, high, dizzying cliff and she'd spent ten years fighting hard to keep from toppling off. Because she still had no idea what might become of her if she fell.

"You really are gloating," she said, folding her arms over her chest and frowning at him. It was more of a smirk than a smile, she thought as she eyed him warily, and that too-bright gleam of a warmth like honey in his dark coffee gaze. "I don't know why that surprises me, coming from you."

"I'm not sure that *gloating* is the word I'd choose."

He was lethal, pure and simple, and his dark gaze was too intent. It took everything she had to keep from turning and bolting for the door. *This day was always coming,* she told herself harshly. *Accept it, because you can't escape it.*

Though she'd tried. God, but she'd tried.

"The first time I asked you to marry me you were how old?" he asked, his voice almost warm, as if he was sharing a fond reminiscence instead of their long, tortured history. "Twenty?"

"I was eighteen," Mattie said crisply. She didn't move as he roamed toward her. But she wanted to. She wanted to bolt for her childhood bedroom on the second floor and lock herself inside. She made herself lock her gaze to his, instead. "It was my debutante ball and you were ruining it."

Nicodemus's mocking little smile deepened, and Mattie fought not to flush with the helpless reaction he'd always caused in her. But she could still remember that single waltz her father had insisted she dance with him that night. Pressed up against his big body, much too close to his fierce, demanding gaze, and that mouth of his that had made her nothing but…nervous. And needy.

It still did. Damn him.

"Marry me," he'd said instead of a greeting, almost as if he'd meant to let out some kind of curse, instead.

"I'm sorry," she'd said, holding Nicodemus's dark, dark eyes as if they hadn't bitten deep into her, making her chest feel tight. She'd been a brash girl when she'd wanted to be, back then, forever attempting to get her father's attention, but her voice had been small. He had terrified her. Or maybe that wasn't terror, that overwhelming thing that had swamped her, fierce and instantaneous, but she hadn't known what else to call it. "I don't want to marry you. Or anyone."

He'd laughed as if she'd delighted him. "You will."

"I will never want to marry you," she'd told him stoutly, some kick of temper—or self-preservation—in her gut making her bold. She'd been eighteen. And it hadn't been lost on her that Nicodemus was not one of the silly boys she'd known then. He'd been very much a man.

He'd smiled at her as if he knew her and it had connected hard to her throat, her chest, her belly. Below. It had made her toes cramp up inside her ferociously high shoes.

"You'll marry me, princess." He'd seemed certain. Amused, even. "You can count on it."

He seemed even more amused now.

Nicodemus closed the distance between them almost lazily, but Mattie knew better. There was nothing lazy about him, ever. It was all misdirection and only the very foolish believed it.

"Have we ever determined what was wrong with you that you wanted to marry a teenager in the first place?" she asked him now, trying to divert whatever was coming. But he only stopped a scant few inches in front of her. "Couldn't find a woman your own age?"

Nicodemus didn't reply. He reached over and raked his fingers through the long, dark hair she decided instantly she needed to cut off, then wrapped it all around his hand, like he was putting her on a leash.

Then he gave it a tug. Not a gentle one. And she felt it deep between her legs, like a flare of dark pleasure.

Mattie wanted to smack his hand away, but that glinting thing in his dark gaze dared her to try, and she didn't want to give him the satisfaction when she was already tilting her head back at an angle that made a dangerous heat kindle to bright life inside her. Then build.

"That hurts," she told him, horrified that there was a hint of thickness in her throat when she spoke. That gave him ammunition. It couldn't be allowed.

"No, it doesn't." He sounded as certain as he had when she'd been eighteen, and it was infuriating. No matter if it made everything inside her tilt again and then tighten.

"I realize I've been bartered off like chattel," she bit out. "But it's still my hair. I know how it feels when someone pulls it."

His smile deepened. "You lie about everything, Mattie," he murmured, the slap of the words at jarring odds with the way he crooned them, leaning in close. "You break your word the way other women break their nails."

"I break those, too." It was like she couldn't stop herself. "If this has all been a bid for the perfect, polished trophy wife, Nicodemus, you're going to find me a grave disappointment."

He laughed softly, which wasn't remotely soothing, and tugged again, and it wasn't the first time Mattie regretted the fact that she was both tall and entirely too vain. Five feet ten inches in her bare feet, and the gorgeous black boots she was wearing today put her at a good six feet and then some. Which meant that when Nicodemus loomed over her and got too close to her, that mouth of his was *right there*. Not miles above her, which was safer.

Within easy reach—and she imagined he was deliberately standing this close to her because he wanted to remind her of that.

Like she—or her shuddering, jolting pulse she could feel in a variety of worrying places—would be likely to forget.

"I told you a long time ago that this day would come," Nicodemus said now.

"And I told you that I wasn't going to change my mind," she replied, though it cost her a little more than it should have to keep her chin up and her gaze steady on his. "I haven't. You can't really believe that this grotesque, medieval form of blackmail is the same as me surrendering to you, can you?"

"What do I care how you come to me?" he replied in that low, amused voice of his that kicked up brushfires inside her as it worked its way through her and made her feel a delicious sort of weak. "You mistake me for a good man, Mattie. I'm merely a determined one."

And despite herself, Mattie remembered a long, formal dinner in Manhattan's Museum of Natural History for some charity or another and her father's insistence that she sit with Nicodemus, who, he'd informed her when she'd balked, was like another son to him. *A far-better-behaved one,* he'd added. Mattie had been all of twenty-two—and infuriated.

"I'm not trying to change your mind, princess," Nicodemus had told her in a voice pitched for her ears alone, at odds with the way he'd spoken to others that night—mighty and sure, bold and harsh. He'd shifted in his seat and pinned her to hers with that knowing dark glare of his she'd come to know far too well. "We both know how this will end. Your father will indulge you to a certain point, but then reality will assert itself. And the longer you

make me wait, the more I'll have to take it out of your rebellious little hide when you're where you belong. In my
bed. Under my…" He'd paused, his dark eyes had glittered,
and she'd felt it as if he'd licked the soft skin of her belly.
Like a kind of glorious, transformative pain. His lips had
crooked. "Roof."

"What an inviting fantasy," Mattie had retorted, aware
he hadn't meant to say *roof* at all. "I can't imagine what's
keeping me from leaping at the opportunity to experience
that great joy."

"Suit yourself," he'd replied. He'd shrugged, but she'd
been far too aware that every inch of him was hewn of
steel, that he was himself a deadly weapon. She'd felt the
power he wore so easily like a thick, hot hand at her throat.
Worse, she'd been aware of that part of her that craved it.
Him. *More.* "I have a very long memory, Mattie, and a
very creative approach to retribution. Consider yourself
forewarned."

"Be still my beating heart," she'd snipped at him, and
then had tried her best to ignore him.

It hadn't worked then. It didn't work now.

"Will we reminisce all day?" she asked, injecting a note
of boredom into her voice that she dearly wished she felt
while he continued to hold her immobile. "Or do you have
a plan? I'm unfamiliar with the ins and outs of blackmail,
you see. You'll have to show me how it's done."

"You're free to refuse me yet again."

"And lose my father's company in the process."

"All choices have consequences, princess." He
shrugged, much the same way he had at that benefit dinner. "Your father would have been the first to tell you that."

That he was right only infuriated her more.

"My father was misguided enough to consider you like
a son to him," Mattie said, and there was no keeping the

emotion at bay then. It clogged her throat, made her eyes heat. But she didn't care if he saw this, she told herself. *This* wasn't the emotion that would destroy her. "He adored you. He thought more highly of you than he did of Chase, at times." She paused, as much to catch her breath and keep from crying as for effect. "And look how you've chosen to repay him."

She'd expected that to be a blow to him, but Nicodemus only laughed again then dropped his hand from her hair, and it took everything Mattie had not to rub the spot where he'd touched her. The worst part was, she didn't know if she wanted to wipe away his touch or hold it in. She never had. He canted his head to one side as he studied her face and then laughed some more.

"Your father thought I should have dragged you off by your hair years ago," he said with such lazy certainty that Mattie flushed with the unpleasant understanding that he was telling the truth. That Nicodemus and her father had discussed her like that. "Especially during what he liked to call your 'unfortunate' period."

She flushed even darker, and hated that it hurt. And she suddenly had no trouble at all imagining her father discussing her regrettable, motherless and rudderless early twenties with Nicodemus, no matter how much it scraped at her and felt like a betrayal.

"I did the best I could," she bit out, and she broke then, because that was scraping a bit too close to truths she didn't dare voice, and that terrible guilt that lay beneath everything. She stepped back and would have put even more distance between them, but Nicodemus's hand shot out and wrapped around her upper arm, stopping her that easily.

She refused to think about the impossible strength in that hand, much less its dark heat, no matter that it blasted into her through the soft, black cashmere knit of her dress.

She wouldn't think about it and she wouldn't react to it. *She wouldn't.*

"You know very well that you did not do anything remotely like your best," he said evenly, with only the faintest hint of old tempers and half-remembered harsh words in his voice. "You made it your business to shame your father. I would say you shamed your family name, but we both know your brother had that well in hand. How a great man like your father managed to raise two such useless, ungrateful, overly entitled children remains one of life's greatest mysteries."

Chase was right. Her father might have agreed with Nicodemus while he'd lived, but Mattie couldn't let herself live down to those low expectations any longer. She could smell the leather again, feel the heat of the South African sun. Then the screech—

"Almost everyone is useless, ungrateful and overly entitled in their early twenties," she told him, forcing herself to face him, to hold that judgmental gaze of his, and not try to jerk out of his hold. She suspected he wouldn't let go, and then what? "The trick is not *remaining* any of those things."

"Some of us had far more serious things to do in our early twenties, Mattie. Like survive."

So pompous. So full of himself. But better that than he know anything real or true about her. That was the only way she was going to make it through this.

"Yes, Nicodemus," she said with an exaggerated sweetness he couldn't mistake for anything but sarcasm. "You're a self-made man, as you're the first to point out at every opportunity. Alas, we can't all be you."

His fingers flexed against her arm and she hated the arrow of fire that shot from that faintest contact straight into her sex. She hated that her body had never cared how dangerous this man was, no matter how panicked her brain might be.

He'd proposed again when she'd been twenty-four.

Mattie had been dancing for hours in a dress that was really more of a wicked suggestion with a few cleverly placed straps, a cheeky selection for a night out in London. Then she'd walked outside the club to find *him* waiting there at the private, paparazzi-free back entrance, leaning up against a muscular little sports car parked illegally in the alley with his arms folded over his powerful chest.

For a moment, Nicodemus had only stared at her, his mouth a sardonic curve and his dark, honeyed gaze alight with a fire that did not bode well for her.

But Mattie hadn't been a teenager anymore, so she'd dug out a cigarette and lit it as if his presence didn't bother her at all. Then she'd blown out a stream of smoke into the cool night air, like it was a defensive weapon she could use against him.

"Why bother with those pointless scraps of fabric at all?" he'd asked her, his voice a scrape against the night and a scrape straight down the middle of her, as if his words had their own claws. "Why not simply walk around naked?"

"It's cute that you think it's your business what I wear," she'd said with deliberate nonchalance. As if he'd bored her. She'd wished, not for the first time, that he had.

Nicodemus's gaze had slammed into her then, making her feel hollow. Dizzy. As drunk and as dangerously out of control as she'd been trying to remain during these blurry, pointless, post-collegiate years. It had reminded her who and what he was. Harshly.

"Oh," he'd said dangerously. "It's my business, Mattie. It's all my business. All the men you let touch you. All the nights you flaunt that body of yours for the world to see.

The courtesan's ring in your belly you show off every time you let them photograph you in various states of undress. That tattoo I warned you not to put on your body. Those filthy cigarettes you use to pollute yourself. Believe me, it's my business."

He'd straightened from his obnoxiously hot car while he spoke, and then he'd stood over her, one of the few men she knew who was taller than she was despite her dramatic heels, and she'd told herself she hated the way he made her feel—that shivery, panicky, out of control fire that had burned through her when his dark eyes had fixed on her.

He could take everything, she'd thought then. He could take all of her and she'd be lost, and then what happened when he discovered the truth? What happened when this fire was gone and there was nothing between them but the awful truth of what she'd made happen?

"If you were as smart as you pretend to be, you might realize that I don't care what you want or what you think," she'd told him while her heart had slowed then beat harder. Much harder. "Because I don't. You should find someone who does. I'm sure there's a website for compliant little girls looking for big, bad billionaires to obey. You could be playing lord and master of your own private castle in a week, tops."

His lips had quirked, which on any other man might have meant laughter, but it was Nicodemus, with those stern, dark eyes that had drilled into her with all of his disturbingly fierce patience. It had disrupted her breathing.

"Marry me, Mattie. Don't make this even worse on yourself than it already is."

"Why?" she'd asked, almost helplessly.

"Because I want you," he'd said, sounding very nearly grim, as if it was an imposition, that wanting. A trial for him. "And I always get what I want."

"I'd rather swallow my own tongue," she'd replied, a wave of a kind of despair swelling in her, because she knew better than to consider the things *she* wanted. What was the point, when she couldn't have any of them? "I'd rather impale myself on a—"

"You're a very foolish girl." He'd shaken his head, muttering something dark in Greek. "But you're mine."

Then he'd jerked her toward him with one hand on her shoulder, knocked the cigarette from her fingers with the other and slammed his mouth to hers.

And all of that dark wonder had simply *burst* within her. Hunger and heat. That damned harsh mouth of his like a kind of miracle against hers. Claiming her. Branding her.

Shaking her to her core.

But she'd kissed him back, despite everything. She'd tasted him until she'd thought she really was as drunk as she sometimes acted. She'd fallen apart in his arms as if she'd been waiting her whole life for him to taste her. As if she'd always known it would be like that.

On some level, she had.

Fire. Panic. An instant and impossible addiction that had already gnawed at her, even while he'd still been taking his lazy, devastating fill of her mouth, as lethal and sure in the way he'd kissed her as in everything else.

"I told you," he'd growled into her mouth when she'd been limp and useless against him. "You're mine. You always have been. You always will be. How long do you plan to draw this out?"

Mattie had stared at him, unable to speak with all of those dark and wondrous things moving in her, and he'd smiled then, as close to tender as she'd ever seen him. It had transformed his dark face. It had made him something far more dangerous than simply gorgeous.

So she'd run in the opposite direction.

"Play your games, princess," he'd said, harsh and amused as she'd fled from him. *Certain,* the way he always was. "When you come to me, I will make you crawl."

She'd believed him.

"No," he said, yanking her back into the dangerous here and now. His hand was on her arm, and that heat was stampeding through her and this time, there was no hope of escape. "We can't all be me. But you can certainly learn how to please me, Mattie. And if I were you, I'd learn it fast."

It was another threat. Or more of a promise, she supposed. Because despite everything, despite how long and how far she'd run from this man, he'd won. The way he'd always told her he would.

"I've never really been a quick learner," she told him with a kind of manic cheerfulness, because she couldn't let herself think about what *pleasing him* might entail. God help her, but she didn't dare. "Oops. One more disappointment for you to swallow, I'm afraid."

CHAPTER TWO

HE'D WON.

That was what mattered, Nicodemus told himself as he looked down into the lovely, rebellious face of this woman who had defied him and haunted him across the years, and somehow willed himself not to put her over his knee. Or under him right here on the library floor.

He took a breath, the way he would if this was as simple as the business deal he was pretending it was. Then another, and still she watched him like he was an animal, and she was half-afraid she might pick up a few fleas if she stood too close.

Nicodemus couldn't understand why he didn't feel jubilant. Wildly triumphant. Instead of this same dark fury that always beat in him when she looked at him like this, so recklessly defiant when the fact he would win could never have been in any doubt.

He made himself let go of her, though it was hard. Too hard, when everything inside him beat like a tight, taut drum and he wanted nothing more than to bury himself in her, at last. To ride out his victory until she screamed his name the way he'd always known she would, to taste her and learn her and take her, over and over, until this vicious hunger was sated.

Because he was certain it would be sated once he had her. It had to be.

But that would come later.

"Sit," he ordered her, jerking his chin in the direction of two deep, dark brown leather armchairs before the nearest fireplace. "I'll tell you how this will work."

"That doesn't sound like a very promising start to the marriage you've been threatening me with for years," she said in her usual flippant, disrespectful way that he really shouldn't find as amusing as he did. Like it was foreplay. "In fact, if you ask me, it sounds like the kind of marriage that will lead to a very big, very public divorce in approximately eighteen months, or as soon as I can escape and file."

"You won't escape," he said, nodding toward the chairs again, and less politely. "Though you're welcome to try. I'd be happy to chase you down and haul you back."

He was rewarded with that dark blue glare of hers that had been making him ache with a driving need for almost as long as he'd known her. He smiled and was rewarded with the faintest hint of a shiver that she tried to hide.

She settled herself in the far chair with that wholly unearned grace of hers that he'd found nothing short of marvelous since the day they'd met. Mattie Whitaker had never suffered through any awkward phase as far as Nicodemus could tell. She'd been a gleaming bright beacon at sixteen, with her half-American, half-posh-British accent she'd wielded like a sword, even then. At eighteen, she'd been magnificent, pure and simple. From her glossy blue-black hair to her rich, dark blue eyes, to that wide mouth that should have been outlawed. She'd had poise and elegance far beyond her years, a consequence, he'd decided long ago, of having had to play hostess for her father after her mother had died when she was only eight.

He'd walked into that silly ball, that leftover nod to some gilded-age American fantasy he couldn't begin to understand, and had been struck dumb. Like she'd been a lightning bolt instead of what she was, what he knew she was: one more pretty little rich girl in a sparkling dress.

But God help him, it was *how* she'd sparkled.

She'd been so careless—thoughtless and spoiled as only wealthy heiresses could be. He'd suffered through that once already back in Greece, with self-centered, deceitful Arista, who'd nearly taken him to his knees and to the cleaners when he'd been twenty-two and a trusting, stupid fool. He'd vowed he'd never trust so easily nor be so deeply foolish again.

But there was something about Mattie that had drawn him in despite that. He'd watched her careen through all her blessings as if she hardly noticed them. He'd studied the way she'd shrugged off her expensive schools and the featherweight jobs she'd taken afterward, in publishing companies or art galleries or the like that paid so little only heiresses could afford to work at them. Or only occasionally work at them, in her case.

Nicodemus watched her now as she leveled that frank gaze of hers at him, her dark eyes serious, though they were the precise color of after-dinner chocolates with that intriguing shimmer of darker blue. She could be flighty and reckless and sometimes attention-seeking, but she was also intelligent. He'd long suspected she liked to pretend otherwise, for her own murky reasons. Another mystery he looked forward to solving.

"I think it's time you told me what this is really about," she said, and she reminded him of her father then, with that matter-of-fact tone and her direct gaze. Nicodemus pulled in a breath. "I mean it," she said as if that had been an argument. "I don't believe for one second that there aren't

parades of more suitable heiresses if an heiress is what you
want. Prettier ones, if that's your thing. Richer ones, certainly. Far more notorious ones and one or two who might
as well have spent their lives in a convent. You've always
struck me as being particularly annoying—" and there
was the faintest hint of that dent beside her mouth that he
knew was a dimple, that he'd spent many a lazy hour longing to taste "—but there's no denying the fact that you'd
be a nice catch. You're disgustingly wealthy. You're very
powerful. You're not exactly Quasimodo."

"What a resounding recommendation," he said, torn
between laughter and incredulity that she dared speak to
him the way she did. She always had. Only Mattie, in all
the world. Maybe that was why she haunted him. "Who
wouldn't marry me?"

She eyed him for a moment that bordered on the uncomfortable. "Why me?"

And what could he tell her? That he'd been hit by something he still didn't understand? He didn't believe that
himself. Nicodemus got what he wanted, no matter what
it took. It was how he'd clawed his way to where he was
today. It was how he'd first claimed Arista, then rid himself of her and her sharp claws. It was how he'd survived
learning the truth about his stern, rigidly moralistic father
and what his exposing that truth had done to his mother.
It was what he did. Why should this woman be any different? He told himself that was all there was to it.

He'd been telling himself that for years.

He forced a smile. "I like you. That's why."

"If you do," she said drily, "then I suspect you might
be mentally ill."

"Perhaps I am." He shrugged. "Does that make me less
of a catch? A little more Quasimodo than you thought?"

He'd meant to simply outline what would happen from

here now that she'd finally come to him. Lay down the law with the supreme pleasure of knowing that this time, she'd do as she was told. Because this time, she had to do it.

And he hadn't lied to her. He never lied. He didn't care how she came to him. Angry or on her knees, whatever worked. Nicodemus didn't waste much time worrying about the cost of Pyrrhic victories. It was the victory itself that mattered.

It was the only thing that mattered.

"It makes you much more likely to find yourself committed to a mental institution by your devoted wife one day," Mattie was saying. She smiled that fake smile of hers. "Depending on the fine print of our prenuptial agreement, of course."

She was eyeing him with a certain mild arrogance, as if she was the one with all the power here. When he could tell—from the way she sat with her legs crossed tight and her arms over her middle, from the telltale fluttering of her pulse at her neck and that faint flush high on her cheeks—that she knew she was on precarious ground.

But then, so many things about this woman were an act. Smoke and mirrors. And he vowed he would find the truth beneath it all no matter how long it took him. He would take her apart and put her back together the way he wanted her.

He'd been waiting for this—for her—for years.

"We marry in two weeks," he said, watching her face as he said it. Something flashed through her dark eyes, but then he saw nothing but that polite mask of hers that he'd always known better than to believe. "It will be a very small ceremony in Greece. You, me, a priest and a photographer. We will honeymoon for two weeks at my villa there. Then we will return to Manhattan, where your brother and I will finally merge our companies, as was the wish of both your father and me." He smiled and let her see the edge in it. "See? Simple. Hardly worth all this commotion for so many years."

"And what is my part of this?" she asked as if she couldn't care less either way.

"During the wedding I expect you to obediently recite your vows," he said silkily. "Perhaps even with a touch of enthusiasm. During the honeymoon? I have a few ideas. And ten years of a very vivid imagination to bring to life, at last."

There was no denying the flush that moved over her face then, or that look of something like panic that she blinked away in an instant. Not touching her then very nearly hurt—though wanting Mattie was second nature to him now. What was waiting a little bit longer after a decade?

Besides, he suspected that his feigned laziness drove her crazy, and he wanted any weapon he could find with this woman he still couldn't read. Not the way he wanted to read her.

"I meant when we return in all our marital splendor to New York City," she said, and it occurred to him to wonder if it was difficult for her to render her voice so loftily indifferent. If it was a skill she'd acquired once and could put on whenever she liked or if she had to work at it every time. "I have my own apartment there. A life, a job. Of course, I'm happy to live separately—"

"I'm not."

She blinked. Then smiled. "I doubt very much you'd enjoy moving into my tiny little two-bedroom. It's very girlie and I don't think you'd look good in all that pink."

She reached into one of the pockets he hadn't realized she had in that dress of hers to pull out a cigarette and a lighter, then lit the cigarette, watching him blandly as she blew out a stream of smoke.

"Enjoy that cigarette, Mattie," he told her mildly. "It will be your last."

She let out another stream of smoke. "Will it?"

"I have very specific ideas about how my wife will behave," he said, and smiled when that coolly unbothered front of hers slipped slightly. "That she will live in my house and that she will not work, if that's what you call it, at that laughable excuse for a public relations firm in all those see-through clothes."

"I see. This will be a medieval marriage, to go along with the Stone Age courtship rituals we've been enjoying thus far. What a thrill."

He ignored her. "I have certain expectations regarding her behavior. Her style of dress, her comportment. The lack of cigarettes sticking from her mouth, making her smell and taste like an ashtray." He shrugged. "The usual."

She held the cigarette in one hand, not looking the least bit worried, though that faint tremor in the hand that held that cigarette told a different story, and stared at him. "I understand that this is all a big chess game to you, Nicodemus, with me playing the role of the most convenient pawn—"

"More the queen than a pawn. Unpredictable and hard to pin down, but once that's sorted, the game is over." He smiled when she frowned.

"I hate chess."

"Then perhaps you should choose a better metaphor."

"I'm a *person*," she told him, and he thought that was temper that made each word like a blade. Her dark eyes blazed with heat. And fear. And yet her voice was cool, and he wanted her with that desperate edge that made him loathe himself. The wanting was fine. The desperation was not. He'd thought he'd outgrown that kind of thing when he'd shaken Arista off. "And this is not, despite all appearances to the contrary, the twelfth century—"

"Then why are you marrying me?" he asked, making no attempt to keep that lash from his voice. "You don't have to do it, as you've pointed out. There's no gun to your head."

"A merger between our two companies will strengthen both, and bolster Chase's position as CEO," she replied after a moment, something shrewd and sad in her gaze. "It changes the conversation he's been having with the board and the shareholders, anyway. And of course, you'd become the COO, and you've proved you're very good at operating companies and making piles of money. But you don't have to marry me to make that happen."

"I don't." He shrugged. "I'm not the one crafting objections to this marriage and looking for explanations. You are."

"But you won't hold up your end of your business arrangement with Chase if I don't agree to do this." Her eyes darkened. "I want to be a hundred percent certain we're both clear about who's pressuring who in this."

"I'm perfectly clear about it." And practically cheerful, as he smiled at her obvious flash of temper. "But this is all more of these games you like to play, Mattie. We both know you're going to marry me. You've known it since we met."

She didn't like that. He could see it on her face, stamped across those lovely cheeks of hers. But it didn't change that simple truth. Nothing ever had.

"I haven't done it yet," she pointed out quietly. "I'm not sure I'd get carried away counting my chickens if I were you."

He laughed then. "I'm going to enjoy teaching you the

appropriate way to respond to your husband, Mattie. I really am." He leaned forward, took that nasty cigarette from her and tossed it into the fire without looking away from her. "I'm marrying you because I want you. I always have. More than that, I want to merge my company with your father's, and I want the link between us to be strong. I want to be part of the family, so there can never be any question about who deserves a seat at the table. That means marriage. Babies. A very long life together, because I don't believe in separations or divorce. Or secrets."

Especially the secrets, he thought, shoving those terrible old memories aside. The lies and the devastation they'd wrought.

Mattie held his gaze for a long moment, something slick and glazed in hers. The only sound was the storm outside, harsh against the windows, and the crackle of the fire. He fancied he could hear her breath below that, too fast and uneven, betraying her—but he doubted she'd let that show and assumed it was only in his head. More wishful thinking, and he should know better.

"What you mean is, I'm a pawn," she said evenly. "You can say it, Nicodemus. It's not as if I don't know it already."

"And you're marrying me because…?" His lips curved when she only glared at him. "You enjoy playing the martyr? You've always wanted to barter yourself? You have a deep desire to prostrate yourself before the ambitions of others?"

"Family duty," she said primly. Piously. "I don't expect you to understand that."

"Of course not," he said, and he wasn't laughing then. "Because everything I have I tore from the world with my own two hands. My father never believed I would amount to anything." *And he did his best to see that I wouldn't,* Nicodemus thought grimly, those same old lies like painful scars deep inside him. "My mother cleaned houses and worked in the factories. The only thing they gave me was life. The rest I worked for."

And held on to, despite the best effort of grasping materialistic little parasites like Arista.

"No one ever said you weren't an impressive man, Nicodemus," Mattie said to him. "But what does it have to do with anything? You've been chasing me for so long, I think you don't even know why you started."

"No, Mattie," he said gently. Too gently, maybe. He thought that might have been the trouble from the start. He'd treated her like she was made of glass, and she'd done nothing but cut him with her own sharp edges. It was time he remembered that.

It was time he took control of this.

Her cheeks were flushed and her mouth was so close, and he'd waited *so long*. He could see the panic in her eyes as she looked back at him, the rise and fall of her perfect breasts against that unfathomably soft dress she wore. He couldn't stop himself from reaching over and taking her hot cheek in his hand, holding her there and tracing her lips with a single restless movement of his thumb.

He watched her redden, felt himself tighten at once in reaction, and it was like that lightning all over again. A bolt, brilliant and true, burning him alive where he sat.

It had damned them from the start. It had made all of this inevitable.

And made it worth it. He'd been sure of that, too.

"I've always known why," Nicodemus told her, and it was as close to the truth as he could get. The rest hung around them in all that white-hot heat, wrapping them both in the same wild hunger. He could see it in her face, in that bright blue sheen in her dark eyes. He felt it in his own flesh. He smiled. "It's you who have been confused. But you won't be for very much longer."

They were high over the Atlantic Ocean with nothing but darkness on all sides before Mattie gave up on her internal battle and the magazine she hadn't read a single word of no matter how fiercely she'd scowled at it. She finally stopped pretending and looked down the creamy, gold-edged interior of the private jet to where Nicodemus sat, looking for all the world like the wholly unconcerned king of his very own castle.

He was sprawled out at the table, sheaves of papers spread out before him and his laptop at his elbow, looking studious and masculine and very much like the deeply clever, world-renowned multimillionaire she was grudgingly aware he was. His dark hair looked tousled, like he'd been running his hands through it, and despite herself, her breath caught.

And he either felt her gaze on him or he heard that telling little catch, because his dark eyes snapped to hers at once.

"Has the silent treatment ended, then?" he asked, dry and amused and so very, very patronizing. "And here I'd got used to the quiet."

Mattie had been doing such a good job of ignoring him up until then. He'd left her in her father's house that day with no more than an enigmatic smile, and that had been that. He'd simply…let her stew for the next week and a half with no further threat or argument or input from him.

Mattie had considered running away, naturally. She'd dreamed it at night. She'd gone so far as to plot it all out. One day she'd even booked a plane ticket to Dunedin, New Zealand, tucked away on the bottom of the planet, the farthest place she could find on the map. But despite her wildest fantasies and several more detailed internet searches involving far-off mountain ranges and remote deserts, when Nicodemus had appeared at her door to whisk her off to Greece earlier this evening, Mattie had been there.

Waiting for him, as promised, like a good little arranged bride. Like the daughter she'd never been while her father was alive, as she'd been too busy veering between acting out or acting perfect to get his attention. She'd even packed.

Nicodemus had shouldered his way into her airy, comfortable apartment, walking in that lethally confident way of his that had made a shiver whisper down the length of her spine. She'd assured herself it was anxiety and not something far more feminine and appreciative. Her apartment was in a prewar building on Manhattan's Upper West Side, replete with lovely old moldings, scrupulously maintained hardwood floors and soaring ceilings that made the place seem twice its actual size. And yet Nicodemus made it feel like a closet-size studio simply by standing in it. Like a tiny, claustrophobic box. He was too *alive. Too much*. He'd nodded at her bags, his people had whisked them away and then he was simply…standing there in a very small, enclosed space. *Her* space.

Like it was already his. Like she was.

Mattie had refused to entertain that crazy little part of her that had melted at the notion. It would all be so much easier if he was less brutally gorgeous, she'd thought furiously. He wore a dark, fine sweater that did marvelous things for his already too perfect torso and an open wool coat cut to add warmth and elegance, not bulk. And his dark trousers looked both rugged and luxurious at once. He was a remarkably attractive man. There was no getting around it. She'd hated the fact she couldn't ignore that truth. Even when she'd known perfectly well he'd been there, shrinking down her living room and making her skin feel two sizes too tight, for the singular purpose of towing her off to do his bidding.

The fact that she'd be married to him in a handful of days had felt impossible. *Ludicrous.* And every time she met his too-knowing gaze, she felt like he'd lit her on fire and tossed her headfirst into a vat of gasoline.

"None of this is pink or even particularly girlie," he'd said, his harsh mouth curved with that sardonic amusement that had made her feel much too jittery. She'd felt stretched thin between a reckless hunger and a driving panic already, and she'd been back in his clutches all of five minutes. His dark eyes had held hers, hard and mocking at once. "You really do lie about everything, don't you?"

"Are you really starting out our glorious Two Weeks of Love by calling me a liar?" she'd asked, and she didn't care how brittle she sounded. How cold and obvious. She'd let out a laugh that hadn't sounded any better. "That bodes well."

"I suppose it must be me," he'd said quietly, eyeing her in a way that had made her feel flushed and flustered while something deep in her gut knotted into a red-hot fist. "If I stood in the pouring rain you'd tell me the sky was the brightest blue you'd ever seen. I inspire this in people, apparently. Especially women. I think you should worry about what will happen, Mattie, when I figure out how to read the truth no matter what lies you choose to tell me. Because I will."

"I've worried about very little else since that delightful meeting at my father's house," she assured him.

"Another lie."

"That was actually the truth. Amazing, I know."

And he'd reached over and taken hold of her chin like that was his right, the way her body had seemed to think it was as it had burst into all those hectic fireworks and roaring brushfires, nearly knocking her from her feet where she stood.

"That's not what you're worried about," Nicodemus had said, much too close and entirely too sure, as if he could taste that humming need in her that she'd wanted so badly to deny.

Mattie had decided right then and there that she needed to stop talking to him. It was too dangerous. Especially if it led him to put his hands on her.

She'd told herself she was relieved when he let her go again without pressing the issue, but it wasn't quite that simple. There were the aftershocks to consider—the rumbling, jagged tectonics that shifted and reshaped everything inside her no matter that she didn't want any of it.

But Mattie was nothing if not pointlessly stubborn. She'd maintained her silence all through the car ride out to the private airfield in the suburbs of Manhattan, through the boarding of the sleek Stathis company jet that waited there and their several hours of flight en route to what he'd called *my small, private island in the Aegean Sea.*

Because *of course* Nicodemus had *an island*, the better to make absolutely certain that Mattie was completely and utterly trapped with him, truly forced to marry him if she ever wanted to leave it again. That or hope she could swim for the mainland. Across the Aegean Sea. In October.

"That wasn't the silent treatment," she said now, stretching her legs out in front of her as if she felt as carefree and relaxed as he apparently did.

He shook his head in that way of his that reverberated inside her like another press of his strong fingers against her skin. "I don't understand why you bother to lie when you must have realized by now that I can see right through you."

"I merely ran out of things to say to you," Mattie said

loftily. "I imagine that will happen quite often. Yet one more sad consequence of a forced marriage like ours—a lifetime of boredom and silence while stuck together in our endless private hell."

His lips twitched. "It's not your silence I find hellish."

She nodded as if she'd expected that. "Resorting to insults. Quiet little threats. This is what happens when you blackmail someone into marrying you, Nicodemus, and we're not even married yet. I did try to warn you."

"There's no reason to resort to anything quite so unpleasant," he said silkily, leaning back in his chair. He tossed his pen down on the polished wood surface, and then the heat in his gaze made the narrow walls of the plane seem to contract in on her—or perhaps that was nothing more than the wild drumming of her pulse. "I'm sure we can find any number of things to do that don't require words."

Mattie rolled her eyes. "Veiled sexual threats aren't any less threatening simply because they're sexual," she said. "Quite the opposite, in fact."

"Is that why you're turning red?" he asked lazily. "Because you feel threatened?"

"Yes."

He shook his head again, slower this time. "Liar."

She reminded herself that just because he was right it didn't mean anything. He didn't *know* that he had this insane effect on her. He only *hoped* he did.

"I'm assuming you have some idea of how this works," she carried on, because now that she'd started poking at him, the idea of returning to that heavy silence was stifling. She was afraid it would crush her. "Now that you're in the process of isolating me from everything familiar, as most men like you do."

"Men like me," he said, and there was a dark current in

his voice that was either laughter or something far more treacherous, and she felt the uncertainty, the edginess, everywhere. "Are there many? And here I'd considered myself a special snowflake—almost an American, I'm so remarkably unique."

"It's a typical pattern," she assured him and smiled kindly. "Run of the mill, really."

"If you're attempting to shame me into releasing you," he said drily, "you have seriously misjudged your target."

"No one is *actually* shameless, Nicodemus," she said, and her voice softened somehow—lost that cool, mocking edge. She had no idea why. "No matter what they pretend."

"Perhaps not," he agreed, shifting slightly against his seat, though he never took that hot, hard gaze from hers. "But you don't know me well enough to even guess at the things that crawl in me and call my name in my darkest hours. You wouldn't recognize them if you did."

There wasn't a single reason that should take her breath away, or why her stomach should flip over, and so Mattie told herself it was a patch of turbulence, nothing more.

"You seem to want to make this a squalid little transaction," he said when she didn't throw something back at him, and she couldn't read the expression on his face then. He lounged back in his chair, propping his head up with one hand, and looked at her. Just *looked* at her. As if her layers of clothes and even her skin were no barrier whatsoever. As if he could see straight through to what lay beneath. "As painful and as horrid as possible."

"It is what it is," she said. "I have no idea how these barbaric arrangements work. Will you check my teeth like I'm a horse? Kick my tires like I'm a used car you bought off the internet?"

Something sharp and hot, a little too much like satisfaction, flared in the honeyed depths of his dark gaze, and his harsh mouth pulled into a very dangerous curve.

"If you insist," he said, lazy and low.

Mattie went still. She felt her eyes widen and could see from that gleam in his gaze that he saw it.

For God's sake! the hysterical part of her—currently occupying almost every part of her save her big mouth—shrieked. *What is the matter with you? Don't* challenge *him! Stop this right now before it gets out of hand!*

"Oh, I'm sorry," he practically purred, reading her much too easily. Again. "Was that yet another example of your mouth getting you into trouble? It's either lying to me or provoking me, I notice. It does make me wonder what it would be like to put it to better use."

He was right, Mattie realized. If he was truly the man she'd been treating him like he was, she'd be significantly more respectful and careful around him, wouldn't she? The truth was, she knew he wasn't. She couldn't believe that he'd really do this. She *didn't* believe it, even though she was currently suspended somewhere over the ocean on her way to Greece.

Granted, he was doing an excellent job of acting like a scary, overwhelming, my-way-or-the-highway barbarian, but she'd known this man for years. More important, her father had genuinely liked him. Had even considered him a good match for his only daughter. She simply couldn't make herself believe that Nicodemus would honestly *force* her to marry him.

Much less any of the other things he wasn't *quite* threatening to do, that were pressing into her so hard now that she was certain they'd leave marks.

"I wasn't kidding," she said, and she stood up then, un-coiling herself to stand there in the aisle before him. She opened up her arms and spread them wide, as theatrically as possible. "I'm sure the third richest man in Greece—"

"That's rather less of a salutation than it might have been once," he pointed out, that cool amusement in his gaze. "I can't tell if you mean it as compliment or condemnation."

"—doesn't buy one of those crotch-rocket motorcycles of his without making sure it lives up to each and every one of his exacting standards," Mattie continued as if he hadn't interjected anything.

She'd seen him on a Ducati once, roaring up a winding country lane in France to a weekend party in a friend's chateau she never would have attended if she'd known he'd be there. She'd escaped shortly thereafter, but she'd never been able to get that image out of her head. A powerful man on such a sleek and dangerous machine, like lethal poetry etched against the backdrop of vineyards turning gold in the setting sun, as if they'd been doing it purely to celebrate him.

She glared at him and held her crucifixion position. "Well? Here I am."

Nicodemus's dark eyes glittered, and he didn't move, yet Mattie felt as if he'd leaped up and yanked her to him. She felt surrounded, smothered. And lit on fire.

He raised his shoulder in that profoundly Mediterranean way of his, then dropped it lazily.

"Go on, then," he said, his voice *this close* to bored, though his gaze burned through her, churning up too much heat and that dangerous hunger she'd been denying for years now. "Strip. Show me what I've chased across all these years and bought, at last."

CHAPTER THREE

MATTIE GAVE UP her charade of even, calm breaths. She stared at him—and he only smirked back at her.

Because he didn't think she'd do it, she realized. He thought he'd push her the way he had outside that club in London—until she broke and ran.

Not this time, Mattie thought icily. If he wanted to act like the kind of man who bought wives, she'd act like the kind of woman who could be bought.

She dropped her arms and shrugged out of the long red sweater jacket she'd been using as much like a blanket as a coat. She tossed it on the leather bench beside her, then kicked off her short boots.

Nicodemus said nothing.

Mattie pulled her cashmere V-neck up and over her head, aware as she did it that a fair swathe of her belly was exposed as she stretched her arms over her head. She thought she heard him mutter something, but when her head was free again he was still right where she'd left him, still watching her as if this was the safety demonstration on a commercial flight and about as entertaining.

So she peeled off her tight T-shirt, too, and refused to allow herself a single shiver of response when his gaze dropped to move over her breasts and the burgundy-colored bra she wore. She didn't move a muscle on the outside—

but her stomach pulled itself into a tight, hard little ball and she could hardly breathe around the fire of it. She stood there, so hot and so long she was sure her skin matched the bra, and still, he took his time returning his gaze to hers.

"Do you like the merchandise?" she asked coolly.

"How can I tell?" he asked in a similar tone. "It remains covered. Surely not an attack of modesty, Mattie? Not after that topless shot that so entranced your adoring public two summers ago?"

"There's nothing wrong with sunbathing topless on a yacht in the middle of an ocean," Mattie said, and only when she heard her own voice did she realize how defensive she sounded. "I thought I was alone. Am I supposed to live my life wrapped up in a shroud on the off chance there might be a helicopter above me?"

"Perhaps you could simply pay slightly more attention to how you display your body," Nicodemus suggested, with a hint of steel in his voice. "Particularly now that it's mine."

He watched her for a moment, and she felt too obvious, too exposed. He was right. It was silly. She'd worn dresses to banquets that covered less than what she was wearing right now. Why should this feel so much more intimate?

She decided she didn't particularly want to explore that line of thought.

But she'd started this. She'd push it all the way to the finish. She'd push *him*.

"Do you have any other awkward, pathologically possessive remarks to make?" she asked, nothing but brisk politeness in her tone. "Do you perhaps feel the urge to fire up your company logo and brand it into my skin?"

That curve of his harsh mouth. That bright, hot gleam in his dark eyes. That languid, offhanded way he lounged there, as if he was something other than the most physically powerful man she'd ever let this close to her.

She swallowed, hard. Betraying herself. Nicodemus smiled.

"I'll let you know," he said, and then he inclined his head in a regal sort of way that was as infuriating as it was strangely attractive, silently bidding her to continue.

Mattie despaired of herself. But she leaned over and pulled off her socks then stood again and shimmied out of her skinny black jeans, kicking them out of her way when she was done. And then she stood there. In nothing but her bra and panties.

And told herself—over and over again—that it was like a bathing suit. It was fine. It was *nothing*.

Nicodemus's gaze was so hot it hurt. But he still didn't move.

"I can't tell if this is modesty or a dramatic pause," he said after a moment, his voice insultingly bland. "But it bores me."

For the first time, a little trickle of fear dripped down the length of her spine, and it occurred to Mattie to wonder who was pushing who.... But she only lifted her chin up then reached behind her to unclip her bra. She pulled it from her body slowly, exposing one breast and then the other, and then she dropped it. He watched, a kind of fierce concentration stamped over his strong face. So she hooked her fingers in the sides of her panties and tugged them down to her knees, then let them fall the rest of the way to the floor so she could move them aside with her foot.

Then she was standing naked in front of Nicodemus Stathis, the bane of her existence, who was now her fiancé. Who would soon be her husband, if he had his way. Her mind shied away from all of that. The terms themselves. The reality.

And she was still completely and utterly naked.

Which was really not the best time to question the decision-making that had led her to this point—so Mattie held her head at a belligerent angle and waited, as if she was perfectly comfortable hanging around planes in the nude with infuriating men.

Nicodemus let out a low sound that wasn't quite a laugh, and then he stood up. Mattie's mouth went dry and for a stark, spinning second her mind blanked out.

He was too big for the plane—*for the world,* she thought wildly when she could think again, and certainly much bigger than he'd seemed when she'd had her clothes on—and he only took a single step closer then braced himself on the ceiling above them and left the rest of his lean, powerful body angled away from her. Looming and not looming at the same time.

It didn't make him any less dangerous. Mattie didn't feel remotely safe. But she didn't dare examine what she felt too closely.

He frowned down at her, and it occurred to her that she should have paid more attention to the things he'd said before. About how little she knew him when they both knew he'd studied her very closely indeed over the past decade. It put her at a distinct disadvantage.

That and the fact she was naked.

"Why are you standing there?" She only blinked at him in confusion, and he made a spinning motion with one long finger. "Turn, please."

She told herself he only wanted to humiliate her. To break her. And she was still holding out hope that he wouldn't take this as far as he could. That this was all some kind of extended practical joke. Or, if not a *joke,* precisely, that he wanted to teach her some kind of lesson for rebuffing him all these years. He'd back down. He had to back down.

But that meant she couldn't.

Mattie turned, and she took her time doing it. She even put her hips into it, so it was a little bit of a show—

Then she felt his hands on her. And froze.

It took her a moment to understand that it wasn't a random touch, or even a particularly sexual one. He was tracing the delicate tattoo that flowed over one hip and up her side to cradle the lower edge of her ribs.

"It's a phoenix," she blurted out, and hated that her voice was so quiet and so rough. Like this was getting to her—his too-warm hands on her skin, his terrifying and intoxicating closeness, her ill-conceived nudity.

"I know what it is," he said, his tone curt, and she couldn't see anything she recognized in his face when she turned the rest of the way around to face him. "What I don't know is how it applies to the charmed life you've always led."

Mattie had no intention of ever telling him. Or anyone.

"Nicodemus—" she started, but he shook his head.

And she had no idea why she fell silent. Why she obeyed him when everything inside her was a blistering, shattering scream.

"And that cursed belly ring," he muttered, still in that short, dark way, and she steeled herself when he reached over and tugged on the little silver ring, gently enough. So gently it shouldn't have seared through her the way it did, burning a path from her navel to the molten core of her. Making her *melt*.

She managed to keep herself from making any sound, but his lips twitched again and she was sure that somehow he knew, anyway.

He shifted closer, and her heart exploded, pounding at the wall of her chest like it might break free, and that was the least of her worries. She was too hot, too cold. Her breasts ached then *hurt* when he brought his hands up beneath them, spanning her waist, holding her. *Caging* her—

"Nicodemus," she started again, and she couldn't contain her panic or her need, or keep either from her voice. She hardly recognized herself.

"Is this what you wanted?" His voice was gruff and dark, shocking her with the force of it. "Next time, the little dance isn't necessary. You can simply ask."

And then he leaned in, as if she'd begged him to do it and he had all the time in the world, and took her mouth with his.

It was better than he remembered.

Much better.

Mattie tasted like smoke and heat, some kind of perfect whiskey that was all woman and only her, and Nicodemus felt knocked sideways. Drunk for the first time in more years than he could count.

He let go of the sweet indentation of her waist and sank his fingers deep into that glossy hair of hers, widening his stance so he could pull her off balance to sprawl across his chest. And they weren't in London this time. There were no bouncers nearby, no fear of exposure.

Nicodemus could finally take his time.

He could test this angle and then that one. He could taste her again and again, kissing her with a fury and a longing that took him over, making him wild and desperate and intoxicated with every drugging slide of his tongue against hers.

Mine, declared that primitive voice inside him, the way it had done so many years ago at that fateful ball. And ever since.

And she was perfect.

That spill of thick, beautiful, dark hair that fell around her shoulders and felt like raw silk against his palms. That rangy body of hers, so tall and taut, with her proud, rose-tipped breasts to the inviting swell of her hips. She made his mouth water. Even that damned tattoo he'd ordered her not to get stamped into her pretty skin suited her, as delicate and mysterious as she was, in a swirl of bright colors he longed to taste.

And that belly ring that made him think of long, hot nights and the sweet undulation of feminine hips.

He'd never wanted another woman like this. Not even Arista. He'd never *wanted* like this.

That sent a chill spiraling through him, and it was the only thing that penetrated the delirious, pounding need that threatened to take him over there and then. He pulled his mouth from hers then ran his hands down the silken length of the arms she'd wrapped around his neck, continuing down the perfect line of her spine to cup that sweet, delectable bottom in his palms. Her eyes were closed, those sooty lashes a distraction. Her lush mouth tempted him, full and slick from his. Her breasts pressed against him and he marveled, once again, at how right she felt in his arms. Not so short he had to stoop, not so slight he was afraid he might break her. *Perfect.*

Nicodemus thought he might die, then and there, if he didn't get inside her. If he didn't taste her. If he didn't *do something* about the thing that howled in him, fanged and clawed and desperate for more.

He ordered himself to set her aside, to hold off, to wait until he had every last bit of the power he was after, but Mattie shifted against him and made a small, needy sound in the back of her throat—

And he was only a man. He could only take so much.

He lifted her arms from around his neck and guided her toward the leather couch along one wall of the jet. He sat her down then knelt between her legs, shouldering her knees apart so he could see every part of her.

"Wait," she said, her eyes fluttering open then, sounding as breathless as she was flushed. "Are you—?"

"Hold on," he ordered her, bending down to her, inhaling the rich scent of her arousal, the sweetness of her skin.

"Nicodemus." But her voice was so insubstantial, a token protest at best when she was still open and arched before him, and he was so close. *Too close.* "I don't—"

"I do," he muttered, the way a religious man might utter a fervent prayer.

And then he simply worshipped her. He pulled her long and lovely legs over his shoulders, wrapped his hands around her hips and buried his face in her heat.

The way he'd longed to do for a thousand years. More.

She made the most beautiful noise he'd ever heard, something like a gasp and a scream at once, and Nicodemus growled against the slick, hot core of her. She tasted sweet and wild. Like honey. Like *his.* He could feel her quiver beneath his hands, and he licked his way into her, teasing her and tasting her, until he felt her hips begin that lush dance against his tongue.

"Oh, no," she moaned, but even as she said it, she raised her hips to meet his mouth. She threw her arms over her face, hiding right there in plain sight, and he was too lost in the exquisite pleasure of tasting her at last to do anything but let her.

And then she was crying out his name, tense and even more beautiful as she bucked against him. She sobbed out words he didn't understand, almost as if he was bringing her to this delectable edge against her will when he could taste her need—

Until she shattered. Into a million pieces the way he'd always dreamed she would, long and loud and calling out his name.

All mine, Nicodemus thought with a deep satisfaction

that felt like something else. Like a truth he didn't know how to name—so he didn't try.

Not here. Not yet.

Mattie hated herself.

It took her a long time to open up her eyes. When she did, she found she was curled up on the leather couch, her sweater jacket draped over her like a blanket and Nicodemus sitting beside her with his long legs taking up the whole of the aisle and an air of smug confidence she didn't have to look at his face to see. And he was turned, she found when she dared sneak a look, anyway, so that he could watch her with those stark, too-incisive, dark eyes of his that seemed to burn straight through her to all the places she most wanted to hide.

She pulled in one breath. Then another, just as shaky as the first. And she still didn't understand how she'd allowed this to happen. How had he *done* that? It was as if he'd used her own body against her—and in that moment, Mattie couldn't think of a single thing that frightened her more.

She shoved her hair back from her face with one hand, using the other to keep the sweater in place, which she didn't need that small gleam in his gaze to tell her was absurd, at this point.

Ruined, she thought then. She felt utterly ruined. Wrecked from within, like a stranger inside her own skin.

The silence stretched out, filling the jet, drowning out the sound of the engines, not comfortable in the least.

And beside her, Nicodemus radiated that heat and menace that made him who he was: the most dangerous man she'd ever met. She'd always known he was exactly that—and now he'd proved it. His dark eyes tracked her, and she was afraid to look too closely—afraid of what she'd see.

"Is this what it takes?" he asked in a quiet voice that

seemed to crack her foundations deep inside her. "This is what I must do to see behind all the masks you wear?"

She was terrified that he really could. She was terrified of what had happened here, full stop, especially because she could still *feel* his mouth against that most private part of her. She could still *feel* the aftershocks. The lush, impossible wave of joy and pleasure that had rent her in two. She shook her head—once, hard, as much to snap herself out of this fugue she was in as anything else—and found she was scowling at her lap.

"I doubt there will be a repeat of that unfortunate demonstration," she said, but her voice lacked its usual force even to her own ears. "Once was enough."

"Once," he said, and his voice, by contrast, was alive with fire and that sharp edge that sliced deep into her, "is by no means enough. That was only the beginning, Mattie."

"I said I'd marry you," she heard herself say, as if from some far-off distance. She didn't recognize that voice that came out of her mouth. Soft. Pleading. As if he'd licked her into a different person—and she was deeply afraid he really had. "That doesn't mean you can claim marital rights like some eighteenth century relic. I'm not sure you can even really call me your *wife*, since you're essentially purchasing the title."

"Look at me."

She didn't want to do that, and she couldn't understand, then, why she did it, anyway. She felt much too raw, like her heart was a throbbing thing that might rip her wide open in a moment, and yet she looked at him. Because he'd told her to. And she bit back something she was terribly afraid was a sob when he reached over and brushed her hair from her face.

With devastating gentleness.

"Are you afraid of me?" His voice was softer than it

had been a moment ago, but Mattie couldn't allow herself to melt into that the way her body wanted to do. The way her body *did*. She couldn't let herself topple over into the way he was looking at her. She couldn't let this happen. She couldn't risk this kind of thing—this kind of softness.

Mattie knew what came next. First the softness, the intimacy, the love. Then loss. And all that darkness ever after.

"Why would I be afraid of you?" she asked, her voice a bitter little scrape against the taut thing that hung between them, against that softness making his eyes gleam like gold. Against the darkness she hid away inside her and yet held before her like a shield. "I love it when men I don't want spirit me away on private planes and then put their mouths wherever they like on my body. It's my favorite thing."

"Ah, Mattie," he said quietly, and if he'd been someone else, if she'd been someone else, she might have thought he truly cared about her then. That she was something different, something more, than a long-sought trophy he aimed to put high on the shelf of his choosing. "I don't know if it's your favorite thing or not. But it just became mine."

Something swelled in her then, making a new, hectic kind of heat prickle all over her exposed skin and, worse, lodge behind her eyes with too much dampness. Mattie didn't know what she'd do if she actually cried in front of this man. She didn't know how she'd survive any of this—how she'd possibly remain intact when he had all of this shocking power over her—but particularly not if he saw her cry.

"I don't want this," she gritted out at him, so desperate to keep the tears from spilling over that her hands clenched into fists, and her fingernails dug deep into her own palms. "I don't want any part of this. I never have, and you know it."

She didn't know what she expected. Not that long, oddly

shattering look Nicodemus gave her then, that she might have called *hurt* on a less-dangerous, less-inscrutable man. Not another brush of his hard fingers against her cheek, making a different sort of heat warm to a glow inside her.

"You know it," she said again, more insistent, and his mouth moved, pulling to one side.

Like he knew her better than she did. "So you have said."

Mattie moved, jerky and strange, as if she was a marionette someone else was operating on very stiff strings. She found her panties and pulled them on, feeling immediately better. Her bra. Her jeans. Her T-shirt. As if it was all armor-plated instead of merely from Barney's, and could keep her safe from this man. As if anything could.

Nicodemus only leaned back against the leather sofa and watched as she pulled on her V-neck sweater and then stamped her feet into her boots.

"I didn't mean for that to happen," she said when she was clothed and felt somewhat more like herself than she had before.

"I know what you meant to do." Still that too-dark, too-painful look. "Perhaps in future you'll listen to me. When I told you it was impossible for you to shame me, I meant it."

"Then you are a far worse creature than I imagined," she said. "Wholly irredeemable."

"If you say so," he said. He rubbed his hands over his face. "Your problem is that you expect these pronouncements to wound me." And when that dark gaze of his met hers again, it seemed to slam into her. Another gut punch, hard and deep. "You're a decade too late. I've watched you for too long. I know that you'll say and do anything to try, even now, to escape the inevitable."

"Maybe you should ask yourself why you're so dead set on marrying someone who wants to escape you," she pointed out. "Why a man who could have any woman chooses to buy one, instead. All to become president and COO of a company that isn't even his. Don't you think that's a bit sad?"

It was as if the longer she wore her clothes, the more she reclaimed herself. Or the more she could pretend she couldn't still *feel* him in that betraying softness at her center, so hot and wet even now, pulsing with that destructive need that could destroy her. That would, if she let it.

That already has, something whispered.

"Is this where you appeal to my reason?" His mouth was harder then. Lethal. And she could still taste it. "My good side?"

"Or the part of you that doesn't live in the Stone Age."

"But where you are concerned, I do." His voice even sounded like stone, as if to underscore the harsh way he said that and the way his dark honey eyes gleamed, all menace and certainty. "I don't mind the dance, Mattie. Twist yourself into as many convoluted shapes as you like. Try out all your last-ditch attempts to save yourself. Keep going. See what happens."

"I refuse to believe you're really going to force me to marry you," she threw at him. Accusation and desperation, rolled into one.

"I'm not." That tug in the corner of his mouth, not quite a smile. Not anything that pleasant. "I didn't drag you from your apartment in handcuffs. I didn't kidnap you. No one made you come with me. Just as no one will make you recite your vows."

Mattie was shaking again. Why couldn't she make it stop? How had she managed to completely lose all her self-control? She crossed her arms over her chest, but that only served to make her far too aware of her breasts, which still ached. For him, she knew. Always for him.

"You're splitting hairs," she said. "And you know it."

"No." And his voice was no less stern for that gentle look he aimed at her. "I am a very simple man. I keep the promises I make. I don't have to force you to do anything. I don't *want* to force you. I told you before—you're free to do as you like. You always have been."

"Free to have you hunt me down all these years? Free to have you make nasty little bargains with my brother that you know I'd have to be a selfish monster to refuse?"

Nicodemus didn't quite shrug. "Freedom is never without cost."

"And what was—this?"

She jerked her chin in a hard little gesture that she hoped encompassed what had happened right here on this plane. She certainly didn't want to think about it, much less let those images chase through her head, or move like wine in her veins. She didn't want to feel the aftereffects, all those leftover flames still dancing just beneath her skin.

She didn't want to admit that he'd knocked down a lifetime of her defenses that swiftly, that easily. With her participation and help, no less.

"I thought you wanted me to take you for a test drive, Mattie," he said, horribly, and even laughed when she scowled at him. "Was that not enough of a test? Should we try a higher gear?"

"I," she said very distinctly, very deliberately, "would rather throw myself out of this plane right now."

"That would be unfortunate," he said, without sounding in the least concerned she'd try. "And undoubtedly painful, before your inevitable death."

"I don't want to have sex with you." Her voice was much too strident.

As usual, Nicodemus didn't do what she'd expected he might. He only shook his head at her as if she was a child.

"That is a lie," he said quietly. "As I think you must know I am well aware, having tasted what you want right here."

"Are you going to manipulate me into that, too?" she demanded, uneven and too loud. "Are there more hideous consequences if I don't lie down and take it the first time you order me to do it?"

Nicodemus blinked. "I can promise you that there will never come a day when I will order you to *lie down and take it,* as intriguing as that image might be."

"Don't avoid the question."

Nicodemus studied her, and, not for the first time, Mattie had the prickly sense that he saw all the things she'd spent her life working so hard to conceal. All the things she'd shoved aside, hidden, buried deep.

"No," he said, and he didn't break that uncompromising gaze. "I'm not going to force you. I'm not going to manipulate you."

"I wish I could trust you," she said.

"I've never lied to you," he said, in that same inexorable, impossible way, as relentless as an incoming tide. "You can't say the same. I suspect it's you that you can't trust."

She rubbed her hands up and down her arms and moved to sit in one of the comfortable chairs across the aisle, pulling her feet up beneath her in as close to the fetal position as she could get while still upright.

"I have no idea what you mean."

"Mattie." He might have been laughing again. She could see it in his eyes , could hear it, rich and thick and entirely too beguiling in his low voice. "I don't have to force you or manipulate you or strip off my clothes in a clumsy little challenge, do I?" His smile then was beautiful, truly. Stunning and shattering at once, and it poured into her, through her, like light. Like a nuclear blast. Like a death knell, and she knew it. "I only have to touch you, and you're mine. You've always been mine. Perhaps it's time you admitted it."

They arrived on his island a little before noon the following day after a helicopter ride from a private airfield outside Athens, and it took every shred of control Nicodemus had left inside him to keep from simply tossing Mattie over his shoulder and ravaging her the moment they stepped inside his villa. Exactly the way he'd told her he wouldn't.

This has been a very long game, but the end is in sight, he reminded himself fiercely. *Don't lose your advantage now.*

She had to come to him, one way or another. She had to surrender. She had to be complicit in his triumph over her, or he wouldn't truly win her at all. He knew this as well as he knew his own name. On some level, he supposed he'd always known it.

Nicodemus had bought this island not long after seeing Mattie for the first time at that damned ball of hers, flush with his own burgeoning success and sense of purpose. He'd planned to remake the world in his image and to a large extent, he'd succeeded. He'd built the vast, sprawling villa in the intervening years, making it as much a monument to his own growing power and influence as to the stunning views it commanded from the top of the rocky hill that made up the bulk of the small island, tucked away in a sleepy part of the tourist-heavy Cyclades islands.

It was the kind of house he'd dreamed of while growing up in a crowded flat in the port city of Piraeus outside Athens, mired in his father's strict rules and then, afterward, the mess of his father's lies. It was a house filled with light and art and the sea, not the clamor and struggle of the busy, working-class neighborhood of his childhood.

Quiet elegance and wealth were evident in every last detail, from the dizzyingly high ceilings to the recognizably famous canvases he'd installed on his walls. All it needed was the perfect gilded lily of a woman to live in it with him, as glossy and as bright and as expensive as the view he'd worked so hard to claim as his own.

Not any woman, he knew. He'd tried simply glossy and pedigreed once, and it had brought him Arista, who had wanted his money and his power and his prowess in bed, but not his ring or his name. It had taken him much too long to see her true face, to understand what it had meant that her family sneered at him and his lower-class roots. Mattie was different—because he'd always seen her true face. He'd known from the start that she was lying about her aversion to him. He'd held her in his arms in that ballroom and felt her tremble even as she'd denied him. More than that, claiming her meant claiming a place deep in the bosom of her family. He knew exactly how highly her father had thought of him, because Bart Whitaker was a self-made man who'd married above his station, too.

It was as if Mattie had been crafted specifically for him.

And now she was here. Right where he'd wanted her for a decade. Standing in his house, contained by the walls he'd designed and built himself, the last component of his dream come true sliding into place with a *click* he thought was nearly audible.

Few things in life were as good in fact as they seemed in theory, Nicodemus knew from painful experience, but this—*she* was one of them. He didn't know what surged in him then, some wild concoction made of equal parts lust and satisfaction and *at last,* and he simply stood there in the foyer and let it beat through him. As simple and as poignant as joy.

He watched her as she turned around in a circle in the

great room that opened up in front of him, that too-pretty face of hers unreadable in the bright fall sunlight. She tipped her head back, as if to bask in all that sunshine, but then she caught him looking and stopped. Hid. Again.

Because there was always another game where Mattie Whitaker was concerned. Always another lie.

It was good he remembered that now, he told himself sternly, before he forgot himself entirely and did something foolish. Like pick her up in his arms and swing her around, as if she'd come happily and willingly to this marriage. As if this was some kind of love story.

His own sentimentality should not have surprised him. It was nothing new. This was the culmination of his last remaining dream. He'd already achieved all the rest, one after the next. Mattie was the last thing he'd wanted that he hadn't yet had. The very last. It was his own burden that he also wanted her to be *real*.

"I would ask you if you like this place," he said, aware of the chill in his voice and doing nothing to modify it, because better she should hear that than what lurked beneath, betraying him completely, "but it doesn't really matter, does it?"

"Apparently not." Her dark eyes met his, then moved away again—too quickly, as if she feared what he'd see if he looked too closely. Or perhaps he only hoped that was why. "If you say so." Her mouth shifted into something far more recognizably bitter. "Is this how you prefer I address you, Nicodemus? As submissively as possible? Should I curtsey?"

"There is very little submissive about you, Mattie," Nicodemus said with a great patience only slightly marred by his clenched teeth and the rigid way he held himself too still. "Especially when I can hear you choking back your temper as you speak."

"A natural reaction to my circumstances, I'd imagine," she retorted, her arms crossed tight over those beautiful breasts of hers, and it didn't help that he now knew what they looked like when they were taut with need. He knew how she tasted, and it might very well be the ruin of him. "I'd see about forming a support group, but I suspect the taking of war brides went out with the last century. If not well before."

"This is the history of the world," he said, with what he thought was admirable patience. He thrust his hands deep in his pockets so he'd keep them off her, and roamed across the marble floor in her direction, the room in blues and whites with hints of darker woods as accents, and Mattie's glossy black hair a startling midnight in the middle of it. *Perfect.* "We aren't doing anything particularly new, you and I. People have always done things like this, for the same reasons, all throughout the ages."

"You mean *women* have always *been forced* to do things like this," she corrected him, but he was closer now, and her voice wasn't as strident as before. He saw the remains of all that exuberant heat still there in her lovely eyes, and he wanted to taste her again more than he wanted his next breath. But he only waited, and watched her pull in a long, ragged breath. "Women are forced to bend, or kingdoms break. Women are made to surrender, or nations and corporations and *men* fall apart."

"Consider this a history lesson, if you must. If that makes it easier for you. More palatable."

She glared at him. "And what about what I want, Nicodemus?"

"What about it?" He shook his head when her glare deepened into a scowl. "We both know that you aren't as opposed to this as you pretend. Did we not prove that in scorching detail at thirty-thousand feet?"

"You're wrong. Again. Why am I not surprised?"

"Have I beaten you?" he asked, his voice a lash in the vast room, and she jolted slightly, as if she felt its edge in long, red stripes against her skin. "Abused you in some way?" She looked as if she was about to speak but he kept going. "There are a lot of men who might have taken that impromptu strip show on the plane as an invitation to indulge whatever appetites they liked."

"Didn't you?" she accused him, and he laughed.

"Remind me, in future, never to restrain myself where you are concerned." He shook his head. "Particularly when you take it upon yourself to get naked in inappropriate places."

"I didn't want that!" she hissed at him, with as much force as if she'd have preferred to scream it. Her hands were clenched tight. She was rigid and obviously angry and Nicodemus's curse was that he found her beautiful. Distractingly so. Even—especially—when she was attempting to defy him. "I didn't want any part of what you did."

"This I could tell by the way you screamed my name as you climaxed in my mouth," he said with arid impatience, and she flinched as if he'd slapped her.

"I thought you would stop." It was a harsh whisper.

"Because I always have before?" The laugh he let out then was devoid of humor. "Then you've learned a valuable lesson. Don't test me again." The look on her face was mutinous and miserable at once, and so unnecessary when they'd come this far already—but he bit back the more earthy reaction he had to it. "Your body doesn't tell the lies you do, Mattie. It's significantly more honest."

"Just because my body has some insane chemical reaction to you doesn't mean *I* want to indulge it," she threw at him. "The world doesn't work that way."

"Yours does," he said flatly. "The sooner you accept

that, the happier you'll be." She made a sound that was as close to a growl as he'd ever heard her make, and he really did laugh then. "This is like your very own, personal fairy tale," he told her. He swept an arm through the air, inviting her to truly take in her surroundings. "Blue sky, perfect Greek sea, a little castle on a hilltop, and all of it yours. All you have to do is marry a man with whom you have all of this inconvenient chemistry. No glass slipper required. You should look a bit happier."

She turned slightly to look out at the view, through all the sweeping glass that let in the glory of the Greek islands on three sides and all that sunshine from above, but her mouth pressed into a flat line.

"You're thinking of Disney fairy tales, I think," she said, those dark eyes fixed on Kimolos, the nearest island, as if she was calculating how far it would be to swim to it. "This feels a bit more Grimm Brothers, where everything ends in pecked-out eyes and a river of tears."

He waited until she turned toward him, which took a few tense moments, and when she did, he only shook his head, slowly. A dark scowl like a thundercloud rolled across her lovely face, ferocious and fierce. It only made him want her more.

"I'm pleased to see that you've accepted the reality of the situation with such grace," he said smoothly. "And while we're on that topic, I'll show you to our room so you can get settled."

She blinked. Went entirely too still, the way he'd known she would. "*Our* room?" she asked.

And Nicodemus smiled.

CHAPTER FOUR

THREE DAYS LATER, Mattie dutifully mouthed a set of vows that might as well have been gibberish for all they resonated in her, high on a rocky cliff with a view of nothing but the deep blue Aegean Sea and the next island over, which Nicodemus had informed her boasted a population of less than a thousand souls and the only nearby ferry to Athens.

"Should you wish to swim for it," he'd drawled that first night when he'd installed her in the bedroom he'd claimed they were to share, with its stunning view of the shifting sea and the green hills of the other island, "you should know that it's several miles and there's a vicious current. You could wind up in Tripoli by morning."

"And wouldn't that be a shame," she'd sniped back at him, because she was incapable of biting her tongue at the best of times—and especially when facing him over the wide, vast expanse of the giant bed his amused expression had told her he had every intention of sharing with her. "This close to the wedding of the century."

Nicodemus had only laughed and left her there, to seethe and plot and try her best not to fall apart.

Mattie still didn't believe this was real. That this was really happening.

Not when Nicodemus had looked her up and down in

that dizzying, glassed-in great room of his obnoxiously perfect villa earlier today, his mouth crooking slightly as he took stock of the dour gray dress she'd opted to wear for the occasion.

"Are you in mourning already?" he'd asked, that rich amusement making his voice deeper, darker. It had washed through her like another devastating lick of his talented tongue, and with the same explosive effect. She'd tried valiantly to fight it off, though his expression indicated she hadn't been particularly successful.

"It seemed appropriate," she'd replied coolly. "It was the only one I could find on such short notice that screamed *forced to the altar*. Don't you agree?"

Nicodemus had only laughed. *At* her, she'd been well aware, the way he'd done a great many times since that day in her father's library. Since her eighteenth birthday, for that matter. Then he'd taken her by the arm and led her over the smooth stones toward the priest and the two members of his household staff who were standing in as witnesses to this quiet little tragedy out on his covered marble terrace.

Mattie had told herself that none of this was happening. That none of this was real. That none of it *mattered*.

Not when Nicodemus took her hands in his. Certainly not when he recited his own vows in that powerful voice of his that seemed to echo deep in her bones, however unreal the words seemed to her. Not when the priest spoke in English and then in Greek, as if to make certain it took. Not when one of his staff took a series of photographs that Mattie was sure she didn't want to see. Not when Nicodemus pulled her close to him to press a coolly possessive kiss to her mouth, more matter-of-fact than anything else.

Not that her treacherous body had cared how he kissed her, so long as he did—and she hated that she couldn't lie to herself about that. That the proof was right there in the rowdy, insistent pounding of her heart and the blistering heat at her core, telling her truths she didn't want to accept. Especially when he left her there on that achingly lovely terrace to escort the priest and the two witnesses back into the villa, as if it had never crossed his mind that she might consider jumping from that cliff, to swim or to drown or to be swept off to Tripoli with the next tide, to escape him by any means necessary.

It was no more than another nightmare, she thought, and she was well-acquainted with those. *That didn't really happen.* But even as she thought it, she looked down at her hand at the heavy set of rings that he'd put there, sliding one on right after the next. A square-cut diamond raised high above two sapphires next to a ring of flatter diamonds around a platinum band. The kind of rings reality show "housewives" wore, she thought uncharitably, though she knew that wasn't fair. They simply weren't the sort of hushed, restrained rings her mother had worn all those years ago, the sort Mattie had always imagined she'd wear herself one day.

Not that Nicodemus had asked what she'd wanted. And the rings he'd given her still fit perfectly, she noticed, no matter how she scowled at them.

The October afternoon was cool, or maybe that was her. Mattie had never been one of those wedding-maddened girls, forever imagining *her perfect day* and flipping through bridal magazines in the absence of a groom, but she'd always imagined that at least one of her parents would be there when it happened. That neither of them was alive to know she was married, much less to have witnessed it, ached—and ached deep.

And while she'd known that this situation with Nicodemus was part of a much wider bid to retain control of the family company and all the high stakes that implied, Mattie really had imagined that Chase might have made it from London to watch her sacrifice herself for his benefit, rather than sending her an underwhelming text with his apologies.

Then again, she and Chase hadn't been close in a long time. And she'd always known whose fault that was.

It was a good thing she'd frozen solid, she thought then, because if she hadn't, she might have been tempted to indulge that great, heavy sob building up somewhere inside her. And that might wreck whatever little of herself she had left.

"Reflecting on your good fortune?" Nicodemus asked from behind her, and Mattie congratulated herself on managing, somehow, not to jump at the sound.

"Something like that," she said, as coolly and unemotionally as she could.

Down below, she heard the roar of a motor before she saw the small boat take off in the direction of the island of Kimolos a few miles away. She frowned when she saw three figures on the deck. The priest and both witnesses, clearly, which meant she was alone here with Nicodemus.

Alone. And married to him. *Married.*

Mattie turned, very slowly, to face the man who stood behind her, his hands deep in the pockets of the loose-fitting tan trousers he wore. His crisp white shirt highlighted his olive skin, the contrasting beauty of his dark eyes and almost wild hair, and though it didn't cling to him at all, it still somehow emphasized his powerful chest. He should have looked anything but elegant. But somehow, on him it all worked, and brought out his power and his ruthlessness instead of undermining it.

There was something different about him then, she realized. Something even more dangerous than before. It made the tiny hairs on the back of her neck and down her arms prickle in uncomfortable awareness. It was almost as if—

But then she understood. *He'd won.* Just as he'd always promised her he would.

Her throat was dry. Too dry.

And Nicodemus Stathis was her husband.

"Come inside," he said, his gaze as dark as it was patient, and that made something very deep inside her shudder.

"I'm fine right here."

It was a profoundly stupid thing to say. It made her sound like an infant and she knew it the moment the words passed her lips. Nicodemus's hard face softened, and that only made everything worse.

"You're afraid that if you come inside with me, that means we'll immediately consummate this marriage," he said after a moment. His head canted slightly to one side, as if he was imagining it, sending a fist of need punching into her belly, then clenching tight. "Does it happen on the marble floor, in your half-terrified, half-longing fantasies? Up against the wall beneath the paintings? Sprawled out across the couches, to really settle in and take our time?"

"I don't think anything of the kind." But she did. She really did, and his scalding-hot images didn't help matters, not when she knew how he'd hold her, how he'd tease her and torment her. How he'd take her places she'd never dreamed she could go. "We've shared a bedroom the past two nights and you haven't attacked me. I'm not afraid of you."

His mouth moved into that mocking little crook. "Of course you're not. That's why I've found you sleeping in the guest suite one night and on that sofa in the solarium the next. Because you are so unafraid."

Mattie had no intention of telling him about the nightmares—the screech of tires, that endless singing, that empty stretch of road—that had ripped through every night for as long as she could recall, torn it and her apart. It was why she'd never shared a bed with anyone.

And while she might have realized pretty quickly that first day that fighting with Nicodemus on the topic of separate bedrooms was futile, that didn't mean there weren't ways around it. She'd done what she'd always done before when faced with unacceptable sleeping arrangements, whether here or in boarding school or wherever she found herself along the way: she pretended to sleep where she'd been put, then snuck away to somewhere her inevitably violent awakening wouldn't attract any notice.

"You 'worked'—" and she crooked her fingers in the air to hang quotation marks around that word "—both nights until dawn. What do you care where I slept?"

He studied her the way he did much too often—the way that made her wonder yet again how she'd failed to realize that he'd spent these long years figuring her out while she'd only been focused on avoiding him. And worse, made her remember what it had been like to wake both nights to find herself lifted into his strong arms then carried through the house against the sweet torture of his magnificent chest. *Safe,* a rebellious part of her whispered. Like when he'd placed her back in that huge bed in the master bedroom that he made feel so tiny and so crowded when he slept beside her for an hour or two, his arms around her like he could fight off whatever came their way.

These are not helpful thoughts, she told herself sternly.

"I care that you continue to be disobedient when I've made it fairly clear that there will be consequences for disobedience," he said, so silkily she nearly missed what he'd actually said. "But you should ask yourself why—if

I knew I had to work all this time, and I did—I insisted you sleep in the master bedroom at all."

"If I cared as much about sleeping arrangements as you seem to do," she said icily, "I would have asked you."

"Because I know you far better than you think I do," he answered for her, those dark honey eyes gleaming hard, his voice even darker, even smoother, confirming a whole handful of her worst fears. "And everything with you is easier if it is introduced slowly, and in stages."

She really, really didn't want to think about that, and everything it implied. About their history. About him. About what was going to happen here, between them, if he had his way.

"I'm not a headstrong mustang you can break with a few muttered words and a carrot," she snapped at him. "You're definitely not a cowboy, and this isn't the Wild West."

"I think you should consider the fact that if I was happy to allow you to get naked on a plane, I'm unlikely to stand much on ceremony on my own island, where no pilot or air steward lurks a few feet away," he replied, that voice of his lethal. "If I want you, the fact you're standing outside is hardly going to put me off."

"Thank you," she gritted out. "That's very comforting."

"If you want me to comfort you, you need only ask, Mattie." He paused, his dark eyes searching hers, and that soft thing in them again that would be the undoing of her. "Just ask."

And that was worse. That hint of emotion in his voice, of something like understanding. *Sympathy.* It choked her, black and thick and terrible.

"What if what I need comfort from is you?" she asked, her voice a jagged little bit of sound, hardly there at all with the sea crashing into the rocks below and a few hardy seagulls cartwheeling in the air around them as if it was still summer. It matched that almost-smile he aimed her way, that sent a bolt of something a great deal like sorrow arrowing through her. As if she'd already lost something here.

"Come inside," Nicodemus said again. It wasn't a request.

If you can't be in control, Mattie's father had always said, *you can at least be practical.* So she gathered herself together as best she could. She kept her spine straight and her head high, and she marched through the open glass doors like she was proceeding straight off a plank into shark-infested waters.

He slid the doors closed behind her. Mattie heard the *click* when they shut like a gun to her ear. She walked to the seating area nearest the great windows and sat down in an armchair with great deliberation, so Nicodemus couldn't sit next to her. He watched her, his mouth twitching again as if he could read her mind as easily as breathe, and then went to the bar tucked into a cabinet to the side and poured two flutes of champagne.

"Take this, please," he said when she only glared at the glass he brought over and held out to her.

She felt numb, but she took it, staring at it as if it was poison.

"Eis igían sas," he said. When she frowned up at him, he lifted his champagne in a toast she was certain was mocking. "To your good health."

"I'm not sure good health is anything I should be aspiring to, in my situation," she said crisply. She set the flute down on the vast, glass-topped table before her with a decisive *clink* without so much as tasting it. "It seems to me that a tidy little virus that will carry me off with a minimum of fuss is what I ought to be hoping for. It might be my only escape."

"I'm sorry to tell you that with great wealth comes immediate access to the best physicians across the globe," Nicodemus said, seeming perfectly content to *stand* there, tall and dark and *her husband*. "I'd make certain you were cured."

"Exactly how long am I to be trapped in this marriage?"

"You should have paid better attention earlier. Until death," he said quietly, and there was something in the way he looked at her that made that heavy knot low in her belly flare to life again, hot and needy. Longing and betrayal at once. "Forever."

"*Until death is not the same as forever.*"

"Then yes, Mattie," he said in a mild tone that made her feel like a tantruming toddler. She supposed it was meant to do exactly that. "You may have all the freedom you could possibly desire. In the grave."

"Wonderful." She treated him to a tight, fake smile. "Well. This has been delightful. Every girl dreams of being hurriedly married across the planet from all the people she cares about. And half in a language she doesn't understand. If you'll excuse me, I think I'll take a nap to recover from the thrill of so much fairy-tale glamour at once."

"You've taken quite a few naps since we arrived here." He moved then, draping that absurd body of his on the nearby couch, at an angle to her, and her heart kicked into a higher gear. "I wonder why?"

"Jet lag?" Mattie supplied tartly. It wasn't as if she'd slept during those *naps* she'd claimed she'd needed, of course. She'd been keeping as far away from him as possible.

"Perhaps." His long fingers toyed with the delicate crystal he held, and she remembered, with startling accuracy, the feel of those fingers dancing across the skin at her side, tracing the sweeping lines of her tattoo. "Or perhaps you are merely trying to avoid the consequences of the past ten years, to say nothing of what happened on the flight over."

"You talk a lot about these consequences," Mattie said in as unbothered a tone as she could manage. "But I already feel humiliated. That happens when one is forced into a marriage she doesn't want. What's a little in-flight entertainment on top of that? I hope you filmed the whole thing and are planning to upload it to YouTube. Sixty million page views and a host of vile and insulting comments are about the only thing that could make this any worse."

"That's more your province than mine, I think," he said, his dry tone reminding her of that unfortunate video a "friend" of hers had uploaded when Mattie was twenty-three and very drunk. "I've never graced the internet without my knowledge, as far as I'm aware."

"Do you own the internet, too? Or just every person who might post on it?"

"I'm so pleased," he said after a moment, "that none of this has dulled your sense of drama."

Mattie found that her hands were in fists again, stuck in the voluminous dark gray skirt of the dress that had seemed like such a good idea when she'd packed it in New York, and now felt nothing but childish. Just as he'd accused her of being, directly and indirectly, a thousand times. It made her heart ache and her head pound today.

Being near him made her feel as out of control and panicky as it ever had. As perilously close to losing herself and all those tightly held spiked things she carried in the deepest, darkest part of her. Worse, now, that he'd kept so many of his promises. That he'd won.

That he kept winning.

"Did you send your staff away with that priest?" she asked. Her voice was quieter. More raw. Too telling by far.

And she thought he heard that, because he studied her for a long moment without speaking.

"I did." She didn't understand that particular light in those honeyed dark eyes of his. She didn't want to. "We are very much alone, though there will be deliveries to the dock each morning should you require something. Do you?"

"A ride to Athens?"

His lips crooked. "Other than that."

"I don't know what you want from me."

"You do." He smiled, and she told herself the chill that snaked down her back was fear, not anticipation. Never that. "Everything, Mattie. I want everything, as I've told you from the start."

She shook her head. "That was all a game. A dare stretched out across the years. Stupidity." She broke off and tried to find the right words, or, when that failed, *any* words. "This is different. It's not a game anymore. I don't *want* this, Nicodemus."

He leaned forward to put his empty glass on the table and then sat back again, and she still couldn't get that raggedness inside her under any kind of control. She still couldn't do a thing about that wild red tide that rose inside her, as relentless and unstoppable as he was.

And he simply sat there, unmoved and unbothered, as if everything between them was unfolding according to his plan. She supposed it was, and that made her feel even more trapped, even more hunted, than before.

"I don't believe you," he said, with that remarkable, maddening calm. "But even if I did, it's done."

"I did what you wanted," she gritted out. "I married you. Why can't that be enough?"

Again, that smile, much too knowing. Much too dangerous. "You know why."

Mattie didn't mean to move. She had no intention of doing anything but continuing on as she was and hoping that somehow poked holes in his smooth, impenetrable armor....

But instead, she simply *burst*—reaching out and slapping her full glass of champagne with all of her might and an open hand. It flew through the air, spraying the amber liquid all around and then smashed into pieces on the white marble floor some six feet away.

And for a moment, the only sound was her own harsh breathing and the drumming of her pulse in her ears.

Nicodemus's too-calm gaze tracked the arc of the champagne glass, stayed on the shattered glass rather longer than it should have then finally cut back to her.

"Ah, Mattie," he said. Soft. Lethal. And something like kind, which made it that much worse. It told her exactly how much trouble she was in, on the off chance she couldn't guess. "You really shouldn't have done that."

Nicodemus decided he was enjoying himself, after all.

"You're going to clean that up," he told Mattie, who had her chin set at that mulish angle that he found far more amusing than was wise, and all that murder in her eyes. "But first, of course, there must be punishment."

"Punishment," she repeated, as if she'd never heard the word before.

"It's what happens when one throws temper tantrums," he said. "As you would have realized had your father not shipped you off to stuffy British boarding schools for half your life and treated you with benevolent neglect the rest of the time."

She stiffened, and her lovely, dark eyes flashed with outrage. "You're insane."

Nicodemus smiled and settled back against the couch, lazily at his ease.

"I'm feeling benevolent myself, as this is our wedding day," he told her, injecting a note of magnanimity into his voice, purely to watch the fireworks in her gaze. "So I'll give you a choice. Either you subject yourself to the task of my choosing, or I spank you."

For a moment, she didn't react. Then his words clearly penetrated. She flushed hot. He saw the pulse in her neck leap as she jerked back against her chair.

"You can't *spank* me!" But there was that note in her voice, and that heat in her eyes, and he wondered what images she was playing with in that complicated head of hers. If they matched the ones in his.

"Can't I?"

"You can't simply…do whatever you want!"

"By all means, Mattie, complain to the local authorities." He nodded toward the windows and the sea beyond. "It's a bit of a swim, as I've said, but I'm sure you'll receive a perfectly warm welcome in Libya when you come in with the tide."

"Don't be absurd!" she snapped.

But he could see that she wasn't as sure of herself as she'd been in all their previous encounters, and that amused him more than anything else could have. Perhaps it had dawned on her that for all the years they'd played their game of cat and mouse, she'd relied as much on the fact they were in public while they danced around each other as she had on his restraint. And now they were stranded here, together.

This was his home. His rules. His game.

"Act like a child and I will treat you like one," he told her after a moment, when he thought he could have heard her heart thumping if he'd only stopped to listen. "I'm not your father, Mattie. I'm far more proactive. I'm not going to spoil you on the one hand, ignore you on the other and hope for the best."

A best that had included Mattie's well-photographed "wild phase," which still irritated Nicodemus more than was warranted or, he was aware, fair. A best that had also included making no provision for his own children in the event of his own death. What had Bart been thinking?

"You're not really going to *beat* me." She'd reverted to that bored tone of voice again, but he could see the hectic sparkle in her eyes.

"It's not a beating if you end up begging me for it, I don't think. Certainly not if you enjoy it. Though you can call it that if you like."

"I won't submit to something like that, obviously," she said coolly, though her gaze was anything but. "It's barbaric."

Nicodemus smiled, and he realized it was with actual fondness, which should have terrified him. It should have brought back his history with Arista and all the red flags he'd ignored that first time. But instead, he filed it away and concentrated on the woman before him, whose outrage had thawed the frozen shell she'd been wrapped in since their wedding ceremony. *Another victory,* he thought.

"Is it?" he asked then. "If I reach between your legs, will I find you as desperate for me as you were on that plane? Wet and needy and mine already?"

She did nothing for a long moment but breathe, trembling where she sat, all fists and fury and that sizzling lightning just beneath it, blinding him. Tying him in knots. Making him nothing at all but greedy.

Soon, he promised himself. *It will be soon enough.*

"I'll clean up the glass," Mattie said in a low voice. "But there will be no spanking."

"Not today, then," he said, relaxing back into the sofa. "I understand. Trust takes time."

She looked at him with loathing—or what would have been loathing, had he not been able to see that spark of need in her dark eyes. Not only for sex, he thought—which was one of the reasons she got beneath his skin. All the *more* that lurked in her, that called to him. She got to her feet stiffly and started toward the mess she'd made, and he let her walk a few steps. He doubted she knew how she looked in that dress. Not at all like a widow or a wraith as she'd obviously intended. The gray suited her, made her flashing eyes and glorious hair something like glimpses of clear sky through lovely clouds, and he wondered why any bride wore white, instead. But then, not every bride could possibly look like his.

God help him, the ways he wanted this woman. Only the fact he'd held on to his composure for so long already allowed him to keep doing it.

"Stop," he said when she'd moved far enough into the center of the room, and though she scowled at him when she turned to look back at him, she obeyed. And he liked that as much as if he truly was the barbarian he knew she thought he was. "Stand right there."

He simply studied her, watching as her scowl deepened. And then, moments later, as she shifted from one foot to the other, in some mixture of impatience and anxiety, and he wanted to taste both.

"What now?" she asked tightly. "Aren't menial chores and threats of physical abuse enough for one day?"

"Don't move," he ordered her. "I told you there were two options. And if you are as adamantly opposed to my spanking you as you've claimed, that means you've chosen the other by default."

"Is it really necessary to play these dictatorial games,

Nicodemus?" she asked, and there was something more than her usual provocation in her voice then. Something real. Raw.

"I don't know. I asked myself a similar question many times over the past ten years. Do you have an answer?"

"I wasn't playing games. I didn't want you. I don't."

"That's what I thought you'd say." He smiled. "You seem very fidgety, Mattie. Almost nervous."

"You obviously want me to be nervous," she snapped.

"Perhaps you should be. Perhaps it's past time you took this seriously."

And he could see that she was as nervous as he could hope. Finally. But it wasn't as simple as nerves. There was that longing beneath, that need. And that other, electric current that looked a great deal like anticipation.

He'd spent a long time learning how to read this woman. It was finally paying off.

"You used to tell me how much you liked to dance," he said when he could see it had built in her to a fever pitch, and he wasn't sure what she'd do next. "Do you remember? Every time you explained to me why it was necessary for you to spend *quite* so much time falling in and out of clubs."

She clenched her hands tight, then opened them.

"Yes." He hardly recognized her voice when she finally spoke. "I like dancing. Is that another manufactured crime you can claim you need to punish me for?"

"Then dance." It was a dare. A command. He waved a hand, taking in the vast, empty room, nothing in it or the whole villa but the two of them and this bright, greedy thing that grew tighter between them with every breath. "For me."

"I...what?"

But she swayed where she stood, in unconscious obedience, and it sent a spike of pure need straight through him, deep and hard. She might not know how much and how deeply she wanted him. She might not be able to admit it. But Nicodemus knew. He'd known since that very first dance they'd shared all those years ago now.

How much different would all of this be—would *they* be, he wondered, if she'd allowed him to claim her then? If she hadn't led him on this merry chase across the years?

"Pretend," he invited her, and it was as if the space between them shrank. Disappeared. "Pretend you want me so much it's like a fist in your gut, making it hard to breathe. Pretend you desire me almost as much as you fear me, like a terrible flu you worry might carry you off. Pretend you can claim a little bit of your power this way, by beguiling me and seducing me." His gaze was hard on hers, the way he wished his hands were. "Do it well enough, my sweet little wife, and perhaps you won't be pretending. Do it better than that, and perhaps we won't need to call any of this *punishment,* after all."

CHAPTER FIVE

INSTEAD, MATTIE FLED.

She ran through the sun-bathed halls of the villa, past the awe-inspiring paintings she refused to look at too closely for fear they would tell her things about their owner she didn't wish to know. She ran all the way to the master bedroom and that huge bed she didn't want to share with him, and then she locked herself in the bathroom.

Like a child. Again.

And then she waited there, her heart pounding so hard she could feel its staccato rhythm when she swallowed, for Nicodemus to storm in on her. For him to pound on the door, rage and shout on the other side, even break it down before him—

But he did none of those things. She couldn't even tell if he'd followed her wild dash through the house or if he was still sitting where she'd left him, that harshly seductive mouth of his crooked to one side and his low voice urging her on.

Pretend you desire me almost as much as you fear me.

Mattie didn't have to pretend when it came to Nicodemus, and she was terribly afraid he knew that, the way he seemed to know everything else.

She still didn't understand *how* he knew. How he'd always known.

The shadows lengthened. The bathtub was a grand affair, set high on its own dais with a wide window facing the slumberous expanse of the sea, and Mattie curled up there, taking an austere sort of comfort from the rigid porcelain beneath her. She watched the sun sink toward the horizon, then disappear in a blaze of brilliant reds and oranges. She watched the stars come out, only a few as twilight stole the bright colors of the sunset away, then too many to count as nighttime fell in earnest.

She fell asleep eventually, then woke in her usual state of tumult and desperation, the nightmare clinging to her as she tried to fight her way free of its sinewy grip. The crash. The horror. The hours trapped in that backseat with her face pressed into the leather and Chase holding her there, both of them shaking—

Mattie wiped her eyes, waited for the same shaking to pass in the present, then fell back asleep.

And when she woke in the morning, the light was pouring in, dazzling her, so it took her a few critical moments to realize that she was no longer in the bathtub. She was in the big bed in the master bedroom and Nicodemus—*her husband*—was stretched out beside her.

Just like every morning since they'd arrived here, only this time, Mattie had no memory of him carrying her from the bathtub to the bed. She could remember nothing but the nightmare. How had he moved her without her knowledge? Had she told him the truth while she slept? And what else had happened that she couldn't recall?

Mattie jackknifed to sitting position, tearing back the covers to make sure she was still wearing her sour version of a wedding dress. She made no attempt to hide her sigh of relief when she discovered it was still on, as were the bra and panties she'd worn beneath.

"Let me assure you," Nicodemus said in that low,

amused voice of his that seemed to wind through her, setting her alight, especially when it sounded as sleepy and as *close* as it did just then. "If anything of that nature had happened, after all these years, you would not have to check."

She swallowed, feeling much more fragile than she should have. She cast around for her outrage, her fury—but there was only that same old panic he always kicked up in her. Simmering there inside her, more mellow, somehow. Or more resigned.

Almost as if it wasn't panic at all, but something else entirely.

"So I am to have no privacy whatsoever," she said, her gaze trained on her lap. The yards and yards of gray that had failed to protect her.

"I apologize," he said in that arid way of his that was no apology at all. That mocked the very notion of an apology. "Were you comfortable in the bathtub? My mistake. You looked cold and underfed. And I think you were having a nightmare."

Mattie went cold. Her mind cleared. No one had ever been near her during one of her nightmares, and she certainly couldn't let it happen again. What if she told him what had happened? What if he knew what she'd done?

She felt ill at the very idea and didn't want to think about the contradiction there.

"No privacy," she said crisply, as if reading off a list. "Spankings presented as reasonable resolutions to conflicts. Threats issued. Told to dance for your pleasure and to perform chores at your command." She stared at him. "You'll understand if somehow, I found the bathtub more inviting."

"You made a mess, princess." His dark eyes probed hers, and for once she couldn't find any laughter lurking there, only that implacable iron that made her shake down deep inside, and she couldn't lie to herself and pretend it was fear. It wasn't. "I had every intention of making sure you cleaned it up."

"Oh, right," she replied. "You mean that in the broader sense, I gather. I'm supposed to spend this sick joke of a marriage paying penance for not racing into it sooner? That's the mess I made?"

He was quiet, and that wasn't any good. It allowed Mattie time—and she didn't want time. The morning sun spilled over him like a radiant, clinging lover, bathing his perfect form in too much light to bear. The trouble was—had always been—he was flawless. He wore nothing but a low-slung pair of boxer briefs this morning, and in truth, he had nothing to hide. Every inch of him was stunning. The taut, lean muscles in his arms, his flat pectorals and ridged abdomen, those tough, strong thighs. He was dusted with dark hair that thickened and then disappeared beneath his boxer briefs, and she told herself she didn't notice the rest of him.

Certainly not the part of him that stood ready, huge and impatient and barely contained, right where she absolutely refused to look.

"You've been crying," he said gruffly, and for a dazed moment she didn't understand what he meant. He reached over and ran a thumb beneath one of her eyes and she jerked her head away. "Why?"

She blinked, oddly off balance. "I can think of a thousand reasons."

"Pick the one that's true," he suggested, still in that rough way that, perversely, made her imagine he cared. She hated that she wished he did.

And Mattie couldn't tell him the truth. Her nightmares were her business—and anyway, she told herself, he didn't really care, no matter that note in his voice. He only wanted to make certain she had nowhere to hide.

"It doesn't matter what I say." She shifted away from him. "You've already decided that I'm a liar. You decided it a hundred years ago, so why should I bother saying a word?"

"Or you could try not lying."

He rolled toward her, closing the distance she'd put between them and propping himself up on one elbow, and she could have done without that play of all his beautiful muscles beneath his sleek skin, *right there* in front of her. She could have done without the unearned, unwanted, terrible intimacy of this. It felt like a great and awful weight, pressing down hard on her chest, like he was holding her down with all his obvious strength when what was far, far worse was that he didn't have to.

"I've been bartered off to save a company, as if I were nothing more than a collection of shares in human form," she said instead of any of the other things she could have said. "A spreadsheet with legs. Anyone would shed a few tears."

But his dark eyes only lit up with all that golden amusement, sending a shiver straight through her.

"This could all have been very different," he said lazily. "If you had married me the first time I asked, I would have treated you like you were made of spun glass, not shares. I would have worshipped the ground you walked upon. Bent the whole world before you, to service your every whim."

Worried that if she tried to get out of the bed he'd reach over and stop her, which would involve touching her—and she had no idea what she'd do then—Mattie pushed herself back until she was leaning against the headboard, curled her knees beneath her and tried to stare him down.

"I was eighteen," she said, not sure where that urgency in her voice came from when she'd wanted to match his nonchalance. "I was a kid. I had no business thinking about getting married and you shouldn't have asked. The only reason you *did* ask was because you wanted an in with my father. Let's not pretend your heart was involved, Nicodemus. It was your wallet first and then, when I refused you repeatedly, your pride. It still is."

He reached over and pulled the hem of her dress between his fingers, and she bit back the rebuke that hovered on her tongue. What did it matter if he touched her clothes? There were far worse places he could put those clever fingers of his, and she knew that all too well now.

"Perhaps I simply wanted a Whitaker as my wife, and all the shares and spreadsheets that go along with that. Sadly, you are the only one available."

"I'm told I have distant cousins in Aberystwyth. I'm sure one of them would have suited you fine." She scowled at him when he laughed. "And I don't think you should try to get too much mileage from the term *wife*."

He shook his head at her as if he knew exactly where she was going with that. "Did you knock yourself on the head in the bath? That was an actual wedding yesterday. All very legal, I assure you."

"That might have been a wedding, but this isn't a real marriage," she insisted, surprised to hear how loud her voice sounded in all that dizzy Greek sunshine that filled the room. "In the real world, marriages don't involve threats and promises of high-ranking positions in corporations as some kind of twisted dowry. You're going to be COO and President of Whitaker Industries, Nicodemus. Those are the titles you care about. *Husband* and *wife* are just words."

He moved then. He reached over and hauled her to him, rolling with her until she was beneath him, he was pressed between her thighs and braced above her, and she could do nothing at all but gape up at him.

She thought she was having a heart attack, but it kept *pounding* like that, jarring and huge and whole-bodied, and it took her long, shuddering moments to realize that this *was* living through it. That it only felt like it was killing her.

That if it killed her, that might be better, because everything that was happening to her right now—everything he was *doing* to her—she was all too aware he could *see*.

"Does this feel real, Mattie?" he asked roughly, his gaze on her mouth. "Marital enough for you? *Real?* Because neither your father nor your brother are in this room. It's only me and you and your heart has gone mad inside your chest. I can feel it."

"That's panic," she threw at him. "And a little bit of revulsion."

But she made no attempt to fight him off. No attempt to roll out from under him, or to dislodge the sleek, solid weight of him from on top of her, from that place where he rested against her as if they were already joined. And she knew, somehow, that if she'd tried any of that, he'd have let her go at once. She didn't try.

You can't let this happen! cried that voice inside of her, the way it always did—but this time, she knew on some deep, feminine level she'd never accessed before, was for completely different reasons.

This wasn't some overeager boyfriend she had to placate and put off. This was Nicodemus.

This was *Nicodemus* and she couldn't even manage to pull her gaze away from his. And that profound failure to act told her things she didn't want to know about herself—that and what felt like a slow-motion detonation from that molten-hot place between her legs outward, making her burn from her navel to her fingernails. Making her nothing but heat and wonder and that thing she liked to tell herself was fear. Pounding, driving, consuming fear that wasn't *fear* at all.

Nicodemus did nothing but gaze down at her, fierce and demanding and still. And Mattie wasn't afraid of him the way she knew she should have been, because *she* was the one who closed the distance between them. *She* lifted her lips toward his. *She* found she was begging with every part of her except her voice—

"First you must ask," he told her, his gaze a dark fire and his voice like gravel. "Out loud, so there can be no mistake."

"Ask?" She hardly understood what he'd said, much less what she'd repeated. As if she'd never heard the word in her life. And all she could see was that beautiful, harsh mouth of his, bold and hard and so deliciously close to hers—

"I'd prefer it if you begged," he said, low and rough and needy, but absolute. Implacable. "But if you ask nicely, I'll let it slide. Just this once."

And then there was a very long moment where Mattie couldn't think of a single reason why she didn't do exactly that. Not one single reason.

She opened her mouth—but then reality asserted itself inside her, blinding and brilliant, bringing with it a kind of desperate reason, and she didn't care if he saw all of it in her eyes. Intimacy with this man meant losing herself first, and then losing him. She'd known that for years. She knew it the way she knew he'd wanted her, always. Deep in her bones. Immutable and irreversible. A simple, searing truth.

"I'm not going to ask you nicely," she promised him, though her voice shook. "And I'm certainly not going to beg. That might be your conception of marriage, but it certainly isn't mine."

"I thought this wasn't a real marriage," he murmured,

all silk and fire. "No need to fight for equality in a sham like this, is there? Just surrender, Mattie. I promise you, you'll like it."

She believed him. That was why she scowled at him again. Harder.

"No begging," she snapped. "Unless you plan to get down on your knees and try it yourself?"

His hard mouth crooked. "I hope you're prepared to suffer." He was so big, hard and gorgeous and almost entirely naked as he pressed her to the bed yet kept the bulk of his weight on his arms on either side of her, as if he was the only thing protecting her from what they both wanted. "Because that's the only way I'll touch you again."

"You're touching me now, I can't help but notice."

"Splitting hairs won't take the ache away, Mattie," he all but crooned at her, as if he knew how badly she already did. As if he could *see* all the ways she longed for him. "It will only draw this out."

He laughed, and it was that same dark victor's laugh, but this time it rolled through her differently. Because his mouth was so close to hers, maybe. It swept inside her like an inexorable wave, and she didn't know if she wanted to weep or scream or betray herself entirely and beg the way he wanted her to do.

Anything to get him to touch her again without her having to ask—without her having to thereby prove that he was right about her.

She hated herself for that twisted little thought.

"Let me go," she whispered then, furious at both of them, but he only laughed again, in exactly the same way.

"I don't know why, when you obviously want me as badly as I want you, you go to these lengths to deny it. But none of that matters."

"Because you've seen the error of your ways and are

setting me free from this absurd pseudo-marriage?" she asked with all the bravado she wished she felt.

He leaned in and nipped at the soft place beneath her chin, punishment and seduction at once, and Mattie could do nothing but jolt and then shudder. Showing him too much, she understood. Proving herself the liar he already thought she was.

The liar she'd proved herself to be again and again and again. Every time he touched her, she lied.

"Pick a new strategy, Mattie," he told her, and then moved up and off her in a breathtakingly smooth shift of athletic grace, giving her an unwanted object lesson in all of that divine, stunning strength of his. "The problem with this one is that I'm bored with it."

"Heaven forbid I *bore* you," she snapped out. "You've blackmailed me, threatened me and manhandled me into this sham of a marriage—but all of that pales in comparison to *boring* you. A fate worse than death!"

"You dance too close to the edge again and again," he said as if she hadn't spoken. "You treat me to your sharp tongue whenever you feel like it, you run and hide when I return the favor, then you repeat the pattern ad nauseam. All without any consequences, until now."

Nicodemus was standing then, by the side of the bed with the morning sun casting his face in shadow, but she had no trouble seeing that gleam of honey in his gaze. That dark *knowing* thing behind it. She felt it everywhere.

Worse than his mouth on her. Deeper. Infinitely more destructive.

"Without consequences?" she asked, her voice shakier than she liked. She raised up her hand with its heavy rings. "What do you call this?"

His mouth curved. "I can do this for another decade if I have to, and I'll still win. It's entirely up to you."

* * *

He was right. She was going about this all wrong.

Mattie came to that conclusion in a near-violent rush while she stood in the spacious shower, her hands braced against the lovingly crafted stone wall and her head tipped back, letting the water fall down on her like rain. She'd spent all this time treating Nicodemus like he was an unfightable force of nature, some impossibly powerful creature made of myth and magic, when the truth was he was a man.

Just a man, like all the rest.

And when she put her wildly beating heart aside, when she shoved off the things he made her feel against her will and the very real fear that she was already coming undone because of him, she knew that she'd been playing this the wrong way from the start. Because he'd taken her breath away when she was still eighteen without even trying, and she'd forgotten the simple truth she'd known even then: men were easy.

Men were creatures of simple needs and impulses that could be directed and finessed and yes, used. Fathers, brothers, boyfriends—it was the same thing, really, if different tools. Mattie had learned that a long time ago in the glare of cameras usually wielded by men, none of whom were immune to the judicious application of a little bit of feminine charm. It was easy to flirt or flatter her way out of trouble, to misdirect, to indulge in a little sleight of hand. It was easy to change the conversation from the things she didn't wish to give up to other things she didn't much mind surrendering.

Mattie hadn't been able to do much about her guilt. But a little bit of charm had gone a long way with Big Bart, especially because she'd been willing to move back to the States and under his thumb. And if she could charm her father, who she'd hurt so terribly twenty years ago, she knew she could charm anyone.

If she wanted to gain back any of the ground she'd lost in these explosive few days, Mattie needed to treat Nicodemus like any other man she'd ever known. Mortal. Manageable.

She started by dressing for him.

Mattie tried to remember every single thing he'd ever said to her about her appearance—all of it negative, generally, and delivered in that withering tone of his—and dress around it. She ended up in a soft, cocoa-colored cashmere sweater that was airy enough for the Greek sun and warm enough for the hint of autumn chill beneath it. She layered it over a pair of white trousers and left her feet bare in a touch of feminine vulnerability. She twisted her hair back into a casual chignon with a few strands left loose, and when she was done she looked a good deal more like the kind of woman Nicodemus had always seemed to think she should have been than she usually did. The kind of woman she might have been naturally had she not felt compelled to dress in dark, moody colors and clothes he found inelegant to convey her defiance every time she saw him.

And then she squared her shoulders, reminded herself how many times she'd done something like this before when she'd needed to appease one of her boyfriends who'd grown too demanding and went to find him.

He was only a man, she reminded herself again as she moved through the villa. No matter how he made her feel. No matter that he'd somehow managed to make her forget herself completely almost every time he touched her. No matter that he'd taken a piece of her no one else ever had.

None of that mattered. She had to even this playing field, or she'd disappear.

He sat with his laptop at the gleaming counter in the

expansive, light-filled kitchen on the lower level of the villa, a Greek coffee steaming at his elbow. She hesitated in the doorway, assuming he'd heard her approach the way he always had before, though he didn't glance her way.

And for a moment, she forgot about her strategies and her plans. She forgot what he was or wasn't. What she could or couldn't do. Because he was staring off into space with an unguarded, wholly un-Nicodemus-like expression on his face. Not fierce, not hard. Not myth or magic.

She couldn't categorize it. She didn't recognize it.

Mattie only knew it made her throat feel too tight.

But then it was gone as if it had never been, and all the dark steel she recognized as pure Nicodemus returned. He shifted slightly in the high stool, frowning at the screen before him.

"Has the funeral ended so soon?" he asked mildly enough, making her wonder exactly when he'd seen her there in the arched doorway when he still didn't bother to look her way. "I expected to see you draped in shrouds and mantillas for at least the next week."

"I suppose I had that coming," she agreed in a soft voice, and that made him look up and focus on her, those dark eyes narrowing immediately.

He's just a man, she reminded herself as that look seared into her. *He can't read a single thing in you unless you let him. He doesn't have the slightest idea what you dream about.*

And if she redirected his attention, he never would.

She walked into the kitchen as if she was unaware of that faint frown between his eyes and settled herself gingerly at the counter with him. Not across from him as she would have done before, but on the stool next to his, the way she would have done if he was someone else. *Right* next to his, and it was hard—almost too hard—to keep her head in this game instead of losing her cool.

He was so big, so solid. Sleek and fierce and this close to him, she felt him—all that dark, restless power, all his stark ruthlessness—like an electric hum beneath her own skin.

"Still," she continued in the same soft voice once she was seated, ignoring all the rest, "I thought you'd appreciate that I've attempted to dress more to your taste."

He trained his simmering dark gaze on her, and she felt simultaneously very small and very exposed. Instead of striking out, she let it show. Men liked softness and small, helpless things. They liked to feel large and mighty. She'd watched this same scene play out a hundred times.

He is the same as all the rest, she chanted to herself, like that could make it so.

"By that I assume you mean that I should applaud the fact you're actually wearing something attractive?" Nicodemus asked silkily. "Rather than displaying your wares to any and all who venture near or wrapping yourself in the sartorial equivalent of a cocoon? What a gift, indeed."

It actually hurt to gulp back the sharp retort that appeared on her tongue, but Mattie did it. Men were all about pride and fury. And they were all brought low by lust. Nicodemus was no different, despite the fact his barbs struck harder. Deeper than anyone else's ever had.

"Nicodemus," she said, as calmly as she could. "Maybe we can stop all of this. Maybe we can just…talk."

"Talk." He shook his head as if amazed. Then he shut his laptop with a quiet slap that made her think of ferocity restrained. "You want to *talk.* All these years later."

She shrugged and let her sweater slide down one shoulder as she did. "I want to start over."

His gaze moved over the exposed curve of her shoulder,

then he aimed it at the ceiling and made a sound that was somewhere between exasperation and laughter. He crossed his arms over his broad chest—happily covered in a soft shirt now, though with too many buttons left undone for her peace of mind—and regarded her with that darkly honeyed gleam in his eyes that promised nothing but trouble.

"Let me guess what this is. You think that you can charm me into dropping my guard with you, because your usual games and stunts aren't working." He sighed. "And I've never seen your charm except from a distance, and always aimed toward others, so who knows? This might be an excellent plan."

Mattie ordered herself to breathe. To think before she spoke. To *stay calm*—because God knew she'd spent ten years completely out of control around this man, and what had that ever gotten her? Married against her will and trapped on an island in the middle of nowhere, that was what.

Adapt or die, she snapped at herself. *Right now.*

"I want to get to know you," she said, and she even smiled. It was easy if she simply *pretended*, as he'd suggested. Though Mattie doubted he'd intended that she should pretend he was someone else. Someone far less… *him.*

His gaze was far too shrewd. "Whatever for, I wonder?"

She turned toward him and extended her hands out in front of her, making sure she almost touched him—but didn't. It was a gesture of supplication. Of something like surrender.

"Because there's no one here but you and me, Nicodemus, and as you've pointed out several times, you know me already. I think it's time I stop fighting this and return the favor, don't you?"

He shifted in his stool so that he was more standing than

sitting, and facing her completely. He was so tall. Dark and beautiful, and she had to do this. She had to wield the only weapon she had or he'd tear her wide open, sift through her hidden places and see everything. She had to put them back on common ground—any common ground at all—or she'd lose herself. For good.

And she couldn't risk him finding out the truth.

"What do you want, Mattie?" he asked softly.

You on a platter, she thought, but did not say. She would get there. She could wreck him, too. She was sure of it. Chemistry went both ways, surely.

She took a deep, ragged breath that she didn't have to fake, and then she reached over and put her hands on his rock-hard thighs. He didn't appear to move at all, but she felt him tense beneath her. And he was so hard. So absurdly perfect in every way it made her feel something like drunk.

"I'll ask you again," he said, in a voice gone fierce and hot and lethal. "What do you want?"

She slipped from her stool and stood too close to him. Not quite leaning into him, but not losing contact with him, either. Then she slid her hands to the waistband of his trousers and felt him turn to stone beneath her palms.

"If you truly did fall and hit your head, you should tell me now," he said in that dry way of his that she was afraid would be the death of her, because he might make her laugh and that would make this all much more difficult. Much more *real*. "Before I assume the worst and have you treated for a concussion."

And Mattie understood, then, in a sudden flash that made her wonder how she'd missed it before, that she had far more power here than she'd imagined. That he was as off balance as she was. That perhaps he always had been, and she'd never noticed. She'd never *allowed* herself to notice. She told herself she could use that—and ignored the sudden hollow place in the vicinity of her chest.

She didn't speak. She shifted closer and let her hands drift down, until she could cup the bold length of him through the fabric of his trousers. He didn't groan. He didn't push her away. But he was hot—*so hot*—and he let out a very long breath as if it hurt him.

As if she did.

"Mattie." His voice was brutal. Clipped and hard. His hands came up to wrap around her upper arms, but he didn't move her off him. And his touch was gentle, belying the tension she could feel in every part of him. "What the hell are you doing?"

She tilted her head back and looked up at him through her lashes, testing the length of him against one palm while he shook slightly, very slightly, and scowled back at her.

"I don't know," she told him.

But she did know. She'd never felt anything quite like this before, like every time she stroked him and felt him tense, the same shudder he fought to conceal worked its way through her. She felt molten, wild. And she'd hardly done anything yet.

She thought he was at the edge of his control and she didn't know what might happen if he tipped over, so she moved quickly. She unzipped his trousers and reached inside, freeing him, holding him in her hands at last. *At last.* He was velvet and steel. Hot and silken to the touch, and so powerfully male it was difficult to breathe.

And she didn't know who was shaking more at that point, her or him.

That was as terrifying as it was thrilling, and she didn't want to examine it. His eyes were so dark now they looked like the small hours of a long night, and he was muttering in Greek, almost beneath his breath, oaths and invocations. Curses and prayers, if the look on his face was any guide.

"Mattie." Like her name was another curse, a heftier one.

She sank down to her knees, never breaking eye contact with him, never letting go. He was big and heavy everywhere, hotter than should have been possible, and she forgot that this was supposed to be a weapon. *Her* weapon. She forgot what game she was playing, or why. She wanted to taste him so badly she thought she'd do anything, say anything—

"What is this?" he asked, his accent heavier than she'd ever heard it, his voice thick, but he didn't push her away. He didn't stop her. His chest was rising and falling too fast to mistake, and the sight made her feel almost as needy, almost as molten bright and greedy, as he'd made her feel with his mouth.

"An apology," she whispered, which wasn't what she'd meant to say and had more truth in it than she liked, and so before she could think about it or betray herself further she leaned forward and took him deep into her mouth.

CHAPTER SIX

HE WAS DYING.

Or dreaming—but Nicodemus had had this dream a hundred times before or more, and it had never, ever been this good. *Never*.

Mattie's mouth was so hot, her tongue so delicate and wicked at once as she licked him and tasted him. Tracing patterns, then taking the whole of him deep inside. She moved as she knelt there before him, the culmination of a thousand fantasies and far better than any of them, rocking slightly as if she really was dancing for him, at last, and he died.

Again and again, he died, and she kept going.

Nicodemus was no fool. This kind of sudden reversal made no sense, especially not from Mattie. But he couldn't seem to care about that.

And it would take a far better man than he was to do anything about it now.

He sunk his fingers deep in her thick hair, loosely holding on to her as she tormented him, as she worshipped him. Letting her build the fire in him higher and higher, letting her take him, letting her have him any way she pleased.

Mine, he thought with every stroke of her wicked tongue. *Finally mine*.

And when he fell off the side of the earth and shattered

into a thousand pieces, he shouted out the glory of it in words he knew she couldn't understand.

When he opened his eyes she was still on her knees before him, those marvelous eyes big and wide and focused only on him. Another trillion dreams shattered by a far better reality, he thought. Her lush mouth was swollen slightly, and there was that flush across her cheeks that told him she was as affected by this as he was. For a moment he only stared at her, this woman who had haunted him for so long.

This woman he still didn't understand at all.

Then Nicodemus tucked himself away and zipped up his trousers, the fire still roaring inside him. He wanted to haul her to her feet and bend her over the counter. He wanted to lick his way into her heat again, then lose himself in it, until they were both as shattered as that glass she'd thrown.

He wanted all of her. Here, now.

But he'd waited so long—and he couldn't trust her sudden capitulation. He reached down and slid his hand along her jaw, holding the side of her face, the soft satin of her cheek warm against his palm. Something like tenderness, but with so many lies between them.

Always the lies. Always so many damned lies.

"I think I like you kneeling, princess," he said, not wanting to face that yet. "I may make it a daily requirement."

She didn't like that. He could feel it in the way she quivered, could see it in the way her pretty dark eyes narrowed. But she didn't throw something back at him the way he could see she wanted to do. She stayed there, passive and accommodating and not at all the Mattie he knew.

Not that he was complaining. Not at the moment. Not when he was still breathing hard.

"Wasn't that…okay?" she asked, with breathy concern.

But he could see the calculation in her eyes, and it helped bring him back to reality.

"You don't listen," he told her coolly. "I've told you before—I don't care how I have you. I'm not that proud. If you want to kneel down before me and pretend it's an apology instead of a manipulation, I won't stop you." He shrugged. "I didn't."

He was impressed with how she held herself so still. "I don't know what you mean."

"This kind of about-face would be suspicious in anyone, but is especially so in you." She started to move, and he shook his head, made his voice harsh. "Stay where you are."

"So you can indulge your domination fantasies?" She rolled her eyes. "No, thank you."

"This is not a fantasy." He smiled, enjoying the fury in her gaze because that was the *real* Mattie behind whatever sugar-coated, undeniably hot game she was playing out. "This is a fact."

He was fascinated by the way her face changed, one emotion after the next and none readable. Eventually, her shoulders dropped. She let go of the ripe tension drawing her body so tight, blowing it out in a long sigh that drew his attention back to her mouth, which he knew, now, could make him her slave. Easily. And then she smiled at him in that way she had before, so that the exquisite little dent beside her mouth revealed itself anew.

As if she was made entirely of sunshine and sweetness.

He didn't believe it, of course. But it made that heat flare again inside him, pooling in his groin with as much force and need and hunger as if he'd never let her use her mouth on him in the first place. As if he'd never found such sweet release.

"I'm sorry," she murmured. "You make me feel—" She

shook her head, as if she couldn't bring herself to name it. "I don't know how to react to it."

"That may be the most honest thing you've ever said to me." Her hair had tumbled down from the little twist she'd put it in, thanks to his hands and the madness of the way she'd brought him over the edge like that, and he brushed the silken mass of it back from her face. "But I doubt very much that's why you're saying it."

"Fine." She settled, relaxing her bottom on her feet, looking less like she was kneeling and more like she happened to be doing some kind of yoga near him. "You're the expert on me, or so you keep telling me. So what terrible, underhanded reasons do I have for doing what I just did? Maybe you can explain why you did the exact same thing to me on the plane. Will our reasons be the same?" Her mouth curved, challenging him. "Or will you decide, the way you always seem to do, that I'm devious and motivated only by plots and schemes and deceit while you— and only you—are nobly called to action by nothing more than the purity of your intentions?"

"I might be less sarcastic, were I on my knees," Nicodemus observed.

That curve in her mouth deepened, her eyes were bittersweet chocolate with that blue besides and still seemed like sunlight next to the glossy midnight fall of her hair, and he knew that this could go on forever. That it would.

It made him inexpressibly sad.

They'd been sniping at each other for a decade, and there was no end in sight. Playing power games, raising the stakes. He'd forced this marriage and she'd only today touched him for the first time entirely of her own volition—and not, he understood and hated that he did, because she'd been overcome with the longing to do so.

He'd told her he didn't care how she came to him, and

on some level, that was true. But it was also true that there was a restlessness in him, like an uneasy winter wind, and a howling expanse inside that he didn't want to admit was there.

Finally, everything was exactly how he wanted it. Everything was in its rightful place. He had every single thing he'd ever desired—and yet this was still nothing more than an echoing, cavernous house filled with *things*. The world in his pocket, the woman of his dreams at his feet with his rings on her finger, and he was still as entirely and utterly alone as when he'd realized what Arista really was all those years ago. What she'd really wanted from a low class man with high class aspirations and too much money too fast.

How was this any different?

He realized, then, the depths of the fantasy he'd built up around Mattie Whitaker. The things he'd imagined she could do, the magic she could work, and why? Because she'd been the prettiest thing he'd ever seen when he was twenty-six and so far away from the ugly little place he'd come from. Because, as she'd accused him, he'd wanted that access to her father and to Whitaker Industries. Because he'd wanted *her* and had convinced himself that he'd already learned his lesson with Arista. That he'd never repeat those mistakes.

Nicodemus was, as he had always been, the king of the damned. A lie his father had told and nothing more. And the worst part was that he knew he wouldn't change a thing he'd done to get here. Not one thing. Not even this.

Especially not this.

"Are we going to stare at each other forever?" Mattie asked, her voice easy but those dark eyes of hers intense. "Or is it that you don't have an answer?"

"I have an answer." He thought he sounded far smokier,

darker, all the way through, but she didn't seem to notice any difference, and why would she? She didn't know him. No one ever had, and he understood then that no one ever would. Especially not this woman he'd made his wife, a word she'd claimed was meaningless, anyway. He believed her. Finally, he believed her. "I doubt you'd like it."

Nicodemus dropped his hand from her face and when she rose to her feet in a lithe sort of ripple that made all sense desert him for a beat of his heart, then another, he didn't object. She reached over and helped herself to his coffee, swirling the traditionally thick mixture around in the cup before taking a dainty sip.

"This is about control, isn't it?" she asked. But it wasn't really a question, and he found he was preoccupied with the fact that the soft, airy sweater she wore matched the darker parts of her eyes. "You're obsessed with making sure I don't have any."

"No," he said. He wanted to be the coffee cup she pressed to her lips. He wanted to lick the little bit of moisture away when she lowered it. He wanted her to *want* him, and not because she thought she could leverage it. Maybe that was all he'd ever wanted. More fool, him. It was Arista all over again, and he wasn't twenty any longer. He had no excuse this time. "This is about lies. It always is. And I'm afraid you've miscalculated."

She raised her eyebrows at him, but didn't speak, not even when he reached over and traced a path along her delicate jaw, over that little dent that made him foolish with longing, then on down the elegant line of the aristocratic neck she'd inherited from her titled English mother. Then he found his way along the collarbone that led to her exposed shoulder. Her skin was so soft, so warm. She was still so pretty, as gleaming and lovely in his house as in her father's.

And she was no more than what he'd made her inside his own head. A stranger with a perfect face. One more critical mistake in a long line of them.

Another damned lie and this one all the worse because he'd told it to himself. For years.

"I've known for a long time that everything you said to me was untrue," he said after a moment, and he wasn't playing up that dark note in his voice then, like grief. That was what this was. What he'd lost. "But your body, I believed. I told myself it whispered the truth no matter what you said."

The more dramatic papers claimed she'd lured him into this marriage, that she was a siren who'd enslaved him with her infamous charms, that she was her brother's instrument sent to bring him to heel. He watched her now and wished that any of that were true. That he could fool himself for a little bit longer.

"My body and I are not separate entities," she said, grittier than whatever too-sweet voice she'd been using, but at least that was real. At least that was *her*.

"And now I know it," he said quietly. He dropped his hand and stepped back, away from her, the way he should have done when she'd come to him in the first place. The way he should have done ten years ago when he'd found himself drawn to yet another pointless, pretty little heiress who would never do anything but look down her nose at him. "Which means there's not a single thing about you I can believe, Mattie. And from this moment forward, I promise you, I won't."

That shouldn't have hurt her, given how deliberately she'd played out this scene, and it certainly shouldn't have sat on him the way it did, so heavy and dark he thought it might crush him, but there was no mistaking the ravaged look on her face then.

"I wouldn't have—" She stopped, and he got the impression she'd surprised herself by speaking. "Nicodemus, if I didn't want—"

But she didn't finish. Her expression was equal parts misery and resignation. What he would have called longing, before, when he was still clinging to all his fantasies. When he'd still imagined that this was a game he could win.

That she was.

"Nothing's changed," he said . "I finally see this for what it is."

"A mess?" she supplied bitterly, and he smiled.

"Just another lie," he told her. And he'd had his fill of them so long ago, hadn't he? How had he done this to himself? "But it's our lie, Mattie, and there's no escaping it now."

He knew he had to leave her there in the kitchen before he made himself a liar, too. Before he forgot what he was doing and lost himself in her, instead, that gorgeous deception she'd offered on her knees with a smile. That marvelous deceit he wanted to believe more than he wanted his next breath.

More than he wanted anything.

Nicodemus didn't know how he made himself walk away. Only that he did.

"If I had known that you planned to work through our honeymoon, such as it is," Mattie said in a very bored tone, lifting her gaze from the tablet computer, where their wedding pictures were splashed across all the tabloids, and glared at Nicodemus's profile as if it was *his* fault she looked besotted and in love in every one of them, "I might have brought my own along."

Nicodemus had his laptop open before him on the glass-topped table between them, his smartphone in his hand,

and he didn't bother to look over at her. As if they'd been unhappily married for years, Mattie thought darkly.

"Your work?" he asked, perfectly politely. "I was unaware that you had more than a passing acquaintance with the term."

And that right there was the problem. He'd been nothing but *polite* since that scene in his kitchen almost a week ago now. Nicodemus was scrupulously courteous. Unerringly distant. And that gleaming thing she'd taken entirely for granted, she only realized now that she couldn't see it, was gone from those dark eyes of his.

He insisted she sit with him. Sleep in that bed with him whenever he was in it. Eat all her meals with him. He was still attempting to *gentle* her, like she was an obstreperous cow. But the Nicodemus she hadn't realized she'd come to know—and, on some level, depend upon—was gone.

Mattie hated it.

"You know perfectly well that I work in PR," she said now. "I can think of at least three occasions in the past five years you've referenced it directly."

She was curled up in a corner of the sofa in the great room while Nicodemus sat in one of the armchairs, leaning forward now to tap at his keyboard. He still didn't look at her. Not even to point out that none of the references he'd made to her career were positive.

"You do not *work in PR*," he said when he finally deigned to answer. That harsh mouth of his didn't curve the way it would have, once. There was no hint of that rich laughter in his low voice. "You get paid to attend parties with the paparazzi in tow. You get paid more to call up your equally rich, bored and pointlessly famous friends to come along with you. You raise the profile of already sensationalized events by your exalted presence. Is that PR? Or a slightly more sanitized version of prostitution?"

Ouch.

"The tabloids claim you've stolen me away and married me without Chase's permission, because you're business rivals fighting over the company like a couple of wild dogs." She eyed him. "Making me the bone in this scenario."

The old Nicodemus would have smirked at that. This one didn't bother, and Mattie hated that she felt it like an acid inside her, eating away at her. Leaving nothing but gaping holes and a kind of hollowness behind.

"They also claim you've been secretly in love with me for years." He kept typing whatever it was he was typing, ruling his world from a distance and not sparing her a single glance as he spoke. "That your father opposed our relationship and only now can we be together, the Romeo and Juliet of the business world. Or that you're actually the conniving power behind Chase, and this union was all your idea to throw off your father's creditors. I'm not sure which version I find more laughable."

HAS MATTIE BEEN FAKING IT ALL ALONG? screeched one article, which had hypothesized that Mattie was actually some kind of corporate Mata Hari, slithering from one rich man to the next while hiding herself in plain sight as a vapid tabloid train wreck. She thought that one might actually be the most insulting of them all.

"I thought the witnesses to our wedding were household staff with the odd smartphone camera," she continued, changing the subject slightly from the obnoxious headlines that showed no signs of abating as the days passed. "Imagine my surprise to discover that one was a photographer so talented he made that sad little exercise look like a romantic moment."

"You're a far better actress than I ever gave you credit for," Nicodemus said, and he did glance over at her then, but she saw nothing on that fiercely beautiful face of his but impatience. "But then, why shouldn't you be? It's not like you know anything about reality."

"Like you do, you mean," she retorted, and waved a hand around them to indicate the sprawling villa and the stunning views in all directions. "Because this is reality."

"The difference is that I earned this." His cell phone buzzed and he frowned at it but didn't answer, and Mattie hated how she clung to that. Like it meant something. "I built this. I came from nothing and believe me, I remember what it was like to have no reason to live but dreams that someday, it might be better. I don't imagine you can say the same."

"Everybody's had to fight, Nicodemus," she said, and she was horrified at what she heard in her voice. That rawness. That telling darkness. The memories that came with it, and then the guilt. Always the guilt. "Everyone. Even someone you find as useless as me."

He looked at her then, but it was different—so damned different—from the way he'd studied her all these years. She didn't understand why it made a clawing panic rise inside her, making her chest tight and her throat hurt. She didn't understand any of this. She only knew that she'd played her best weapon and won—but lost something, too. Something she hadn't realized she could lose. Something she certainly hadn't realized she'd miss.

And suddenly, she was afraid to hear what he might say next.

"Is it in your grand plans that I continue to work?" she asked languidly, as if she wasn't affected by any of this at all. "When we get back to New York, I mean. Does your great and glorious male dignity demand that I become some kind of housewife, instead? I read an article that claimed you've abducted me against my will and hypnotized me to force me to act against my brother. Just FYI. There could be questions if I don't turn up at the office."

"I don't believe you possess any of the skills I might require in a housewife," Nicodemus said, and there was the faintest hint of his dry humor there. It made Mattie's heart kick at her. "Can you cook? Clean? Do a single thing you're told?"

She settled back against the couch. "A man of your wealth has a housekeeper for all that, surely."

"Yes, and my housekeeper obeys me. *She* is a gem without price."

"So am I to perch on your arm and be decorative?" Mattie asked. "That sounds delightful. Very intellectually stimulating, I'm sure. What will we tell the tabloids? What new stories will they create? That you took me to Greece to lobotomize me?"

He ran his hand over his face and for a moment—just a moment—looked tired. Sad, even. It reminded her of that unguarded moment she'd stumbled upon that day in the kitchen, and, like then, she didn't know what to make of it. Or of her own response, which was outsized and strange. *Unwieldy.*

If she could, she thought—if she was someone else—she would reach over and try to soothe him with her hands. She scowled down at her fingers, clenched around the tablet with too many tabloids and still sporting those too-bright rings he'd put there, as if they'd betrayed her.

"You can do whatever you want, Mattie," Nicodemus said, and she hated everything about this. That she felt caught up in whatever this new thing between them was, tighter and harsher and so much narrower. That she hurt—and more for him and that light she missed seeing in his eyes than anything else.

She didn't dare ask herself what that meant.

"And if I want to leave you?" she heard herself say, because she couldn't stop.

"Anything but that," he said, his voice harsh, and when his phone rang again he swiped it up from the table, though his dark eyes stayed on her. "We'll suffer in this together. I know I already made that clear."

And then he directed all of his attention back to his work, and Mattie knew she had no one to blame for that dark and heavy thing squatting on her chest but herself.

That night they worked together in the kitchen, putting together one of the simple meals they'd been living on here. A fresh salad. Homemade pita bread warmed in the oven and placed in a basket. A plate with a hunk of feta and tangy local olives, drenched in a gold-green olive oil. Lamb that Nicodemus had prepared matter-of-factly and quickly on the grill, then placed on the plates Mattie carried out to the table on the terrace.

It occurred to her as they settled across from each other that they'd developed their own rhythm in these past days. That this was what married couples *did*, this quiet dance of shared food and a laden table. Candles against the cool October air and no need for conversation.

It occurred to her that despite everything, despite what she'd done to avoid it, this was the most intimate she'd ever been with a person she wasn't related to.

The insight was like a slap to the head and she sat there for a moment, staring at Nicodemus in dismay. Because this was precisely why he was doing all of this, she understood. Even if he was angry with her, he was still creating bonds between them that had nothing to do with their decade of games or that sexual tension that burned between them even now. He was making this—*him*—a habit.

This was exactly what she didn't want. What she couldn't allow.

"What now?" he asked, reaching out to drag a soft square of the pita bread through the olive oil, then popping it in his mouth. He sat back in his chair as he chewed, but the way he looked at her was anything but indulgent.

"I think it's time you explained to me what happened the other day in the kitchen," she blurted out. "Most men would be transported with delight if they received an unsolicited blow job."

Was that a muscle that twitched in his jaw? Or did she only want it to be because it indicated she still affected him? How could she know her own motivations so little?

"I am not most men."

"Obviously." She sat much too rigidly in her seat, and found that her appetite had deserted her. She shoved the perfectly grilled lamb around on her plate. "You've been punishing me ever since."

"Don't be so dramatic." He seemed unperturbed, and continued to eat with every appearance of contentment. "Punishment can take many forms, but none, I think, involve whiling away your days on a beautiful island with nothing to do but relax."

"That depends on the company."

"Here's the thing, Mattie." His gaze flared into something else. Something so blisteringly hot it robbed her of breath. "I've done all this before. The pretty girl. The endless, circular lies. I already know how it ends."

She didn't like that flare of prickly heat that washed over her, because she knew exactly what it was, and she'd never been jealous of anything before in her life. *Damn him.*

"Are you trying to tell me that I don't measure up to your ex?" she asked tautly. "They say comparison is the thief of joy, Nicodemus. Maybe that's why you're so grumpy all the time."

He looked like he wanted to bite at her, and she shouldn't have thrilled to that.

"I don't find all the insults and digs and snide remarks amusing anymore," he grated at her.

"Why not?" she asked, and she didn't know how she dared. Or why her voice was so tiny when she did. "I thought you knew how it ends."

"What I thought was a game we were both playing was something else entirely to you," he said with a quiet menace that rolled through Mattie like a seismic event, and paled in comparison to that look in his dark eyes. "I wasn't lying. You were."

"But what if I'm not?"

She hadn't meant to say that. She didn't even know where it came from—and yet it was there between them, stretched out prone on the small table, surrounded by the flickering flames of the candles and the rich Greek night all around them.

"There are always consequences," he said after a moment. "In this case, I don't believe a single thing you say. You wanted to manipulate me and you were willing to go as far as possible to do it."

"You're one to talk," she managed to reply, though her eyes felt glazed and she was half-afraid the rest of her had turned to stone. "Where do you think I learned how to use sex as a weapon in the first place?"

"You're such a liar." It came out somewhere between wonder and despair, and she'd never heard him use that tone of voice before. It tore at her. "You lie to my face about things I know are not true. I was there. I've never *used* sex. I've simply admitted the attraction I feel and occasionally acted upon it. There's a difference."

"Because you say there is!" she threw at him. "That doesn't make it so!"

"I've been dreaming of getting my mouth on you for years," he growled at her, looking much too dangerous for a man who still appeared to do no more than lounge there across from her. "I didn't ask you to strip for me, Mattie. You did that."

"But you were happy to take advantage, of course."

"I'm not going to have this argument," he told her then, that colder note of impatience back in his voice. Shifting, she thought, from potentially emotional husband to unamused CEO in an instant, and she loathed it. "Because we both know you know better—and that I wasn't the one playing games."

"Nicodemus—"

"Eat your dinner," he told her. He picked up his own fork and speared a piece of lamb with barely repressed violence.

"This is fake," she gritted out, and was surprised to discover that her hands were in fists in her lap, and her throat was so tight it hurt to speak. "This is nothing but a game of make-believe. We might as well be the tabloid stories they make up about us. How is this any better?"

"This is a marriage," he retorted, all of that ferocity in his voice , and darkening his gaze, and she was sick enough to exult in that, because at least she'd reached something in him. "Our marriage. You should count yourself lucky I've decided it should be so goddamned civil."

Nicodemus woke in a rush.

He didn't need to reach out to the empty mattress beside him to realize that Mattie wasn't in the bed. He knew immediately. But his hand moved over the spot she normally occupied—as far away from him as she could get and still technically be in the same bed—and he found it cold. Utterly devoid of her heat, telling him that she'd slipped away again. She always did.

He swung his way out of the bed and onto his feet, not bothering to turn on the lights. Outside, the moon was flirting toward fullness, creating a rippling path across the dark water, and Nicodemus was furious.

He would have asked himself what the hell was wrong with him, but he knew. It was always Mattie, always this same woman lodged in him like a pebble in his shoe. Or a knife in his side, if he was more accurate, and he had no idea how he was maintaining his control. If it didn't bother her so much when he went cold and distant, he acknowledged to himself in the predawn quiet of his empty bedroom, he would have broken already.

So maybe he played as many games as she did, after all.

But it was this particular game of hers—this nightly ritual—that he thought might drive him to the brink of madness.

Every night she deserted their bed. Every night he would either wake to find her missing or come to bed after another round of irritating international conference calls to find she wasn't there. Every night he would hunt her down, find her sleeping somewhere else in this sprawling place and sometimes muttering and thrashing in a way that suggested anything but sweet dreams, and carry her back with him.

Every single night, and they never discussed it.

Nicodemus assumed it was her last gasp of rebellion, and on some level he couldn't help but admire her hardheadedness and persistence. But it wasn't admiration he felt tonight as he failed to locate her in any of her usual spots. She wasn't in any of the guest suites. She wasn't in the great room, the solarium or on the leather couch in his office. He went through every room of the villa without finding her, and it was only when he stood near the wall of windows outside his private gym and indoor lap pool that he realized she'd escalated things and left the building.

He thought she might be the death of him one of these days, he really did.

Nicodemus let himself out into the cold night, the October wind and the watching moon piercing him as he walked across the flagstone patio that made a ring around the outdoor pool that he'd need to close for the season soon. He felt the coming winter in the stones beneath his bare feet, and he felt like a caveman when he wrenched open the door to the pool house and saw her there, where she shouldn't have been.

She was in a ball on the summer chaise in the corner, and for a moment, he thought she was awake and speaking to him—

But then he saw the tears. And the look of abject terror on her face.

She wasn't speaking, he realized. She was crying the same word over and over and over.

Nicodemus didn't hesitate. He wasn't *civil*. He simply closed the distance between the door and the chaise in two strides. He picked her up, blanket and tears and all, and cradled her in his lap.

She was ice cold and distraught and she wasn't, it finally dawned on him, awake.

So he simply held her. He rocked her gently, murmuring old words he half remembered from a childhood he would have said had held no softness of any kind. He smoothed her hair back from her face and let her sob into his neck.

And he pretended he would do the same for any woman he encountered, any person at all. That he would feel this same sense of immensity and something very nearly like awe that she was letting him hold her, this same ache that she was in pain. This same pounding understanding—like his own heart in his chest—that he would fight off anything that threatened her, even if it was inside her own head.

Slowly, the sobbing subsided. Her breaths came smoother, slower. And Nicodemus knew the moment she came fully awake and aware of her surroundings, because her whole body went tense.

"You're all right," he told her quietly, glad it was so dark in the pool house. Glad there was no chance she could see the expression he was afraid he wore much too plainly on his face. "I'll keep you safe."

He chose not to investigate how deeply and wholly he meant that.

"What—what happened?"

Nicodemus had never heard her stutter, he thought then, nor sound so terrified. Not his Mattie, who careened through the world like Don Quixote but with a far sharper tongue. He rubbed a hand over that aching thing in his chest, then smoothed it over her hair again—but she was awake now, and she pulled away.

And he had no choice but to let her.

"Do you have these nightmares often?" he asked as she scrambled up and out of his lap like she was on fire, then wrapped herself in that blanket as if it could protect her. From him or from whatever dire thing stalked her dreams? He couldn't tell. "Is that why you creep out of our bed every night? You've been upset before, but not like this. You usually quiet down when I hold you."

"What?" Her voice was sharper then, but no less panicked. More so, he'd have said. "What do you mean?"

"You were having a terrible nightmare," he said slowly, aware from the taut way she stood and the sudden spike of tension in the room that he'd stumbled into something here. Something important. "You were sobbing. Screaming, I think. The same word again and again."

"How strange," she said, and though her voice was cooler then, he could hear all the panic and the leftover nightmare beneath it. "I must have eaten something that disagreed with me."

Another lie, Nicodemus thought, but he couldn't summon up the usual fury at that sad little truth. She was so brittle; she was acting so tough—but she hadn't faked those desperate sobs. She hadn't faked those tears that he could still feel against his collarbone, the night air turning his dampened skin cold. Like proof.

He stood and saw the way she jerked her chin back, as if she had to fight herself to stay still. He wished, then, they were different people. Or that they could start this whole thing over the way she'd pretended she wanted to do that day in the kitchen. He wished that he could trust her—or that she could trust him, even a little, with who she really was.

He wished this hadn't all been set in stone so many years ago now.

He didn't touch her, though he wanted nothing more. But he didn't think he'd stop at a mere touch, and that was the last thing she'd allow. He could almost *see* the defensiveness prickle around her, like she'd grown spikes where she stood.

"I don't think it was food poisoning," he said after a moment. His voice was matter-of-fact in the dark room. "You were crying out for your mother."

She made a sound like she'd been socked in the gut. "My mother?" she asked, much too softly. "That doesn't make any sense. You must be mistaken."

"No, *agapi mou,*" he said, and he was only distantly aware that he'd called her *my love.* It hardly seemed important, though some part of him registered it would be.

Eventually. He reached over despite himself and wrapped a strand of her black hair around his finger, pleased that it retained a small bit of her warmth. Wishing he could, too. "All you said was *mama*. Over and over again."

CHAPTER SEVEN

WHEN SHE WOKE up it was morning, and Nicodemus was gone.

For a moment, Mattie blinked at the side of the bed where he normally sprawled, all of his masculine perfection on mouthwatering display. But then her memory caught up with her in a sickening rush, and so did her headache.

She felt hungover, though she knew she wasn't. Dreadfully, hideously hungover, from the pounding at her temples to the desert where her mouth should have been. And there was panic like a stomach cramp, deep in her belly, growing more acute by the second.

A shower—long and hot and almost punishing—didn't help. Neither did sneaking down to the kitchen and fixing herself a huge mug of coffee to stave off the fog in her head. Mattie crept down the long hall that led to Nicodemus's office and stopped when she heard his voice from within. Powerful, commanding. Certain.

"I've already signed the papers," he was saying, and Mattie imagined boardrooms all over the world filled with corporate disciples in three-piece suits, leaping over each other to do his bidding. "I will be forced to view any further delays or dragging of feet as hostile, am I clear? *Endaxi.*"

His voice lulled her into a false sense of security, like

he could handle anything—even her, and she knew she couldn't risk that.

She slipped back down the hall and climbed back up to the master bedroom. It took her only a moment to locate her things in the vast walk-in closet, and she pulled the cigarette packet out of the bottom of her purse with a small sigh of relief. The packet had crumpled on the side and the three cigarettes that remained within were bent almost to breaking, but that hardly mattered. She pulled one out, then rummaged around for her lighter.

She didn't go out on the balcony that wrapped around the master bedroom on three sides. Instead, she retraced her steps through the villa and then continued on into the long wing where all the guest suites were. It was there, at the farthest point of the house, she snuck out onto a little patio, found a small iron bench not directly visible from inside and indulged in her filthiest habit.

Mattie pulled her legs up beneath her and tipped her head back, letting the chilly air and the warm sunlight battle it out. Slowly, surely, she felt better. The cigarette tasted stale, but that didn't matter. It wasn't about the taste. It wasn't even about smoking.

It was, if she was honest with herself, purely about reminding herself that Nicodemus couldn't control this. *Her.* That he didn't know her, no matter what he'd thought he'd heard last night. That she still had whole parts of herself she was keeping at bay, keeping hidden, that he couldn't reach no matter how many meals they shared or nightmares he soothed away. That he cast the illusion of safety, but it was only that: an illusion.

Because that had to be true, or she was well and truly lost.

And if there was a growing part of her that wanted to simply surrender to him, to lose herself in him, to see if someone as strong and formidable as he was could help her carry the weight of all her secrets—

"Don't be an idiot, Mattie," she said out loud.

"I am afraid it is much too late for that."

She jumped against the iron bench and swiveled to see Nicodemus standing there in the French doors that led to the guest room. Tall, dark. Grim.

And furious.

Mattie looked at the cigarette as if she'd never seen it before, then looked at him. *That will be your last cigarette,* she remembered him saying so long ago in her father's library. Her heart was wild against her ribs. But she couldn't back down. She'd already given too much away.

So she held his dark gaze while she put the cigarette to her mouth again, took a long drag and then blew the smoke out. At him.

For a moment, everything stopped. The world on its axis. The air around them. *Everything.*

Then Nicodemus threw back his head and laughed.

It was the last thing Mattie expected; it filled the morning with its golden, infectious sound, and maybe that was why she didn't think to move when he closed the distance between them, rounding the bench to stand in front of her.

And then it was too late. He leaned over her, trapping her against the high back. He plucked the cigarette out of her fingers the way he had once before, and this time he stubbed it out beneath his foot. Then he caught her where she sat with an arm on either side of her, bringing his face dangerously close to hers.

There was a fire in his dark gaze. And it lit her up with what she chose to call fear, though that molten thing down deep in her core knew better.

"Was I unclear?" he asked in a mild tone at complete odds with the fierce look in his face. "Because I remember telling you that smoking was unacceptable. Did I dream this conversation?"

"I never agreed to obey you, Nicodemus," she said, amazed she had the power of speech when he was so close and so obviously furious with her. "You simply decided I should, the way you've decided any number of things since the day we met." She didn't know where she got the courage—or foolishness—to shrug like that, like he bored her. "And you're welcome to decide whatever you like, but that doesn't mean I have to agree with your decisions. Much less follow them like gospel."

He looked at her for what felt like a very long time. And then he smiled.

"Thank you," he said, almost formally.

She was almost afraid to ask. "For what?"

"For making this easy."

She didn't see him move. He only shifted, and then she was in the air, unable to make sense of what was happening to her until the soft curve of her belly hit the rock hardness of his shoulder. He was already inside the villa and moving swiftly through the guest wing by the time she registered that he'd simply picked her up and thrown her over his shoulder.

Mattie fought. She kicked at him and beat at his back with her fists, and he only laughed and smacked his hand down on her bottom. Hard.

Then he tipped her upright again and dropped her. She cried out in the instant before she bounced in the center of their bed. *His* bed, she corrected herself furiously, desperately scrabbling to catch herself and sit up—

To see Nicodemus standing there at the foot of the bed, his arms crossed over his chest and his eyes like stone as he glared down at her.

"We've had a week of lies and strained civility," he said,

and there was nothing cool about his voice. Nothing measured or *polite*. "Now we do this my way."

"This has all been your way already!"

"Mattie," he said, harsh and certain and more like steel than she'd ever heard him. "Be quiet."

She told herself she wasn't obeying him. That she was simply trying to calm her racing heart, stop her ragged-edged gasping for breath. She told herself that *if she'd wanted to*, she would have screamed at him. But whatever the reason, she fell silent.

Nicodemus could have been carved from marble.

"What do you suggest I do with a woman who acts like a disobedient child?" he asked, his voice a low rasp.

"I take it that's a rhetorical question?"

He ignored her. "It doesn't take a psychiatrist to figure out that you have Daddy issues, Mattie. The question is, do I play that role? Is that what it will take?"

Her jaw ached. That was how she realized she was clenching her teeth.

"I," she bit out, so angry it was like a living thing clawing its way out from within her, "do not have *Daddy issues*. The only issue I have is you."

"This is what you need to understand," Nicodemus said in that ruthless way that made something shiver through her, settling low in her belly and becoming a pulse of heat, mixing with that anger and changing it into something she couldn't recognize. Or she didn't want to recognize. "I will win. No matter how long it takes, no matter what I have to do, no matter what games you play. I will win because winning is what I do."

"You don't get to order me—"

"It is time for you to stop running at windmills," he told her in that same ruthless way. "We are not living in your world, where you can order everyone around and have them dance to your tune. We are in mine. And I find my interest in indulging these tantrums is over."

She couldn't speak for a long moment. There was that terrible yearning deep inside her, too deep and too dark. It would eat her whole, she knew, and what would be left of her on the other side? What would happen when he got what he thought he wanted and really, truly knew her?

Why did she want to find out when she knew she'd regret it?

"The fact that you think you have the right to expect obedience is a problem, Nicodemus," she said, scowling at him, hoping she could bluster her way through this the way she always had before. "The fact that you think you can manhandle me? Also a problem."

He was dressed all in black today, she couldn't help but notice. A black T-shirt that strained over his muscled arms and black trousers that clung to his narrow hips and showed the faintest hint of his olive-toned skin at the waistband. He looked like he could singlehandedly take down a terrorist cell if he felt like it—which meant cowing her should be the work of a few moments. The idea made her limbs feel like liquid. Hot and slippery when she wanted to be strong.

"And the fact that you call anything I do that you don't like *a tantrum*," she continued, her chin rising up as she refused to let herself look away from him, "is certainly a big problem, as well. It's wildly condescending, for a start."

"Here is what will happen," he said in a perfectly calm, conversational tone, as if there was no tension in the air, no beating, throbbing, white-hot *thing* wrapping tighter and tighter around them both. "I told you I was going to spank you. You had the option to dance for me, instead, but you chose to run away, as usual. Leaving me to clean up yet another one of your messes. Also as usual." He smiled faintly. "Did you think I had forgotten these infractions?"

"Is this boarding school all over again?" she demanded, still going for the bluster even as that hot, slippery, *yearning* thing made her worry she might turn into a puddle on the bed. "Will I get detention for smoking that cigarette? Will I have to write lines? Scrub the floors?"

"I have something significantly more corporeal in mind."

"You say you want obedience but you didn't like it much when I actually got on my knees, did you?" she snapped at him, telling herself that fire in her was fear, not desire. Because she didn't want to be fascinated by this. She wanted to be afraid. "And I'm not calling you *sir*, by the way, no matter how many shades of crazy you show me."

A careless shrug. "You made your body fair game in this little struggle of ours. Why shouldn't I do the same? I think we'll do this my way and see what you call me when I'm done. You might be surprised."

"If you spank me," she told him, low and fervent, "I really will let that current sweep me off to Libya. I mean it, Nicodemus."

"Note to self," Nicodemus said mildly, sounding completely unimpressed with her threat. "Tie wife to the bed."

He moved then, putting his knee on the mattress as if he meant to crawl toward her. And everything seemed to slide sideways in a dizzy sort of shift. The world went red. Mattie thought something blew up inside her—knocking out reason. Knocking out everything save that grinding, expanding, whole-bodied *desire* for anything and everything he might give her.

She panicked.

Mattie dove for the side of the bed, already envisioning

her escape. Into the bathroom, where she could lock the door and, if all else failed, crawl out on the roof and try—

But he simply reached out and caught her with one large hand around her hip, yanking her back into the center of the bed.

"Be still," he told her.

So instead, Mattie fought.

She flailed and she kicked, she bucked and she twisted, and she was lost for what seemed like a very long time in the haze of it. But then the fever seemed to lift, and Mattie had to face the unpleasant realization that, as ever with this man, she'd only made it all that much worse.

Because he hadn't fought back. He'd simply pinned her to the bed with his superior strength. And waited.

She was out of breath. Nicodemus was impassive.

He was stretched out above her in absolutely the worst position she could imagine. His chest pressed against hers, flattening her breasts in a way that made her simultaneously hot and very, very worried. His hips were flush against hers, his legs on the inside of hers, and he made no attempt at all to hide the fact that he was hard. Ready. Aroused.

He was so strong. So perfectly formed. Beautiful even when he held her down, his fingers threaded with hers, her arms up and over her head and flat against the mattress.

"You're only making this worse for yourself," he told her.

And she was sick, she decided, because she didn't want to fight him any longer. She wanted to melt into him. She wanted to shift so that his hardness pressed more directly against the core of her. She wanted to lift her mouth and press it against his. She *wanted*—and she knew that it was more destructive by far than anything he could do to her.

"Nicodemus." But she was whispering, and even she

could hear the longing in her voice. And the fact she didn't demand that he release her.

"You claim you won't surrender to me by choice," he said, in that firm, relentless way that made a rush of heat wash over her, turning her restless and liquid and *yearning* beneath him. "And yet it has been obvious to me for some time that surrender is what you need above all things. Think about it. You, completely out of control. No manipulations. No schemes. No plotting. Just your bare bottom and my hand. Imagine what we can learn from an interaction so elemental?"

It took her long moments to realize that she was shaking, over and over, as if something had gone loose inside her and could no longer be contained. As if he was already doing the things he'd painted so vividly. As if she was already that far gone. That lost. As if she could truly surrender the way he wanted her to do. The way she wished she could do. She shook, hard and deep.

But she didn't say no.

"Or," he said, in that dark, low way, "you can tell me one true thing." His gaze locked with hers. "Just one. The truth, Mattie, or my hand. Your choice. But I'll have some kind of surrender from you, either way."

And that was when Mattie realized what she had to do.

Because it was the only thing she had left. And she didn't know why she'd been avoiding it for so long. As Nicodemus had taught her too well in this last fraught week, there were intimacies much more shattering than sex. The world was filled with one-night stands, bedpost-notchers and all kinds of people who used sex to hide from intimacy, not to enhance it.

She could do it. She should have done it long before now. She should have realized it was the only possible way she could get the upper hand with him.

Mattie swallowed, hard. She searched his face for any give, any softness, any sign that he was something other than this: hard, demanding, implacable. But it was the Nicodemus she knew staring back at her, and the sheer, startling *rightness* of that—of him and of this decision she'd made so effortlessly after all these years of agonizing—washed over her. It made her remarkably calm for someone who was pinned to a bed and literally trapped between a rock and a hard place.

But it also made it easy. Or maybe that was because it was him.

Maybe, a small voice whispered inside her, *it's always and only been him, and you should have admitted it a long time ago.*

Mattie didn't want to think about that, or all the things it could mean.

"One truth," he said, as if he thought she wasn't going to answer him. "That's all it will take to clean the slate. Can you do it?"

She pulled her fingers out of his, faintly surprised when he let her. Then she reached up and slid her palms along his hard jaw, letting the sensation crash into her. She liked the fact he hadn't bothered to shave in days, that his skin was rough to the touch. She liked that gleam in his dark eyes. She liked that she was closer to him now, almost too close to bear.

"I want you," she whispered.

And Nicodemus froze.

For a shimmering moment, everything was taut. Stretched thin on the edge of a knife—or maybe that was him, holding himself above her, her words like a shout ricocheting within him.

Nicodemus didn't ask her to repeat herself. Not because

her words were burned into him, though they were. Not even because he knew he couldn't possibly hear her over the racket inside him, the clamor of his heart and the shout of his blood in his veins.

But because he had never seen that look on her face before, in her pretty eyes. Wide open. Clear. Determined, perhaps, and more than a little anxious. Bright.

True.

It moved over him like a wave. Like an ocean's worth of tides, dragging at him, blessing him or condemning him, and Nicodemus wasn't sure he cared which. He reminded himself that Mattie was a liar. That like the only other people who had ever meant anything to him, she would lie to him as easily as she breathed. That there was no point in believing her now, when she was only telling him what she thought he most wanted to hear.

When she was right.

She moved then. She slid her hands from his face and wrapped her arms around his shoulders, and then she shifted her hips against his, dancing for him again. Making him wish that this once, he could believe her.

"Nicodemus," she whispered. "I always have."

And he was still only a man, despite everything. He was as weak as any other. Perhaps even as weak, in his own way, as the man he'd always hated the most—his father. And Mattie Whitaker had been crawling in him like an itch for all these years, whispering his name in his darkest hours whether she knew it or not, and promising him exactly this in every last one of his favorite fantasies.

How could he resist her?

He stopped trying. He simply dropped his head and crushed his mouth to hers, and who cared what came after? If she proved—the way he assumed she would, because she always did—that even this was a lie?

For the first time in his life, Nicodemus didn't care.

She tasted like fire and longing and all of the wildness that had swirled between them all this time. He kissed her again and again, glutting himself and losing himself at once, feeling that lush, lithe body of hers pressed against him, soft where he was hard, tall and long and perfect.

Mine, he thought, reveling in the word, in her exquisite warmth in his arms and that pounding, beating, hungry demand inside him, spurring him on, making him half crazed with need.

Her hands traced shapes down his back, tested the heft of his biceps, then found their way to his hips. Everything was the heat of her mouth, the glory of her taste, the maddening slide of her body against his. He pulled back to peel off his shirt and she made a soft sound of distress.

Nicodemus thought he might very well eat her alive.

He threw his shirt away, then tugged hers off. He peeled the skintight black denim from her endless legs, feeling as delirious at the sight of all that lovely flesh as he had been when she'd done this for him in midair. He reached out and traced her phoenix tattoo again, attuned to the soft sounds she made, the way she caught her breath and then let it out hard as he leaned in close and licked his way over the riot of color.

He took his time. He settled in and followed every line, tasting every part of that magical, mystical creature she'd inked into her skin. When he was done, she was shifting and rolling beneath him as if she couldn't help herself. As if she was as needy and insane with it as he was.

But it wasn't enough.

Nicodemus pulled her bra down, one cup at a time, so he could worship each of her breasts in turn. He remembered the thrust of her nipples, the sweet rose of them, but this time he savored each one. He used his tongue and his lips and even the scrape of his teeth, until she was thrashing against the mattress and muttering what sounded like his name. Or perhaps it was an endless stream of something very much like a plea.

Either way, it moved in him like the finest music.

He shifted then, following a meandering path down her abdomen until he reached her pierced navel and could admit, at last, that he liked it. He more than liked it. It made her even sexier, something that he'd have thought impossible. He wanted her—all of her, all of these bright colors and sexy rings—entirely to himself.

The possessiveness wasn't new. But the simple beauty of her surrender, her body wide open beneath him, quivering for his touch—made him feel like a god. He would do anything for this, he understood then in a way that might have worried him had he allowed himself to consider it, and yet at the same time he doubted he'd ever drink his fill of this woman. He couldn't see how he'd ever come close.

Mine, he thought again, the way he always did, though this time it felt darker. Hotter. Much more intense.

Because it felt like truth, at last.

When he reached the dainty lace thong that stretched to contain her femininity, her fingers dug into his hair. Hard.

"No." He only watched her, though he went still, however difficult it might have been. "I want you," she said again, even more beautiful this time because her voice was so ragged, and he knew he'd done that to her. "Inside me, Nicodemus. Please."

"Be certain," he told her, still crouched over her, his mouth a scant inch above that sweet, hot core of hers he longed to taste again. But he didn't care what she did or what she said, what she let him do at the moment or what she held in reserve, as long as she didn't stop. *Please don't stop.* "This is one among many things you can't take back."

Did he imagine her eyes darkened then? But it didn't matter, because she was moving, rising to her knees to take off the bra he'd only shoved out of the way, then wiggling out of her panties, as well.

"I don't want to take anything back," she said huskily, her eyes never leaving his.

And he believed her. God help him, but he believed her.

He reached out and tugged her closer, so they were kneeling together in the center of the bed he'd always imagined would be theirs one day. She kissed him with a passion and a wonder that echoed in him, making him that much wilder, that much closer to losing control.

He sank his hands into her hair and held her where he wanted her, where he could plunder her mouth while her hands worked between them, pulling open his trousers and freeing him. When her hands closed around him, he groaned, resting his forehead against hers. He was too hard. It had been too long. It had been forever.

Still, he let her test the length of him in her palms. Once. Twice. But at that third slide of rough silk and all that ferocious, impossible hunger, he pulled her hands away.

"But I want—"

"You already told me what you want," he told her, gruff and dark, "and you won't get it if you keep that up."

And perhaps he'd gone completely delusional, after all, but the smile she gave him seemed to fill the whole room. And him, too, kicking through the shadows that lurked inside him and letting light into the darkest places—

This was the real danger, he knew. It always had been. *He wanted to believe.*

Nicodemus stretched out on his back, kicking his trousers off as he went, and pulled her down beside him. Then he pulled one of those long legs of hers up over his hip and took her mouth again, feasting on her as his hands roamed.

One anchored in that thick, sweet-smelling hair of hers. The other moved lower, making its way to her core.

Where she was molten hot, wet and soft, and there was no doubt at all that she wanted him. That this was real. That whatever she might be lying about still, and he was sure she was because she always was, it wasn't this.

This was real. This was true.

This was finally happening.

Nicodemus stroked his way into her, finding her shockingly tight and incandescent all around his gentle entry. She shuddered against him, and he tried another finger beside the first, twisting his hand so that every time he rocked into her, he pressed hard against that jutting center of her need.

And Mattie went wild.

She thrust against him. Her hips were like lightning and he didn't want to contain it—he wanted to glory in the storm. He held her mouth to his as she moaned, holding her when she would have pulled back, feeling her tighten everywhere as she melted into his hand. Feeling her shudder and twist, hearing her make the wildest, sweetest noises imaginable, until she choked out something that sounded like his name and catapulted straight over the side of the world—consumed in all that glorious fire while he watched, fierce male satisfaction and that terrible need pouring through him, setting him aflame.

"You are mine, *agapi mou*," he told her then, pulling his hand from her clenching heat and shifting her over to her back even as she shook and cried out in his arms. "You have always been mine."

And then, at last, he slammed his way into her, hard.

He felt the tightness, then the tear as she gave way. Felt her go rigid even as she cried out, and no longer in anything like passion.

Impossible, he thought.

But the sound she'd made was sheer pain, threaded through with shock. Her eyes were dark and glassy, and her hands came up to slam against his chest, and he didn't think she knew she hit him, much less that hard—

She was a virgin.

CHAPTER EIGHT

IT HURT.

Mattie only realized, as that strange, overstretched fullness went on, as the burning part felt like it might drown her
and her thighs felt like someone else's, with so much of him
hard and prodding and huge between them and *in* her, that
she'd convinced herself it wouldn't. Not after all this time.

Not with him.

Dimly, she realized that he was much too still. That it
could only mean that her fantasy of him not even noticing had failed to come true. That he had, indeed, noticed.

And worse, stopped.

"It's okay," she said in a bright sort of voice that even
she could hear sounded strained and awful and much too
loud. "It can only get better. Right?"

She gave an experimental roll of her hips and had to
suck in a breath, because it wasn't better. It was...pierced
and heavy and *full.* Much too *full,* and so much more *physical* than she'd imagined.

"Even here, you find a new way to lie to me," he gritted
out, his voice a scrape of sound and painful to her ears.
"When I'd have told you it was impossible."

He did not sound remotely lighthearted or amused, or
darkly thrilled, all of which she'd imagined as alternate
scenarios to him simply failing to register it at all.

And it still hurt.

"I didn't lie," she told him, surprised that she could speak when *so many things* were happening to her, *in her,* far too many to process—and yet none that looked anything like what she'd seen online and in all those movies. She even managed to sound faintly offended. "You never asked me if I was a virgin."

He was still holding himself motionless, stretched there above her, every inch of him managing to *bristle* somehow, as if she'd betrayed him. She didn't like the tiny little tremor that moved through her, like something in her agreed.

"How?" He bit it off in a dark voice so filled with storms that Mattie shivered again, and hated that he was right there. That he saw it. The way he saw everything.

"The usual way," she said, shifting beneath him, trying to find a comfortable way to lie there with a man *inside* her. "Which mostly involved never doing this."

She could *feel* his gaze boring into her, burning her, accusing her.

"You are twenty-eight years old. *Twenty-eight.* I would sooner expect to see the face of God appear on the side of a dinner plate than a twenty-eight-year-old virgin."

"It's not like there's a law that everyone has to lose their virginity at a certain age."

"No." His voice then could have stripped paint. "But there is something called reality. To say nothing of your very public relationships, all conducted in the glare of a thousand cameras."

"What happens in front of the cameras is theater and misdirection, Nicodemus," she said hurriedly. "A game. You know that."

"You mean lies."

"That's not the word I'd use."

His fingers tapped at her chin, which was when Mattie realized she'd been frowning at the center of his neck this whole time.

And when she finally saw his face, she almost gave in to that hectic heat that threatened to spill over from her eyes. He looked drawn and furious at once. Something like wounded, and haunted around the eyes.

She had done that to him, she knew, though she shoved that aside and concentrated on the fact that once again, Nicodemus was not like other men. He wasn't like anyone else she'd ever known, and she hated that acknowledging it made her feel that much more raw.

"How?" he asked again, his voice far more clipped.

It occurred to Mattie then that she hadn't thought this through—mostly because she'd assumed that she was so old that none of the usual virginity concerns would apply. She certainly hadn't anticipated having to defend something she'd hardly dared admit to herself had even been happening all these years, that seemed that much more silly and pointless now, when it *hurt* and he was looking at her like she'd *done something* to him.

"Why am I not surprised?" she flared at him. "Give the man a blow job and he has an extended temper tantrum. Give the man *virginity*—which I believe some women sell for astronomical prices on the internet, by the way, so prized is it in this modern age—and he acts like it's some kind of communicable disease. My God, Nicodemus. What's the matter with you?"

"You are an idiot," he retorted, in a tone she'd never heard him use before. "I begin to believe it is entirely on purpose. A willful and deliberate course of action you choose to cause the most harm."

"I'm not an idiot," she retorted, stung, which only made her feel like one.

"Did you want me to hurt you, Mattie?" he gritted out. "Is that was this was—a carefully orchestrated scene to make certain I would feel nothing but guilt and regret and make you my victim, at last? Congratulations. You have succeeded admirably."

He moved then, and she realized he was about to roll off her. About to end this whole strange experience—and that shot through her like a bullet, clearing out that terrifying rawness that hovered within her like a fragile thing and leaving only a desperate flare of fury in its wake.

"Don't you dare!" She tightened her legs around him as if that could keep him where he was, that or her sheer panic that if she let him go, she'd lose him forever. She opted not to consider why that would bother her so much. "If you stop now, all it will ever be is this. Painful and weird."

"You have no idea what you're talking about," he told her bitterly, though he didn't pull out of her. He'd stopped moving away, just as she'd asked. And she felt a deep relief she hadn't earned, and wasn't certain she even understood. "As you have demonstrated, going so far as to hurt yourself in the process."

She realized her hands were on his chest, balled into fists, and she opened them, spreading her fingers wide and soaking in the heat of his skin, that chiseled perfection that was only Nicodemus. She felt his heart thundering there, under one palm, and became aware, then, of the way he breathed. Harsh. Like this hurt him, too. Experimentally, she moved her hips against his.

She couldn't claim it felt *good*. But it didn't make her want to cry, either.

"Make it better," she ordered him, and his dark eyes widened slightly, in a kind of shock he hid almost as soon as she saw it. And then, behind that, she saw that heat she recognized.

Male. Primitive. Fire and need.

She wanted that back.

"What makes you think I can?" he asked, but there was less of that grimness in his voice, she thought. Less of that impenetrable darkness. And she clung to it.

"Because you've already proved that you can."

Mattie didn't know why she was whispering. She knew only this. Him, still and strong above her, holding himself off her with his fists dug into the mattress. She wanted him lower. Closer. She wanted him to *do something* with this strange yearning inside her, somehow physical and emotional at once. Twined and nonsensical, but all his fault.

Deep inside her, she felt him twitch, and it made her break out in goose bumps, all the way down her arms. She shuddered.

His dark eyes narrowed.

"And if I do this," he said then, as if he was choosing his words carefully, "what do I get in return?"

Mattie frowned at him. "An orgasm, presumably. Unless something goes horribly wrong. Isn't that what you usually get out of it?"

She thought she saw a glimpse of that dark, honeyed gleam, that amusement that she thought was only hers, and it made that fullness in her—that quivering stretching place inside her that he still claimed—seem to shudder, too. It wasn't quite heat, but it didn't hurt. Not as much as before.

And then, when he shifted against her—once and then again, in a lazy sort of almost rhythm that made her freeze, then relax, then let out her breath in a rush—she realized that he really did know what he was doing in ways she couldn't possibly have imagined.

"This isn't about orgasms, Mattie," he said softly, with an undercurrent of pure, male confidence. "Orgasms are what happen when chemistry and skill unite. That isn't in question here."

"That," Mattie said very seriously, "is not at all what I've read."

His mouth curved then, and she felt it everywhere. In the places where their bodies clung together. In the core of her, where his quiet little movements were making her feel soft again, and warm. In that raw heat that was too much for her eyes to hold, she was sure of it, and might at any moment overflow and betray her.

"You are killing me," he whispered. "And I may kill you yet myself. But first, I see I must show you the difference between reading and living."

He bent his head and licked one of her nipples, and she could feel his smile against her skin when it responded to him at once, pulling taut in a way that drew a rippling sort of line directly from his mouth to her core. A line and with it, a kind of fire.

"You will enjoy the lesson." He used the edge of his teeth on her other breast, and she found she was shifting against him again, around that relentless hardness inside her, and it felt a whole lot better. "Then, princess, we will talk."

He rolled his hips on hers, somehow hitting her right in that needy little button that only he had ever managed to find, much less use to such effect, and she suddenly realized *why.* Why it was all connected. Why she felt him *everywhere.* Why they were built like this, so oddly and so perfectly, so obviously for each other.

Nicodemus pulled out, then thrust back in, slow and steady, and it all made a glorious kind of sense.

"Keep doing that," she whispered, amazed to find her voice was shaky, "and we can talk all you want."

He laughed then, long and low, and that, too, was its own blaze inside her.

Mattie didn't know when it all changed. One moment she was counting all the things that *weren't* painful—and then the next, she couldn't count, because it was all too much. It was fire and glory. It was beautiful and wild. It was a perfect storm of pure insanity, and Nicodemus was orchestrating it all.

His hands, his mouth. That lazy and yet somehow demanding rhythm he chose, rocking them both closer and closer to something *huge*. Mattie had had an orgasm before. She'd even had more than one with him. But she understood, somehow, that the place they were headed together was different. Immense and life-altering. Too intense to survive—

"Nicodemus—" But she didn't sound like herself, and he laughed again, as if this was all part of his plan. "I can't—"

"You will," he said, his mouth at her ear, and then he really began to move.

And Mattie felt it everywhere. She felt it curl up from some dark and wondrous place inside her she'd never known was there, spreading out like a brushfire until there was nothing but him, nothing but the way he moved and the way she met each thrust. Nothing but this beautiful light they made together.

Nothing but love.

An alarm rang in her then, but she ignored it, too far gone to care.

"I can't," she said again, but this time her voice was a sob and she hardly knew what she said.

"You must," he told her, so dark and so sure. And she believed him. "Now."

And then he reached down between them and pressed down hard just above her entrance, never stopping that delicious rhythm of his, and Mattie exploded. Shattered into nothing but slivers of that same great light, cast out to the heavens.

Shattered into nothingness, but not before she heard him shout her name, and follow.

It was not until the night fell again outside that Nicodemus finally left her, and even then, it very nearly proved impossible.

She was so warm. Pliant and perfect as she lay against him, her face in his neck and her breathing solid and even. A perfect fit, even now.

But he made himself do it. He pulled away and sat up on the edge of the bed, almost wishing she would wake as she'd done so many times before, tempting him back to her side so he wouldn't have to think. Wouldn't have to consider what to do next. Wouldn't have to accept what he already knew he would have to do.

It had been a long day.

A very long day, and all of it moved in him, slow and sweet, making him want her anew when he'd have thought it impossible. He'd finally explored every inch of her delectable body. He'd taken her again and again, even after he'd thought she must surely have had enough—but all she had to do was whisper that she wanted more in his ear and his self-control deserted him.

He knew how she tasted now, everywhere. He knew what sounds she made when she was close and what cries she let out when she was feeling frustrated and deliciously greedy. He knew how she threw back her head, how she went liquid and wild then burst into flame.

And he was the only man who knew. The only man who had ever touched her like this, had her, claimed her— and Nicodemus knew he was every inch of him caveman enough to revel in that. His possessiveness roared in him, almost drowning everything else out.

Almost.

"Is this the talking part?" she asked from behind him, her voice husky in the shadows.

He could have said no. He could have simply turned, swept her into his arms again, lost himself in her the way he wanted to do. He could have put this off for the night, for the rest of their time here. Forever.

But he didn't. He couldn't.

"You are a liar," he said, and this time, it wasn't that same accusation. It was a simple statement of fact, and he heard her shift against the sheets behind him.

"Does this qualify as pillow talk?" she asked. "Because if so, I think you suck at it."

Delivered in that way of hers that made him want to laugh, and he understood that this was why she was so dangerous. Even more dangerous than he'd thought she was when he'd only longed for her from afar. Unlike Arista, who had only ever been what he'd projected on her, Nicodemus *liked* Mattie.

He liked her wry humor. He liked how profoundly unafraid of him she was. He liked how willing she was to mock them both, as if all of this was simply a game they were playing instead of so terribly real and important it made him ache inside. He liked a thousand things about her that had nothing to do with how pretty she was, or how terribly he craved her, or his merger with her father's company and the work he'd do with her brother in the coming months.

Yet none of that mattered, because she couldn't stop lying and he couldn't live with it. He'd had more lies in his life than he could bear. And he couldn't help noticing she hadn't denied it.

"That wasn't meant to be anything but a simple truth," he said then, shifting around so he could look at her. "It's the central core of who you are, Mattie. You lie. Always. About everything. Even this."

She frowned at him, though her mouth looked vulnerable, and he had to steel himself against reaching for her.

"You can't demand that someone let you into their private thoughts. That takes time and—"

"Why did you save yourself for me?" he asked her, swift and brutal.

Her frown deepened. "It was an accident."

"That's a lie, even as we sit here discussing lying." She flushed, confirming it as surely as if she'd openly admitted it. "Let's try again. What are your nightmares about?"

She looked miserable then, and he wanted that to be enough. He wanted that to matter. But she swallowed, looking down and moving her hands beneath the sheet she'd pulled over her so he couldn't see them. He didn't need to see; he knew she'd made them into fists.

He knew too much about her now. That was the trouble.

"I had one nightmare," she said in a low voice, and she couldn't even look at him. "And you woke me."

He felt like he was cracking open, breaking apart. Like that final lie was the last nail into a sheet of glass and it shattered everything.

"I thought I could reach you," he said quietly. "I thought it was all a game and you'd stop playing it when we were here, alone. All this time, I thought that beneath everything, this mattered."

She lifted her dark eyes to his, and they were bright with tears he had no expectation she'd ever shed. He couldn't even be certain they were real, no matter how much he wanted them to be.

"This does," she whispered. "This matters."

"Then tell me one true thing, Mattie," he said, more urgently than before. "One that isn't a trap. One that doesn't take us down your little rabbit hole of lies within lies until we are nothing but twisted into knots. *One thing.*"

"You know everything that matters," she said instead. "I'm here, aren't I? This all happened. I saved myself for you, and what does it matter why? What more do you think you need to know?"

He shook his head , and the battle to keep himself from touching her became pitched and nearly violent. He stood, moving away from the bed to slap on the lights that lit the room with a golden glow—but it was better than all those shadows. All that too-intimate darkness, where he was too likely to imagine he saw what he wanted to see instead of what was.

Mattie sat in the center of the bed, wrapped in his sheets, blinking in the sudden onslaught of light. And he still longed for her, despite everything. He was still as hungry for her as if he hadn't spent an entire day indulging that appetite.

He understood, then, that this would never change. That she'd had this hold on him since the first and always would. That he loved her as he'd loved no other, and it still didn't matter.

He never did learn his lessons.

"My father was a strict, grim man," he told her, though he didn't know why. But then, he didn't want to leave her in any doubt as to his motives. "He came in and out of our flat in a dark cloud, and my mother rushed to appease him, no matter what he did or said. For a long time, I didn't understand why his moods were the only important ones in our home."

He studied her as she sat there, her eyes wide and fixed

on him. "No smart little interjections, Mattie? I'm surprised."

"You never talk about your past," she said simply. "Only what you own."

He accepted that as a hit, though he wasn't certain it was meant as one. It stung, nonetheless.

"As I grew, my father took an interest in my character." He folded his arms over his chest and stared at her, though what he saw was that crowded little flat and the angry man who dominated it with his temper and his cruelties. His ability to find fault in everything. "He could smell lies on me, he told me. And when he did, he took it upon himself to beat them out of me."

"So we are both liars, then," Mattie said, and he thought her voice was warmer than it should have been. Warmer than made any sense.

"He was given to great lectures he punctuated with his fists," Nicodemus continued. "He had very distinct ideas about what was wrong and what was right." He smiled, not nicely. "Needless to say, I was a grave disappointment to him in all ways."

She let out a small sound that was something like a sigh. "It's hard to imagine you subject to someone else's whims. Much less a disappointment to anyone."

Nicodemus didn't want to continue with this. He wanted to explore that soft note in her voice, instead. He wanted to pretend none of this mattered to him. He wanted to bury himself in her and let that be enough. It almost was, after all.

Almost.

He wanted more than *almost.* He'd accepted *almost* for the whole of his life. From his parents, from Arista. From Mattie. He couldn't do it any longer. He wouldn't.

"Luckily, my father did not stay with us all the time," he

said, instead. "Often he was gone for weeks. My mother would tell me he was away on business, and that he loved us very much, as if she thought I needed soothing, but the truth was, I preferred it when he was away. The only time my mother ever hit me was when I said so out loud."

"I don't mean to overstep," she said quietly. "But I can't say I'm forming a positive impression of your parents."

He saw his mother's stunningly beautiful face, those flashing black eyes and that lustrous fall of hair she'd spent so many hours brushing and curling and tending. He saw the creams she'd only used when his father wasn't there, the drinks she'd favored while alone that were liberally laced with the alcohol she otherwise only served his father. He could picture her, pretty and breakable, staring out the windows as if looking for ships at sea—though they hadn't had a view of the sea from their flat. And the only one who ever came to visit them was his father.

"One day when I was twelve, I decided to follow my father when he left us," Nicodemus said then, because he couldn't seem to stop. "I don't remember what brought this on. I'd like to think he'd given himself away somehow but I suspect the truth is, I was twelve. I was bored. He had come less and less that year, and the less he came, the more it upset my mother. She coped by drinking and spending her days further and further away inside her dream world."

"Who took care of you?" Mattie asked.

He smiled. "Did your father take care of you himself while running Whitaker Industries?" he asked. "I imagine not."

"We had a series of excellent nannies," she shot back, tilting her chin up as she did, reminding him of all the ways he couldn't have her. "And a fantastic housekeeper that Chase and I consider a member of the family."

"My mother did not work, though she told stories of

when she'd cleaned houses before I was born. There were no nannies or housekeepers. I took care of myself." That look on her face made him feel something like claws inside his chest, so he pushed on. "But that day, I followed my father. I followed him up into the hills where the houses were bigger. Prettier."

Nicodemus found himself moving without meaning to do it, ranging toward the windows and pausing there, his back to the bed, because he wasn't sure what he'd do if she kept looking at him with all that softness in her gaze. He didn't know what would become of his conviction, his purpose. Of him.

"And when I peeked in the windows of the big house he'd gone inside," he said quietly, as much to the sea as to the woman behind him, as much to his memory as anything, "I found he had a whole other family." There was no sound from behind him, not even a breath against the air in the room. "I didn't understand at first. I couldn't make sense of it. There was a woman, three children. One was a boy who looked about my age. And they all called my father *Babá.*"

He had never said that out loud. And even now, he refused to admit that it tore at him, like knives into flesh. That he could still feel such an old betrayal so keenly, even after all these years.

"That is the word for *Dad,*" he clarified. And he heard her then. She breathed out, long and hard, like she hurt for him, and his curse was, he wished she did.

"I don't know how long I watched them through their big windows." He remembered it being a long time— months, even—though he supposed that could have been the vagaries of memory, playing tricks on him. "I went back day after day. And watching them, I learned to want. I wanted all of it. The parties that seemed to bore them.

The fancy toys they never seemed grateful for. The great big house with whole rooms they didn't enter for days at a time, if at all."

He turned back to face her then, leaning one shoulder against the wall to the side of the window. She hadn't moved. She still sat where he'd left her, more beautiful now than any woman had the right to be. Her hair was a tousled mess, tumbling down her back in its midnight glory. Her mouth looked ravaged and her eyes gleamed with emotion. And he wanted her. God, how he wanted her. The way he'd always wanted her. The same way he'd wanted that other life he'd glimpsed through his father's windows.

He should have known better then. He did know better now, and still, here he was. It was as if he'd learned nothing, after all.

"The next time my father beat me for my supposed lies, I asked him about his." Mattie frowned, as if she could see what was coming in that small, sharp-edged curve of his mouth he allowed himself. "I knew it was a secret, but you see, I had no secrets of my own. He'd seen to that. So it never crossed my mind to consider the reasons secrets like his might be better kept hidden."

"Nicodemus," she said softly, like she could see straight through him to his guilt. His lingering fury. "Whatever happened, you were a child."

"I was twelve," he corrected her. "Not quite a child, not where I grew up. And certainly man enough to receive the vicious beating my father gave me for questioning him, following him, calling him out. I was his sin, you see. The living, breathing emblem of his betrayal of his wife with the low class servant girl who had cleaned his house. He was very self-righteous when he told me that he had come to us all these years purely in an effort to wash the stain from my soul. To help me become a better man, because left to my own devices, I'd no doubt become a whore like my mother." Nicodemus didn't look away from Mattie as he said this, laying out the history he never spoke of so matter-of-factly. And he didn't crack when she winced at that ugly word. "He made me thank him as I lay there, bloody on the floor. And then he walked out the door and he never returned."

"Never?" Mattie asked, shock coloring her voice, her gaze. "But he was your father!"

"Worse, he stopped supporting us," Nicodemus said. "That meant I had to leave school to work wherever I could, and it meant my dreamy, useless, fragile mother had to work in the factories. Thread, mostly. And it killed her."

Mattie didn't say his name again, but she made a small noise that sounded almost too rough, too raw. It made him want to touch her, hold her, almost more than he could bear.

"When I went back to my father's great big house on its sparkling hill, to ask him to help once my mother had collapsed, he had me arrested."

It was amazing how remote he could sound, he thought. As if these things had happened to someone else. But he could still feel his father's security guards' hands on him, his father's foot against his neck, as he was held facedown in the dirt. He still remembered the stink and the din of that grotty cell.

"While I sat in jail, my mother died. And when I got out, Mattie, I dedicated my life to making certain that no one would ever use their wealth or power to get the better of me. And that no one would ever lie to my face again. I was sixteen, and I maintained this position for at least a couple of years. And then, when I was twenty and full of myself and all the new money I'd made running construction sites, I lost my head over the boss's daughter."

"Nicodemus," she said in that thick, ragged way that he feared would be his undoing.

"Her name was Arista and she was much too pretty," he said. "It blinded me. She took my money and my adulation and she liked what I could do for her in bed, but when it came time for her to marry she chose a rich boy from her social circle and laughed at me that I'd expected anything else. I was something stuck to the bottom of her shoe, nothing more. I thought I'd learned my lesson, at last."

She looked at him for a long time, and Nicodemus wished things could be different. Wished all of this was different. And wishing had never led to anything but trouble.

His smile felt bitter. "And then I came to the States and I saw you. And you were everything I ever wanted, Mattie. More than I dared dream. Your father treated me better than my own ever had, and I could see all that heat in your eyes when you looked at me, and I knew you were the one I wanted. You and no one else."

She jerked slightly. And when her gaze met his again, it was something more than troubled.

"You wanted a pretty girl you saw dancing at a party," she said, very carefully. Very distinctly. "I could have been anyone. I could have been that girl in Greece. You didn't know anything about *me*. You still don't."

"I love you," he told her, because there was no point pretending any longer, and it didn't matter, anyway. "And everything you've ever told me is a lie."

Her breath caught, then came fast, like that flush across her cheeks and the upper slopes of her breasts. Her mouth opened, but she snapped it closed, and he saw a whole world of misery in those bittersweet eyes of hers.

Still, she said nothing. But then, had he expected anything else?

"And when I tell you I cannot abide liars, Mattie, I mean it. I mean this. I mean you."

Everything had gone too dark, despite the golden light that made the room seem so cheerful, so bright. Too raw. Too stark. And she looked at him like he'd broken her heart. Like he'd torn her in two.

It said terrible things about him, he knew, that he wished he had. That he wished he could. That he wished she felt something for him when he knew—*he knew*—that would only make this that much worse.

"Tell me the truth," he said then, his voice final, and he could see she heard it. "I won't ask again."

It was as if a thousand words fought inside her, pushing at her throat and making it feel tight, turning into the tears that pricked at the back of her eyes, running over her skin and into her veins like some kind of poison—but Mattie knew she didn't dare open her mouth. She didn't dare try to speak.

She knew, somehow, that she wouldn't stop.

And the idea of that—of spilling her guts the way Nicodemus had done, of letting out all the brutal things that had lived inside her all this time—swelled in her like a terrible wave.

She couldn't do it. She would rather he hate her forever for the things he *thought* he knew about her than tell him the truth and see it right there on his face. Unmistakable and real.

Mattie fought back a wave of panic and crawled to the edge of the bed, then onto her feet. Only then did she let the sheet drop, and was rewarded for that with the sharp sound of Nicodemus's indrawn breath.

"Don't play these games with me," he warned her. "You didn't like how it ended the last time you tried to manipulate me with sex."

But he didn't move from where he stood near the window, and that was what she focused on.

I love you, he'd said, and the words tumbled around and around inside her, picking up mass and speed with every second until she thought they were all she was. That and all the things she *couldn't* say in return.

She moved closer to him, feeling that pull, that electricity that called to her whenever he was near. And now she knew what it meant. What it was promising.

"Mattie." He took her hands in his when she would have put them on his bare skin, and his face was grim again. Dark and forbidding, and that thing inside her that she'd always thought was broken because it only ever responded to him pulled taut. As attracted to his darkness as his light. Attracted, no matter what. "Just tell me the truth. Any truth, damn you."

But she couldn't do that. She didn't know how.

All she'd ever done with Nicodemus was fight. Fight and lie, just as he accused her. It hadn't been a strategy— it had only ever been survival.

And so, she told herself, was this.

She melted against him. She turned her head to kiss her way along his strong forearm, amazed when she felt him shudder. She tipped forward until her breasts pressed into his chest—and she smiled when he let out a stream of dark, evidently filthy Greek.

He let go of her hands.

And Mattie told him all the truths she knew in the only way she could.

She loved him with her mouth, her fingers, her cheeks against the expanse of his abdomen. She loved him the way she understood, now, she always had. He'd cast his shadow across the last ten years of her life, and she finally understood why.

Why she'd waited. Why she'd had boyfriends but had never felt right about taking that last step with them. Why she'd run so hard in the opposite direction every time she'd seen Nicodemus.

It was *this*. The things he wanted were uncompromising, exhilarating. The things she felt were the same.

Too much. Everything.

She couldn't open herself up like that. She didn't dare. But she could give him this.

Mattie showed him what lurked in her heart, what she'd never dare say aloud. She lavished him with all the beauty and terror and sweet, hot need he'd introduced her to so expertly. She led him to the bed and crawled over him, leaving no part of him untouched. As if she could press all the things she felt directly into his skin. As if she could tattoo him with her own mouth.

As if this was better than the truth he wanted.

And then, finally, when everything had tightened beyond bearing and both of them were desperate, she climbed on top of him, wincing slightly when she took him deep inside her.

"This is too much," he gritted out, even now, when she knew he was pushed to his limits. "You are new to this."

Mattie only held his gaze. And then she began to move.

She built her rhythm slowly, carefully, and then, when she was more comfortable, she picked up her pace. His hands gripped her hips as he met her, thrusting hard and deep and beautiful.

And this, she thought and had to bite her lip from saying, was better than simply true. This was truth itself and this was *right* and surely, he must feel it. Surely, he must know all the things she felt, yet couldn't say.

Surely, he must understand how desperately she loved him.

This time, when the fire built and built until it finally

burned them both alive, they flew off that glorious edge together.

But when Mattie woke from a shockingly uninterrupted sleep, it was another perfect gold and blue morning outside the windows, there was a servant bustling around in the kitchen downstairs with unwelcome efficiency and cheer, and Nicodemus was gone.

CHAPTER NINE

NICODEMUS'S ENTIRE LIFE mocked him.

There were the papers he'd signed in a grim fury the day he'd returned from Greece to merge the Stathis Corporation with Whitaker Industries, despite that burning thing in him that had wanted nothing more than to fly to London and punch Chase Whitaker in the face, because Chase was the closest thing on the planet to Big Bart. He still didn't know how he'd managed to keep himself in check. How he'd returned to Manhattan and his office there without causing any international incidents, such was the temper he'd been in when he'd left his island.

There was the brownstone in New York's West Village he stood in now, that he'd bought and painstakingly renovated years ago and had been calling *home* when his real home should have been in Athens near his own head-quarters. There was even this damned mood he was in, black and dangerous like the autumn storm outside the windows, pelting the city with the same bitter cold he felt inside himself.

It was all about her, and he felt it like one of her mocking little laughs, lighting him up and ripping into him at the same time.

You have to put this behind you, he ordered himself. Over and over again. But it didn't seem to work.

The sad truth was, everything he did and everything he'd done for years revolved around Mattie Whitaker, and the fact he hadn't noticed it even as he'd done it galled him. The fact he'd never seen her for what she was ate at him. At first, perhaps, it had been unconscious. He'd wanted a woman *like* her, he'd told himself. And he'd admired her father, the first man who'd ever treated Nicodemus as something other than a trashy upstart. The man who'd encouraged him to educate himself and had given him the tools to do it.

But at some point along the way he'd stopped pretending. And now he was married to a woman he couldn't trust, tied up in a thousand legal knots with her family business, and completely screwed.

Literally as well as figuratively, he admitted darkly, and let out some rendition of a laugh.

And she'd been a virgin.

He still couldn't believe it. He still couldn't handle all the implications of that—the one thing she couldn't fake or lie about. He didn't know what was worse—his absolute disbelief, because her virginity meant he didn't know her as well as he'd thought he did, or that primitive part of him that simply wanted to claim her as his, now and forever.

It stood to reason that now he finally had her, now that he'd made her his in every possible way, he didn't see how he could let himself keep her.

Another blustery autumn night had fallen over Manhattan, blanketing the city with a thick darkness that looked almost soft from inside the office he'd built on the second floor of the brownstone, despite the rain that still pounded down, making the trees along the city street bend and sway.

And Nicodemus ignored the insistent beeping from his laptop that indicated one incoming email after the next.

He ignored the buzzing of his mobile phone. He stared out at the cold, wet dark and tortured himself.

One scalding-hot image after the next, as relentless as the freezing rain outside, and as brutal.

Mattie kissing him, using her mouth all over him, beguiling him and enslaving him. Mattie sitting astride him, the most beautiful creature he'd ever beheld, riding them both into all of that white-hot wonder.

Mattie, Mattie, Mattie, the way it had been since the moment he'd seen her in her long-ago ball gown, sparkling so brightly she'd eclipsed the whole of the world.

And that was when the truth of things hit him, making him feel something like sick.

After all this time, after all the effort he'd put into never, ever becoming a man like his father, he'd neglected to recognize that it was his other parent's influence he should have guarded himself against.

Because he was no different from his sad, discarded mother, was he? She'd taught him how to pine. How to spend years longing for someone who would never return the feeling. Arista had been a mere practice run. He'd built a whole life around his hopes and dreams about Mattie.

"How can you consider taking him back, after all of this?" Nicodemus had railed at his mother in those terrible days after that last scene with his father, when his mother had still maintained her vigil and her beauty regimen as if those things were sacred rituals that would bring him back. "How can you weep for him?"

"The heart is more forgiving than you imagine," his mother had told him, humming to herself as she'd combed out her hair. "And far more resilient."

And he'd hated her for it.

He could admit that now, after all these years had passed. After he'd exacted his revenge when he'd gutted his father's company and stripped him of the better part of his wealth. After he'd gone on to far outshine the man who had ruined them both. God, how he'd hated her. He'd hated her almost as much as he'd loved her, in that same helpless way, so unable was he to fix what was broken in her or save her once his father had abandoned them.

"He is never coming back," he'd told her when she'd ended up in the hospital and had insisted that he dress her in something nicer than a hospital gown, in case his father deigned to stop by when Nicodemus had known full well he wouldn't. "He doesn't care if we live or die."

"Love is not always a straight line, Nicodemus," she'd replied in that reedy voice of hers, so thin even he'd known, at sixteen and before the doctors had taken him aside to confirm it, that she hadn't had much time left.

And the guilt he'd felt over how much he'd hated her obliviousness, her dogged optimism, her reckless belief in one so deeply unworthy of her notice, had led him to approach his father that last time.

His reward for that had been a month in jail, and his mother had died alone.

Nicodemus couldn't shake aside these old ghosts. He felt as if he was that twelve-year-old boy again, miserable and astonished, with his face pressed to the gates of a fancy house high in the hills above Piraeus. He'd done exactly what he'd set out to do then. The houses. The expensive toys. Whatever he desired was his—precisely as he'd dreamed when he'd first seen the true life his father led. When he'd understood that he and his mother were the dirty secrets.

But he'd forgotten—or chosen to ignore—that the heart that beat inside his chest was softer.

As foolish and as suicidal as his mother's had been.

"You must stop this," he ordered himself, only aware

that he spoke out loud when he heard the resounding silence that followed his words.

He cursed beneath his breath, pushing back from the desk, ignoring his ringing phone. Ignoring the hours of work he had left to do today. Ignoring everything but that darkness inside him that he wished he could excise with his own two hands.

He wished. He still wished and that, Nicodemus understood, was his problem. Perhaps it always had been.

He had to decide what to do with Mattie now. It occurred to him, standing in yet another home he'd made with every expectation that she would live in it with him one day, that this was the first time in a decade that he'd had any doubts. He'd always known exactly what to do with Mattie Whitaker. He'd always had a plan. That plan had changed in its particulars over the years, but essentially, it was always the same: isolate the two of them from the rest of the world and let their insane chemistry do the rest.

He'd always imagined that would be enough.

But now—he'd tasted her innocence. He'd seen truths in her beautiful eyes that she'd refused to speak out loud. He'd soothed her in her restless, broken sleep and he'd held her in his arms as she'd cried. He'd watched her rebel, and he'd watched her surrender, and he couldn't have said which part of her he liked most.

He'd loved her from afar for ten years. He loved her even more now.

And it still didn't matter.

He couldn't trust her. He didn't believe her. She was made entirely of secrets and lies, and he couldn't do it. He knew where it led. *Exactly* where it led. He'd already done this, more than once.

Which meant that somehow, after all these years and all the things he'd done to get them here, the lives he'd built for them to live in and the dreams he'd been fool enough to think he could indulge, he had to find a way to let her go.

"You must have done something," Chase said over the phone, with what sounded like sheer irritation in his voice. It made his British accent that much more pronounced.

It made Mattie want to reach through the phone and slap him, all the way across the Atlantic Ocean in his London office.

This is your beloved big brother, the only family you have left in all the world, she cautioned herself. *None of this is his fault,*

None of this is your *fault, either,* she replied to herself staunchly—though she imagined that depended on which of her faults was under discussion. And with whom.

Mattie took a deep breath as she stood in her same old living room on the Upper West Side, now its usual size without Nicodemus looming in it to shrink the dimensions around him. His absence lanced into her, a sharp and searing pain, no less bearable for the fact it wasn't anything new, and she deeply regretted returning her brother's call.

"Would you like a point-by-point analysis of how I executed my duties as Nicodemus's arranged bride?" she asked, her voice almost as clipped as his, and her accent had gone American years ago. "I should warn you in advance. Some parts get a little bit naked. That's what happens in marriages whether they're arranged or not, or didn't you know?"

It was easy to keep her voice cool and even. Or arch and brittle, more accurately. Because ever since Nicodemus had left her to make her own way home from his island, Mattie had felt...nothing. Not when Chase called. Not when the papers speculated about her and her marriage. Not at all.

She was a polished piece of glass, she told herself now. Hard and smooth. Impervious to harm.

"I don't need this bloody headache," Chase muttered.

It was almost under his breath. And Mattie therefore *almost* pretended that she hadn't heard it. But there was that raw thing inside her that felt like a poisonous snake, coiled tight and ready to strike, and Chase was setting himself up as the perfect target.

"I apologize that the marriage you pushed me into for business purposes has turned out to be less than blissful," she said in that same bright and hard tone. "You'll remember how thrilled I was about it in the first place. Who could possibly have predicted that this might happen?" She pretended to wait a beat, as if considering the question. "Oh, right. I did."

Chase sighed at her sarcastic tone. Mattie's fingers clenched so hard around her phone receiver that it hurt, her rings biting into her flesh, and it wasn't her brother who she was angry at, she knew. He had nothing to do with all the things that had happened between her and Nicodemus on that island—all the things she couldn't tell him. Or anyone.

All the things she wasn't entirely ready to admit to herself, even now.

"I spoke to Nicodemus not three days ago and he gave me no indication that there was anything wrong with your marriage," Chase said, sounding impatient, which made that thing inside her pull tight. Coil harder. "In fact, you didn't even come up."

"Oh, I see," she gritted out. "That must mean that I hallucinated the past month of my life, then."

She heard the sound of papers rustling, and then a keyboard tapping, and it filled her with a completely unwarranted fury that Chase could simply…go about his business while she was nothing but stuck.

Not that she'd entirely admitted that to herself in the week or so since she'd returned home from Greece. She hadn't allowed herself to think such a thing while tossing herself back into the life she'd left behind here and wanted so desperately to believe still fit like a glove.

But that didn't make it any less true.

"Although, now that I think about it, he did seem particularly focused on business," Chase said, almost grudgingly. "He's usually a little more friendly. Only a little."

Mattie waited, but Chase didn't offer up any other details. She realized she was clenching her teeth, and forced herself to stop.

"Thanks," she said mildly, though inside, she was so terribly raw and too hot and shattering into jagged little pieces. "I'll write you a note, shall I? And the next time you see him or talk to him, you can give it to him, and we can all pretend we're in grade school together."

"Mattie—" Chase began.

"I don't want to hear whatever you're about to say," she told him, and there was nothing smooth or glass-like about her voice then. She only wondered how she'd held it together so long. "I did what you wanted me to do, and you couldn't even do me the courtesy of showing up to witness it. And I only called you back today because I thought you should know the state of things between Nicodemus and me. Foolishly, I was worried that it might affect the business. I'm delighted to hear that while Nicodemus may have broken a promise or two to *me,* all is well where the company is concerned." She laughed, and it was not a nice sound. "As ever, that's all that matters."

"It's not all that matters." Chase sounded tougher than the brother she knew. Harder. Colder. "But it's the only thing we have left. And if that doesn't mean something, Mattie, then I don't know what does."

It's not the only thing, a tiny voice whispered inside her. *It's a company. It's not us.*

And Mattie realized then that she was miserable. Pure and simple.

She let that unfortunate truth trickle through her, filling her up until she hardly recognized herself, as if it had changed her from the inside out. Altered her. It made her want to throw her phone across the room and watch it break into pieces. It made her want to curl into a ball and cry for days, as she'd only done one other time in her life.

She'd been a liar for most of her life because there was one truth she couldn't tell. And she wondered why she'd never noticed that keeping that secret had changed her. Turned her inside out. Made her the kind of woman who could look at a man she loved and be too afraid to admit it, even to herself.

That thudded into her. Like a sledgehammer. Like Nicodemus's heartbeat beneath her palm. Like one more true thing she couldn't tell him, couldn't say out loud, couldn't let herself believe.

"Do you think about that day?" she asked Chase, because they were what was left. The company was incidental. Or it should have been.

His silence told her he knew exactly what day she meant. And more, that he did think about it. But they hadn't spoken of it. Not in twenty years. Not since it had happened.

And she didn't want that guilt anymore, the guilt that had always convinced her that it was her fault they had this distant, strained relationship. That it was her fault they were like this.

"I get that you're upset, Mats," Chase said after an uneven moment, when there'd been nothing but that heavy silence between them that she wasn't sure he'd break. "But I don't see any point in revisiting old ghosts. Particularly those ghosts."

"I'm guessing that means *you* don't wake up every night of your life screaming, then," she heard herself say, as if from a far-off height. "Calling out for her again and again."

"What is the point of this?" And she'd never heard him sound like this, not in years. Like there was something raging beneath his skin, too. "What is there to be gained? I'm sorry that you still have the nightmares, I am. But dragging ourselves back through this swamp is only going to—"

"I don't understand why we lied about being there," she whispered, because she couldn't seem to stop now that she'd started. "What was the point of *that?*"

"You were eight years old," Chase said succinctly. "I was thirteen. I don't think we remember the same things. We did her a kindness. As well as us."

"I'm not eight anymore, Chase. Tell me what you remember."

"Our mother died in front of us," he said, and she couldn't identify what she heard in his voice then. Pain, yes. That same horror she still felt herself. Grief and fury and then something so much darker beneath it. "On the side of a road. But you and I are safe. I don't know what else you want."

"I want the truth," she said, and maybe it shouldn't have surprised her that her legs were too shaky, that she had to sit down. That the world felt as if it was breaking apart all around her, and she wasn't sure she wanted to know why.

Or maybe she was afraid she already did.

"Leave it, Mattie," Chase told her, his voice hard again. He sounded like a different man entirely today, raw and grim, and it changed everything. It changed her. Or maybe it was Nicodemus who had done that. "There are some stones it isn't worth turning over."

And she wasn't surprised when he claimed he had another call and disconnected moments later. She sat where she was for a long time.

Mattie had been protecting something she didn't fully understand since she was eight years old. She'd been held hostage to those memories. And the only way she'd figured out how to do that and carry on living was to hold herself at a distance from anyone and everything that ventured near. Let nothing and no one close, she'd reasoned, and they couldn't know her. Or hurt her, the way she'd been hurt the day they'd lost her mother.

Or learn things they shouldn't. Things so terrible that her relationship with her father and with Chase had never recovered after that awful day.

But Nicodemus had never been one for distance, until now. She shook her head slightly, as if trying to clear it, and understood that was part of what was happening to her. Why she felt like an empty echo chamber. Why she was so miserable.

He wasn't there.

For ten years, Nicodemus had always been there. If not right in front of her, then nearby. She'd known it. She'd expected it—perhaps even come to depend on it. He'd made certain she did. He'd been a fact of her life, like the weather, like the inevitability of fall into winter. He'd been relentless. He'd been *Nicodemus*.

He'd pushed and pushed, and he'd made it so very easy to push back—

Mattie didn't know what to do with herself now. Not when she'd given him everything, more than she'd ever given anyone, and it still wasn't enough. Not when she'd pushed back the way she'd always done and he'd walked away instead, leaving her with no choice but fall forward on her face. Leaving her where she landed on the ground.

Leaving her, at last, the way she'd always claimed she'd wanted him to do.

After everything, it shouldn't have surprised her so much that he was right. She really was a liar.

Glass, she told herself frantically as she felt all of this surge inside her, so close to bursting out. She was smooth and she was hard all the way through and she was *glass*—

But what she felt was broken.

Mattie waited for him in the decidedly sleek and modern waiting room of his Manhattan office, high in one of those Midtown buildings that housed everything from doctors to lawyers to international multimillionaires like Nicodemus in varying shades of lush, dark wood and understated gilt edges.

"Mr. Stathis may be some time," the gatekeeping receptionist said pleasantly enough from behind her fortress of a high, curved desk, if not for the first time. "He doesn't encourage walk-ins."

"Mr. Stathis will see me," Mattie assured her with a grand sort of bravado that she did not feel at all. Also not for the first time.

"I really do need your name, ma'am," the woman replied, her professional smile showing signs of strain.

"I'll say it once more." Mattie raised her voice so that all the people around her pretending not to listen to this interchange—business associates of Nicodemus's, she could only hope, waiting for their meetings with his various staff members and capable of all kinds of gossip should he ignore her for too long—could hear her. And recognize her, she had no doubt. And wonder. "Just tell him there are consequences to his behavior, and they are sitting in his lobby."

The woman's lips all but disappeared, she pressed them together so hard, but she didn't say another word.

And Mattie waited. She used her smartphone to page through tabloid articles heralding the quick end to her hasty marriage and did her best to look as relaxed and confident as she wanted to look—as she'd dressed.

Once again, for him. Killer heels not suited for New York City sidewalks in the wet, slippery fall, a pencil skirt that made poetry of her long frame and a silk blouse that wrapped around her torso lovingly yet failed to show anything a possessive Greek husband might find objectionable.

At least, Mattie fervently hoped he was still both of those things. Possessive and her husband. Or this meeting she'd engineered was going to be significantly more devastating than she was prepared to handle.

But it was still a very long time before a sharp, expectant sort of silence descended over the waiting room, like the fall of an ax. Mattie sat a little straighter in her chair, but she didn't look up. Not while she heard a low, quick conversation in a voice she knew all too well, one that made her whole body shiver into immediate goose bumps. Not when she felt a very familiar dark glare sear into her flesh from across the room, making it difficult to sit still.

Not until he was looming over her and she had no choice whatsoever but to crane her head back and look up that mouthwatering length of him, packaged to extremely gorgeous effect in one of the dark suits he favored that made him look like he really was king of the goddamned world.

He wasn't smiling. His eyes were cold—colder than she'd ever seen them before.

And both of those things hurt in ways Mattie hardly knew what to do with.

"Are you pregnant?" he asked. Not at all gently, or even politely.

She didn't blush. She didn't look around to see if anyone had heard. She knew Nicodemus well enough by now to know he never would have said that if anyone was listening.

Or she hoped she did.

"No," she said, very calmly, which wasn't at all how she felt.

"Then I fail to understand what *consequences* there could be that require not only my presence upon demand, but your theatrical appearance here at all."

If he was having trouble with all of that subzero wind chill that dripped from his low voice and oozed from every taut, unwelcoming line in his body, he certainly didn't show it.

Trust only went so far, Mattie decided, and snuck a glance around him to see that—as she should have expected, because he might be furious with her but he was still Nicodemus—he'd dismissed the receptionist and cleared the room.

"I'm not happy with you," she informed him.

Something in his hard jaw twitched. "I will cry myself to sleep over that, Mattie, I promise you. But in the meantime, I have a company to run and a merger with an unpleasant family company I regret already to oversee. I left your histrionics and your lies in Greece for a reason."

"And I slept with you," she retorted.

He hadn't expected that—she could see it in the way his dark eyes widened slightly, then narrowed. He frowned at her, and there was something wrong with her that she saw that as a kind of progress. Better than all that ice, anyway.

"Thank you," he said, in such frozen tones she almost missed the fact that his accent was heavier—also a good sign. "But my memory works perfectly."

"I'm twenty-eight years old and I've never slept with

anyone but you," she said, and she pushed up out of the chair then, so she could face him. So he wasn't towering over her, especially not with the shoes she had on. So she could look him in the eye, the way that had always made her feel so strong and so weak at once. Today was no different. "You gave me one night and then you disappeared."

His stunned pause was so brief that she almost missed it.

"I'm reliably informed that is the plight of many a young woman in this dark, dirty city," he told her, with all that menace and ruthlessness in his voice, in the way he looked at her, and her curse was that it moved through like a long, low lick of heat. "You should count yourself lucky I didn't make you walk home from Greece."

"I waited a long time to have sex," she said, keeping her chin high and her eyes on him. "I want more of it." She felt more than saw the way he caught his breath at that, but she had no trouble identifying that flash of murder in his dark gaze. "And I'm married to you, which means that if I head out for the bars like so many young women in this big, bad city, I'd be committing adultery."

"That," he said, his voice a mere rasp of darkness despite the bright lights all around them, "and I'd kill you."

Mattie smiled. "So you see my predicament."

He stared at her for a long time. Too long. Then he reached over and wrapped his hand around her upper arm, sending a bolt of that wildfire straight through her. There had to be something wrong with her that even a touch like that made her melt—but she didn't care. She was too busy reveling in it.

"Once again," Nicodemus said in that same dangerous tone that was wreaking havoc with her nervous system, "you play with things you cannot possibly understand."

"Play with me or I'll play with whoever I want," she countered, fairly bursting with all of that fake bravado, because it was the only thing she'd been able to think of that would push him enough, and quickly. "Those are your choices, Nicodemus, though you claim I never give you any."

His hand tightened around her arm, and he hauled her, gently yet inexorably, around the side of that fortress of a desk that was currently missing its gatekeeper. He towed her down the long hallway, while his employees leaped from his path and did a terrible job of pretending not to stare, until he reached the great, big office in the far corner.

It had a long, deep view of the city along the outside walls, and when he closed the door behind them, they were trapped there together. A wall on one side to block them from prying eyes and the canyons of Manhattan right there on the other.

He let go of her, but she could still feel his fingers and the heat of his skin, like brands into her flesh.

"I don't know what I'm going to do with you," he told her, his accent under control again, but this time she sensed how hard it was for him to maintain it. "But it will not involve bargaining for sex like an animal."

"Not like an animal," she protested mildly. "Unless, of course, you think that's fun. I'm willing to try anything once. Even spanking. I think."

He shook his head and leaned against the massive granite desk that should have fallen through the floor beneath it, so gargantuan did it look, and yet somehow it suited him. He ran his hand down his front as if to straighten the tie he wore that didn't require any straightening, and it would have been easier if he'd glowered at her.

But he didn't. If anything, he looked sad and tired, the way he had before, and like then, it made her heart clutch inside her chest.

"I don't want to play games with you anymore," Nicodemus said quietly. Too quietly. "For too long, I thought this was all a game, and that I knew how to win it in the end, but I was wrong. I'm not accustomed to that. It might take some adjustment."

She'd expected temper. Accusation and heat. Not this.

But she didn't know how to do anything with this man but push back.

"Does that mean divorce?" she asked in her same nearly flippant tone, so at odds with the one he'd used. "Or no divorce? I can't keep track. Though the fact you ran away from Greece rather suggests the latter, if I had to guess. You're usually far more direct."

"I did not *run away*," he corrected her, his dark gaze narrowing with a temper he didn't let color his voice. "I had work to do, and let's be honest, Mattie, though I know that's a stretch for you. You can't give me what I want."

If he'd shoved a red-hot fire poker into her chest, he couldn't have hurt her more, and she couldn't control how stricken she felt. He saw it and shook his head as if it hurt him, too.

"I'm not trying to hurt your feelings," he said after a moment, his voice a fraction less cold. Less painfully precise. "Perhaps it was never fair of me to want the things I demanded of you. I don't know. Maybe you were right when you said any pretty girl would have done. I can't take any of that back. But I can stop chasing a person who doesn't exist."

This was worse. This made the misery she'd felt without him pale and wither away, and she had no idea what that was that swamped her then in its place. Only that it felt too much like despair.

"And what am I supposed to do?" she asked, and she didn't understand why she sounded so muffled and squeaky at the same time until she felt that heat trickling down her cheeks. She was crying. After all this time, she was crying in front of him without a nightmare to blame it on, and she didn't even care.

Nicodemus looked hewn from stone, propped up there against that granite desk with the city laid out at his feet. His gaze was dark and troubled, but he didn't move.

"I don't understand," he said after a moment, and there were too many undercurrents in that voice of his, too much Mattie knew she couldn't comprehend. "I thought you would rejoice at this. You've wanted me to leave you alone for years."

"But you never did," she said, or sobbed, and she didn't care which. How could she not care? After all these years so desperate to keep him from seeing any hint of vulnerability? But all she cared about was him. "You were always there. You were always pushing at me, and I got used to it. To you. What am I supposed to do when I push back and there's nothing there?"

He stared at her then, for so long that she thought she'd almost reached him—but then he shook his head. Once. Hard. Like he was waking himself up.

"I don't want to spend any more time than I already have, loving someone I made up inside my head." He looked tormented as he said it, torn apart, and it made Mattie feel like she was falling to pieces herself. "I know where that ends. I know what it looks like. I can't do it. Not again."

He'd gotten louder as he said that, more the Nicodemus she knew and less that creature made of stone and blame and judgment, and it was absurd how very nearly giddy that made her then, a dizzying hope like a great, bright beam of light inside her.

"That's a lie," she said, wiping at her cheeks and then holding his incredulous, thunderstruck gaze with hers, brave suddenly, because she recognized this. "And I would know. You're afraid."

CHAPTER TEN

"I BEG YOUR pardon?" His voice was a harsh warning, but Mattie ignored it.

"You heard me," she said, forging on. "What happened to the Nicodemus who told me that our marriage would last forever? Babies and no divorces?"

"I also told you there would be no secrets," he bit out. "But you can't do it. You prefer to play your games, trying to manipulate your way out of anything honest with sex."

"So do you."

In the silence that fell between them then, Mattie could hear her own heart, catapulting itself so hard against her ribs she worried it might break right through. Slowly, very slowly, his dark gaze fixed to hers, Nicodemus straightened from his desk, and she was reminded how very dangerous he was. How lethal when he chose.

"You know you do," she said. "Any game I might have played with sex, you've played yourself. The fact that you think you had different motives doesn't change anything. It's the same game."

"It most assuredly is not."

"This has been the same pattern from the start. You push, I push back. Around and around we go, and we've been doing it for years. You had no reason to think anything would change when we went to your island—but then it turned out that I wasn't who you thought I was. And if I was a virgin, you couldn't stay up there, all warm and comfortable on your moral high ground."

"You can twist this any way you like, Mattie," he said in that same harsh tone. "That doesn't make it true."

"There are a thousand ways we could have handled this marriage," she said, searching his face for the man she'd glimpsed in Greece, the man who'd been discarded by his father and had still made so much of himself. The little boy he must have been once, who'd made himself into a king of sorts, by the force of his own will. "It could have been a team effort. But instead, you threatened me and crowded me. Gloated about your victory over me."

"You're unbelievable." He took a step toward her, then appeared to think better of it and stopped. "Are you truly standing here today, claiming that had I approached you differently you would have—what?" He shook his head in amazement. "Come to this marriage dancing and singing?"

"I don't know," she said. "But I do know that you couldn't risk it. How could you possibly pretend to open up to me and then retreat like this if I was interested in a real partnership? That might make you something less than the upright and honest one here, and then what would happen?"

She couldn't help the bit of sarcasm that snuck in there at the end, and she saw him register it with a scowl.

"Let me guess," he said, witheringly. "Somehow, this is all my fault, yes? Isn't that where you're headed?"

"Not at all." It was hard to keep her head up high, her gaze on his, but she did it. "You *wanted* me to respond the way I did. Because that way, you get to be the martyr, and I'm still the spoiled brat who even managed to remain a *virgin* to spite you."

"Then why?" And there was nothing controlled about

his voice then. Nothing concealed in his expression. She could *feel* the kick of it. "If not for spite—for another point in this endless game?"

"Why do you think, you idiot?" she hurled back at him, and she threw her hands up as if she wanted to hit him or encompass all of Manhattan or maybe because she couldn't stand still. "Because of you!"

Nicodemus stared at her, his beautiful wife and this warrior creature who'd taken her over, making her lovely cheeks flush and her bittersweet eyes glitter wildly. She looked perfect in her stunningly feminine clothes, from head to toe his living, breathing, fantasy—and she'd just called him an idiot.

"What do you mean, because of me?" he asked, because he couldn't process any of this. It was like he was learning English all over again, and missing half the meaning.

"I mean, because of you," she said, and her voice was a little too thick and too uneven. "You were always there, weren't you? Since I was eighteen. And how could any of the boys I dated compete?" He only stared at her. "Whatever I felt for you, Nicodemus, it was consuming. I spent more time worrying about how to avoid you than I did about the boys I was supposed to be in love with. It never seemed right to take things any further when you were always there, lurking around in my head or at the next party. Always *so sure* that I'd end up with you."

"Careful, Mattie," he said, unable to do anything about that dark thing inside him that colored his voice, bitterness and confusion and all these years, all these long years, "or I may be tempted to think you care."

"That's what I'm trying to tell you," she snapped back at him. "Obviously. Since I'm standing right here, in your office, after you left me on a Greek island half a world away." She was scowling at him now. "Why else would I be here?"

"Sex?" he supplied acidly. "As you mentioned in the reception area?"

"Right," she said, her voice so dry it hurt. "Because after waiting twenty-eight years to have sex, it makes perfect sense that I'd suddenly want to whore it up all over Manhattan. Like it's a faucet I can turn on or off and *oops!* You left it on! Like it had absolutely nothing to do with you at all." She looked so furious for a moment that he wouldn't have been at all surprised if she'd swung at him. Instead, she crossed her arms over her chest again, which didn't help him at all, as he already found those perfect breasts distracting. "You really are an idiot."

"I let that slide once," he bit back at her. "Don't push me."

"That's the only thing I know how to do!" she shouted at him. "And God knows, Nicodemus, it's the only thing you ever respond to!"

He moved toward her then, but she backed away, her eyes stormy as they fixed on him.

"Don't touch me," she ordered him. "That confuses everything."

He recognized the things that flowed through him now, though he couldn't quite believe any of them. Triumph, yes. Hope, which was harder to stomach. That same old wild desire—and he knew too much, now. He knew that the reality of her trumped his fantasies, and then some.

"You wanted honesty," she was saying, still watching him too intently, as if all of this was hurting her. "You can't cut it off in the middle because it doesn't fit the story you've already told yourself about how this would go."

She'd backed up all the way to that wall of windows, and stood there, bracketed by another perfect autumn afternoon in New York City. The light was tipping over toward gold, and it poured over her, making her look like something out of a dream.

His dream, he realized. He'd had this dream.

He stood and waited though he thought that it was perhaps the most difficult thing he'd ever done.

"My mother died when I was eight," she said, and for some reason, Nicodemus felt a chill go through him. "But you know that already."

"Of course," he said, not sure why he felt so uneasy all of a sudden. "Lady Daphne was in a car accident while your family was on holiday in South Africa. It was a tragedy."

"It was a tragedy," Mattie said in a whisper that wasn't at all soft. "It was my fault."

Nicodemus only watched her. She swallowed hard, her gaze on his like she was searching for condemnation. She must have seen something on his face that encouraged her, because she cleared her throat and continued.

"I was in the backseat with Chase. Mama was in the passenger seat in front, talking with the driver. I was singing. Chase told me to stop. They all told me to stop. And I hit him."

Her eyes darkened, and he realized that this was her nightmare. This was what he'd found her reliving that night in the pool house.

"I'm sorry," he said quietly, when it seemed she'd gone somewhere inside her head. "But I don't understand how you could have caused a car accident from the backseat."

"I hit Chase," she said again, and it tore at him, how she said that so matter-of-factly, as if, inside her head, she'd conducted whole trials and found herself guilty again and again. "And he teased me, and I hit him again. They told me to stop and I didn't. I was too mad. And then I hit the driver and everything…flipped. And then we were on the side of the road and Mama—" She shook her head instead of finishing that sentence. "It was my fault, Nicodemus. I hit the driver and made him lose control of the car. He died, too."

"Mattie," he said softly. "It was an accident."

"Nothing was the same afterward," she whispered. "No one could look at me. Chase, my father. We all pretended, but I knew. They even made us lie about what had really happened." Her eyes welled up then. "And every time I told someone that Chase and I weren't in the car, that it had happened to her while she was on her own, it made it worse. I did this horrible thing. I ruined my family and killed an innocent man. And yet I was protected."

He couldn't hold himself back then and he stopped trying. He crossed to her, pulling her into his arms and holding her the way he'd always wanted to hold her—the way she'd only let him the night he'd found her sobbing and in the grip of her internal terrors.

She shook against him, and he held her so he could look down at her, at those pretty eyes slicked with tears again, at all that guilt and misery he understood, now, had been behind all of this from the start.

"And you wanted me so badly," she whispered. "But I knew you wouldn't, if you knew."

He shifted so he could cup her face in his hands.

"There is nothing you could do to make me want you any less," he said gruffly. "Much less this revelation that when you were a child, you acted like one. There was a terrible accident. You survived."

"What kind of person kills their own mother, Nicodemus?" she asked harshly.

"Me," he said after a moment. "I'm as guilty of it as you are."

Her face flushed. "It's not the same."

"Yes," he said. "It is. If I was a child who couldn't be held responsible for what followed my recklessness, so were you. Maybe it's time we both forgave ourselves."

Her eyes searched his. She took a deep breath that he could feel move through him, too.

"I'll try if you will," she whispered.

And then, at last, he kissed her.

It wasn't until the second kiss, that sweet fire, that easy press of his mouth to hers, that Mattie realized she hadn't truly believed he would ever kiss her again.

When she felt him smile against her mouth, her neck, she realized she'd said that out loud.

"I should have kissed you at that ball a hundred years ago and spared us both all this wasted time," he muttered. "And all this unnecessary guilt."

Mattie lifted her head then and opened her eyes, and couldn't quite fathom what she saw on that hard, fierce face of his. Shining openly from those dark eyes. It lodged in her chest. It melted all that hard, cold glass inside her as if it had never been.

"You gave up on me," she said, very seriously. "On us. Don't do it again."

His smile deepened. "My version of giving up involved signing a major merger with your family's company and returning to the city where you live." His fingers moved near her temple, playing with a strand of her hair, and the look in his dark eyes made her want to cry again. "I don't think you have to worry."

"I never sleep through the night, Nicodemus," she said. "Never. But I did that night in Greece. And when I woke up, you were gone."

"I don't want any more of these games we play," he told

her, and the words were like a song inside her, buoyant and melodic, sweet and perfect. "I only want you."

"You can have me," she promised him, and these, she understood then, were her real vows. These pierced straight through her, leaving tangled roots in their wake. Binding her to him forever. No witnesses. No pictures for the hungry tabloids. Only the two of them. And the truth. "But I want the same in return."

"I'm yours, Mattie," he told her, and he pulled her close again, lifting her up as if she weighed nothing and holding her there, like she was a miracle. Like this was, this thing between them that finally made sense. That meant everything. "All you had to do was ask."

"I love you," she said softly, threading her arms around his neck and smiling down at him as if he was the whole world. Because he was. He was hers. "But to tell you the honest truth, Nicodemus, I think I always have."

She kissed him then, and there was nothing between them but light.

And the love that had been there for all those years, waiting for them to notice it.

The summer sun poured in through the high window, and Mattie woke slowly, letting the gold of it warm her and run all over her like her husband's clever hands. She reached out to feel for him across the vastness of that great, Greek bed, and woke further when she heard his low chuckle from beside it.

"Do you miss me already?"

She opened her eyes to find Nicodemus standing there in nothing but a towel, and smiled at him, feeling lazy and happy.

"Always," she said. "You should have taken me with you."

It was amazing what a full night's sleep could do—much less three years of the same. Three years of learning how to love this man as he deserved. Three years of learning how to let him love her back.

The best three years of her life.

"The last time I attempted to take you into the shower before you were ready, you acted like it was an attempt on your life," he reminded her. "You've become appallingly lazy, princess."

"I have," she agreed with a grin. "And so demanding."

She crooked her finger at him, letting the instant gleam of dark honey in his eyes warm her.

Nicodemus crawled across the bed to her, taking her mouth with that marvelous ferocity that made her sigh against him while everything else turned molten and hot.

"I love you," she whispered when he pulled back marginally, and smiled when he kissed her again, harder and deeper than before.

"I love you, too," he replied. "Which is why you'll understand that I cannot tolerate any secrets between us. Was I unclear on this in the past? I feel certain I wasn't."

"I have no idea what you're talking about," she lied. "I'm a model wife. What more could you ask? I'm the perfect decoration."

"The decor does not normally start its own PR firm and find itself too busy to tend to its primary purpose, which is standing about looking pretty," he pointed out, shifting so he could take her in his arms and roll them both, until she was on her back and he was sprawled out beside her. "You've become entirely too professional."

"I apologize." She wasn't sorry at all, and the little nip he gave her, at the tender place beneath her ear, made her laugh. "I know you preferred it when I was pointless and spoiled."

He propped himself up on his elbow so he could look down at her, and she loved him so much it felt like a wave that crashed over her, again and again, bathing her in its sweetness. Its goodness. She loved the smile he wore so often now and that gaze of his that was always more honeyed than grim. She loved how well she knew him and how, astonishingly, he'd come to know her, as well.

Intimacy, it turned out, was worth all the trouble it took to get there. All the fear and all the pain. That sensation of being turned inside out, vulnerable and exposed, was only the beginning. Every day it deepened. Every day it got worse.

And better. So much better. So exquisitely, miraculously better.

"Tell me," he said, grinning down at her. "Because I already know."

"Then why must I tell you? Surely, your psychic powers are their own reward."

"Confession is good for the soul," he said, letting one big hand travel over her warm body, heating it as he went, from her tender breasts to the bright phoenix that flirted with the curve of her belly that wouldn't stay trim much longer. "Especially yours."

"Maybe you should spank it out of me," she suggested, taking his hand in hers and holding it where it rested, hot and right, above the place far within where their baby already grew.

"How kinky you've become," he said, pretending to chide her. "Spanking was meant to be a punishment, Mattie, not a pleasure."

"Liar," she teased him, and he grinned back at her.

"I love you," Nicodemus said, his gaze another vow, and it warmed her all the way through. "You and that baby, who you should have told me about weeks ago."

And then he made her pay, in the delicious way only he could.

The way he always did.

The way she knew—as she knew the sun would rise in the morning, as she knew she'd loved him a lifetime already, as she knew this child of theirs would be a little boy whose father would never, ever lie to him or leave him— he always would.

* * * * *

SECURING THE GREEK'S LEGACY

JULIA JAMES

Julia James lives in England and adores the peaceful verdant countryside and the wild shores of Cornwall. She also loves the Mediterranean – so rich in myth and history, with its sun-baked landscapes and olive groves, ancient ruins and azure seas. 'The perfect setting for romance!' she says. 'Rivalled only by the lush tropical heat of the Caribbean – palms swaying by a silver sand beach lapped by turquoise waters…What more could lovers want?'

CHAPTER ONE

ANATOLE TELONIDIS STARED bleakly across the large, expensively furnished lounge of the penthouse apartment in the most fashionable part of Athens. It was still as untidy as it had been when his young cousin Marcos Petranakos had last walked out of it a few short nightmare weeks ago, straight to his death.

When their mutual grandfather, Timon Petranakos, had phoned his older grandson he had been distraught. *'Anatole, he's dead! Marcos, my beloved Marcos—he's dead!'* the old man had cried out.

Smashed to pieces at twenty-five, driving far too fast in the lethal supercar that had been Timon's own present to Marcos, given in the wake of their grandfather's recent diagnosis with cancer.

The death of his favourite grandson, whom he had spoiled lavishly since Marcos had lost his parents as a teenager, had been a devastating blow. Timon had since refused all treatment for his cancer, longing now only for his own death.

Anatole could understand his grandfather's devastation, his mind-numbing grief. But the fallout from Marcos's tragic death would affect more lives than their own family's. With no direct heir now to the vast Petranakos Corporation, the company would pass to an obscure Petranakos relative whose business inexperience would surely, in these parlous economic times, lead inevitably to the company's collapse and the loss of thousands of jobs, adding to the country's sky-high unemployment levels.

Though Anatole had his own late father's business empire to run—which he did with tireless efficiency and a pressing sense of responsibility—he knew that, had Marcos lived, he could have instilled a similar sense of responsibility into his hedonistic young cousin, guiding him effectively. But the new heir—middle-aged, self-important and conceited—was resistant to any such guidance.

Frustration with the fate awaiting the Petranakos Corporation—and its hapless workforce—Anatole started on the grim process of sorting out his young cousin's possessions. Bleakly, he began his sombre task.

Paperwork was the first essential. As he located Marcos's desk and set about methodically sorting out its jumbled contents a familiar ripple of irritation went through him. Marcos had been the least organised person he'd known—receipts, bills and personal correspondence were all muddled up, demonstrating just how uninterested Marcos had been in anything other than having a good time. Fast cars, high living and an endless procession of highly temporary females had been his favoured lifestyle. Unlike Anatole himself. Running the Telonidis businesses kept him too occupied for anything more than occasional relationships, usually with busy, high-powered businesswomen he worked with in the world of finance.

Frustration bit at Anatole.

If only Marcos had married! Then there might have been a son to inherit from Timon! I'd have kept the Petranakos Corporation safe for him until the child grew up!

But to the fun-seeking Marcos marriage would have been anathema! Girls had been for casual relationships only. There'd be time later for getting married, he'd always said.

But there was to be no later…

Grim-faced, his honed features starkly etched, Anatole went on sorting through the papers in his cousin's desk. Official in one pile, personal in another. The latter pile was not large—not in this age of texting and the internet—but one drawer revealed a batch of three or four envelopes addressed to Marcos in cursive Roman script with a London postmark and UK stamps. Only one had been opened.

Anatole frowned. The lilac-coloured envelopes and the large, looping script suggested a female writer. Though Marcos's dramatic death had been splashed across the Greek tabloids, a British girlfriend might not have heard of it. It might be necessary, Anatole thought reluctantly, for him to let her know of Marcos's fate. That said, he realised as he glanced at the envelopes' postmarks, none of these was dated more recently than nine months ago. Whoever she was, the affair—or whatever it had been— was clearly long over.

With a swift impatience to be done with the whole grim business of sorting through Marcos's personal effects Anatole took the folded single piece of paper from the one envelope that was open. He flicked open the note and started to read the English writing.

And as he did he froze completely…

Lyn made her way out of the lecture hall and sighed. It was no good, she would far rather be studying history! But accountancy would enable her to earn a decent living in the future and that was essential—especially if she were to persuade the authorities that she was capable of raising a child on her own: her beloved Georgy. But for now, while she was still waiting so anxiously to learn if she could adopt him, she was only allowed to be his foster carer. She knew the welfare authorities would prefer for him to be adopted by one of the many childless couples anxious to adopt a healthy baby, but Lyn was determined that no one would take Georgy from her! *No one!*

It didn't matter how much of a struggle it was to keep at her studies while looking after a baby as well, especially with money so short—she would manage somehow! A familiar regret swept over her: if only she'd gone to college sooner and already had her qualifications. But she hadn't been able to go straight from school because she'd had to stay home and look after Lindy. She hadn't been able to leave her young teenage sister to the indifference and neglect which was all her mother had offered. But when Lindy had left school herself and gone to London, to live with a girlfriend and get a job, her mother had been taken ill, her lungs and liver finally giving in after decades of abuse from smoking and alcohol, and there had been no one else to look after her except Lyn.

And now there was Georgy...

'Lyn Brandon?'

It was one of the university's admin staff.

'Someone's asking to see you,' the woman said briskly, and pointed to one of the offices across the corridor.

Frowning, Lyn walked inside.

And stopped dead.

Standing by the window, silhouetted by the fading light, was an imposing, dark-suited figure. Tall, wearing a black cashmere overcoat with a black cashmere scarf hooked around the strong column of his neck, the man had a natural Mediterranean tan that, along with his raven-dark hair, instantly told Lyn that he was not English. Just as the planes and features of his face told her that he was jaw-droppingly good-looking.

It was a face, though, that was staring at her with a mouth set in a tight line—as though he were seeing someone he had not expected. A frown creased his brow.

'Miss Brandon?' He said her name, his voice accented, as if he did not quite believe it.

Dark eyes flicked over her and Lyn felt two spots of colour mount in her cheeks. Immediately she became conscious of the way her hair was caught back in a stringy ponytail. She had not a scrap of make-up on, and her clothes were serviceable rather than fashionable.

Then suddenly, overriding that painful consciousness, there came a jolt of realisation as to just who this clearly foreign man must be—could only be…

The Mediterranean looks, the expensive clothes, the sleekly groomed looks, the whole aura of wealth about him… She felt her stomach constrict, filling with instinctive fear.

Across the narrow room Anatole caught the flash of alarm and wondered at it, but not nearly as much as he was wondering whether he had, after all, really tracked down the woman he'd been so urgently seeking ever since reading that letter in Marcos's apartment—the woman who, so his investigators had discovered, had most definitely given birth to a baby boy…

Is he Marcos's son? The question was burning in hope. Because if Marcos had had a son then it changed everything. *Everything!*

If, by a miracle, Marcos had a son, then Anatole had to find him and bring him home to Greece, so that Timon, who was fading with every passing day, could find instead a last blessing from the cruel fate that had taken so much from him.

And it was not just for his grandfather that a son of Marcos's would be a blessing, either, Anatole knew. This would persuade Timon to change his will, to acknowledge that his beloved Marcos had had a son to whom he could now leave the Petranakos Corporation. Infant though he was, Anatole would guard the child's inheritance, keep it safe and prosperous for him—and save the livelihoods of all its employees.

Tracking down the author of the letters had led him first to a council house in the south of the country and then, through information given to his detectives by neighbours, to this northern college, where he'd been told the young woman he was so urgently seeking—Linda Brandon— had recently moved.

But as his eyes rested now on the woman he was addressing he felt doubt fill him. *This* was the woman he'd trekked to this grim, rainswept northern town to find in a race against time for his stricken grandfather? Marcos wouldn't even have looked twice at her—let alone taken her to his bed!

'*Are* you Miss Brandon?' he asked, his voice sharper now.

He saw her swallow and nod jerkily. Saw, too, that her entire body had tensed.

'I am Anatole Telonidis,' he announced. His voice sounded clipped, but his mission was a painful one—and an urgent one. 'I am here on behalf of my cousin, Marcos Petranakos, with whom I believe you are…' he sought the right phrase '…acquainted.'

Even as he said it his eyes flicked over her again doubtfully. Even putting aside her unprepossessing appearance, Marcos's taste had been for curvy blondes—not thin brunettes. But her reaction told him that she must indeed be the person he was looking for so urgently—she had instantly recognised Marcos's name.

And not favourably…

Her expression had changed. Hardened. 'So he couldn't even be bothered to come himself!' she retorted scornfully.

If she'd sought to hit home with her accusation she'd failed. The man who'd declared himself Marcos Petranakos's cousin stilled. In the dark eyes a flash of deep emotion showed and Lyn saw his face stiffen.

'The situation is not as you suppose,' he said.

It was as if, she realised, he was picking his words carefully.

He paused a moment, as if steeling himself to speak, then said, 'I must talk to you. But the matter is…difficult.'

Lyn shook her head violently. She could feel the adrenaline running through her body. 'No, it's not difficult at all!' she retorted. 'Whatever message you've been sent to deliver by your cousin, you needn't bother! Georgy—his *son*!—is fine without him. Absolutely fine!'

She saw emotion flash in his dark eyes again, saw the shadow behind it. Out of nowhere a chill went through her.

'There is something I must tell you,' Anatole Telonidis was saying. His voice was grim, and bleak, as if he were forcing the words out.

Lyn's hands clenched. 'There is nothing you can say that I care about—!' she began.

But his deep, sombre voice cut right through hers. 'My cousin is dead.'

There was silence. Complete silence. Wordlessly, Anatole cursed himself for his blunt outburst. But it had been impossible to hear her hostility, her scorn, when Marcos lay dead in his grave…

'Dead?' Lyn's voice was hollow with shock.

'I'm sorry. I should not have told you so brutally,' Anatole said stiffly.

She was still staring at him. 'Marcos Petranakos is *dead*?' Her voice was thin—disbelieving.

'It was a car crash. Two months ago. It has taken time to track you down…' His words were staccato, sombre.

Lyn swayed as if she might pass out. Instantly Anatole was there, catching her arm, staying her. She stepped back, steadying herself, and he released her. Absently she noticed with complete irrelevance how strong his grasp had been. How overpowering his momentary closeness.

'He's dead?' she said again, her voice hollow. Emotion twisted in her throat. Georgy's father was dead…

'Please,' Anatole Telonidis was saying, 'you need to sit down. I am sorry this is such a shock to you. I know,' he went on, picking his words carefully again, she could tell, his expression guarded, 'just how…deep…you felt the relationship was between yourself and him, but—'

A noise came from her. He stopped. She was staring at him, but the expression in her face was different now, Anatole registered. It wasn't shock at hearing about Marcos's tragic death. It wasn't even anger—the understandable anger, painful though it was for him to face it—that she'd expressed about the man who had got her pregnant and then totally ignored her ever since.

'Between him and *me*?' she echoed. She shook her head a moment, as if clearing it.

'Yes,' Anatole pursued. 'I know from your letters—which, forgive me, I have read—that you felt a strong… attachment to my cousin. That you were expressing your longing to…' He hesitated, recalling vividly the hopelessly optimistic expectations with which she had surrounded her announcement that she was carrying Marcos's baby. 'Your longing to make a family together, but—'

He got no further.

'I'm not Georgy's mother,' Lyn announced.

And in her bleak voice were a thousand unshed tears.

For a moment Anatole thought he had not heard correctly. Or had misunderstood what she had said in English. Then his eyes levelled on hers and he realised he had understood her exactly.

'What?' His exclamation was like a bullet. A blackening frown sliced down over his face. 'You said you were Linda Brandon!' he threw at her accusingly.

His thoughts were in turmoil. What the hell was going on? He could make no sense of it! He could see her shaking her head—a jerky gesture. Then she spoke, her voice strained.

'I'm…I'm Lynette Brandon,' Anatole heard her say.

He saw her take a rasping breath, making herself speak. Her face was still white with shock with what he'd told her about Marcos.

'Lindy…Linda—' she gave her sister's full name before stopping abruptly, her voice cutting off. Then she blinked.

Anatole could see the shimmer of tears clearly now.

'Linda was my sister,' she finished, her voice no more than a husk.

He heard the past tense—felt the slow, heavy pulse of dark realisation go through him. Heard her thin, shaky voice continuing, telling him what was so unbearably painful for her to say.

Her face was breaking up.

'She died,' she whispered. 'My sister Linda. Georgy's mother. She died giving birth. Eclampsia. It's not supposed to happen any more. But it did…*it did…*'

Her voice was broken.

She lifted her eyes to Anatole across a divide that was like a yawning chasm—a chasm that had claimed two young lives.

Her mind reeled as she took in the enormity of the truth they had both revealed to each other. The unbearable tragedy of it.

Both Georgy's parents were dead!

She had thrown at Anatole Telonidis the fact that his uncaring, irresponsible cousin wasn't wanted or needed by his son, but to hear that he had suffered the same dreadful fate as her sister was unbearable. As unbearable as losing her sister had been. Tears stung in her eyes and his voice came from very far away.

'You should sit down,' said Anatole Telonidis.

He guided her to a chair and she sat on it nervelessly. His own mind was still reeling, still trying to come to grips with what he had just learnt. The double tragedy surrounding Marcos's baby son.

Where was he? Where was Marcos's son?

That was the question he had to have answered now! A cold fear went through him. Newborn babies were in high demand for adoption by childless couples, and a fatherless baby whose mother had died in childbirth might have been just such a child...

Had he been adopted already? The question seared in Anatole's head. If so, then he would have a nightmare of a search to track him down—even if he were allowed to by the authorities. And if he had already been adopted then would his adoptive parents be likely to let him go? Would the authorities be likely to let him demand—*plead*!—that they accede to his need for Timon to know that he had an heir after all?

He stood looking down at the sister of the woman who had borne his cousin a child and died in the process. He swallowed.

'Where is my cousin's son?' he asked. He tried not to sound brusque, demanding, but he had to know. *He had to know!*

Her chin lifted, her eyes flashing to his.

'He's with *me*!' came the answer. Vehement, passionate.

Abstractedly Anatole found himself registering that when this drab dab of a female spoke passionately her nondescript features suddenly sharpened into life, giving her a vividness that was not drab at all. Then the sense of her words hit him.

'With *you*?'

She took a ragged breath, her fingers clutching the side

of the chair. 'Yes! With me! And he's staying with me! That's all you need to know!'

She leapt to her feet, fear and panic impelling her. Too much had happened—shock after shock—and she couldn't cope with it, couldn't take it in.

Anatole stepped towards her, urgency in his voice. 'Miss Brandon, we have to talk—discuss—'

'No! There's nothing to discuss! *Nothing!*'

And then, before his frustrated gaze, she rushed from the room.

Lyn fled. Her mind was in turmoil. Though she managed to make her way into her next lecture she was incapable of concentrating. Only one single emotion was uppermost.

Georgy is mine! Mine, mine, mine!

Lindy had given the baby to her with her dying breath and she would *never*, never betray that! *Never!*

Grief clutched at Lyn again.

'Look after Georgy—'

They had been Lindy's final words before the darkness had closed over her fevered, stricken brain and she had ebbed from life.

And I will! I will look after him all my life—all his life—and I will never let any harm come to him, never abandon him or give up him!

'Just you and me, Georgy!' she whispered later as, morning lectures finally over, she collected him from the college crèche and made her way to the bus stop and back home for the afternoon.

But as she clambered on board the bus, stashing the folding buggy one-handed as she held Georgy in the other, she completely failed to see an anonymous black car pull out into the road behind the bus. Following it.

Two hours later Anatole stood in front of the block of flats his investigator had informed him was Lynette Brandon's place of accommodation and stared bleakly at it. It was not an attractive building, being of ugly sixties design, with stained concrete and peeling paint. The whole area was just as dreary—no place for Timon Petranakos's great-grandson to be brought up!

Resolve steeling, he rang the doorbell.

CHAPTER TWO

LYN HAD SAT down at the rickety table in the corner of the living room and got out her study books. Georgy had been fed and changed, and had settled for his afternoon nap in his secondhand cot, tucked in beside her bed in the single bedroom the flat possessed. She was grateful for Georgy's afternoon sleep, even though if he slept too much he didn't sleep well at night, for it gave her an hour or two of solid homework time. But today her concentration was shot to pieces—still reeling with what had happened that morning.

Hopefully she had made her position clear and the man who had lobbed a bombshell into her life would take himself off again, back to Greece, and leave her alone. Anxiety rippled through her again. The adoption authorities believed that there was no contact with Georgy's father or any of his paternal family. But since this morning that wasn't true any more...

No, she mustn't think about that! She must put it behind her. Put behind her all the dark, disturbing images of the man whose incredible good looks were such a source of disturbance to her. For a moment his image formed in her mind, overpowering in its masculine impact. She thrust it impatiently aside and started reading her textbook.

Two minutes later she was interrupted. The doorbell had sounded. Imperative. Demanding.

Her head shot up. Who on earth…? No one called on her here.

The bell rang again. Warily, heart thumping suddenly, she went to the door, lifting up the entryphone.

'Who is it?' she asked sharply.

'Miss Brandon—we need to continue our conversation.'

It was Anatole Telonidis.

For a moment Lyn remained motionless. *Don't let him in!* The childish, fearful words sounded in her head, but she knew she could not obey them. She had to get this conversation over and done with. Then she could send him away and never see him again—never be troubled again by the existence of Georgy's father's family. Nervelessly she pressed the entry buzzer, and a few moments later opened her front door.

He was just as tall and formidable as she remembered. Taller, it seemed, in her poky flat. But it was not just his size and demeanour that pressed on her senses. His physical presence was dominating more than just the space he stood in. It was making her horribly aware all over again of his dark, devastating looks.

Desperately she tried to crush down her awareness of them. It was the last thing she should be paying any attention to right now!

Besides, a vicious little voice in her head was reminding her to think about what *he* was seeing! He was seeing a plain-faced nobody who was wearing ancient baggy jeans and a thick frumpy jumper, with her hair tied back and not a scrap of make-up. A man like him wouldn't even look once, let alone twice!

Oh, for God's sake, what are you even thinking of? Focus—just focus! This is about Georgy and what this man wants—or doesn't want.

And how quickly she could get rid of him…

She stared at him. He seemed to be looking about him,

then past her into the small living room, with its shabby furniture, worn carpet and hideously patterned curtains. Her chin went up. Yes, the place was uninviting, but it was cheap, and it came furnished, and she wasn't going to be choosy. She couldn't afford to be—not until she was earning a decent salary. Till then Georgy didn't care that he wasn't anywhere nice. And neither did she.

This man who had dropped a bombshell into her life, however, looked as if he cared—and he didn't like what he was seeing.

'I hope,' he said evenly, 'that you have now had a chance to come to terms with what I told you this morning, and that you understand,' he continued, 'how imperative it is that we discuss my cousin's son's future.'

'There's nothing to discuss,' she replied tightly.

Anatole's mouth tightened. So she was still taking that line. Well, he would have to disabuse her of it—that was all. In the meantime there was something that was even more imperative. He wanted to see Marcos's son—see him with his own eyes. He looked around the room.

'Where is the baby?' he asked. He hadn't meant it to sound like a demand, only a question, but it seemed to make the girl flinch. Seeing her now, like this, had not improved her looks, he noted absently. She was still abysmally dressed, without any attention to her appearance.

'He's asleep,' she answered stiffly.

The dark eyes rested on her. 'I would like to see him.'

It was not a request. It was a statement of intent. His eyes went past her to the half-open bedroom door and he stepped towards it. Inside was a cot beside a bed, and in the cot the small figure of a baby nestled in a fleecy blanket. In the dim light from the drawn curtains Anatole could not make out the baby's features.

Are you Marcos's son? Are you the child I've come to find? The questions burned in his head. Instinctively he moved to step into the room. Immediately a low-voiced hiss sounded behind him.

'Please don't wake him!'

He could hear a note in her voice that was not just a command but a plea. Abruptly, he nodded, reversing out of the cramped room, causing her to back away into the equally small living room.

Once again she felt his presence dominate the poky space.

'You had better sit down, Miss Brandon,' he said, indicating the sofa as though he, not her, was the host.

Stiffly, she did so. Somehow she had to find a way to make him go away—leave her and Georgy alone. Then it came to her just why he might be here. What he might be after.

'If you want me to sign papers saying I forfeit any claim to his father's estate, I will do so straight away,' she blurted out. 'I don't want any money, or maintenance, or anything like that. Georgy and I are fine as we are—we're all sorted!' She swallowed again, altering her tone of voice. Her eyes shadowed suddenly. 'I'm sorry to hear that your cousin is…is dead…but—' her eyes met his unflinchingly '—but it doesn't change the fact that he was not in the slightest bit interested in Georgy's existence, so—'

Anatole Telonidis held up a hand. It was a simple gesture, but it carried with it an expectation that she would cease talking.

Which she did.

'My cousin is…*was*,' he corrected himself painfully, 'the only Petranakos grandson of our mutual grandfather, Timon. Marcos's parents died when he was only a teenager and consequently…' Anatole paused. 'He was very precious to our grandfather. His death has devastated him.' He took another heavy breath. 'Marcos's death came as a viciously cruel blow—he was killed driving the car that our grandfather had given him for his birthday. It was a birthday Timon knew would likely be the last he would see, because...' Anatole paused again, then finished the bleak saga. 'Because Timon had himself just been diagnosed with advanced incurable cancer.'

He fell silent, letting the information sink in. Lynette Brandon was sitting there, looking ashen.

'You will understand, I know,' he went on quietly, 'how much it will mean to Timon to know that, although he has lost his grandson, a great-grandson exists.' He read her expression. It was blank, rejecting. He *had* to convince her of the argument he was making. 'There is very little time,' he pressed. 'The cancer was very advanced at the point of diagnosis, and since my cousin's death my grandfather has refused all treatment—even though treatment could keep him alive for a little while longer. He is waiting to die—for with the loss of his grandson he has no reason to live at all. Not even for one single day.' Then he finished what he had come to say. 'Your sister's baby—my cousin's son—gives him that reason.'

He stood looking down at her. Her face was still ashen, her hands twisting in her lap. He spoke again, his voice grave. He had to convince her of the urgency of what had to happen.

'I need to take Georgy to Greece with me. I need to take him as soon as possible. My dying grandfather needs to know that his great-grandson will grow up in the country of his father—'

'*No!* No, I won't let you!' The words burst from her and she leapt to her feet.

Anatole pressed his lips together in frustration. 'You are overwrought,' he repeated. 'It is understandable—this has come as a shock to you. I wish that matters were not as urgent as they are. But with Timon's state of health I have to press you on this! The very last thing I want,' he said heavily, 'is to turn this into any kind of battle between us.

I need—I *want*—your co-operation! You do not need me to tell you,' he added, and his eyes were dark now, 'that once DNA testing has proved Marcos's paternity, then—'

'There isn't going to *be* any DNA testing!' Lyn shot back at him.

Anatole stopped. There was something in her voice—something in her face—that alerted him. There was more than obduracy in it—more than anger, even.

There was fear.

His antennae went into overdrive. *Thee mou*, might the child not be Marcos's after all? Everything about those plaintive, pitiful letters he'd read indicated that the baby's mother had been no promiscuous party girl, that she had fallen in love with his cousin, however unwisely. No, the child she had been carrying *was* his. He was certain of it. Timon, he knew, would require proof before he designated the baby his heir, but that would surely be a formality?

His thoughts raced back to the moment in hand. The expression on Lynette Brandon's face made no sense. She was the one objecting to any idea of taking Marcos's son back to Greece—if the baby were not Marcos's after all surely she would positively *want* DNA testing done!

He frowned. There was something else that didn't make sense, either. Something odd about her name. Its similarity to her sister's. Abruptly he spoke. 'Why is your sister's name so like yours?' he asked shortly. He frowned. 'It is unusual—confusing, as I have found—for sisters to have such similar names. Lynette and Linda.'

'So what?' she countered belligerently. 'What does it matter now?'

Anatole fixed his gaze on her. His antennae were now registering that same flash of emotion in her as he'd seen when he had mentioned DNA testing, but he had no time to consider it further. Lynette Brandon was launching into him again. Her voice was vehement, passionate.

'Have I finally got you to understand, Mr Telonidis, that your journey here has been wasted? I'm sorry—sorry about your cousin, sorry about your grandfather—but Georgy is staying here with me! He is *not* going to be brought up in Greece. He is *mine*!'

'Is he?'

His brief, blunt question cut right across her. Silencing her.

In her eyes, her face, flared that same emotion he had seen a moment ago—fear.

What is going on here?

The question flared in his head and stayed there, even though her voice broke that moment of silence with a single hissing word.

'*Yes!*' she grated fiercely.

Anatole levelled his gaze at her. Behind his impassive expression his mind was working fast. Since learning that morning about the double tragedy that had hit this infant, overturning his assumption that Marcos's son was with his birth mother, he had set his lawyers to ascertain exactly what the legal situation was with regard to custody of the orphaned boy—and what might be the outcome of any proposition that the baby be raised in Greece by his paternal family. He had no answers yet, but the baby's aunt had constantly—and vehemently!—expressed the fact that *she* had full legal charge in her sister's place.

But *did* she?

'And that is official, is it? Your custody of Georgy?' His voice was incisive, demanding she answer.

Again there was that same revealing emotion in her eyes, which was then instantly blanked.

'*Yes!*' she repeated, just as fiercely.

He frowned. 'So you have adopted him?'

A line of white showed on her cheekbones. 'It's going through,' she said quickly. 'These things take time. There's a lot of paperwork. Bureaucracy and everything. But of *course* I'm adopting him! I'm the obvious person to adopt him!'

His expression did not change, but he could see that for the British authorities she would be the natural person to adopt her late sister's son if she were set on doing so. Which she evidently was! Anatole felt a ripple of respect for her determination to go through with it. Her life could not be easy, juggling studying with childcare and living in penny-pinching circumstances.

But for all that, he still had to find a way to convince her that Marcos's son just could *not* be raised by her in such penurious circumstances. It was unthinkable. Once Timon knew of his existence, he would insist with all his last strength that his beloved grandson's son be brought home to Greece, to be reunited with his father's family.

Just how, precisely, Marcos's son was to be raised—how a small baby, then a toddler and a schoolboy was to grow up—was something that could be worked out later. For now, just getting the baby to Greece, for his grandfather to see him—make him his heir—before the cancer claimed Timon was his only priority.

And to do that he had to get this totally impossible intransigent aunt to stop blocking him at every turn!

But how?

A heavy, unappetising thought forced its way forward. His mouth tightened. There was, of course, one very obvious method of attempting to stop any objections to what he was urging. A way that worked, as he knew well from his own business experience, to win compliance and consensus and agreement.

A way he did not want to use here, now, for this—but if he had to...if it worked...?

He must. If nothing else he must attempt it. He owed it to Timon, to Marcos—to all the thousands employed by the Petranakos Corporation whose livelihoods were threatened.

Reluctantly, for what he was about to say went against the grain, he spoke. His tone of voice was measured, impassive. 'I know full well that Timon will insist on thanking you for your care and concern for his great-grandson—that he will fully appreciate the accommodation you make towards granting his fervent wish for Marcos's son to grow up with his paternal family—and that he will wish to settle a sum on you in respect of his gratitude and appreciation such that your financial security would be handsomely assured for the future.'

There—he had said it. He had said outright that if she stopped stonewalling him her life of poverty would be over for good. He let the words sink in, not taking his eyes from her.

Her expression was blank, however. Had she not heard what he'd said?

Then she answered him. 'You want to *buy* Georgy from me?' Her voice was as blank as her eyes.

A frown immediately shaped Anatole's face. 'Of course not!' he repudiated.

'You're offering me money to hand him over to you,' the same blank voice intoned.

Anatole shook his head. Did she have to put it in such unpalatable terms? 'What I am saying,' he spelt out, 'is that—'

'Is that your grandfather will pay me if I let him have Georgy to bring him up in Greece.' Her voice was flat.

'No! It is not like that—' Anatole's voice was sharp.

Suddenly the blank look in her eyes vanished utterly. She launched herself to her feet, anger blazing in her eyes.

'It is *exactly* like that!' she cried. 'How *dare* you? How dare you sit there and tell me you'll *buy* Georgy from me? How *dare* you do such a thing?' Her voice had risen; her heart was thumping furiously. 'How *dare* you come here and offer me *money* to hand my dead sister's son over to you? How dare you?'

He was on his feet as well. He filled the room, intimidating and overpowering. But she would not be intimidated! Would not be overpowered! Would not be paid to part with Georgy!

She took a heaving breath, words pouring from her.

'I swore to my sister on her *deathbed* that I would never, never abandon her baby! That I would never hand him over to *anyone*! That I would always, *always* look after him and love him. Because she was not going to be able to do it! Because she was dying, and she knew she was dying, and she was never going to see her baby grow up, never going to see him become a boy, a man—never, never, *never*...'

Her voice was hoarse, the words torn from her, from the very depths of her being. Her hands were clenched into fists at her sides, as if she could—and would—and *must*—fight off the whole world to keep Georgy with her!

For a second there was silence. Absolute silence between them. Then into the silence came a high, solitary wail.

With a cry of consternation Lyn wheeled about. Oh, no—now she had gone and woken Georgy! With all this awful arguing about what was never going to happen—because she was never giving Georgy up! *Never!*

The wail came again. She rounded on Anatole. 'Please go!' she said. 'Please—just go!'

She rushed from the room into the bedroom, where Georgy was wide awake, his little face screwed up. She scooped him up with a hushing noise, soothing and rocking him in her arms until he had quietened.

The feel of his strong, solid little body, so familiar, so precious, calmed her too. She took long slow breaths, hugging him tightly, and felt his warmth and weight in her arms like a blessing, a benediction.

How could anyone think to ask her to give him up? She loved this little child more than anyone in the whole world! He was everything to her—and she was everything to him.

Love flowed from her, enveloping and protective, as she cradled him against her, her eyes smarting, her throat tight. Slowly the heaving emotions in her breast, her heart, eased. Georgy was safe. He was in her arms. He was with her. She would never let him go, never abandon him. Her hectic pulse slowed. Cradling him, her hand curved protectively around his back, she crooned soothingly at him, wordless sounds murmuring, familiar and comforting. The rest of the world seemed very far away...

'May I see him?'

The voice behind her made her spin round. Anatole was standing in the doorway of the bedroom.

But there was something different about him. Something quite different. She'd seen him only as dark and tall and formidable—telling her things she did not want to hear, his very presence a terrifying threat to everything that she held most dear.

Now, as she gazed at him, her expression stricken, across the dimly lit curtained room, he did not seem formidable at all. Or threatening. He seemed merely—tense. As if every muscle in his body were pulled taut. In the dim light the bone structure of his face was stark.

She felt Georgy lift his head from her shoulder, twist his neck so that he could see where the voice had come from. He gazed at the figure in the doorway with eyes just as dark as those which were fixed on him.

For a moment the tableau held all of them immobile. Then, with a gurgling sound, Georgy lurched on her shoulder, his little arms reaching forward towards the man standing in the doorway. The man with eyes like his own.

The man who was kin to the father he had never known. Never would know now....

As if in slow motion, Anatole found his hand reaching inside his jacket pocket, drawing out something he had brought with him from Greece. It was a silver photo frame from his grandfather's opulent drawing room, displaying one individual alone. Slowly he shifted his gaze down to the photo he held in his hand, then back to the baby cradled so closely in his young aunt's arms.

'He is Marcos's son.' Anatole's voice was flat. But there was emotion in it. Powerful emotion. His gaze cut suddenly to Lyn. 'Look,' he instructed, holding up the photo.

It was an old one, pre-digital, an informal shot and unposed, but the likeness to the baby in it was unmistakable. The same wide brown-eyed gaze. The same-shaped mouth and head. The same expression.

How was it, Anatole found himself thinking, emotion rising in his chest, that the genes Marcos had carried could be so clearly visible even at this tender age? What was it about the human face that revealed its origins, its kinship? Yet so it was—this scrap of humanity, less than a year old, stared back at him in the baby he himself could just dimly remember from his own boyhood.

'I couldn't be sure,' he heard himself saying. 'Knew that I must get DNA testing. Knew there would be doubts that necessitated such measures.' He paused. 'But I have no doubts—not now.' His voice changed, and so did his expression. 'This is my cousin's son—his *only* son! The only trace left of him in this life! He *must* be part of his father's family.' He held up a hand as if to pre-empt what he knew would be her response to that unarguable statement. 'But we must find a way...there must be one—' He broke off, taking a sharp breath, his focus now on Lyn.

'I am sorry—sorry that I said what I did just now. It

was offensive, and you have every right to be angry.' He paused. 'Will you accept my apology?'

His eyes met hers, seeking a way past the stormy expression in them. Slowly, painfully, Lyn swallowed. There was a large stone in her throat, but it was not only from her anger at his vile offer. It was because of the way he'd stared at Georgy...the emotion in his eyes...his voice.

He was seeing his dead cousin in the baby she was holding in her arms...

Just as I see Lindy in him.

She felt her throat close—felt something change, somehow, deep within her. Slowly she nodded, taking a ragged breath.

'Thank you,' he said in a low voice.

His eyes went from her face back to Georgy. That expression returned to them, making her breath catch as the same emotion was aroused in herself.

Warily Lyn made her way past him into the living room, heading for the sofa onto which she sank down on shaky legs, her heart rate still ragged. But something had changed. She could feel it—sense it as clearly as if the wind had changed its quarter, as if the tide had turned in the depths of the sea. It was in his voice, his stance, his face, as he sat down at the far end of the sofa.

And it was in her, too, that change. Was it because she was finally accepting that Georgy was more than her dead sister's son? That he had a family on his father's side too, to whom he was precious—as precious as he was to her?

She did not want to accept that truth—had tried to fight it—but she had to. Must.

For a moment—just a moment—as Anatole Telonidis lowered his tall frame on to the sofa, he seemed far too physically close to her. She wanted to leap to her feet—away from the intensely physical presence of the man. But even as she fought the impulse she could feel Georgy using his not inconsiderable strength to lean forward, towards this interesting addition to his world. And as he did so, he gave another crowing gurgle, his little arms stretching forward towards his father's cousin.

And then Lyn saw something quite extraordinary happen.

Before her eyes she saw this tall, dark, forbidding man who had walked uninvited into her world, catalysing her deepest fears with his demands, his assumptions, all the power of his wealth and family, transform. Greek words sounded from his mouth and then slowly, as if he were moving through thick, murky water, she watched him reach a hand out towards the infant. Immediately a little starfish fist closed around the long, tanned finger and tugged it hopefully, if ineffectually, in the direction of his mouth.

'Hello, Georgy,' said Anatole. His voice sounded strained, as if his throat weren't working properly. 'Hello, little fellow.'

There was, Lyn could see as plain as day, extraordinary though it was, a look of stunned wonder on his dark, formidable face.

She felt emotion stab at her but did not know what it was. Only that it was powerful. *Very* powerful…

Her eyes could not leave his face, could not stop staring at the transformation in the man. But Anatole had no eyes for her stunned scrutiny of him. He had eyes only for one thing—the baby in her arms who had brought him here. His dead cousin's child.

Lyn heard him murmur something in Greek. Something that sounded soft and caressing. Something that felt like a warm touch on her skin even though it was not directed at her. It drew a response from her, all the same, and she felt a strange, potent flickering of her senses.

Then Georgy was wriggling impatiently in her arms, tugging on the finger he was clutching. She loosened her hold automatically, so that he could gain his objective, but now he had seen something more enticing to clutch, and he dropped the finger he'd been gripping. Instead he made a lunge at the dark silk tie dangling so tantalisingly close to him as its wearer leant forward. To his own considerable pleasure he made contact, grasped it greedily, and pulled the end into his mouth, sucking vigorously.

A burst of laughter broke from Lyn. She couldn't help it. 'Oh, Georgy, you monkey!' she exclaimed ruefully.

She lifted a hand to disengage the tie, conscious as she did so that the gesture brought her disquietingly closer to the man wearing it. Deprived of his tasty morsel, Georgy gave a howl of outrage. Lyn took his tiny hands and busied herself in remonstrations that enabled her to straighten up, increasing the distance between herself and this most disturbing of men.

'No, you can't have it! You little monster, you! Yes, you are! A little monster!' She nuzzled his nose with an Eskimo kiss and set him laughing. She glanced across at Anatole at what was doubtless a hideously expensive tie now somewhat soggy at the end. 'I'm sorry about that. I hope it's not damaged too much.' Her voice was apologetic, constrained with an embarrassment that was not just due to Georgy's misdemeanours but also to the awkward self-consciousness of sharing a sofa with Anatole Telonidis.

Anatole surveyed the soggy item. 'It is of no consequence,' he remarked.

Then, before Lyn realised what he was doing, he was unfastening his gold watch and offering it to Georgy. Eyes widening in disbelieving delight, Georgy snatched up the shiny treasure and clutched it to his chest, gazing wide-eyed at the giver of such largesse.

'You're mad!' exclaimed Lyn, throwing a shocked glance at Anatole. 'He'll try and eat it!'

But Anatole merely looked at the baby. 'Georgy. No eating. A gentleman does not eat his watch. Understood?'

Georgy stared, his eyes wide in wonder. This stern, deep voice had clearly made a deep impression on him. Dutifully, he made no attempt to ingest the Rolex, contenting himself with continuing to clutch it while staring riveted at this oracle of good advice.

Anatole cast a long-lashed sardonic look at Lyn—a strangely intimate glance that sent a quiver through her. Then the next second his moment of triumph evaporated. With a jerky movement Georgy slammed the watch to his mouth.

'Georgy—no!' Both adults moved fast but, alas, Anatole's belated attempt to remove his watch incited outrage in the infant, whose little face screwed up into angry tears.

Hastily Lyn fumbled in the plastic toy bucket beside the sofa to fetch out Georgy's favourite—a set of plastic keys—and managed to swap them, with some difficulty, for the precious gold watch. Charily, she handed the latter back to its owner, avoiding eye contact this time, and then busied herself settling Georgy in her lap as he chewed contentedly on his keys. She felt unbearably awkward, and yet she knew that something had changed. Thawed.

Imperceptibly, she felt a tiny amount of the tension racking her easing. Then, into the brief silence, a deep voice spoke.

'So, what are we to do?'

CHAPTER THREE

LYN'S EYES FLEW upwards. Anatole Telonidis was looking at her, and as he did so she knew for sure that something had definitely changed between them. She was still wary, yes—wariness was prickling through her every vein—but that wash of rage and outrage against him had gone. His tone of voice was different too. It was more—open. As if he were no longer simply dictating to her what must happen. As if he were truly asking a question of her.

A question she could give no answer to other than the one she had hurled at his head five minutes ago. She could not—*would* not—ever give Georgy up!

She gave an awkward shrug, dropping her eyes again. She didn't want to look at him. Her self-consciousness had soared suddenly, and whereas before she might have found refuge in animosity and resentment and rage against him and his autocratic demands, now she felt raw and exposed.

Anatole watched her sitting there, with the baby on her lap, her attention all on the infant who was busily chewing on his keys and chuntering away to himself. Emotion poured through him, powerful and overwhelming. Even without the formality of DNA testing his heart already knew that this was Marcos's son. And already he felt a powerful urge to protect and cherish him.

Which is what she feels too! That is what is driving her!
Her obduracy, her angry outburst, were both fuelled

by the deepest of emotions—emotions that he understood
and recognised.

Love and grief.

She could not give up the child. Not now. Not like this.
It was impossible for her to conceive of such a thing. Impossible for her to do anything other than what she had
done—rage at the very notion of it! A flicker of a different emotion went through him—one he had not envisaged
feeling. One that came again now as he let his eyes rest on
her while her attention was on the baby in her lap.

There was something very moving about seeing her
attend so tenderly to the tiny scrap of humanity she was
engaged with. Her face seemed softer somehow, without
that pinched, drained, defensive look that he'd seen in it.
The contours of her profile, animated by her smiles of affection for the infant, were gentler now.

He found an irrelevant thought fleeting through his
head. *If she had her hair done decently, took some trouble over her appearance, she would look quite different—*

He reproached himself. What time or funds did she have
to pay any attention to her appearance? She was studying
full-time and looking after a baby, on what was clearly a
very tight budget. And it was obvious, too, from the circles under her eyes, that she wasn't getting enough sleep.

A sudden impulse went through him.

*I could lighten her burden—the load she is carrying
single-handed.*

But not by taking from her the baby she was so devoted to.

He heard himself speaking. 'There must be a way we
can reach agreement.'

Her eyes flew to his. Back in them, he could see, was
the wariness and alarm that he was so familiar with.

'You're not taking Georgy from me!' Fear and the hostility raked through her voice, flashed in her eyes.

He held up a hand. His voice changed, grew husky. 'I can see how much Marcos's son means to you. But *because* he means so much to you I ask you to understand how much he means to his father's family as well.' He paused, his eyes holding hers, willing the wariness and resistance to dissolve. 'I need you to trust me,' he said to her. 'I need you to believe me when I say that there has to be a way we can resolve this *impasse*.'

She heard his words. Heard them reach her—strong, fluent, persuasive. Felt the power of that dark, expressive gaze on her, and the power, too, of the magnetism of the man, the power of his presence, the impact it had on her. She felt her senses stir and fought them back. But she could not fight back the intensity of his regard—the way those incredible eyes were holding hers, willing her to accept what he was saying to her.

He pressed on. 'I do not wish,' he said, making his words as clear as he could, 'for there to be animosity or conflict between us. A way can be found. I am sure of it. If…' He paused, and now his eyes were more intense than ever. 'If there is goodwill between us and, most importantly, trust.'

She felt her emotions sway, her resistance weaken.

As if he sensed it, saw it, he went on. 'Will you bring Georgy to Greece?' he asked. 'For a visit—I ask nothing more than that for now,' he emphasized. 'Simply so that his great-grandfather can see him.'

His eyes searched her face. Alarm flared again in her eyes.

Lyn's hand smoothed Georgy's head shakily. 'He hasn't got a passport,' she replied.

'That can be arranged,' Anatole responded promptly. 'I will see to it.'

Her expression was still troubled. 'I…I may not be allowed to take him out of the country—?' she began, then stopped.

Anatole frowned. 'You are his aunt—why should he not travel with you?'

For a second—just a second—he saw in her eyes again that same emotion he had seen when he had challenged her as to whether she had adopted Georgy or not.

'You said that the process of adoption is not yet finalised,' he said. 'Does that affect whether you can take him out of the country?'

She swallowed. 'Officially I am still only his foster carer,' she replied. There was constraint in her voice, evasiveness in the way her gaze dropped from his. 'I...I don't know what the rules are about taking foster children abroad...'

'Well, I shall have enquiries made,' said Anatole. 'These things can be sorted.' He did not want her hiding behind official rules and regulations. He wanted her to consent to what he so urgently needed—to bringing Marcos's son to Greece.

But he would press her no longer. Not for now. Finally she was listening to him. He had put his request to her—now he would let her get used to the idea.

He got to his feet, looking down at her. 'It has been,' he said, and his voice was not unsympathetic now, 'a tumultuous day for you—and for myself as well.' His eyes went to the baby on her lap, who had twisted round to gaze at him. Once again Anatole felt his heart give a strange convulsion, felt the pulse of emotion go through him.

There was so much of Marcos in the tiny infant!

Almost automatically his eyes slipped to the face of the young woman holding his infant cousin. He could see the baby's father in his little face, but what of the tragic mother who had lost *her* life in giving *him* life? His eyes searched the aunt's features, looking for an echo of similarity. But in the clear grey eyes that were ringed with fatigue, in the cheekbones over which the skin was stretched so tightly, in the rigid contours of her jaw, there was no resemblance that he could see.

As his gaze studied her he saw colour suffuse her cheeks and immediately dropped his gaze. He was making her self-conscious, and he did not want to add to her discomfort. Yet as he dropped his gaze he was aware of how the colour in her cheeks gave her a glow, making her less pallid—less plain. More appealing.

She could be something...

The idle thought flicked across his mind and he dismissed it. He was not here to assess whether the aunt of the baby he'd been so desperately seeking possessed those feminine attributes which drew his male eye.

'Forgive me,' he said, his voice contrite. 'I can see my cousin so clearly in his son—I was looking to see what he has inherited from his mother's side.'

He had thought his words might reassure her that he had not been gazing at her with the intention of embarrassing her, but her reaction to his words seemed to have the opposite effect. He saw the colour drain from her face—saw, yet again, that emotion flash briefly in her eyes.

Fear.

He frowned. There was a reason for that reaction—but what was it? He set it aside. For now it was not important. What was important was that he took his leave of her with the lines of communication finally open between them, so that from now on they could discuss what must be discussed—how they were to proceed. How he was to achieve his goal without taking from her the baby nephew she clearly loved so devotedly.

He wanted his last words to her now to be reassuring.

'I will leave you for now,' he said. 'I will visit you again tomorrow—what time would be good for you?'

She swallowed. She had to make some answer. 'I have lectures in the morning, but that's all,' she said hesitantly.

'Good,' he said. 'Then I will come here in the afternoon. We can talk more then. Make more plans.' He paused, looking into her pinched face. 'Plans that we will *both* agree to. Because I know now that you will not give up Georgy—you love him too much. And *you* must surely know that since he cannot be taken from you without your consent, for you are his mother's sister and so the best person to adopt him, that you have nothing to fear from me. Whatever arrangements we make for Georgy's future it will be with your consent and your agreement. You have nothing to fear—nothing at all.'

Surely, he thought, *that* must give her the reassurance that would finally get her to make long-term plans for the infant's upbringing?

But her expression was still withdrawn. Anatole felt determination steal through him. Whatever it took— *whatever*!—he would ensure that his Georgy was reunited with his father's family.

Whatever it took.

He took a breath, looking down at the baby and at the aunt who held him.

'I will see myself out,' he told her. 'Do not disturb yourself.'

Then he was gone.

In the silence that followed his departure the only sound was Georgy contentedly chewing on his plastic keys. Lyn's arms tightened unconsciously around him. She felt weak and shaky and devastated. As if a tsunami had swept over her, drowning her. Her expression was stark.

An overwhelming impulse was coursing through her, imperative in its compulsive force.

The impulse to run. Run far and fast and right away! Run until she had hidden herself from the danger that threatened her—threatened her beloved Georgy! The danger that was in the very person of the tall, dark figure of Anatole Telonidis.

Fear knifed through her.

Anatole threw himself into the back of his car and instructed his driver to head back to the hotel. As the car moved off he got out his mobile. It was time—most definitely time—to phone Timon and tell him what he had discovered.

Who he had discovered.

He had kept everything from Timon until now, loath to raise hopes he could not fulfil. But now—with or without DNA testing—every bone in his body was telling him that he had found Marcos's son.

The son that changed everything.

As his call was put through to his grandfather, and Timon's strained, stricken voice greeted him, Anatole began to speak.

The effect was everything he'd prayed for! Within minutes Timon had become a changed man—a man who had suddenly, miraculously, been given a reason to live. A man who now had only one overriding goal in his life.

'Bring him to me! Bring me Marcos's boy! Do anything and everything you need to get him here!'

Hope had surged in his grandfather's voice. Hope and absolute determination.

'I will,' Anatole replied. 'I will do everything I have to do.'

But as he finished the call his expression changed. Just what 'everything' would need to be he did not fully know. He knew only that, whatever it was, it would all depend on getting Lyn Brandon to agree to it.

As the boy's closest living relative—sister of his mother—his current caregiver and foster mother, with the strongest claim to become Georgy's adoptive mother, it was she who held all the aces.

What would it take to persuade her to let Marcos's son be raised in Greece?

Whatever it was—he had to discover it.

As his mind started to work relentlessly through all the implications and arguments and possibilities a notion started to take shape within his head.

A notion so radical, so drastic, so...*outrageous* that it stopped him in his tracks.

CHAPTER FOUR

'Are you sure he is not cold?' Anatole frowned as he looked down at the infant sitting up in his buggy.

Lyn shook her head. 'No, honestly, he isn't. He's got lots of layers over him.'

She glanced at the tall figure sitting beside her on the park bench they had walked to. It was a drier day than previously, but spring was still stubbornly far off and she could see why someone used to warmer climes would think it very cold. But it was Anatole Telonidis who had suggested that they take the baby outdoors. Probably, Lyn thought tightly, because a man like him was not used to being in a place as shabby as her flat. Not that this scrappy urban park was a great deal better, but it had a little children's play area where Georgy liked to watch other children playing—as he was doing now.

Even though they had the bench to themselves, it seemed too small to Lyn. She was as punishingly conscious today of Anatole Telonidis's physicality as she had been the day before.

How can he be so devastatingly good-looking?

It was a rhetorical question, and one that every covert glance at him confirmed was unnecessary. It took an effort of will to remind herself brusquely that it was completely irrelevant that she was so punishingly conscious of just how amazing-looking he was.

All that matters is that he wants Georgy to go to Greece...

That was all she had to hold in her mind. Not how strange it felt to be sitting beside him on a chilly park bench, with Georgy's buggy pulled up beside them. A flicker went through her. Others would see a man and a woman in a children's park with a baby in a buggy.

As if they were a family.

A strange little ripple went through her—a little husk of yearning. She was being the best mother she could to Georgy, her beloved sister's son, but however much she tried to substitute for Lindy there was no one to do the same for Georgy's father.

She pushed the thought away. He had *her*, and that was what was important. Essential. Vital. Whatever Anatole wanted to say to her this afternoon, nothing on earth would change that!

'Have you given any more thought to what we spoke of yesterday?' he opened. 'Bringing Georgy out to Greece to meet his grandfather?' He paused minutely. 'I spoke to Timon yesterday.' Anatole's voice changed in a moment, and Lyn could hear the emotion in it. 'I cannot tell you how overjoyed he is to learn of Georgy's existence!'

Lyn's hands twisted in her lap. 'I don't know,' she said. 'I just don't know.' Her eyes went to the man sitting beside her, looking at him with a troubled expression. 'You talk about it being just a visit. But that isn't what you said initially! You said you wanted Georgy to be brought up in Greece! What if you simply don't let Georgy come back here with me? What if you try and keep him in Greece?'

He could hear, once again, the fear spiking in her voice. Resolve formed in him. 'I need you to trust me,' he said.

'How *can* I?' she cried wildly.

Anatole looked at her. Was it going to be like this the whole time? With her doubting everything, distrusting him, fearing him—fighting him? Because he didn't have time for it—and nor did Timon. Timon had undertaken to talk to his oncologist, to find out whether he was too weak to try the strong drugs that he would have to take if he wanted to keep death at bay, even for a little while. For long enough to see his great-grandson and make him his heir, as Anatole so fervently wanted him to do.

He took a deep, scissoring breath that went right down into his lungs. He had promised he would do whatever it took to get Marcos's son out to Greece, to ensure his future was there. But with the baby's aunt resisting him every step of the way, so it seemed, was it not time to take the radical, drastic action that would dispose of all her arguments? All her objections?

It would surely disarm her totally. Yet he was balking at it, he knew. The idea that had sparked in his mind the afternoon before was still alight—but it was so drastic that he still could hardly credit that it had occurred to him at all!

But what else would it take to get her to stop fighting him all the time on what had to happen?

'I understand your fears,' he said now, keeping his voice as reassuring as he could. 'But they are not necessary. I told you—there must be a way to resolve this *impasse* that does not entail conflict.'

Her eyes were wide and troubled. 'I don't see *how*!' she exclaimed. 'You want Georgy to be brought up in Greece, with his father's family. I want to keep him here with me. How can those two possibly be resolved?'

Anatole chose his words with care. 'What if you came with Georgy?' he asked.

She stared at him blankly. 'Brought him out to visit your grandfather?'

He gave a quick shake of his head. 'Not just to visit—to live.'

'To *live* in Greece?' she echoed, as if she had not heard properly. 'Georgy and me?'

'Why not?' Anatole's eyes were studying her reaction.

'But I'm British!' she replied blankly, because right now it was the only thing that occurred to her.

The corner of his mouth curved, and irrelevantly Lyn thought how it lightened his expression—and sent a pulse of blood around her veins. Then he was replying.

'Many British people live very happily in Greece,' he said dryly. 'They find the climate a great deal warmer!' he said pointedly, glancing around at the bleak, wintry landscape.

'But I haven't got any accountancy qualifications yet, and even when I do I probably wouldn't be able to practise out there. And besides, I don't speak any Greek! How could I make a living?'

Anatole's eyebrows rose. Had she *really* just asked that question?

'It goes without saying,' he said, and his voice was even drier, 'that there would be no necessity for you to do so.'

His reply was a flash of her grey eyes that gave animation to her thin face.

'I'm *not* living on charity!' she objected.

Anatole shook his head. 'It would not be a question of charity!' he retorted. His tone of voice changed. 'Timon would insist that you have an allowance.'

Her mouth pressed together. 'So I'd be Georgy's paid nursemaid? Is that what you're saying?'

'No!' She was taking this entirely the wrong way, he could see. He tried to recover. 'How could you be a nursemaid when you are going to be Georgy's adoptive mother?'

He had thought his words would be reassuring to her, yet for a second there was again that flash of fearful emotion he had seen before in her eyes. His gaze narrowed infinitesimally. 'Tell me,' he heard himself saying, 'is there some problem with your application to adopt Georgy?'

It was a shot fired with a calculated aim to expose any

weaknesses in her claim. Weaknesses, he knew with grim resolve, he would have to exploit if she reverted to being as obdurate and uncooperative as she had been yesterday. But surely that would not be so—not now that they had finally reached the stage where they could at least discuss Georgy's future without her flying into an emotional storm!

He watched her face, saw her expression close. His shot had hit home, he could see.

'What is it?' he asked bluntly.

Lyn's hands twisted in her lap. Unease and fear writhed in her. But she had to reply—that much was obvious.

'From the moment Lindy died,' she said, her voice low and strained, 'the authorities wanted Georgy taken into care and put up for adoption. Adoption not by me but by a childless couple. There are so many desperate for a baby!'

A cold spear went through Anatole. It was just as he had feared the moment Lyn Brandon had said that she was not Georgy's birth mother!

'Even now,' she said tightly, 'if I dropped my application they would hand him over straight away to a married couple!'

'But you are his maternal aunt. That surely gives you a priority claim to him!'

The fear darted in her eyes again. 'They say I'm too young, that I'm a student still, that I'd be a single mother—' Her voice broke.

For a moment Anatole was silent.

'But I'm not giving in!' Lyn's voice was vehement now. 'I'll *never* give in—no matter what they say or how much they drag their heels! I'll never give up Georgy! *Never!*'

Her hands spasmed in her lap, anguish knifing inside her. Then suddenly her hands were being covered by a large, warm, strong hand, stilling their convulsion.

'There is a way.' Anatole heard himself speaking but

did not quite believe he was doing so. 'There is a way that could solve the entire dilemma.'

Lyn's eyes flew to his. He felt their impact—read the fear in them.

'You say that two of the arguments being used against your adopting Georgy are that you are still a student— unwaged and unmarried,' he said. Part of his brain was still wondering whether he would truly say what he was about to hear himself saying. 'What if neither of those things were true any more? What if you became a stay-at-home mother who could devote her days to Georgy—who had a husband to provide for you both and be the father figure that Georgy needs?'

She was looking blank. Totally blank.

'I don't understand,' she said.

Anatole's hand pressed hers. 'What if,' he said, 'that husband—that father figure—were me?'

For a timeless moment she simply stared at him with huge, blank eyes. Then, with a jolt, she moved away, pulling her hands free from his. They felt cold without his covering clasp, but that didn't matter. All that mattered was that she say what was searing through her head.

'That's insane!'

Anatole gave a quick shake of his head. He had expected that reaction. It was, after all, exactly the reaction he'd had himself when the notion had first inserted itself into his brain yesterday, as he sought for ways to sort out the infernally complicated situation he was in.

'Not insane—logical.' He held up a hand. 'Listen to me—hear me out.' He took a breath, his eyes going absently to Georgy, who was still, he was glad to see, totally absorbed with chewing on his beloved set of keys while avidly watching the toddlers tottering about on the park's play equipment.

'This is what I propose,' he said, turning his gaze back to Lyn.

She had gone white as a sheet, with the same stark expression in her face he had seen yesterday. It did not flatter her, he found himself thinking. But he brushed that aside. Her looks were not important right now. What was important was getting her to see the world his way—as fast as he possibly could.

'If we were to marry, it would solve all our problems in one stroke. For the authorities here it would dispose of their objection to you being a single mother, as yet unable to support a child financially. Moreover, in addition to your being Georgy's maternal aunt, the fact that you would be marrying someone who's the closest thing to Georgy's uncle as can be has to be compelling! And finally—' his voice was dry now '—there would be absolutely no question about my ability to support a family financially!'

She was still staring at him as if he were mad. 'But you're a complete stranger! I only met you yesterday!'

And you are about as far removed from anyone I am likely to marry as it is possible to be!

That was the consciousness that was burning in her most fiercely, making her feel hot and cold at the same time, overriding all that he had been saying about the logic behind his insane idea!

Anatole gave a shrug. 'All married couples were strangers once,' he pointed out. There was still a sense of disbelief within him. Was he *really* saying this to the girl sitting beside him? Seriously talking about *marrying* her?

Yet the logic was irrefutable! It was *the* most effective way of achieving what had to be achieved—getting Marcos's son out to Greece, to be raised as Timon's heir.

'Think about it,' he urged. 'I'll give you time—obviously! —but I beg you to give it serious consideration.'

As he looked at her he thought, privately, that right now

she couldn't give serious consideration to anything short of a tornado heading for her—she was still staring at him totally blankly.

'I can't *possibly* marry you! It's…it's just the most absurd thing I've ever heard!' Her voice was high-pitched with shock.

'It isn't absurd—' he began.

'Yes, it is! It's completely absurd—and…and…'

She couldn't go on, was bereft of speech, and he took ruthless advantage of her floundering.

'The purpose of our marriage would be solely to ensure Georgy's future,' he said. 'Once that has been achieved, then…' he took a breath, never taking his eyes from her '…then there will be no need for it to exist.'

She blinked. 'I don't understand.'

'This is what I envisage,' Anatole explained. 'Marriage between us will surely secure Georgy's adoption—we are the closest living relatives he has—but once he has been adopted then there will be no compelling reason why we have to stay married. We can get divorced.' His expression changed. 'Provided Georgy continues to be raised in Greece.'

'Why is that so important?' she asked.

'Timon will insist,' he answered. He paused a moment. 'Timon will make Georgy his heir. He will inherit the Petranakos Corporation when Timon dies—just as Marcos would have done, had he lived.'

Lyn frowned. 'But *you* are his grandson too,' she said. 'Why won't you inherit?'

Anatole gave a quick negating shake of his head. 'I am Timon's *daughter's* son—I am not a Petranakos. I have my own inheritance from my late father and I do *not*,' he emphasised, 'seek Georgy's. What I *do* seek—' he took a scissoring breath '—are the powers required to run Petranakos until Georgy's majority.' His eyes rested on Lyn.

'I do not need to tell you how very grave the economic situation is in Greece at the moment. Unemployment is rife and causing considerable distress. The situation at Petranakos is…difficult. And it has become more so since Timon's illness. Worse, when Marcos was killed Timon decided to make a distant Petranakos cousin his heir—a man who, quite frankly, couldn't run a bath, let alone a multi-million-euro business in a highly precarious economy! If he inherits,' Anatole said flatly, 'he'll run it in to the ground and thousands will lose their jobs! I will *not* stand by and watch that happen!'

He took another breath and kept his eyes on Lyn, willing her to understand what was driving him. 'I know exactly what I need to do to get it on track again and safeguard all the jobs it provides. But for that to happen Timon will insist that Georgy grows up in Greece.'

She heard the steel in his voice, the determination. Yet that did not change her reaction to what had to be the most absurd, insane suggestion she'd ever heard in her life! Even if he was wishing they could divorce later…

She opened her mouth to say so, but he was still speaking.

'You can see just why a marriage between us makes sense! Not only does it keep the adoption authorities happy, but it keeps Timon happy too! He will know that Marcos's son will be raised in Greece, under my guardianship, once his days are gone.'

And that, Anatole knew, would be exactly what Timon would want. He would expect Anatole to take care of Marcos's son, raise him as his own.

That is what I want, too!

The realisation hit him as his eyes went once again to the diminutive figure in the buggy. Emotion welled through Anatole. Of *course* he would look after Marcos's son—there was no question that he would not! He had known of his existence such a short time, known the tiny bundle for even less, but already that tiny bundle had seized upon his heart. He would never abandon him—*never*. That was an indelible certainty now.

Whatever it took to make certain of it!

Whatever...

'It's still impossible! Completely impossible!'

Her voice, still high-pitched and strained, made him twist his head back round to her. She saw his expression change. Something about it sent a shaft of fear spearing through her.

He spoke quietly, but there was a quality to that quietness that made her tense—something about the way his veiled eyes were resting on her. 'Please understand that if we cannot agree on this, then...' he paused a moment, then said what he knew he must say to her, to make it clear that he was set on this course. 'Then I will put in an application to adopt Georgy myself, as his closest, most suitable relative on his father's side.'

He had said it. And it had on her the impact he'd known it must. She paled again, her skin taut and white over her cheekbones.

He pressed on relentlessly. 'Do you really want to take the risk that my claim to Georgy may supersede yours, despite my only being his second cousin, not his mother's sister, as you are?'

She seemed to shrink away from him, and the flash of fear in her eyes was the strongest yet. He could see her face working, her hands clenching and unclenching in her lap.

He covered them again with his own. Set his gaze on her. 'It doesn't have to be like that—truly it does not. I do not want confrontation or conflict. I want you to trust me—trust me that what I am suggesting, that we solve this situation by agreeing to marry, is the best way forward.'

She was still shrinking away from him, her expression still fearful.

'I need you to trust me,' he said again.

She could feel his gaze pouring into her, willing her to accept what he was saying. But how could she? How could she possibly accept it?

He'll try and adopt Georgy himself! He'll use the pots of money he's got—that Georgy's great-grandfather's got—and throw it at lawyers and judges and just go on and on and on...

And it was not just his money that would give him the power to take Georgy from her...

Fear coursed through her again—so familiar—so terrifying.

She gave a little cry, jumping to her feet, pulling free of the clasp that was so warm and strong on her hand.

'I don't want this! I don't want any of this! I just want to go back to the way it was!'

He got to his feet too. A sigh escaped him. He understood her reaction.

'I, too, wish we could go back,' he said quietly, but now the quietness was different. It was threaded with sombre emotion. 'I wish I could go back to before Timon was diagnosed with terminal cancer, to before he gave that lethal car to Marcos, to before Marcos smashed himself to pieces in it. But I can't go back. And neither can you. All we *can* do...' his eyes sought to convey the ineluctable truth '...is go forward as best we can.'

His eyes went to Georgy. Softened. Then back to Lyn, standing there trembling in every line of her body.

'And the best that we want is for Georgy.'

Right on cue Marcos's baby son seemed to hear himself addressed and turned his head enquiringly. Anatole went over and hunkered down to pay him attention. Lyn stood, looking down at them both. Emotion was churning in her over and over, like a washing machine inside her.

Anatole glanced up at her. He could see how over-wrought she was. It was time to lighten the atmosphere.

'Come,' he said, holding out a hand towards her. 'We have had enough heavy stuff for the moment. Let's take a break from it. Tell me,' he asked, glancing towards the swings and slides, 'can Georgy go on any of those yet?'

She nodded, swallowing. 'He likes the slide, but you have to hold him—don't let him go!' she said.

'Great,' said Anatole.

He unfastened the safety belt of the buggy and drew Georgy out. Georgy gave a crow of excitement. Lyn stood watching them interact—Anatole talking to him in what she realised must be Greek. A little pang went through her. Georgy was as much Greek as he was English. Could she truly deny him all that his father's family could offer him?

He will be the heir to a fortune.

She might not care, but wouldn't Georgy want that in-heritance when he grew up? Wouldn't he want to be part of his Greek heritage as well?

Yet what Anatole Telonidis had just proposed was absurd—no one could say otherwise, no one at all!

A chill crept through her. Except if she did *not* agree to that absurdity then he had made it very clear—ruth-lessly clear—that he would seek to adopt Georgy himself.

Fear knifed her. *I can't lose Georgy—I can't!*

The cry—so familiar, so desperate—sounded in her head, her heart.

She watched Anatole carry Georgy over to the slide, hold him on the slippery surface halfway up and then whoosh him down to the end, to Georgy's patent delight. He repeated the whole process over and over again, and she heard his words resonate in her head. She could not go back to the way it had been when it was just Georgy and her. That was over now—*over*. All she could do was go forward. Forward into a future that seemed frighteningly uncertain. Full of risks of losing Georgy for ever.

I have to do whatever I can to prevent that—whatever I can to safeguard him, keep him with me. I have to do whatever it takes.

And if that meant taking the most insane, most absurd decision of her life then she would have to do it…

'If…' Lyn began slowly. 'If we…go ahead…with what you said…then…' She tried to make herself stop talking so hesitantly, but couldn't. 'How long do you think—um—before we could—well—divorce?'

'It depends,' said Anatole. He'd lifted Georgy off the slide and returned to sit next to Lyn, keeping hold of Georgy. It felt good to have the weight of his solid little body perched on his knees. He'd presented Georgy with his favourite plastic keys, and the little hands shot them straight to his mouth to start chewing on them enthusiastically.

He felt his heart clutch, thinking of the tragedy that had befallen his wayward, headstrong young cousin, who had not deserved to die so young, so brutally. Leaving his helpless child behind.

But his son has me now—me to care for him—to guard his interests, ensure his future.

'On what?'

Lyn's thin voice dispersed his memory, his vehement thoughts. He took a breath, focusing on what she'd said, this woman he'd met only the day before whom he was now telling he wanted to marry.

And then divorce again as soon as possible.

'Well, I guess whatever is the minimum time needed, really. I'm not sure what the law is—or if it's different in Greece from here. Obviously the adoption has to go through first, since that's the whole reason for getting married.'

Lyn frowned. 'I think there are laws about not getting married…well, *artificially.* You know—the law says it has to be a genuine marriage.' She swallowed uneasily.

Anatole did not seem fazed. 'Well, it will be, won't it? We will genuinely get married in order to provide security for our orphaned relative. I don't see any problem with that.'

The problem, thought Lyn wildly, was in the very idea of her marrying Anatole Telonidis at all! She swallowed again. 'When…when would it actually happen? The—um—wedding?'

'Ah…' he answered. 'Well, again, I believe there are legal timescales—and, again, I don't know what the law is here on how soon a couple can marry.' His eyes moved to her and held hers. 'The thing is, we will need to marry in Greece. Timon,' he said, 'is not well enough to travel.'

'Greece…' echoed Lyn, her voice hollow.

Anatole's mouth quirked, and Lyn felt that little pulse go through her, as it had when she had first seen humour lighten his face.

'You speak of my country as though it were the far side of the moon,' he said wryly.

'I—I've never been there,' she answered.

'Then you are in for a pleasant surprise. My grandfather lives outside Athens, within commuting distance, on the coast. His villa is at the shoreline, with its own beach, where Marcos and I used to play as children when we visited our grandfather. What I suggest is that you and I make our base not in the main villa—which is massive and very old-fashioned—but in the beach house, which is much more manageable and also goes straight out onto the sand beyond the terrace. It will be ideal for Georgy.'

His voice had warmed and Lyn tried to sound appreciative. 'That would be nice…' she said.

Nice—the word echoed in Anatole's head. Yes, Timon's palatial villa with its luxuriously appointed beach house set in extensive private gardens would indeed be 'nice' for someone whose current accommodation was a cramped, dingy furnished flat in a hideous sixties concrete block…

'Does that reassure you?' he asked.

No! she wanted to shout. *No. Absolutely nothing about this insane idea reassures me!*

But what was the point of saying that? Of course the idea was insane and absurd and outrageous—but Anatole Telonidis was taking it seriously. Talking about it as if it were really going to happen.

Am I really going to go through with this? Go through with marriage to a man I never knew existed forty-eight hours ago?

A man she was a million miles removed from—a man who lived in the distant stratosphere of the rich, while she was an impecunious student struggling along the breadline.

It wasn't as if she were like Lindy, she thought bitterly. Lindy with her lovely blonde hair, her blue eyes and curvaceous figure. No wonder she'd drawn the philandering eye of Marcos Petranakos when she'd lived in London. If Lyn had possessed Lindy's looks she wouldn't feel so abysmally awkward, sitting here talking about something as intimate as marriage to a man like Anatole Telonidis.

But it won't be 'intimate' will it? she castigated herself roundly. *If it's absurd and insane to think of marrying him, it's beyond either to think of anything at all beyond the merest formality. It will be a marriage in name only, solely and simply for the purpose of safeguarding Georgy.*

She and Anatole would be presenting a united front to convince the adoption authorities that they were the best possible parents for him. And if they didn't present a united front…if Anatole applied for Georgy entirely on his own…

Fear stabbed at her. If that happened then he would inevitably discover what she must not let him find out…

Must not!

'Lyn?'

His deep, accented voice interrupted her troubled emotions. She jerked her head up and felt the impact of his gaze, felt the flurry in her veins that came as his eyes rested on her, his look enquiring.

'Are we agreed?' he asked. 'Have I convinced you that this is the very best possible step for us to take?'

She bit her lip. She wanted time—time to think, to focus! But how would that help? The longer she delayed, prevaricated, the more likely it was that Anatole Telonidis would get impatient and set his lawyers to the task of making a formal application to adopt Georgy himself.

She took a breath, ragged and uneven. 'OK,' she said. 'OK, I'll do it.'

CHAPTER FIVE

LYN GAZED AROUND her. The room Anatole Telonidis had ushered her into, Georgy clutched in her arms, was huge. Pale pristine carpet stretched in front of her, upon which was set cream-upholstered sofas and armchairs. Vast picture windows took up one entire wall, looking out over one of London's West End parks. It couldn't have been more different from her cramped little flat. Yet it was where she was going to stay until she went to Athens.

To marry Anatole Telonidis.

She felt the familiar eddy of shock go through her as she faced up to what she had agreed to. But it was too late now—the decision had been made. She had quit her college course, moved out of her flat, travelled down to London with Anatole in his chauffeur-driven car, and her personal belongings had been conveyed by carrier.

He had taken charge of everything, sweeping her along with him so that she hardly knew what was happening any more—except that it was an overturning of everything familiar. Now he turned to look at her as she stared at the luxury apartment he'd rented.

'Come and choose which bedroom you want for you and Georgy,' he said, and led the way back out in to the spacious hallway, off which several bedrooms opened. She knew which one she would choose—whichever was

furthest away from the master bedroom, where Anatole
would be.

A flush went through her. How on earth was she to live
in such close quarters with a man who was a complete
stranger to her? And, worse than that, a man who was,
when it came to physical attributes, a million miles away
from her nondescript appearance.

What on earth does that matter? she robustly admonished herself as she inspected the bedrooms. As she kept
reminding herself, hoping to be reassured, theirs was to be
a marriage in name only, solely for the purpose of adopting Georgy, placating the authorities.

Anatole was speaking again, and she made herself listen.

'There is a gym and a swimming pool for residents
in the basement. The park is accessible directly from the
apartment block, which will be convenient for taking
Georgy out. The apartment is fully serviced, so all meals
can be delivered as in a hotel. Plus, of course, groceries
and anything else you want can be delivered too. Obviously
there's a maid service, so you won't have any housework
to do.' He took a breath and then went on. 'Order whatever you want for Georgy by way of equipment, toys and
clothes. Everything can be taken out to Greece when we
go. A credit card will be delivered to you shortly, and I
am arranging for a new bank account for you, into which
I will pay sufficient funds for you to draw on.'

He paused, and looked at her. She seemed to be taking
it in, but it was hard to tell. She had scarcely opened her
mouth. Well, she was still in a state of shock, he conceded.
Her life had been turned upside down, and she was trying
to come to terms with it. Just as he was....

For a treacherous moment he heard his inner voice re-
monstrating with him, telling him that it was insane to
do what he was doing, but he silenced it. There was no

backing out now. Not for him—or her. They just had to get on with it.

He made his voice soften. 'It's strange for you, I know,' he said, taking a step towards her. 'But you will get used to things soon enough. I am sorry I have to leave you straight away, but it is necessary. I have to see my grandfather and talk to his doctors about what treatment he might be able to have. I have to tell him our plans and urge him to make Georgy his heir, put me in charge of the Petranakos Corporation as soon as possible. Then I have to attend to some urgent business affairs of my own, which have been neglected since I flew to England. In the meantime,' he finished, 'my lawyers are liaising with your social services on an application for Georgy's passport and permission to take him out of the country, as well as everything to do with our forthcoming marriage and how it can accelerate the adoption process. I'll only be in Athens a couple of days. Then I will come right back here.'

He smiled at her in a way he hoped was reassuring. 'I'm sure that you will be feeling more settled by then. You have my personal mobile number, so of course do phone whenever you want if there is anything that worries you.'

A little burst of hysteria bubbled through Lyn. *You mean like anything other than the fact I'm actually going to go ahead and marry you?*

But there was no point saying that. No point doing anything other than nod and clutch Georgy more tightly to her.

'Good,' said Anatole briskly, and lifted his hand to take Georgy's outstretched fingers. This tiny bundle of humanity was what was bringing him and this alien female together. His expression softened. He murmured some infantile nonsense to the baby in Greek, then shifted his gaze to the woman holding him.

'It will be all right,' he said. 'Trust me—please.'

He flickered a brief smile at her, and a warmer one at

Georgy, who was trying to get at his tie again. 'Uh-uh,' he said reprovingly, and chucked him under the chin. 'Be good, young man, and look after your aunt for me,' he instructed.

Georgy gazed at him wide-eyed. Lyn gave an awkward smile.

'See you at the weekend,' said Anatole, and headed for the door.

Behind him, Lyn slowly sank down on to one of the pristine sofas.

She felt completely numb.

Over the next two days she gradually started to feel less numb—less in shock. And gradually, too, she became used to her new surroundings. Although she was worried Georgy might make a mess of the pristine decor, she could not help but find the luxury, warmth and comfort of the apartment very easy to appreciate after the privations of her dingy flat. The milder air of the capital drew her out to the park, with Georgy enthroned in a brand-new, top-of-the-range buggy delivered from a top London store.

She was just returning from such an outing on her third day in the apartment, wheeling Georgy into the spacious hallway, when she realised she was not alone.

Anatole strolled out of the living room.

Immediately Georgy crowed with delight and recognition, holding out his chubby arms. Lyn's senses reeled as she took in Anatole's tall, elegant figure and dark good-looks. He was wearing a suit but had discarded the jacket, loosened his shirt collar and cuffs. The effect of the slight informality of his appearance made her stomach tighten. He looked lean and powerful and devastatingly masculine.

He glanced a smile of greeting at her, and hunkered down to extract Georgy. Hefting him out, he held him

up and swung him high in both hands. He greeted him in
Greek, then did likewise, in English, to Lyn.

'Hi,' she murmured awkwardly, and busied herself folding up the buggy and putting it away in the hall cupboard.

She let Anatole keep Georgy and, taking off her baggy
jacket and hanging it up beside the buggy, followed them
into the living room. It was no longer quite as pristine as
it had once been. One sofa had been covered by a fleecy
throw—more to protect its pale covers than to protect
Georgy—on the thick carpet another throw was spread
out, arrayed with a good selection of Georgy's toys.

She watched Anatole carefully lower the baby down
on to the floor, where Georgy gleefully seized upon one
of his soft toys.

Anatole stood back, watching him. His mood was res-
olute. The time he'd spent in Greece had seen to that. His
grandfather was a changed man, summoning all his doctors and demanding the very latest drugs, determined to
live now for as long as he could. Determined, too, to see
his great-grandson restored to his family. Even if it required Anatole to resort to this drastic strategy to make
that happen.

Timon had seemed to take a moment or two to absorb
Anatole's announcement, his face blanking as if in shock,
but then he had simply waved an impatient hand. 'If it
keeps all the damn officials happy and speeds everything
up, it's worth it,' Timon had said. Then he'd cast a sly look
at his grandson. 'I take it she's got other charms than just
being the boy's aunt?'

Anatole's eyes rested on the figure stiffly sitting herself down on sofa, busying herself playing with Georgy.
No, the charms that Timon had been implying she might
have were conspicuously absent. She still looked just as
she had when he'd first set eyes on her, with her dark hair
pulled back apart from some straggly bits pushed behind

her ears, no make-up, and wearing a shapeless jumper and jeans that bagged at the knees. Yet as he studied her, watched her playing with Georgy, his eyes went to her face and his blighting assessment wavered.

If he dragged his gaze away from her dire hair and worse clothes he could see that her pale skin was clear and unblemished, and her grey eyes were well set beneath defined brows, sparkling now with animation as she laughed with Georgy. The shape of her face was oval, he noted, with a delicate bone structure, and there was something about the line of her mouth that held his glance…

He watched her a moment longer, resolve forming within him. She could not possibly turn up in Greece as his fiancée looking the way she did now, so badly dressed and unkempt.

Well, that could be sorted, but right now he was hungry. He hadn't eaten on the flight, and it was lunchtime. First he needed a shower, a change of clothes and to check his e-mails, and then he would take Lyn and Georgy for lunch.

And after lunch, he resolved, he would take them shopping. Toys for Georgy—new clothes for Lyn.

Everyone would be happy. Including him.

An hour later they were ready to set off. Lyn was not enthusiastic about the expedition, Anatole could tell, but she had acquiesced docilely enough. She'd changed her clothes, though the brown skirt and pale cream blouse were not a great improvement, to his mind. The skirt was overlong and the blouse too baggy. But that didn't matter—after lunch she would be getting a whole new wardrobe.

Over lunch, his sense of resolve strengthened. He would start getting to know her. There must be no awkwardness between them. Georgy united them, and that meant they could not remain strangers. Little by little he had to win her over, get her to relax in his company.

Get her to trust him.

But she was clearly feeling awkward and totally un-relaxed—that much was obvious to him as they made their way into the restaurant he'd selected. A few diners cast disapproving glances at Georgy in his carrier as they took their seats, but since he was looking both angelic and deeply slumberous no one said anything.

Lyn sat down on the plush banquette, feeling acutely uncomfortable. Her dull, chainstore clothes were com-pletely out of place in such an expensive locale, but there was nothing she could do about it. Since she didn't look like the kind of woman a man like Anatole Telonidis would socialise with, there was no point making an idiot of her-self by trying to and failing.

Anatole took charge, ordering drinks and food. Lyn stared around her uneasily, unused to such expensive sur-roundings. She jumped as the wine waiter reappeared and opened a bottle of champagne with a soft pop.

The effervescent liquid was poured out, and as the waiter departed with a bow Anatole lifted his glass. 'Let us drink to Georgy's future,' he said.

He was trying to be encouraging, she could see. Gin-gerly, Lyn raised her glass and took a nervous sip. It tasted very dry, and the bubbles burst on her tongue with a slightly acerbic texture. She set the glass down.

'You don't care for it?' Anatole's voice sounded sur-prised. It was an excellent vintage.

'Sorry, the only fizzy wine I've ever had before has been very sweet,' Lyn apologised.

'This is not "fizzy wine",' said Anatole severely. 'This is champagne.'

Lyn flushed. 'I'm sorry,' she mumbled again.

'There is absolutely no need for apology,' he said promptly.

He started on an explanation of what constituted cham-pagne, and Lyn found herself listening attentively. It wasn't a subject that had ever crossed her path before. As she listened she took some more little sips of the crisp, sparkling liquid, and as she sipped she started to feel that taut wire of tension running down her spine lessening almost imperceptibly.

Their first course arrived—little *rondelles* of salmon pâté lightened with a lemon *jus*—and Lyn found them delicious.

From champagne, Anatole broadened out into discussing wine in general. It seemed a pretty safe topic, in the circumstances.

'Even here in the UK you are starting to produce some very acceptable white wines,' he commented.

'It was the Romans, I think, who first planted vines in Britain,' Lyn ventured. She had to make some kind of effort with conversation. She owed it to Anatole to make this intensely awkward meal less awkward. 'The climate was warmer then—the Roman Warm Period that ended around 400 AD.'

Anatole's expression registered surprise. 'That's very detailed historical knowledge for someone studying accountancy,' he said.

'I really wanted to study history,' Lyn explained diffidently. 'But it's not the best subject for post-graduate employment—especially not since I already count as a mature student, being in my mid-twenties now. Accountancy's far more likely to earn me a good enough living to raise Georgy—' She broke off, conscious that Georgy's financial future was very different now.

'Well, Greece has more history than anywhere else in Europe,' Anatole said. 'And a great deal of it is in Athens.' He spoke lightly, steering the conversation towards classical Greek history. The champagne, he could tell, was starting to help her relax, become more talkative.

'How did you find the service dining in the apartment while I was in Greece?' he enquired as they ate.

She looked up. 'Oh, I haven't used it. It's bound to be very expensive. I've found a small grocery store locally, down a side street, so I've been cooking for myself and Georgy.'

'You really do not have to stint yourself when it comes to the facilities of the apartment,' Anatole said dryly. 'Tell me, have you taken Georgy swimming in the pool?'

She shook her head. 'Not yet,' she said.

'We shall buy him some pool toys this afternoon,' Anatole said. 'All sorts of toys,' he added expansively while he was at it.

Lyn brightened. 'Oh, yes, please—that would be wonderful! He really needs some that are more advanced for the next stage of his development.' She smiled. 'He's very nearly ready to crawl, and when that happens he's going to take off like a rocket!'

The conversation moved on to Georgy, the subject of their mutual interest and the reason for their marriage. As if hearing his name mentioned, Georgy decided to surface from his slumber. Enlivened by his sleep, he made it clear he wanted out of his carrier and into Lyn's arms. Settling him on her lap, she busied herself feeding him from a pot of baby yoghurt she'd thought to bring with her in between taking sips of coffee to finish her meal.

Then, replete and ready for the off, they left—Georgy borne happily aloft as they exited the restaurant, his little arms waving cheerily at what he fondly took to be his admiring fellow diners. Settled into the waiting chauffeured car, they set off for the shops.

The department store they went to was, Lyn resigned herself to accept, one of London's most expensive and luxurious. Since the buggy and baby carrier had been delivered from there, she was not surprised that Anatole seemed to regard it as the obvious place to shop. Certainly the toy department was lavish beyond anything—and so, she very shortly realised, was Anatole's determination to purchase a substantial amount from the infant section of it, much of it way too advanced for Georgy.

'He can't possibly do a fifty-piece jigsaw!' Lyn exclaimed. 'He needs toys that say nine to twelve months—that's all.'

Anatole frowned. 'He is a very intelligent child,' he observed.

'Nine to twelve months,' Lyn repeated firmly. 'Look—that thing there is ideal!'

She pointed to a large moulded plastic construction, a colourful house and farmyard, with big doors and windows and a roof that all came to bits and slotted together again. Around the perimeter was a railway track with a train and truck, containing people and animals for the house and farmyard. A large, baby-operable lever set the train whizzing around the house, ringing a bell as it did so. Lyn demonstrated its mode of operation on the display model and instantly caught Georgy's attention.

Anatole promptly lifted down a boxed unit. 'What else?' he said, looking around him.

Lyn found herself guiding him through the selection process. It felt awkward, initially, having to be so proactive, but she soon realised that she knew a lot more about what was suitable than Anatole did. He deferred to her without demur, and gradually she found that it was getting easier to be in his company like this. It was even, she realised, enjoyable. And Georgy took such enthusiastic interest in this Aladdin's cave of toys, as well as clearly relishing the presence of lots of other babies and infants, that she found her eyes meeting Anatole's as they shared Georgy's enjoyment.

But that sense of communication ended abruptly as they left the toy department.

'While we are here, Lyn, I would like to look in at the women's fashion floor,' Anatole said.

She halted. 'What for?'

He looked down at her face. She had tensed immediately and her expression was wary. Carefully, he sought the right way to say what he wanted.

'I appreciate that your circumstances till now have been straitened financially,' he began, keeping his tone neutral, 'and of course you have had a great deal to cope with, looking after Georgy while pursuing your studies. I can understand those have been your priorities. Now, however, things are different.' He took a breath. 'New clothes for your new life—'

'I don't need any new clothes!'

'Lyn, you need a whole new wardrobe,' he said.

'No, I don't! It's fine as it is! *Really!*'

He could hear the intensity in her voice and found himself wondering at it. Didn't she want something better to wear than what she had to put up with?

'Please,' she went on, with the same intensity in her voice, 'I don't want you spending money on me!'

His mouth pressed tightly. 'Lyn, you are going to be my wife—of *course* I will spend money on you! I have quite a lot to spend,' he reminded her. 'I don't mean to sound extravagant, and I know you have had to be very careful with money—I have a great deal of respect for you for that—but now things are different.' He paused. 'Don't you *want* to have a new wardrobe? I thought new clothes were something all women wanted!' He put a note of humour into his voice, as if to lighten the tension.

It didn't work. She was staring at him, and her expression remained fraught. Did he really think lashing out on expensive clothes would actually do anything for her? Of course it wouldn't! She would just feel awkward and embarrassed and horrible!

'I'm fine with what I've got,' she managed to get out.

Dark flashes glinted in Anatole's eyes, but he veiled them. She might be fine with what she had, but he was not—it was absurd for her to be dressed the way she was. But he took a silent breath. For now he would not pressure her.

'OK,' he said, holding up his hand. 'If that's truly what you prefer.'

'It is,' she said gratefully. Then, casting about to change the subject, she said hurriedly, 'But what I *do* need, however, is some more clothes for Georgy—he's growing rapidly.' She hesitated. 'I'm sure the baby clothes here will be very expensive—I can get them much cheaper elsewhere, so—'

'Here is fine, Lyn,' Anatole interrupted her firmly, and set off towards babywear, next to the toy department.

Lyn hurried after him, pushing the buggy. She felt weak at the narrow escape she'd had. It would have been unendurable to go down to the fashion department and have some snooty vendeuse look pityingly at her while she tried on designer fashions to try and conceal her nondescript looks. She would have writhed with embarrassment and self-consciousness!

Instead, all she had to do now was try not to blanch when she looked at the price tags on the baby clothes that Anatole was holding up for her inspection. If he was going to spend his money at least it would be on Georgy, not her, so she made little objection. Nor did she object when, purchases made, Anatole had them taken down to his chauffeured car. Then, turning to Lyn, he suggested they find the store's tea lounge.

As she sat herself down on a soft banquette, tea ordered

from the waitress and Anatole amusing Georgy with one of his smaller new toys, she found herself observing them.

Emotion moved within her. He was so good with Georgy—naturally attentive and responsive, clearly enjoying interacting with him—and Georgy, too, was clearly enjoying being with Anatole.

That's why I'm doing this, she reminded herself fiercely. *For Georgy's sake!*

Yet even as she said the words in her head she knew, somewhere deep inside her, a little ache had started up, as she gazed at the man holding her beloved Georgy. What if there were no Georgy and Anatole Telonidis, with his amazing looks, his dark, expressive eyes, his lean strength and honed physique, were going to marry her not because of an orphaned baby but for herself alone?

Even as the thought formed she squashed it flat.

Without Georgy Anatole Telonidis would never even have looked her way...

That was what she had to remember. Only that—however crushing the knowledge.

With a silent little sigh, she got on with drinking her tea.

CHAPTER SIX

OVER THE WEEKEND she slowly got used to Anatole being in such close quarters with her. She took Georgy out into the park a lot, now the weather was more clement, leaving Anatole to work, as he told her he must, for he had a lot to catch up with. The apartment had an office, and Anatole disappeared in there, focusing on his laptop and phone. The plan was, he told her, to go to Athens as soon as Georgy had his passport issued and was cleared to leave the country with his foster carer.

'Hopefully,' Anatole had said over dinner that first night, 'my legal team will be able to put sufficient pressure on the authorities to expedite matters. As for Timon—he's now starting treatment, and we must hope that it takes effect. He'll stay in hospital for the time being, since these drugs have side effects he may find it difficult to tolerate and he is an old man in his eighties. But soon—within a few weeks, I very much hope—he will be discharged and able to come home again. And once he's home...' he smiled at Lyn '...we can get on with getting married.'

He paused, looking at her. Her expression was tense again.

'Lyn,' he said, with deliberate lightness, 'this is your *wedding* we're planning—'

'It's not a real one,' she said, and then wished she hadn't. She hadn't wanted to imply that she wanted a *real* wedding to Anatole Telondis! It would be excruciatingly embarrassing if he thought that!

But all he said was, 'Well, it's going to be a happy occasion, anyway. It will secure Georgy's future, and that is what we want.' He took a breath, his expression changing somewhat. 'That said, it can't be a large wedding, as I'm sure you'll understand. That would be…inappropriate, given how recently Marcos died.'

'Of course,' Lyn said immediately, and knew she was grateful not to have to face some huge society bash. That would be as embarrassing as Anatole thinking she wanted her marriage to him to be a real one.

This is all about Georgy—only about Georgy! That's all I have to remember!

Even so, until they were able to divorce she would have to go through with being in such close quarters with Anatole as she was now. It was becoming easier, she'd discovered gratefully. He was obviously making a real effort to try and get her to feel more comfortable, to draw her out and get to know her. It felt awkward for her, but she did her best to co-operate.

'Tell me,' he went on now, moving on from the subject of their wedding, 'why did you not go to college straight after school?'

'Well, it wasn't really possible,' Lyn answered. 'Lindy was only fourteen, and I couldn't leave her.'

Anatole looked mildly surprised. 'You were so devoted to her?'

Lyn swallowed. 'She needed someone to look after her. My mother—well, she wasn't very good at doing that. She'd ended up single, despite marrying twice, because both her husbands abandoned her. After that she spent most of her time in the pub, if I'm honest about it, and I didn't want Lindy to be a latchkey kid, so I stayed at home and did the housekeeping, cooking and so on. By the time Lindy left school Mum was ill. All the years of heavy smoking and drinking too much caught up with her finally, so I stayed to nurse her until the end. Lindy took a job in a wine bar and then, just after Mum died, took off with a girlfriend to London and lived in a flat share, worked in a flash West End wine bar. That's where she met your cousin.' She took a breath. 'When she realised she was pregnant she came back home, just as I was finally about to set off to university as a mature student. Of course I couldn't abandon her then...'

Anatole was silent a moment. A strange sense of recognition went through him. She had shouldered responsibilities not of her making—and he, too, was shouldering responsibilities he could have walked away from. Responsibilities that had brought him to this point: about to embark on a marriage to a woman he would never have known existed had it not been for the baby he'd set out to find...

But it was because of that baby—the baby who had stolen his heart already—that he was doing what he was doing now. The baby was all that was left of his young cousin, all the hope left to his ailing grandfather.

And I will see him right, whatever that takes!

His eyes went to the woman across the table from him. She'd opened up to him just now, more than she had yet done, so he knew he was making progress in gradually getting her to relax, getting her to feel less tense. Getting her to trust him.

He worked away at his goal assiduously, little by little making her feel more comfortable in his company.

Dinner on his second night back in London was a little easier than the preceding one. The main topic of conversation was Georgy, and Anatole could see that when Lyn talked about her nephew her eyes lit up, her face lost its pallor, and the animation in her expression made her seem noticeably more attractive. He found his curiosity as to what grooming and decent clothes might do for her intensifying. He found it curious that she seemed to be so reluctant to be made over. Most women, as he knew perfectly well, would have adored the prospect!

He'd backed off from pressing her the day before, when they'd been in the department store, but that evening he did no such thing.

'How did your swim go this afternoon?' he enquired at dinner, having spent the day working via his laptop. 'You said at breakfast you would take Georgy down to the pool. Did he enjoy the new pool toys we bought him?' he asked encouragingly.

Her reply confounded him.

'Um…the man at the desk said…' Lyn's voice tailed off. What the man at the desk had said still made her squirm.

Sorry, love. Pool's for residents only. Nannies don't count—even if they have their charges with them.

'Yes? The man at he desk said…?' Anatole prompted.

'Well, I think he thought I was Georgy's nanny,' she explained reluctantly.

An explosive noise came from Anatole and his expression darkened.

Immediately Lyn tried to mitigate the situation. 'It's very understandable,' she said. 'I know I don't look like I'm a resident here, so—'

'So *nothing*, Lyn!' Anatole's voice was firm. 'I trust you told the man who you were?'

She coloured. 'Um…no. It was a bit…a bit embarrassing. And I didn't want to make a fuss. He was only doing his job.'

He gave an exasperated sigh. 'Lyn, you must surely see that this cannot continue! Tomorrow I am taking you shopping for clothes and that is that!'

She nodded numbly. Clearly Anatole's patience was at an end. Well, she thought resolutely, not all rich women

were beautiful, but they still wore expensive clothes. Now
so would she.

'Good,' he said. He smiled at her encouragingly. 'Most
women, Lyn, adore clothes-shopping!'

She gave a constrained smile in return, saying nothing.
Thankfully, he let the topic go, and suggested they take
their coffee into the lounge.

She set the coffee tray on a low table between the sofas
and took a seat on the sofa opposite Anatole. He was wearing casual grey trousers and a beautiful soft cashmere
jumper, the sleeves of which he now pushed back, revealing strong, tanned forearms. Immediately, Lyn made herself look away.

'Would you like any music?' she asked, for Anatole had
not turned the TV on.

'Some Mozart, perhaps?' Anatole suggested, stretching out his arms along the back of the sofa and hooking
one long leg casually over his thigh as he relaxed back.

The soft sweater stretched, moulding his torso. Punishingly conscious of his intense masculinity, she crossed to
the music deck and made a suitable selection.

The scintillating tones of the *Linz Symphony* started
to resonate through the room and she came back and resumed her place, curling her legs up under her and pru-
dently removing several of Georgy's discarded toys from
under various cushions, where he'd stuffed them earlier.

She leant forward to pour out the coffee. Black and
unsweetened for Anatole. She knew that now. For herself, weak and milky. She proffered the cup to him and he
reached a long arm forward to scoop it up.

As he did so his fingers touched hers. Jerking, she
nearly dropped the saucer, but managed to avoid it, re-
coiling into her seat swiftly. She knew two spots of colour
were in her cheeks. Covertly, she flicked her eyes across to

the man opposite her. Large table lamps stood either side of the sofa, throwing a pool of soft light over him.

He is just so gorgeous-looking.

It dominated her consciousness, that constant awareness of his physical magnetism. A magnetism he seemed to be unconscious of himself. Or he just took it for granted, probably, she realised. If you grew up with looks like that you *did* take them for granted.

No wonder he wants me to look better than I do!

She bit her lip. Surely once she had got some smart clothes, done her hair, that sort of thing, she would look better than she did now? Not much, she knew dispiritedly, and certainly not enough to put her anywhere near Anatole's league, but surely better?

It was a hope that had to sustain her when, the next morning, back once again in the very swish department store in the West End they'd been to previously, Anatole went with her to the instore beauty salon.

'Hair and all the treatments first,' he told her decisively, 'then clothes and accessories. And while you're doing that…' he smiled reassuringly '…I'll take Georgy back to the Aladdin's Cave of the toy department.'

'He'll love that,' said Lyn, trying to hide her nervousness as the receptionist hovered, ready to usher her into the inner sanctum and the treatment rooms.

'When you're all done we'll go for lunch,' Anatole said, and then, with a final reassuring smile, he wheeled Georgy off.

'This way, madam,' said the receptionist, and Lyn was led away to her fate.

Anatole was enjoying himself. So was Georgy, nestled in the protective crook of Anatole's arm and gazing in open-mouthed delight at the miniature trains hurtling around the elaborate track layout of the vast display centrepiece of the store's toy department. Anatole was giving an explanation of the finer points of rail transport to him, which would probably have drawn indulgent amusement from the other shoppers present, being way too technical for a baby of Georgy's age, had it not been conducted in Greek.

Following Georgy's butterfly attention span, Anatole diverted towards the array of soft toys nearby, drawing the buggy along single-handed. A brief, if one-sided discussion with Georgy as to which soft toy he liked best of all resulted in Georgy becoming the highly satisfied owner of a floppy-limbed teddy bear almost as large as he was, and they set off for yet another circuit of the huge toy department. From time to time Anatole glanced at his watch, but he knew Lyn would not be ready yet.

What would she look like when she emerged? he wondered. He found it hard to envisage. He'd had little glimpses, sometimes, of what she *might* look like—when she wasn't looking tense and reserved and awkward.

But he wanted more than glimpses.

He glanced at his watch again impatiently.

'What about this one?' The stylist's voice was encouraging. 'It will turn heads,' she said enthusiastically, holding up a dress in fuchsia silk jersey.

Lyn stared uneasily.

Sensing it was too bright for her diffident client, the stylist immediately swapped the vivid dress for the same model in a soft coral instead.

'Or this one?' she asked.

'Um…OK,' said Lyn, nodding gratefully. Turning heads was not what she wanted to do—that was far too scary a thought.

But then this whole experience had been scary. For the last two hours she'd been subjected to one beauty treatment after another, and now—finally—with hair, nails and make-up all done, it was time to choose new clothes. The beautifully made dress slipped easily over her and the stylist got to work smoothing it and fastening it, then standing back to view her efforts. Lyn stood meekly, reluctant to look at herself in the mirror. A lot of effort had gone into improving her, and she was not at all sure about the results…

'Now—shoes,' said the stylist, and went to consult the trolley full of shoeboxes that had accompanied the dress rack. She pulled out a pair and held them momentarily against the fabric of the dress, then nodded. 'Yes, these are the ones.'

She helped Lyn into them, even though her client was looking at them, alarmed.

They had a high heel and a very narrow fitting. Yet they felt surprisingly comfortable on—presumably a sign of how scarily expensive they were. But it wasn't her place to object to any of this vast expenditure, so she said nothing. Nor did she say anything when she was presented with a matching clutch and, as a final touch, a piece of costume jewellery consisting of a couple of linked chunks of a copper-coloured stones was draped around her throat.

The stylist stepped back. 'There!' she exclaimed. 'Ready to roll.'

Even as she spoke another member of staff put her head around the door behind her. 'Mr Telonidis is at Reception,' she said.

'Just in time.' The stylist smiled at Lyn.

Stiltedly, Lyn smiled back. 'Um…thank you very much for everything,' she said.

'My pleasure,' said the woman.

Her voice was warm, and Lyn knew she was trying to be encouraging.

'I do hope you're pleased with the results.'

'The clothes and accessories are beautiful,' Lyn assured her, feeling awkward. Then she turned away from the window she'd been standing next to, doggedly staring out over the London skyline beyond, ready to go out and face the man she was going to marry and hope—just hope—that all the money he'd spent on her had not been completely wasted!

As she turned a woman came into view and Lyn halted. Where had *she* come from? She hadn't heard the door open again. She must be the stylist's next client. Curiously, she seemed to be wearing a very similar dress to the one the woman had put on her. Maybe it was a favourite of the stylist's, she thought, confused. It certainly looked wonderful on the other woman, with the soft neckline draping over her bust and the dress lightly skimming her slim hips. The total image was one of effortless chic, from her beautifully cut hair to the elegant high heels and soft clutch handbag.

She gave herself a mental shake. She couldn't stand here gawping. The other woman obviously wanted her to vacate the room, as she was still standing there expectantly. Lyn took a step forward, wavering slightly on the high heels she wasn't used to, and saw the woman step towards her as well.

As if her brain cells were ungluing painfully, the truth dawned on her.

Oh, my God, it's me!

She stopped dead, frozen and motionless. Just staring. Her reflection—because of course, as her brain cells had belatedly worked out, that was what it was—stared back.

The stylist was by the door, holding it open for her, and numbly Lyn walked through and went out into the reception area.

Anatole was there, leaning over Georgy in his buggy, but he straightened as she emerged.

Then, in front of her eyes, he too froze. And stared.

'Lyn?' The disbelief in his voice was evident—he

couldn't hide it—but it was impossible to believe what his eyes were telling him. That the woman walking up to him had once been the drab, badly dressed female he'd handed over earlier. That woman was gone. Totally gone.

And she is never coming back!

The thought seared unbidden through his brain. Unbidden, but undeletable. That old version of Lyn was gone for ever! But this one—oh, *this* one could stay as long as she liked!

From deep inside him came an ancient, powerful emotion. Whatever it was that was calling it from him—the lissom lines of a figure he'd never had the faintest idea was underneath her old shapeless clothes, or the silky swing of freshly styled hair that had been released from its customary straggly knot and now skimmed her slender shoulders—his eyes narrowed infinitesimally as his masculine assessment moved to her face. Quite extraordinarily, the skilfully applied make-up now finally revealed her features—no longer muted but defined, enhanced…

Her eyes! Clear, wide-set, luminous. With delicately arched brows and their sockets softly deepened, the lashes richly lush. And her mouth—yet again Anatole felt all his male hormones kicking in powerfully—her mouth was as tender and inviting as a budding rose.

He murmured something in Greek. He didn't even know what it was, but it was repeating itself in his head as he finally gelled into movement. He stepped towards her and reached for her hand—the one that wasn't clutching a soft leather handbag as if it were a life-preserver—drew her towards him.

'You look fantastic!' he breathed.

His eyes worked over her. And over her again. Disbelief was still not quite dissipated. He took a step back again, and looked again still keeping her hand in his, try-

ing to take in what exactly had been done to her. It was…
everything! That was all he could think. Just…everything.

And yet it must have been there all along…

That was the most remarkable aspect of all. That underneath that wouldn't-look-once-let-alone-twice image there had been *this* waiting to be revealed.

He went on staring—oblivious, for now, of the fact that the expression on her face had reverted to the kind of stiff, self-conscious, tense awkward one she had had right at the beginning, when she hadn't been able to relax in his company even an iota.

Then, breaking into his studied scrutiny, he heard Georgy demanding attention.

Dropping Anatole's hand, Lyn jerked forward. Thank God for Georgy! Thank God for her being able to escape that jet-powered, laser-intense gaze focused on her like that…

She hunkered down beside Georgy and started to make a fuss of him. Behind her Anatole finally surfaced and, with a start, stepped towards the counter to settle up. As he handed over his credit card it came to him that never had his money been better spent. He turned back to Lyn and another wash of disbelief hit him—followed by a very strong male response.

'Time for lunch, I think,' he said as he took the buggy handles and executed a neat turn of the wheels. His voice was warm with satisfaction.

They lunched at the same swish restaurant they had before. Anatole reckoned that Lyn would probably prefer a familiar place. Though this time she looked like a totally different woman! His feeling of satisfaction intensified. Yes, he had done the right thing—absolutely the right thing—in insisting on her having a makeover. To think that this elegant, soigné woman he could not take his eyes off had been there all along! He still found it hard to credit. What he did *not* find hard, however, was having her sitting opposite him like this. It meant he could study her in detail, take in every last dramatic improvement.

The only problem, to his mind, was that she seemed so ill at ease. He wondered why, and asked her right out.

She stared at him as if he had asked a really stupid question. Which, to her mind, he had. Of *course* she was feeling awkward and self-conscious! She'd felt that way when she'd looked awful—badly dressed and shabby—and now she felt that way when she looked the exact opposite! For exactly the same reason.

Because he makes me feel excruciatingly self-conscious all the time! Because I'm just so punishingly and constantly aware of how devastating he is! Because I just want to gaze and gaze at him, but I can't, because that would be the most embarrassing thing in all the world!

The stark truth blazed through her: Anatole Telonidis the man—not the millionaire, nor the man who was Georgy's father's cousin, nor the man she was marrying so she could keep the baby she adored—who sat there, effortlessly devastating from the top of his sable-haired head right down through the long, lean length of his body, was a man who could have an effect on her senses no other man had ever had.

That was why she could only sit there, quivering in every limb, unable to make eye contact, feeling so totally and utterly aware of him on every female frequency any woman could possess!

His sloe-dark expressive eyes were resting on her, expecting some kind of answer to his question. She had to say something. Anything.

'Um…' she managed, fiddling with her cutlery with fingers whose tips were now beautifully shaped with varnished nails. 'I guess I'm just getting used to being all dressed up like this.'

And to being stared at. Not just by you, but by everyone as I walked in here. And not just because we've got Georgy with us. This time they are staring at me, too, and I'm not used to it. It's never happened to me in my life before and I feel so, so conspicuous!

'You are not used to being beautiful,' Anatole answered, his expression softening. 'Don't poker up again. I said beautiful,' he told her, 'and I meant it.'

And he did, too. Her beauty, so newly revealed, was not flashy or flaunting. No, it was subtle and graceful. He wanted to gaze at it, study it.

Enjoy it.

But it was clear she was finding that difficult. Goodness knew why, but she was.

Ever mindful of her sensitivities, he made an effort to stop gazing at her, but it was almost impossible. Thoughts rippled through his head as he made that realisation, eddying and swirling out of the depths of his consciousness. Something was changing, something about the way he was thinking about her—but he couldn't give time to it. Not right now. He would think about it later. Right now he wanted her to feel comfortable. To enjoy lunch with him.

He gave her a smile. The kind he was used to giving her. Kindly and encouraging.

'What do you think you'd like to eat today?' he asked.

He started to go through the menu with her, and the exercise gave them both some time to regroup mentally. So did Georgy's requirements. He'd already had his lunch, in the children's café in the store's toy department. He'd relished it with enthusiasm—if rather more messily than Anatole had been prepared for. But he'd mopped up Georgy—and himself and the tabletop—manfully, and then purchased another top for him to wear, which he was now sporting colourfully. Spotting it, Lyn remarked upon it, and their conversation moved on to an account of Georgy's entertainment that morning.

'Sounds like you coped really well,' said Lyn. It was her turn to be encouraging. Having sole care of an infant could be quite a challenge, but Anatole was not shy of undertaking it.

'It's a delight to be with him,' Anatole said frankly.

He smiled, catching Lyn's eyes in mutual agreement, and a little rush went through her. Oh, Anatole might look like a Greek god, and be a high-powered millionaire business tycoon from a filthy-rich top-shelf Greek dynasty, but his loving fondness for his baby second cousin shone through! It was the one indisputable shared bond between them.

'A delight,' he repeated. 'But definitely full-on!'

'Oh, yes,' said Lyn meaningfully, glancing down at Georgy in his carrier, snoozing peacefully after all the excitement of the morning.

Anatole closed the leather-bound menu with a snap. 'After lunch,' he announced, 'we shall attend to the rest of your new wardrobe. There is a great deal to buy.'

She looked startled. Anatole reached across the table to take her hand. The delicately varnished nails glowed softly, and her skin was soft and warm. It felt good to hold her hand...

'Do not look so alarmed,' he said. 'It will be fine. I promise you. Trust me.'

She gazed at him. She was trusting him with so much already. Trusting him to ensure she could keep Georgy. Trusting him to sort out all the legalities. Trusting him to know the best way to ensure Georgy would never be wrenched from her.

With a little catch in her throat, she nodded. 'I will,' she said.

For a moment their eyes met, gazes held.

Then, with an answering nod, Anatole released her hand.

'Good,' he said. 'That's exactly what I want to hear.'

CHAPTER SEVEN

'IT's A BEAUTIFUL day. Since we can't leave for Greece yet, let's go for a drive in the country,' Anatole announced.

His mood was good—very good. It had been good ever since Lyn had walked out of the beauty salon looking so totally unlike the way she had looked before that he had scarcely been able to credit the transformation.

Now, as he smiled at her across the breakfast bar in the kitchen of the apartment, he still could hardly credit it. She was wearing one of the outfits they'd purchased the previous afternoon after their leisurely lunch, and it emphasised her amazing new look.

His eyes rested on her warmly. Georgy, securely fastened in his throne-like highchair, was waving a spoon around and blowing bubbles. But for once Anatole's primary concern was not Georgy. It was wondering just how Lyn had got away with looking so drab for so long when she could have looked the way she did this morning.

Her hair was clasped back into a loose ponytail, but the new style with its flattering colour tint made all the difference. So did the subtle, understated make-up she was wearing—little more than mascara and lipgloss, but all that was needed to turn her face from a collection of blank features into a face that had contours and depths. As for the sweater she was wearing—well, it was a million years away from the baggy items she'd used to hide herself in.

The soft lambswool jumper she had on, a light caramel, shaped her beautifully.

His eyes slid to her breasts. Before her makeover he'd never even noticed she had any.

But she does—she has beautiful rounded breasts. Slight, but well shaped...

Unbidden, the thought slid between his synapses.

What would she look like bare? Her slender body revealed to me? The sweet mounds of her breasts beneath my touch?

Joltingly he grabbed at his coffee. It was inappropriate to think in those terms.

Up till now he never had. But since her makeover those thoughts, questions, speculations had made themselves conscious in his head.

He pushed them aside.

'So, what do you think?' he said. 'Shall we get out of London today? Take Georgy out for the day?'

Lyn busied herself getting Georgy out of his highchair. The way Anatole was looking at her was making her colour.

I didn't know that was going to happen—I didn't think!

It was confusing—disturbing—to have his sloe-dark eyes resting on her like that. As if he was seeing her for the first time—for the first time as a woman...

Confusing—disturbing—making her blood pulse in her veins...

She forced her mind to focus on what he'd said—not on the effect his gaze was having on her, making her so self-conscious, making her body feel alive, somehow, in a way it never had been. Making her breasts feel fuller, rounder.

'That would be lovely!' she said brightly. 'Whereabouts do you want to go?'

'Heading south sounds good,' said Anatole.

And so it proved. Once across the girdle of the M25,

the North Downs behind them, the Weald stretched before them. With Georgy safely secured in his car seat, Lyn was seated in the passenger seat next to Anatole. She could feel her eyes drawn to the way his strong hands were shaping the wheel, his eyes focused on the road ahead. She wanted to gaze at him, drink him in.

Instead, she made herself tell him what she knew about this part of the country.

'It's called the Weald—from the Saxon word for forest—like the German *Wald*,' she said. 'It's completely rural now, but it was actually the industrial heartland of England for centuries.'

'How so?' Anatole asked, glancing at her. He wanted to go on looking, because in profile she was well worth looking at, but he had to keep his eyes on the road—which he was finding a nuisance.

'The wood was used for charcoal, and that was used for iron smelting,' she explained. 'And many of the trees were cut down for shipbuilding as well.'

She went on to talk about some of the more notable events in English history that had taken place in this part of the country.

'Including the Battle of Hastings?' Anatole said knowledgeably.

'Yes.' She sighed. 'The end of Anglo-Saxon England. The Norman Yoke was harsh to begin with, imposed on a conquered people.'

'Ah…' said Anatole, commiserating. 'Well, we Greeks know about being conquered. We spent nearly four hundred years being ruled by the Ottoman Empire.'

The conversation moved to the subject of Greece's history as the powerful car ate up the miles. From the back seat Georgy gazed contentedly out of the car window, but when they pulled over at a pleasant-looking pub for lunch he was ready to get out. The weather had warmed significantly, and they decided to risk eating in the garden—helped in their decision by the presence of a children's play area complete with sandpit.

'Don't let him eat the sand!' Lyn warned as Anatole lowered him onto its fine, dry golden surface.

'Georgy, a sensible boy never eats sand!' Anatole admonished him, as the baby rashly prepared to break this wise edict.

Memory stabbed at Lyn. In her head she heard Anatole similarly admonishing Georgy not to eat his watch, that first time he'd been with him.

How totally and irrevocably her life had changed since then!

I had no idea then that I would do what I have—that I would be here, now, like this, with him!

How far she had come since those first excruciatingly painful and awkward days as her life changed beyond recognition. Her eyes rested on Anatole now, hunkered down by the sandpit, engaging with his infant second cousin. Emotion went through her—and not just because of the sight of him and Georgy playing so happily, so naturally together. So much at ease.

She was at ease with him too now. Finding his company not fraught or awkward. Well, not in the same way, at any rate, she amended. Having her makeover had set off that intense awkwardness again, but she was getting used to her new look now. Finding it easier to cope with.

Enjoying it…

Because it was good to know she looked good! The novelty of it had lost its terror for her, leaving only pleasure. She'd caught sight of herself in the mirror in the ladies' here and a little ripple of pleasure had quivered through her. The designer jeans hugged her hips and thighs, the ankle boots, soft and comfortable, lengthened her legs, and the caramel lambswool jumper warmed and flattered her.

One of the young male servers came out and took their drinks order. His eyes, as he smiled down at Lyn, told her that she looked good to him too. That little ripple of pleasure came again.

From where he sat, Anatole watched Lyn interacting with the young man. It was good to see her being chilled about the effect she was having on the male population.

If she gets used to it from other men, she will get used to it from me too....

The words slid into his head and he busied himself with Georgy again, who was taking another lunge at the enticingly crunchy sand.

Lunch passed enjoyably, and afterwards they resumed their drive, finally reaching the South Downs. An airy walk on the high chalk expanse, with Georgy hoisted high on Anatole's shoulders, his little fists impaling his hair, laughing heartily, gave them some exercise. They paused at a viewpoint to look out and down over the blue glittering Channel beyond. Lyn tried to make out the coastal geography, hazarding some guesses as to what they were seeing.

'Do you know this part of England?' Anatole asked her.

'It has special memories for me,' she admitted.

Her gaze went out to the coast, and he saw a faraway look in her face—a look that was taking her back down the years.

'We came here on holiday once,' she told him. 'It was just about the only happy holiday I can remember. We stayed on a caravan park, right on the seashore, and Lindy and I were set loose to head down onto the beach every day. It was wonderful! We were so happy, I remember—so carefree! There were some beautiful houses at the far end of the bay, where the gardens opened right out onto the beach, and Lindy and I used to walk past them all and discuss which one we'd live in when we were grown up and had pots of money and no worries and cares.'

Anatole glanced at her. 'That sounds like you had a need for escapism,' he ventured, hoping she might say more.

It was good that she was starting to open up to him—to talk about her own life, herself, and Georgy's mother, too. He wanted to go on drawing her out. It was a sign that she was really starting to trust him, and he needed her to do that. The changes to her life he was imposing on her were so fundamental he did not want her shying away from them, panicking about what she was agreeing to do—bringing Georgy out to Greece and settling him there. So the more she confided in him, the more that trust would grow.

Lyn gave a little sigh. 'Yes, I suppose it *was* escapism, really. I remember that sometimes after that holiday, when things were particularly grim at home, I used to let myself fantasise that Lindy and I had run away to live in one of those lovely seaside houses on the beach—far away from the stress and strain of coping with Mum and all that went with her...'

'Was it *so* difficult when you were growing up?' he asked, his voice sympathetic.

She made a face. 'Well, I know many children have it loads, loads worse! But even so...for Lindy and me it was—well, difficult. That word you used fits the description.' She took a breath. 'Looking back, I can see that Mum probably suffered from depression. But whether it came from inside her, or whether it was because she couldn't really make a relationship last, I don't know. She'd have downers and take off for the pub, drown her sorrows. It's why I ended up more or less bringing up Lindy myself.' Her voice changed. Softened. 'Not that it wasn't a joy to do so. Lindy was always so sweet, so loving! And she had an infectious sense of humour—she could always set me laughing to cheer me up.'

Anatole saw a reminiscent smile cross her expression.

'What is it?' he probed. He let his gaze dwell on how, when she smiled, it lifted her features, lighting up her clear eyes and curving her tender mouth to show pearl-like teeth.

How could I ever have thought her unremarkable? If her sister had half her appeal Marcos must have been lost!

But, much as he might want to indulge himself in gazing at how her lovely smile enhanced the beauty that her makeover had revealed to him, he focused on her answer.

'The caravan park we stayed at was in a place called the Witterings,' Lyn explained. 'It's a pair of villages—East Wittering and West Wittering—and Lindy found the names hilarious! She only had to say them out loud and she fell into fits of giggles—and set me laughing too.'

There was fondness in her voice, and her expression had softened even more, but Anatole could see that faraway look in her eyes again—a shadow of the sadness that haunted her, at knowing her sister had barely made it into adulthood.

Let alone lived long enough to raise the child *they* were now caring for...

'We can go and visit there some time,' he said. 'If you would like?'

Lyn lifted her face to his. 'Can we? Oh, that would be lovely! I would love Georgy to know the place where his mother was happy as a child!'

He felt a spear of emotion go through him. As she gazed at him, her face alight, something moved inside him. He, too, longed for Georgy to know the beach by his grandfather's house, where he and Marcos had played as boys.

'We shall definitely do it,' he said decisively. 'Too far, alas, to include it in today's excursion, but we'll find an opportunity another day.'

He started walking again, and Lyn fell into stride beside him.

She must not let herself be endlessly sad for Lindy, she

knew that—knew that her beloved sister would not want it. Would want, instead, for Lyn to do everything within her power to ensure the son she hadn't been able to look after herself had the very best future possible!

Her eyes went to the man walking beside her. A stranger he might be, but with each day he was becoming less so—and, like her, he wanted only one thing: that Georgy should be kept safe, safe with them, not given to others to raise. And if that meant carrying out this extraordinary and unlikely plan of making a marriage between them, then she would see it through!

Marrying Anatole is the way I can keep Georgy safe with me—that's all I have to focus on!

Yet even as she repeated her mantra to herself she stole a glance sideways and felt her breath give a little catch that was nothing to do with the exertion of walking along these high, windswept downs and everything to do with the way she wanted to gaze and gaze at the compelling profile of the man beside her. At the way the wind was ruffling his sable hair, the way the sweep of his long lashes framed those sloe-dark eyes of his…and the way his long, strong legs strode effortlessly across the close-cropped turf, his hands curled around the chubby legs of Georgy, borne aloft on his wide shoulders.

He is just so incredible-looking!

The words burned in her consciousness and so too did the realisation that today—just as yesterday—she was finally looking like the kind of female a man like him would be seen with. Her style of looks might be quite different from Lindy's blonde prettiness, but she would have been lying if she had not accepted that with her new hairstyle, her new make-up and her beautiful new clothes she drew his approbation.

The transformation he had wrought in her appearance was just one more of the good things he was doing for her!

A sense of wellbeing infused in her and she heard scraps of poetry floating through her head as they walked the iconic landscape. The chalk Downs that ran along the southern coast of England plunged into the sea further east at Dover, and the peerless White Cliffs that defined the country. It was a landscape that had been celebrated a hundred years ago by one of England's most patriotic poets, Rudyard Kipling.

'"The Weald is good, the Downs are best—I'll give you the run of 'em, East to West,"' she exclaimed.

Anatole threw her an enquiring look and then his glance went down to her upturned face. Colour was flagged in her cheeks as the breeze crept up the steep scarp slope from the glittering Channel beyond. It lifted her hair from her face, and her eyes were shining as clear as the air they breathed. She seemed more alive than he had ever seen her. Vivid and vital.

And so very lovely.

A thought slid into his head. A thought that had been building for some time now. Ever since she'd walked out of the beauty salon and blown him away with the transformation in her looks. A thought that, once there, he could not banish. Found he did not want to banish. Wanted, instead, to savour...

Because why not? Why *not* do what he suddenly realised he very, very much wanted to do?

Why not, indeed?

He strode onward. Life seemed very good.

'What would you like to order for dinner?' Anatole enquired solicitously, strolling into the kitchen where Lyn was warming Georgy's bedtime milk.

'To be honest,' she said, 'I'd prefer something light. That cream tea we tucked into was very filling!'

They'd found an olde-worlde teashop in an olde-worlde

Sussex village to round off the day before setting off back to London, and Anatole found himself remembering the way she'd licked a tiny smear of cream from her lip with the tip of her tongue. He'd found it very engaging.

She was speaking again, and he made himself focus.

'If you want,' she ventured, her tone tentative, 'I could just knock up something simple for us both. Pasta or an omelette—something like that.'

His eyes smiled. 'Pasta sounds good. But I don't want to put you to any trouble.'

'No trouble,' she assured him.

'In exchange, I'll get Georgy off to sleep,' he volunteered.

'Thank you.' She smiled too.

He took the bottle from her and headed off.

She watched him go. It was so…contradictory. That was the only word she could find. On the one hand she felt so much easier now in his company. So much more relaxed. Yet on the other hand, since her makeover, 'relaxed' was the last thing she felt!

She felt as if a current of electricity were buzzing through her all the time—a current that soared whenever she saw him or he came near to her.

She took a breath. Well, hopefully, once they'd both got used to her new look it would dissipate—just as her initial stiltedness had.

It had better…

She gave her head a little shake and determinedly yanked open the door of the huge double fridge that occupied a sizeable space in the palatial kitchen. There were several bags of fresh pasta, as well as cream, eggs, butter and smoked salmon. A pot of fresh basil graced the windowsill by the sink, and she busied herself snipping at the fragrant leaves. By the time she had measured out the pasta, whisked some eggs, beaten cream in and chopped up the salmon, Anatole strolled back into the kitchen.

'Out like a light,' he said cheerfully. 'We clearly exhausted him today!' He crossed over to stand beside Lyn. 'Mmm…' he inspected her handiwork. 'Looking good.' He wandered across to the temperature controlled wine cabinet and extracted a bottle. 'I think this should wash it down nicely,' he said.

His mood was good. Very good. They'd had a good day out, Georgy had had fun, and he'd repaid their efforts by falling swiftly and soundly asleep. That left the evening to him and Lyn.

Yes, definitely a good day.

'You OK with eating in here?' he enquired.

'Yes, of course,' she assured him.

The breakfast bar was huge—plenty of room to dine at it. She heard him open the wine and got on with boiling a kettle of water to cook the pasta. Outside, the night sky was dark, but in the kitchen it felt cosy and companionable, warm and friendly.

Happiness filled her.

I didn't realise how lonely I've been since Lindy died…

But she was not lonely now. She had Anatole to be with.

Yet even as she thought that she felt a pang go through her. How long would they be together? This time next year it might very well all be over. His grandfather might have succumbed to his cancer, Georgy's adoption might be finally approved, and she and Anatole might have their mutually agreed divorce underway.

Somehow the thought chilled her.

'Why so sad?' Anatole's voice was kindly. 'Are you thinking of your sister?'

'Yes,' she lied. She poured boiling water into the pasta pan and fed in the spaghetti as it came back to the boil.

She did not want to look at Anatole. Did not want to let her eyes feast on him.

He isn't mine—he never will be. That's what I have to remember. The only thing I must remember.

Not the way her eyes followed him wherever he went. Not the way her breath caught when he smiled at her. Not the way she felt her pulse quicken when he came near her.

Not the way his face was imprinted on her mind, day and night…

'Then let us drink to her—and to my cousin, too.'

He slipped onto one of the high stools that flanked the kitchen bar. One of the ceiling spotlights caught the glint of pale gold in his glass as he lifted it, proffering the other one to Lyn as she took her place opposite him. They toasted their lost ones silently, each thinking their own thoughts about those they had loved who had died so tragically young.

'He wasn't all bad, you know—Marcos,' Anatole found himself saying. 'I know he treated your sister badly, but—well, I've come up with an explanation. It won't make you forgive him, but maybe you'll think of him a little less harshly.'

He looked across at Lyn.

'I think the reason he ignored your sister when she wrote to him is that he thought Timon would insist on him marrying her once he knew your sister was carrying his great-grandchild. Marcos was only twenty-five—and a young twenty-five at that. He wanted fun and no responsibilities. Timon encouraged him in that. He'd spent ten years trying to compensate Marcos for losing his parents at sixteen. A bad age to lose them. I think that learning that your sister was pregnant scared Marcos. Made him hide from it—hope it would all just go away.'

He looked at Lyn.

'I think that, had he not been killed, he would have

faced up to his responsibilities. He'd have come to me and told me first, I'm sure, and I would have helped him deal with it. Got him to make contact with Lindy. I believe,' he finished slowly, 'had your sister not died, he would have asked her to marry him. Made a family with her and Georgy just as she dreamed he would.' He paused again. 'He was a decent kid inside.'

Lyn heard him speak, felt her sympathy rising.

'It's all so sad,' she said. She was feeling choked. 'Just *so* sad.'

She felt her hand being taken, gently squeezed. 'Yes, it is. Sad and tragic and dreadful, and a hideous waste of young lives, their future stolen from them.'

She felt tears spring in her eyes. Felt Anatole's finger graze across her cheekbone, brushing them away. Felt his sympathy towards her.

'I hope they're happy together now, somehow. In that mysterious realm beyond mortal life. I hope,' he said, 'they're looking down at us and knowing their child is safe, his future assured.'

She nodded, blinking away her tears. He patted her hand and then, glancing at the stove, got up to drain the cooked pasta. She got to her feet as well, and busied herself stirring in the creamy concoction she'd prepared. She heaped it into wide pasta bowls and placed them on the bar. Her tears were gone now. Lindy was at peace and so, she hoped, was the man she'd fallen in love with. Who might one day, had they lived, have come to love her back.

Who knew? Who knew the mysteries of the heart? Who knew what life and fate and circumstance could do?

As she took her place opposite Anatole, letting her eyes savour him as they always did, she felt her heart swell.

Not with hope, for that would be impossible, but with a yearning that she could not still.

Anatole broke the moment and got to his feet. 'You

forgot the parmesan,' he said, and went to fetch it from the fridge.

It was such a simple meal, Lyn knew, but it was the most enjoyable she'd yet shared with Anatole. Despite her assurance that she was not very hungry she put away a good portion of pasta, and when Anatole extracted a tub of American ice cream from the freezer she did not disdain that either.

'Let's go next door,' he said, and led the way with the ice cream, leaving her to bring through the coffee tray.

She felt more relaxed than she had ever felt with him. The wine she'd drunk had helped, and it seemed to be giving her a very pleasant buzz in her veins. Carefully she set down the coffee tray and lowered herself onto the sofa beside Anatole as he indicated she should, taking one of the two long spoons he was holding out. He'd wrapped the ice cream carton in a teatowel, to make it easier to hold.

Sharing ice cream, Lyn swiftly discovered, meant getting a lot more up close and personal with Anatole than she'd initially realised. Digging into frozen ice cream was also, she discovered, enormously good fun when done in the right spirit.

'That lump of cookie dough is definitely mine!' Anatole informed her with mock severity. 'You had the last one!'

A giggle escaped her, and she made herself busy to focus on a hunk of chocolate in the icy mix.

'What would make this even more decadent,' Anatole observed, 'would be to pour a liqueur over it.'

'Or golden syrup,' contributed Lyn. 'Lindy and I used to do that as kids. The syrup goes really hard—it's great!' She stabbed at another bit of embedded cookie dough.

Finally, when they'd both OD'd on ice cream, they abandoned the carton and Lyn poured out the coffee. As she leant back, curling her legs underneath her into her usual posture, after handing Anatole's cup to him, she realised that his arm was stretched out along the back of the sofa. She could feel the warmth of his sleeve at the nape of her neck.

I ought to move further away from him, she thought. But she didn't. She just went on sitting there, feeling the heavy warmth of his arm behind her, sipping at her milky coffee.

'What's on TV?' Anatole asked.

Lyn clicked it on with the remote. The channel opened on one of her favourites—an old-fashioned, retro detective series, set back in the 1950s, just starting up.

She felt the arm behind her neck drape lower around her shoulders. He didn't seem to notice what he'd done, and for the life of her Lyn could not alter her position. She felt herself relax, so that her shoulder was almost nestled against him.

It felt good. It felt good to be almost snuggled up against him like this on the sofa, warm and well-fed, relaxed and rested.

Very good.

Another programme came on—this time a history show about the classical world. They watched with interest, Anatole contributing a little and Lyn listening avidly. He read out the Greek inscriptions on the monuments on show and translated them.

'Do you think you could face learning Greek?' he asked Lyn.

'I'll give it a go,' she said. 'The different alphabet will be a challenge, though.'

'It will come to you, I'm sure,' he said. 'I'll arrange lessons for you when we get there. Speaking of which,' he continued, 'it could be sooner than we think. The latest from the lawyers is that there's no objection to Georgy coming abroad with us, so his passport can be issued. We'll fly out as soon as we've got it.'

For a moment Lyn's eyes were veiled, her expression

troubled and unsure. The reality of taking Georgy to Greece was hitting her. It would be soon now—very soon.

Anatole saw her doubts—saw the flicker of unease in her expression. He knew she was remembering her old fears about letting Georgy out of the UK to visit his father's family.

'It will be all right,' he said. 'I promise you. Trust me.'

She gazed into his dark eyes. He was right. She had to trust him. He had done everything he had promised her he would and she must do what she had undertaken. Go out to Greece with Georgy, trusting the man who had taken the responsibility of his care upon his own shoulders.

'I do trust you,' she whispered.

He smiled. 'Good,' he said.

Then, with a casual gesture, he moved her closer. She nestled against him, his hand still cupping her shoulder, as if it were the most natural thing in the world. She found herself getting drowsy, the warmth of the room, the effect of a couple of glasses of wine and the filling food all contributing. Her head sank back against his shoulder, her eyes fluttering as she tried to keep them open.

'You're falling asleep,' Anatole murmured, glancing sideways at her. He flicked off the TV programme.

She smiled drowsily. 'I'd better get Georgy's midnight bottle going. He'll surface for it soon.'

'I'll get it,' said Anatole. 'You head for bed. I'll bring the bottle in when it's warm.'

She uncurled herself and padded off. Five minutes later she was propped up on the pillows, wearing her nightdress, when Anatole entered with Georgy's milk.

'He's just waking up,' she said as he started to stir and kick at his quilt. 'Up you come, then.' She lowered the side of the cot and scooped him up.

'May I feed him?' Anatole requested, looking at Lyn.

'Yes, of course,' she said, slightly confused.

He moved to sit down beside her on the bed and she shuffled sideways against the edge of the cot, hastily putting a couple of pillows behind his back. He leant back, taking Georgy from her and settling him with the bottle. Lyn felt she should get up, but she was between Anatole and the cot. So she went on sitting there. Propped up. Shoulder to shoulder with Anatole. With only the low nightlight for illumination, the physical closeness between them felt very intimate.

Georgy sucked greedily and then, replete, let Lyn wind him gently before consenting to resume his slumbers in his cot. As she raised the side again, to lock it in place, she was burningly aware that Anatole was still beside her. She turned to make some kind of anodyne remark but the words died on her lips.

Anatole was looking at her with dark, deep, long-lashed eyes, his face half in shadow but the expression on it as clear as day. She felt her heart stop, her breathing stop. Everything stop.

Everything in the entire universe stopped except for one thing.

The slow dip of his head to hers. And then the slow, soft brush of his lips on hers. The slow rush of sensation it aroused.

'My lovely Lyn,' he murmured.

Then his kiss deepened.

His hand closed around her shoulder, covered only in the thin material of her nightdress. His hand felt warm and strong, kneading at her flesh as he turned her into his embrace. His mouth opened hers effortlessly, skilfully, and sensation exploded within her. Wonder and disbelief swept over her like a rushing wave.

Was this happening? Was this really, truly happening? Was Anatole kissing her? How could it be?

But it was—oh, it was. It *was*! His mouth was exploring

hers and his free hand was around the nape of her neck, moulding her to him. He was murmuring something in Greek that sounded honeyed and seductive. Warm fire lit within her, her senses flared...soared...and then suddenly he was sliding off the bed, taking her with him. Sweeping her up, striding out of the room with her in his arms, kissing her still.

She could say nothing, do nothing, only let him take her, carry her into his own bedroom, lower her down upon the bed's wide surface. She wanted to speak, to say something—anything—but it was beyond her. Totally beyond her.

He came down beside her, indenting the mattress with his long, lean length. His hands cupped her face as she gazed up at him.

'My lovely Lyn,' he said again. And his mouth came down on hers.

Helplessly, willingly, she gave herself to him, letting him ease her nightdress from her, letting his eyes, so deep and dark, feast on her form, letting his hands shape her breasts, glide along the lines of her flanks, slip under her back at her waist and half lift her to him with effortless strength. And all the while his lips worked their magic on hers, deepening the passion and the intensity.

She was in a state of bliss. Unable to think, to reason, to understand—able only to wonder, only to give herself to the sensations of her body, her yielding, arching body, which yearned and sought and found what she had never dreamed possible: the wonder of being embraced and caressed by this man.

Never had she thought it possible! Never had she dreamt of it in her wildest dreams! Yet now it was real—true. He was sweeping her to a place she had never imagined.

For how could imagination possibly have revealed to her what it would be like for Anatole to make love to her like this? Drawing from her, arousing in her, such incredible feelings that she could hardly keep her senses—so overwhelmed by his touch, his caresses, his sensuous, intimate kisses that sought and found her, every exquisitely sensitive place until her body was a living flame.

A flame that seared into the incandescence of quivering arousal as, stripping his clothes from his heated body, he came over her, his strongly muscled thighs pressing on her limbs, parting them. His hands closed around hers on either side of her head as his body—naked, glorious—arched over her, his questing mouth taking the honeyed sweetness of hers.

His eyes were hazed with desire, molten with urgency, as he lifted his head from her. She arched her hips towards his, yearning for the hot, crushing strength of his body. For one endless moment he held back, and then, with a triumphant surge, he filled her, fusing his body with hers, melding them,

She cried out—a high, unearthly sound—as sensation exploded through her. She heard his voice, hoarse and full-throated, felt the tips of her fingers indenting deeply, so deeply, into his sculpted back. Every muscle strained. Her hips arched against his.

It was like nothing she had ever experienced! It flooded through her, the whitest flame of ultimate consummation, further and further, reaching every cell in her body, flooding every synapse. She cried out again and the cry became a sob, emotion racking through her at the wonder of it, the beauty of it…

And then he was pulsing within her, and she was drawing him in, deeper and deeper, with more and more intensity of sensation, more wonderful yet, flowing and filling her like a molten tide. She clasped him to her, tightly and possessively, holding his body to her as, reaching its golden glowing limit, the tide began to ebb, drawing back through her body, releasing her from its wondrous thrall.

They lay together, their heated bodies limp now, sated, a tangle of limbs half wrapped around each other.

He cradled her to him, murmuring in his own language words she could not tell. But his hand was warm, splayed around the back of her head, holding her. Her breathing slowed and she felt an echoing slowing in him as well—a slackening of his embrace. Wonder washed like the sweetest wine through her fading consciousness as sleep finally overcame her, and she lay cradled and encircled within the embrace of his arms.

CHAPTER EIGHT

IT WAS THE distant, distressed crying of an infant that awoke her from heavy sleep. Fully waking, she heard Georgy's wailing. Instantly she was up, fumbling for her long-discarded nightdress and stumbling from the room towards her own. Stricken, she lifted his squalling body and clutched him tight. She never let him cry—*never*! Guilt smote her and she hugged him, swaying, soothing his little back until he eased, comforted and reassured finally that she was there and all was well. Slowly, very slowly, she eased him back into his cot, stroking his head.

A sound in the doorway made her turn. Anatole was there, naked but for a towel twisted around his hips, a questioning look on his face in the early light of the dawn.

'Is he all right?' he asked.

His voice was throaty, the timbre of it resonant.

She nodded dumbly as memory swept over her, hot and vivid. Dear God, had it really happened? Had she been swept off into Anatole's arms, his bed? Could it be real? True?

Then he was walking up to her, enfolding her in his arms.

'Come back to bed,' he said.

The voice was huskier than before. Its message clear.

Desire was in his eyes.

He kissed her. Soft, then not so soft. Slipped his hand into hers, leading her away...

Much, much later they surfaced.

This time they did not sleep. This time pale daylight edged past the folds of the curtains, proclaiming the day. She lay in the crook of Anatole's arm, half propped on soft pillows, drowsy. Fulfilled.

Hazed still with disbelief.

'Georgy will be waking,' she said. 'He'll be hungry.'

Anatole reached to the bedside table to glance at his watch. 'The day awaits,' he said. He turned back to kiss her softly. His eyes gazed down at her.

'My lovely Lyn,' he said. His eyes caressed her. 'So very lovely.'

Then, with a decisive movement, he threw back the coverings and got to his feet. His nudity was overwhelming, sending her senses into overdrive. Ruffling his hair, as if to wake himself further, he disappeared into the bathroom. Lyn hurried to her bedroom, swiftly showering before Georgy awoke.

In the shower, her body seemed fuller somehow—more rounded. She was still in a daze, yet it had happened. Her body felt it in every stretched and extended muscle, felt it in the warm, deep glow within her. Her breasts were crested, and she could see with amazed wonder the soft marks of his caressing.

As warm water sluiced over her, the shower gel gliding sensuously over her skin, she felt again the echo of the heat that had consumed her.

She dressed hurriedly, pulling on a pair of leggings and shouldering her way into a long, dark blue jersey wool top, loose and comfortable. She dried and brushed her hair out rapidly, not troubling to tie it back, and it tumbled around her shoulders—wavy, wanton. For a moment she caught sight of herself in one of the long wall mirrors in the room, and her reflection stayed her.

Her eyes glowed with sensual memory. Her breasts strained against the soft fabric of her top. She felt desire stir.

Then, with a rattle of cot bars, Georgy was pulling himself up to a sitting position and holding out his arms to her. With a smile, she scooped him up and out, and bore him off to the kitchen for his breakfast.

Anatole was there already, wearing a bathrobe, his hair still damp, fetching cereal and milk, and a baby yoghurt for Georgy. A sudden overpowering sense of shyness swept over Lyn. But he came towards her, bestowing a kiss on her cheek.

'Your tea is brewing,' he told her, smiling, and settled himself on a stool at the kitchen bar. He nodded at Georgy, still held in her arms. 'How is our infant prodigy today?' he enquired humorously.

Georgy responded to his attention by gurgling, and evincing a desire for his yoghurt, which he'd just spotted. Lyn took her seat, Georgy on her lap, and poured milk into her cup of tea, taking a first sip before reaching for the yoghurt. Somehow her shyness was gone.

'So,' said Anatole expansively, 'what shall we do today?'

He knew what he wanted to do. What he had wanted to do, he acknowledged, since the moment she'd walked out of the beauty salon, transformed and revealed. What had been building since then, hour by hour, until last night it had seemed the obvious, the only thing to do. Follow his awakened instincts to their natural fulfilling conclusion.

He was not about to question it, analyse it, challenge it. It was, after all, incredibly simple. Desire—simple and straightforward. And overwhelming.

Quite, quite overwhelming.

He had not expected it. He knew that. Had not thought that it would happen—*could* happen. But it had and he was glad of it! Totally, incredibly glad! It made sense on every level.

He let his gaze rest on her now. Georgy was snuggled on her lap as she spooned yoghurt into his gaping mouth, hungrily gulping it down, ready for more. Her features were soft, tender, as she smiled fondly at her charge.

Well-being filled him.

'How about,' he suggested, 'we take Georgy swimming this morning?'

It proved an excellent idea. Excellent not just because it was so enjoyable to see the fun that Georgy had—his little body safely held in the water with water wings, bobbing merrily as he chuckled gleefully at all the splashing, fully enthusiastic about the exciting inflatable pool toys acquired especially for him—but also because it afforded Anatole the considerable pleasure of seeing Lyn in one of the several new bathing costumes he'd insisted on her buying. True, it was a one-piece, but it was quite sufficiently revealing for him to feel desire stir all over again.

A desire that, when Georgy finally conceded defeat after lunch and succumbed to his nap, Anatole had no reason to defer any longer, and he swept Lyn off to bed.

'We have to take ruthless advantage of Georgy's sleep patterns,' he justified, overcoming Lyn's slight sense of shock at such diurnal amorousness.

But as she journeyed with him to that wondrous place of union she could only agree.

Anything that Anatole wanted was wonderful! Anything at all! She was ardent, adoring, her eyes lit with wonder and pleasure.

I can't think beyond this! It's impossible—impossible! All I can do is go with what is happening.

She was in a haze—a daze of happiness. And beyond each day, each night, she would not think.

Anatole walked out of his office to see Lyn sprawled on the floor with Georgy, who was on all fours, lurching forward in his newly developing crawl.

'The lawyers have just phoned me,' Anatole announced. He took a breath. 'Georgy's passport is being delivered by courier this morning. We fly to Athens tomorrow.'

He came to Lyn, whose eyes had flown up to his, and hunkered down beside her. Her expression was mixed.

'I know you are nervous,' he said, taking her hand and pressing it reassuringly, 'but once we are there you will find it less alarming, I promise you.'

His eyes met hers, but even as they did so they slid past, down to Georgy, intently progressing towards the teddy bear that Lyn had deliberately left out of his reach, to encourage him to try and crawl towards it. Thoughts swirled opaquely in his head. Thoughts he did not want to put into words. Thoughts he banished with the words he always used to reassure her.

'Trust me,' he said. He leant forward and brushed her mouth with his lightly. 'This is the right thing to do,' he said, his voice low, intense. 'It is the best way forward for Georgy—that is all you have to hold on to.'

Yet doubt, unease, still flickered in her face. He kissed her again, more deeply, and felt her shimmer with response. When he took his mouth away the doubt had gone from her eyes, replaced by the glow that was always in them when he kissed her, made love to her...

'That's better.' He smiled a warm, intimate smile and got to his feet. 'Now, do not worry about packing,' he instructed her. 'The maid service here will do that—both for you and for Georgy. We'll enjoy our last day here. Then, tomorrow, we'll be off!'

He headed from the room.

'I'm going to phone Timon—tell him we'll be there tomorrow and get an update from his doctors. They tell me the drugs are kicking in and starting to work, which is just the news I want.'

Lyn watched him go, and as he went from view she felt again that jittery feeling of unease return. It was such a big, frightening step—to leave the UK, to go to a foreign country and put herself entirely into the hands of a man who, such a short time ago, had been a stranger to her.

But Anatole was no longer a stranger! He was the man she had committed herself to with all her body, all her desire. He had swept her away on a wonderful, magical tide of passion and forged an intimacy between them that made a nonsense of her fears, her doubts.

Thanks to Anatole, everything would be for the best now.

Everything will be all right! I know it will! There is nothing to be afraid of—nothing! I must do what he keeps telling me to do—trust him!

And how could she fail to do so? How could she fail to trust him now that he had transformed her life? In his arms, his embrace, she had found a bliss that overwhelmed her with its wonder! There was no more awkwardness with him, no more shyness or diffidence.

Now everything between them was different! Magically, wonderfully different! Since Anatole had swept her into his arms, into his bed, her head had been in a constant daze. It was still so unbelievable, what had happened between them! So unbelievable that she could not make sense of it—could do nothing but simply go with it…with every wondrous, shining moment of it! She would allow herself no doubts, no questions.

The flight to Athens proved straightforward. Georgy took a keen interest in the proceedings, especially all the admiring fuss that was made of him by the cabin staff, and apart from being affected by the change in cabin pressure on take-off and landing had a smooth journey. At Athens airport they were whisked through deplaning and into the chauffeured car waiting for them. Lyn barely had time to take in her new surroundings before the car was leaving the airport, heading for the coast.

'It should take less than an hour, depending on traffic,' Anatole assured her. 'We'll have plenty of time to settle into the beach house this afternoon. As you know,' he went on, 'we have the whole place to ourselves—and I think that will be good. Give you a chance to get used to everything. With Timon still in hospital for the moment, under medical supervision, we can have more time together. That said—' he made a face '—I can't deny that I'm going to have to spend a great deal of time working. Both at my own affairs, which I've neglected, and even more importantly on Timon's business affairs.'

His expression tightened.

'My priority is persuading Timon to relinquish control of the Petranakos Corporation to me. I'm limited at the moment as to what I can and can't do, and I can see that a great deal needs to be done. A lot of the workforce at too many of the sites and premises are very jumpy—they know Timon is old and very ill, they know Marcos is dead, and they don't know what is going to happen. Bankers and investors are restless too, as well as suppliers and customers. None of that is good. I need to take charge—make it clear that I'm going to run the company on behalf of the new heir. And I most urgently want Timon to designate Georgy.' He took a breath. 'Whatever it takes, I *have* to get Timon to hand over the reins of power to me.'

Whatever it takes...

The words echoed in Anatole's head. He had used them so often in these past weeks since Marcos's fatal car crash.

His eyes went to the woman and child seated beside him and he felt them echo again.

Whatever it takes...

Emotion swirled within him. Whatever it took to safeguard Marcos's son and safeguard the jobs of the thousands of people employed by Timon. That was what he must cling to.

His mind refocusing, he started to point out to Lyn the various landmarks they were passing, giving her a sense of the geography of the region.

'We are heading for Glyfada,' he told her. 'It's on the shore of the Saronic Gulf—where, as I'm sure you already know, the famous battle of Salamis was fought in the fifth century BC to defeat the invading Persians. My grandfather's villa is beyond the resort, on a quiet peninsula, well away from all the glitz of Glyfada and its neighbours, like Voula.'

'I see the roadsigns are in the Latin alphabet, as well as Greek,' Lyn remarked.

'That's pretty common in Greece now,' Anatole reassured her.

She frowned. 'It's the hardest part of learning Greek, I think,' she said. 'Having to learn to read a different script.'

'It isn't so bad,' he said encouragingly. 'Lots of the symbols are the same. One or two can be confusing, though—like the Latin capital P, for example, which is our R: *rho*.' He smiled. 'But don't worry. You'll get the hang of it. I'll get a teacher organised, and you can start lessons as soon as you like.'

'Thank you,' she said gratefully. Her heart warmed. He was taking so much trouble to make her feel easier, more comfortable about moving here to Greece.

Yet even so, as the car turned off the main highway, and started to head down smaller roads, threading between what were clearly private and expensive residences all around them then pausing to go through electronically controlled gates to curl around a driveway that led to the huge white villa at the far end, Lyn felt her heart quail again.

But yet again Anatole sought to assuage her fears as she stared, daunted, at the massive ornate mansion.

'Timon likes to live in style,' Anatole commented dryly. 'But the beach house is a lot less grandiose.'

The car took a fork off to the right that went around the main house and down through extensive manicured grounds that led towards the sea, and drew up outside a much more modest-looking building.

'This will be far more suitable for us,' said Anatole.

Lyn could not help but agree.

It was a single-storey, low-level building, with shutters and a terrace to the front, which overlooked the far end of a private beach that fronted the shoreline of the main villa, from which it was separated by formal gardens set with tall cypress trees and a lot of cultivated greenery.

'I've had the beach house opened up, but no one's been here for a while, so it might be a bit musty,' Anatole apologized.

Lyn only smiled. 'It looks lovely,' she said. She definitely felt relieved that she wouldn't have to cope with the huge imposing-looking villa that was Timon Petranokos's residence.

They made their way indoors, leaving the driver to bring in their luggage. Indoors, Lyn immediately felt even more reassured. Although it was clearly a luxury residence the house was small-scale, and simply furnished, but she liked it that way.

'The staff from the main house will do the housekeeping here,' Anatole explained, 'and the kitchen there will always be on call. Tonight,' he went on, 'we'll definitely make use of my grandfather's chef!'

Lyn was grateful, and by the time she had sorted out her unpacking and got Georgy settled in his new nursery in the bedroom next to hers, she was glad to sit down to a dinner that someone else had prepared.

She still felt strange, but knew she must simply get on with settling in. This was to be her life now.

But for how long?

The thought arrowed through her head and she wished it had not. She didn't want to think about the future right now.

All she wanted to do was be with Georgy—and Anatole…

With Anatole's arms around her, his lips kissing her, his hands caressing her, his words murmuring in her ear as he took her to a place that made everything else in the universe disappear…

She wouldn't think about anything else. Just what she had now.

Take each day…each night…and do what he asks you to do. Trust him.

It was all she needed to do.

The following morning they drove to the specialist cancer hospital outside Athens where Timon Petranakos was being treated.

'I hope you do not mind, Lyn,' Anatole said, 'but for this first meeting I want to take Georgy to see Timon on his own.'

Lyn was understanding. 'Of course,' she agreed readily.

It was understandable that he should want that. This would be a very emotional encounter for a man, old and dying, who, still raw with terrible grief, had lost his beloved grandson but who now was to receive a blessing he had never hoped for: his grandson's baby son. She did not wish to intrude on such a special moment.

Anatole was tense, she could see. So much was resting on this encounter, and she did not want to add to that tension. She leant across to give Georgy, already hoisted up in Anatole's arms, a quick final mop of the face, ready to be presented to his great-grandfather, then she stood back, watching Anatole walk out of the visitors' lounge at the swish private clinic. As the door closed behind them, taking Georgy from her sight, a little bubble of anxiety formed inside her. She deflated it swiftly.

What did she imagine was going to happen? That a frail, sick man like Timon was somehow going to whisk Georgy away, never to be seen by her again? Of course he wasn't! She must stop fretting like this. Just as Anatole kept reiterating, everything would be all right…

She sat back on the chair and reached for a magazine to while away the time until Anatole emerged again. She could do little but glance at the pictures, and it strengthened her determination to get to grips with the Greek language without delay. This might only be the first day after their arrival, but the sooner she could cope with the language the better.

It was a determination she found she had ample time to put into practice in the days that followed. Anatole had warned her that once in Greece he would have to focus primarily on work so, like it or not, she had to wave goodbye to him in the mornings as he headed into Athens, leaving her to her own devices during the day. Not that she had any housework to do—maids from the main house appeared and duly disappeared after taking care of all the chores, and food shopping was also taken care of by Timon Petranakos's staff. They all made a huge fuss over Georgy, who clearly revelled in the admiration, and those who spoke English told her, with visible emotion, how like his poor tragic father he was. She herself was treated with great deference as well, as the fiancée of Timon's other grandson, which she found a little awkward. It brought home to her the very different worlds she and Anatole came from.

But it doesn't matter—we are united in Georgy. He bridges any gap between us.

Not that there *was* any gap. She might not see anything of Anatole during the day, but when he came home in the evening he was everything she could desire.

She'd made a point of cooking dinner herself some evenings, for she was reluctant to rely totally on Timon's house staff to do so for her, but she knew her meagre repertoire would soon pall for someone like Anatole, used to gourmet cuisine all his life, so she restricted herself to easy dishes like pasta, leaving anything more complex to the chef from the main house. Baby food, though, she attended to herself, and soon discovered that shopping for fresh fruit and vegetables with Georgy in the nearby little coastal town—to which she was delivered and collected by Timon's chauffeur—made for a pleasurable excursion every day or two. The Greeks, she swiftly realised, were a lot more volubly enthusiastic about infants than the reserved British, and everyone from passing old ladies to shopkeepers made a huge fuss of him whenever she wheeled him along in his buggy, much to his evident enjoyment.

Having bought herself some teach-yourself and tourist phrasebooks for Greek, Lyn steadily tried to put her first stumbling efforts with the language into use as she shopped. They were aided when the teacher Anatole had promised he would organise arrived at the beach house. He was an earnest young man—the graduate son of the brother of Anatole's PA—and with his assiduous help Lyn started to feel less intimated by the Greek script, started to make definite progress with grammar and vocabulary.

While she had her daily lesson one of the housemaids

would look after Georgy. She spoke to him in Greek, as did Anatole quite a lot, and Lyn knew that it was essential that he grow up to be bilingual from the start—a tangible sign of his dual heritage.

But she also knew she didn't want him growing up unaware or under-exposed to his mother's heritage too. It was something that caused her some anxiety now that she was actually here in Greece. It might not matter while Georgy was little, but as he grew to boyhood Lyn knew she would want him to be as much English as Greek. She owed it to Lindy…

She said as much one evening to Anatole over dinner. She felt a little awkward raising the subject, but steeled herself to slip it into the conversation at an opportune moment. He had made some remark about their day out to the South Downs while they'd been in England, and Lyn seized her chance.

'We *will* be able to go back to England some time?' she asked. 'I know we'll have to go back after the wedding at some point, to be present at the adoption hearing, but once that is done do we come back here for good?'

For a moment he stilled completely, and she realised he might have misunderstood her question.

His eyes rested on her. 'Are you not happy here?' he asked.

There was a concerned note in his voice and immediately Lyn replied. 'No, it's not because of that at all—I promise you! I'm settling in, just as you promised me I would! Please, *please* don't worry about that! You've got enough to deal with as it is—with Timon's state of health and all the work you've got to do! I suppose it's simply dawning on me that once Georgy starts talking he's going to have Greek as his predominant language and culture— and I don't want him to lose touch with his English side completely. It would be reassuring to know that he can spend time in England, still—for holidays...that sort of thing! Touch base with that side of his cultural heritage.' She finished hastily. 'But that's all for the future, I know.'

'Yes, it is,' said Anatole. 'But of course I can see why you think about it.' He took a breath. 'We can work something out, I am sure,' he said.

There was reassurance in his voice, but suddenly Lyn saw a veil come down over his expression, as if he were thinking of something he was not telling her about.

She frowned inwardly, and a thread of anxiety plucked at her. It dissipated almost immediately, however, as Anatole's expression cleared.

'I'm going to try and take the day off tomorrow,' he said. 'What's that expression in English? Playing hockey?'

Lyn laughed. 'It's playing *hookey*—but I have no idea what hookey is, or why you play it when you skive off work!'

Anatole gave a quirking smile. *'Skive?'* he queried.

'It's slang for bunking off—which is also slang for going AWOL, I guess...taking a day off work when really you're not supposed to.'

'Well, I think I deserve it,' Anatole said firmly. 'I've been flat out since we got here, and the pressure is only going to get worse when I'm running Petranakos fully. For the moment I'm going to take a long weekend for once.' He looked at Lyn. 'How about if I take you into Athens and show you the sights? I feel bad that you've been stuck away here and haven't seen anything yet.'

Lyn's face lit. 'Oh, that would be wonderful! Thank you! But please, *please* don't feel I've been "stuck" here—this is such a lovely house, with the beach right in front, and the weather is so lovely and warm.'

Anatole looked at her. 'Are you sure you're happy here, Lyn?' he asked.

She could hear the concern in his voice again, and immediately wanted to reassure him. 'Yes, truly I am! It's getting less strange every day. And so is the language.'

'Good,' said Anatole, and relief was clear in his eyes. 'The other good news is that Timon's oncologist tells me he's continuing to do well. The cancer is responding to the drugs and he is coping better with the side effects. He's talking about letting him come home next week, maybe.' His eyes warmed. 'And then, Lyn, we can really get going on our wedding.'

His gaze caressed her, and she felt herself melt as she always did.

'Not that we need to wait for the wedding...' he murmured, and his message was clear—and potent.

Lyn felt a little shimmer as her blood warmed. No, they did not need the formality of a wedding to unite them. It might be needed to expedite the adoption process, which was still progressing back in the UK, but she and Anatole needed no marriage lines to release the passion between them!

Happiness welled through her.

She had everything she could ever dream of here with Anatole, in his arms, in the life he had made for her here with her beloved Georgy!

And if there was a shadow over her happiness, over the future that was yet to come—well, she would not think about that now. Would not let herself be haunted by it.

She would give herself only to the present—this wonderful, magical present that Anatole had created for her!

'There's something else the oncologist was saying, Lyn.'

Anatole's voice penetrated her haze of happiness. She brought her mind back smartly.

'He thinks that Timon is now sufficiently strong to receive visitors—I mean beyond just me and Georgy. I know you've been very understanding that Timon has really not felt up to coping with meeting you yet, and you know how brief I've had to keep my own visits to him, but of course he is keen to meet you. So…' He took a breath. 'How about if on our way into Athens tomorrow we go via the clinic? How would that be?'

His expression was encouraging, and Lyn knew she must acquiesce. She might have her own apprehension about finally meeting Georgy's formidable great-grandfather, the patriarch of the family, but it was something that had to be faced some time. And tomorrow, after all, was as good a day as any.

She dressed the next morning with particular care, and was conscious of a feeling of tension as they arrived at the clinic—conscious, too, of Anatole's warm, strong hand holding hers as they went indoors, dissipating her tension. Georgy was in her arms, and was already a clear favourite with the reception staff, and with the nurse who escorted them to Timon's room.

Anatole went in first, just to check his grandfather was ready for the encounter, and a moment later emerged to escort Lyn inside. He took Georgy from her, hefting him easily into his strong arms, and guided Lyn forward.

'Lyn—come and meet my grandfather,' he said.

She stepped towards the bed, her eyes going to the occupant. So this, she thought, was Timon Petranakos.

A lion of a man, she realised, but one on whom old age, grief and extreme illness had taken a heavy toll. Yet his eyes, as dark as Anatole's, held her with a penetrating regard. For a moment he said nothing, simply looked at her as if taking her measure. Then he nodded.

'It is good to meet you,' he said. His voice was somewhat rasping, and his accent in English strong.

'How do you do?' she said politely.

He gave a short, rasping laugh. 'Not well, but better than I might.' His dark eyes turned to Georgy, who was blowing bubbles at him from Anatole's arms. 'And all the better for seeing *you*!'

He switched to Greek, bestowing what Lyn took to be words of warm affection for Georgy and holding out his gnarled hands for Anatole to place him on his lap. She watched them interact—the old, sick man who had lost both son and grandson before their time and the infant who represented to him all the hope he had for the future. Anatole joined in, speaking Greek as well, and making a fuss of Georgy, who clearly loved being the centre of attention.

Lyn stood at the foot of the bed, feeling suddenly awkward.

Excluded.

Then, abruptly, Timon's head lifted. 'Tell me about his mother,' he commanded.

And it definitely *was* a command, she realised. But she made allowances. A man of his generation, his wealth, the head of a powerful Greek family, would be used to giving commands to all around him.

She swallowed, wondering what to say, where to begin. 'Lindy was…the sweetest person you could know,' she said. 'Loving and gentle.'

It hurt to talk about her, and yet she was glad that Timon Petranakos was asking.

'Beautiful?' he probed.

She nodded. 'Blonde and blue eyed,' she answered.

The short, rasping laugh came again. 'No wonder my Marcos wanted her! He had good taste, that grandson of mine!' There was an obvious note of indulgence in his voice as he talked about Georgy's father. Then the dark eyes went to his other grandson, seated beside him. 'As does this grandson too,' he added.

His gaze slid back to Lyn, and she felt herself flushing slightly. She dropped her eyes, feeling awkward.

'So,' Timon went on, 'you have the wedding all prepared, the two of you?'

Was there something different about his voice as he threw that at them? Lyn wondered uneasily. But perhaps it was just the thickness of his accent.

Anatole was answering him. 'We want you to be out of here first. Back at home.'

Timon nodded. 'Well, the wretches who are my doctors tell me that another week should make that possible.' His eyes went back to Lyn. For a moment there was that measuring expression in them again, and then his face creased into a smile.

'We are going into the city after we have left you,' said Anatole. 'Lyn wants to see the sights.'

Timon's eyes lit. 'Athens is the cradle of civilisation,' he told Lyn. 'No city in the world can compare to it!' His eyes went to his great-grandson. 'It would be unthinkable for Marcos's son to grow up anywhere else. *Unthinkable!*'

'Well,' said Anatole, 'that is what we are making possible.'

He nodded at his grandfather and said something to him in Greek that she did not understand. It was probably, she thought, something to do with the legal issues surrounding Georgy's adoption, because Timon answered in an impatient tone, to which Anatole gave a reply that seemed to have a warning note to it. Lyn could understand how Antole's grandfather might feel irked by the ponderous and exhaustive bureaucracy of the adoption process.

Then Timon's dark, sunken eyes were turned on her again, and once more Lyn felt herself being measured— assessed. She made herself hold the penetrating gaze, though, returning it with a clear, transparent expression. Abruptly Timon's lined face broke into a smile and he nodded.

'Good, good,' he said, in his strong accent. Then he

lifted a hand. 'Go—go, the pair of you.' He turned towards Anatole. 'Take her into the city. Buy her things she likes,' he instructed.

A nurse came bustling in, telling them that Kyrios Petranakos needed to rest now and take his medication. Anatole got to his feet, scooping up Georgy with him. He spoke affectionately to his grandfather in Greek, then came to Lyn as they made their farewells. Lyn was conscious of a feeling of slight relief as they left. Timon Petranakos might be old and ill, but there was an aura of power about him that meant it was more comfortable being out of his presence, however kindly he had been towards her.

As they settled back into the car and set off for the city centre Anatole looked across at Lyn.

'Not too bad, was it?' he asked, cocking an eyebrow at her. But his eyes had a sympathetic glint in them.

'He is quite formidable,' she allowed.

Anatole nodded in agreement. 'He is of his generation,' he said. 'As he demonstrates,' he added dryly, 'by his belief that the way to win a woman over is to "buy her things she likes…"'

Lyn couldn't help but smile. 'You don't have to buy me anything!' she said. Her expression changed as she gazed at him. 'And you've won me over anyway, already—totally and completely!'

His eyes caught hers. 'Have I?' he said softly

'You know you have…' she breathed, her eyes and face alight with everything she felt for him.

He reached across Georgy's infant seat and lightly, so lightly, brushed Lyn's mouth.

'Good,' he said. Then he sat back.

Just for a moment Lyn thought she could see in his air and attitude the same aura of satisfaction she'd seen in Timon's smile.

Well, why not? Anatole is his grandson—of course there will be physical similarities!

Then Georgy was patting at her arm, wanting her attention. She gave it instantly and fully, as she always did, for never, *ever* would she dream of neglecting him—not even for Anatole.

The day they spent in Athens was magical for Lyn. Timon Petranakos had spoken the truth—the city *was*, indeed, the cradle of civilisation, the birthplace of democracy. As they made their way up to the Parthenon Anatole regaled her with millennia of history.

'How extraordinary,' Lyn said as they stood and gazed at the peerless ancient monument that had withstood all the centuries had thrown at it, 'to think that in this very place your ancestors came to worship! Two and half *thousand* years ago!'

Anatole gave his wry smile. 'We take it for granted sometimes and forget how much history we have compared with many other nations.'

She hooked her hand into his arm. 'You'd never run out of history here if you were a student,' she said.

He glanced across at her. 'Tell me,' he asked, 'if I could track down a suitable course of historical study would you be interested in taking it?'

She looked at him doubtfully. 'In Greek?' she asked. 'I don't think I'm anywhere near being able to cope with that.'

Anatole shook his head. 'I'm sure there must be courses in English. The British School at Athens, for example, runs English language summer courses in archaeology, I seem to remember. There are probably other opportunities as well—I'm sure we could find something that would suit you. After all, history was what you originally wanted to study before you had to divert to accountancy.'

'It would be wonderful if I could have a go at history

again!' she enthused. Then she frowned slightly. 'But I don't think it's practical now I'm looking after Georgy.'

Anatole looked at her with his familiar amused expression. 'Lyn—it's one of the many perks of wealth that child-care can easily be sorted! Speaking of which...' His tone of voice changed again, and Lyn looked at him. 'Timon was telling me that he wants to provide us with a nanny for Georgy.'

She looked startled. 'What for?' she said blankly.

He made a slight face. 'Like I said, he is of his generation. To him it is natural for children to be looked after by nursemaids and nannies.'

'I don't *want* to hand Georgy over to nursemaids and nannies!' Lyn exclaimed.

Anatole kissed her forehead. 'Don't worry about it, Lyn.' His tone of voice changed again. 'Now, do you feel up to visiting the temple of Nike as well? Or shall we take a coffee break first?'

They continued with their excursion, and Anatole regaled Lyn with everything he knew about all the monuments they were seeing. By the time they were finished Lyn was glad to set off back home again.

She looked at Anatole as they settled back into the car. 'It will most definitely take more than one visit to see everything in Athens!' she said with a smile.

'In the summer it will get too hot for sightseeing,' he replied, 'so it's best to see as much as possible now, while it's still relatively cool.' He smiled. 'We can drive in again tomorrow, if you like, or if you prefer we could drive out and see more of Attica itself—the whole region that Athens is set in.'

'Oh, that would be lovely!' enthused Lyn.

So they took off the next morning, with Anatole driving this time, touring through the Greek landscape, eating lunch at a little vine-shaded *taverna*, then heading for the majestic temple of Poseidon at Sounion, which stood in breathtaking splendour on the edge of the sea.

The following day they took a launch across the Saronic Gulf to the holiday island of Aegina, and spent a relaxed day there.

It was bliss, Lyn thought happily, to have Anatole all to herself—to spend the day with him, enjoying Georgy between them. Happiness ran like a warm current through her—a contentment such as she had never known. Walking, chatting comfortably, eating ice cream, Georgy aloft on Anatole's shoulders as they strolled along the seafront— it seemed to her so natural, so right.

We're like a real family...

That was what it felt like. She knew it did! And if there were to come a time when they would no longer be united like this for Georgy's sake then it was something she did not want to think about. Not now—not yet.

For now all she wanted to do was give herself to what she had, what there was between them—which was so, *so* much! For now this was enough. This happiness that bathed her in a glow as warm as the sunshine...

CHAPTER NINE

TIMON ARRIVED HOME from hospital at the end of the following week in a private ambulance and with his own large personal nursing team. Anatole had escorted him from the clinic, and when he was safely installed in his master bedroom, with all the medical equipment around him, Lyn brought Georgy in to visit him.

This second visit was less intimidating, and although Timon was polite and courteous to her most of his attention was, understandably, focused on his great-grandson. Now that he was back in his palatial mansion she would wheel Georgy up through the gardens to visit him every day, Lyn resolved.

The following day Anatole arrived back from Athens earlier in the evening than usual.

'We've been summoned,' he told Lyn wryly, kissing her in greeting. 'Timon wants us to dine with him.'

Lyn frowned slightly. 'What about Georgy? He'll be in bed by then.'

'One of the maids can babysit,' answered Anatole, heading for the shower room. 'Oh, and Lyn...' His voice had changed. 'I'm afraid Timon has gone ahead with hiring a nanny for us.'

She stared after him in some consternation.

Immediately he continued, 'Please don't be anxious—she will be based up at the villa, not here, and she will only be for our convenience. Nothing else. Such as for evenings like this.'

Lyn bit her tongue. It wasn't an outrageous thing for Timon to have done, but it was unsettling all the same. And she would have preferred to have had some say in just who the nanny would be. Timon's ideas were likely to run to the kind of old-fashioned, starchy, uniformed nanny who liked to have sole charge of her infant and keep parents—adoptive or otherwise—well at bay.

But she put her disquiet aside. She would deal with it after their wedding—which was approaching fast now that Timon was out of hospital. This time next week she and Anatole would be husband and wife. A little thrill went through her—a bubble of emotion that warmed her veins. But with it came, yet again, that sense of plucking at her heartstrings that always came when she let herself think beyond the present.

This time next week we'll be married—and this time next year we might be already divorced...

She felt her heart squeeze, her throat constrict.

Don't think about this time next year—don't think about anything but what you have now! Which is so much more than you ever dreamed possible!

With a little shake she went to get ready herself for going up to the big house and dining in what she was pretty sure would be a much more formal style than she and Anatole adopted here in the little beach villa.

And so it proved.

Timon might still be an invalid, and in a wheelchair, but he commanded the head of the table in the huge, opulently appointed dining room as he must surely have done all his life. The meal was as opulent as the decor, with multiple courses and an array of staff hovering to place plates and refill glasses. Though she did her best, Lyn could not but help feeling if not intimidated, then definitely ill-at-ease.

It didn't help matters that Timon focused most of his conversational energies on Anatole, and that the main subject under discussion appeared to be a situation that was developing at one of the Petranakos factories in Thessaloniki, in the north of Greece.

Anatole elaborated a little to her, in English, as the meal progressed. 'The workers there are on short time already,' he said to her, 'and now the manager is issuing redundancies. It's not proving popular, as you can imagine.'

'Redundancies are unavoidable!' snapped Timon, interjecting brusquely.

Anatole turned back to him. 'It's been badly handled,' he said bluntly. 'Without any consultation, discussion or explanation. The manager there should be replaced.'

'He's *my* appointment,' growled Timon.

Anatole's mouth set, but he said nothing.

Timon's dark eyes flashed as they rested on his grandson. 'You're not in charge of Petranakos yet!' he exclaimed. 'And I don't *have* to put you in charge, I'll have you remember—'

He changed to Greek, speaking rapidly, with little emotion, and then broke off as a coughing fit overcame him. Lyn sat awkwardly, aware of the strong currents flowing between grandfather and grandson. Anatole looked tense, and she longed to smooth away his worries.

She got her chance when they got back to the beach house finally. After checking on Georgy, thanking the maid who'd babysat and sending her off back to the big house, she went into the kitchen to make Anatole his customary late-night coffee. When she took it into the bedroom he was already in bed, sitting back against the pillows, his laptop open on his knees. He glanced at Lyn, gratefully taking the coffee.

'I ought to be glad that Timon is—very clearly!—feeling better, but I have to say,' he went on darkly, 'it's making him reluctant to relinquish his chairman's role to me.' He made a wry face. 'The trouble is his management style is not suited to the current dire economic conditions. It's out of touch, too authoritarian, and that's far too inflammatory right now!' He took a mouthful of coffee. 'I need to get him to resign from chairing the executive board and put me in his place, so I can sort things out properly, in a more conciliatory fashion, without having all the employees up in arms! But Timon's proving stubborn about it!'

Lyn knelt beside him and started working at the knots in his shoulders.

Anatole rolled his head appreciatively. He caught her hand. 'I'm sorry this is erupting now,' he told her, 'so close to the wedding. But if things don't calm down in Thessaloniki soon I may have to go there. And,' he finished, his mouth tightening, 'I am going to have to do whatever it takes to persuade Timon to hand over the reins of power to me irrevocably! Too much is at stake! He says he wants to wait until Georgy's adoption is confirmed—but I can't wait till then now that all this has flared up. If the workers in Thessaloniki come out on strike it will cost the company millions in the end! I have to stop it getting that far, and to do that I need to have free rein to take what action is necessary!' He took a breath. 'I'm going to tackle Timon tomorrow. Get him to agree to the handover finally!'

He set down his coffee cup, turned off his laptop, and wrapped an arm around Lyn.

'The next few days are going to be tough,' he warned her apologetically. 'It's going to be a race against time to get everything sorted out before the wedding.' He gave a heavy sigh. 'I'll have to be up early tomorrow, just to tell you in advance, and you won't see much of me for the rest of the week, I'm afraid. It makes sense for me to stay in my apartment in Athens until the weekend. There's even a chance that the situation in Thessaloniki will require me to fly up there myself now. I hope not, but I'd better warn you about the possibility all the same.'

Lyn felt a little stab of dismay at the thought of being without Anatole, but knew she must not add to the heavy pressure on him already by showing it. Instead she put on a sympathetic smile and kissed his cheek.

'Poor you,' she said. 'I hope it turns out all right.'

'Me too,' he agreed.

His eyes started to close, and Lyn reached to put out the light. Tonight, sleep was clearly on the agenda.

But in just over a week we'll be on our honeymoon! she reminded herself.

That little thrill of emotion came again as she settled herself down, nestling against the already sleeping Anatole. She wrapped an arm around him, holding him close.

Very close…

'Right, then, Georgy my lad—no use us sitting here moping!' Lyn instructed her nephew and herself roundly as she carried him through into the bathroom to get dressed and ready for the day.

She'd woken to discover that Anatole had, as he had warned her, taken himself off at the crack of dawn to get to his desk, and she had immediately felt her spirits flatten at the dispiriting prospect of his absence for several days to come. Sternly, she'd admonished herself for her craven wish that Anatole were not so diligent in the execution of his responsibilities towards Timon's affairs. She had dramatic testimony that it was those very qualities that she had so much reason to be grateful for. It was, she knew, totally *because* Anatole had such a strong sense of responsibility that he had undertaken so drastic a course of action in safeguarding Georgy's future.

Marrying me! Bringing me here to live with him, with Georgy! Making a home for us here!

Automatically she felt her cheeks glow. He'd done so much more than that!

He's transformed me—transformed my life! Given me a wondrous happiness that I never knew existed! In his arms I have found a bliss that takes my breath away!

Her eyes lit with the light that was always in them when she thought of Anatole and how wonderful he was—how wonderful it was to be here with him.

To think I once feared that he would take Georgy from me! To think that I wished he had never discovered his existence—never come into my life!

Because it was impossible to think that now! Utterly impossible! With every passing day, every hour spent with him, her gratitude and her happiness increased beyond measure! He was doing everything to make her feel comfortable here in Greece, to make her feel at home…valued and cherished.

His concern for her, his solicitude, his thoughtfulness, were all so precious to her!

With deft swiftness she got Georgy ready, then followed suit for herself. It was another warm sunny day, and even if she wished that she could look forward to Anatole coming home, however late he might be, she would not let her spirits sink. She had another Greek lesson in the afternoon, and she was making steady progress in the language—both speaking and reading it. She thought ahead. In the evening she would busy herself reading some of the hefty history books about Greece that Anatole had provided her with in English. She was determined to be as informed as possible when she applied to the history studies course Anatole had suggested she take after the summer.

A little glow filled her again. He was so thoughtful! Despite being rushed off his feet at work he had still found time to think about what she might like to do after they were married, getting her brain engaged again and not neglecting her love of history.

To think that, were it not for him, I'd be stuck studying accountancy and facing making a living endlessly totting up rows and rows of dull figures! I can study at my leisure, study the subject I love most, and it's all thanks to Anatole!

She headed downstairs with Georgy, telling him just how wonderful his big second cousin was—information that her nephew received with equanimity and a familiar chortle. When they reached the kitchen he wriggled in her arms to be set down, but then, as she was about to settle him into his highchair, ready for breakfast, something caught his eye.

It caught Lyn's too.

It was a package on the kitchen table, set in the place she usually sat. It was wrapped in gold coloured wrapping paper and bound up with a huge silver bow. Puzzled, she went round the table to look at it. Georgy immediately lunged for the enticing bow, and she had to busy herself getting him secure in his chair and then hastily unfastening the bow and presenting it to him. He did what he always liked doing best, which was to cram it straight in his mouth to sample. She let him do so absent-mindedly as she undid the rest of the wrapping.

Inside the gold paper was a document case—a tooled leather one—and on the top of it was a card. She lifted it and turned it over. Anatole's familiar handwriting leapt at her.

Timon instructed me to buy you things you like—I hope this fits the bill.

Curious, emotions running, she opened the document case and withdrew its contents.

She gasped.

Attached to some thick, headed paper was a photograph of a house.

An obviously English house in mellow brick, with roses round the door, set in a lovely English garden. In the foreground was a white picket fence, into which a little wicket gate had been set. The photo, she suddenly realised, had been taken from the wide strip of sand onto which the wicket gate opened.

Memory shot through her.

And a spear of emotion with it!

She knew exactly where this house was—exactly where the photo must have been taken! In her head she heard herself telling Anatole about when she had first seen houses like this one.

'Lindy and I used to walk past them all and discuss which one we'd live in...'

She picked up the photo and stared at it. This was certainly one of the prettiest she and Lindy must have seen!

Her eyes dropped to the rest of the contents of the document case and then widened in disbelief. With a catch in her throat she lifted them up.

It was a set of title deeds—deeds to the house whose photo she was gazing at.

Deeds made out to *her*...

Incredulously she let go of the papers, her hands flying to her face, not believing what she was seeing. Yet it was there—all there in black and white. The formal headings and the language was telling her that *she* was the owner of the house in the photo...

She gave a little cry and her eyes lit upon a note clipped to the corner of the deeds. It was in Anatole's handwriting. She picked it up and stared at it, emotion lighting within her.

'So you can always have a place you love in England for yourself.'

'Oh—*Anatole*!' she exclaimed. Incredulity went through her and through her—along with wonder and a wash of gratitude. She could not believe it—for him to have done such a thing for *her*!

She rushed to find her mobile and with fumbling fingers texted him straight away.

It's the most wonderful surprise—and you are the most wonderful man in the world! Thank you, thank you, thank you!

Moments later a reply arrived.

Glad you like it—in haste, A

For the rest of the day she was in a daze of wonder and happiness. If she had thought it a sign of his solicitude and care for her that he wanted her not to neglect her studies, *this* incredible act of generosity and concern overwhelmed her!

That Anatole had taken to heart her concerns that Georgy should not lose all his English heritage—and even more, that he had remembered her telling him about her seaside holiday with Lindy, a precious little island of carefree happiness in a difficult childhood—was a shining testimony to just how wonderful he was!

How am I going to bear divorcing him?

The thought sprang into her head unbidden—unwelcome and unwanted—and she felt it stab at her. She had got used to trying to keep it at bay, for with every passing day spent in her new and wonderful life she knew she was finding the prospect of just how temporary their forthcoming marriage was supposed to be increasingly unwelcome. How simple it had sounded when she had first let herself be drawn into this drastic solution to safeguard Georgy!

But things are now completely and totally different from then! Never in a million years did I imagine just how my relationship with Anatole would be transformed by him! Now the last thing I want to do is for us to part...

The cold wash of knowing that at some point in the future Anatole would extract himself from their marriage, conclude what had never been intended to be anything more than a temporary arrangement solely to enable them to adopt Georgy and settle him out here in Greece, chilled her to the bone.

Words, thoughts, sprang hectically in her brain.

I don't want us to part! I don't want us to go our separate ways, make separate lives for ourselves! I don't. I don't!

She gazed at Georgy, anguish in her eyes.

I want to go on as we are, being together, bringing up Georgy together, making our lives together...

Her face worked.

Maybe Anatole does too! That's what I have to hope— that he is finding the life we are making here as good as I do! That he is happy, and does not want us to change anything, for us to divorce and go our separate ways...

She could feel hope squeezing at her heart—hope and longing.

Let it be so—oh, please, please let it be so!

Didn't that incredible gift of his—the fantastic gift to her of a house of her own, where she could take Georgy sometimes to walk in the footsteps of his mother—show all his generosity, all his thoughtfulness? Wasn't that tangible proof of how much he felt for her?

And how easy it was to spend time with him—how comfortably they chatted and talked! That was good, wasn't it? It must be, surely? And the way they could laugh together, too, and smile at Georgy's antics...

And Georgy—oh, Georgy was beloved by them both. How doting they were to him, how dedicated!

A quiver of fire ran down her veins as she thought of the passion they exchanged night after night, the incredible desire she had for him, that he too must feel for her. Surely that most of all must tell her that what they had between them was not something unreal, temporary, that could be turned off like a tap?

Oh, please, let me mean as much to Anatole as he does to me... Please let it be so!

Anatole rubbed at his eyes as he sat at Timon's huge desk at Petranakos headquarters. God, he could do with some sleep! He was used to working hard, but this was punishing. Non-stop, just about, for the last four days on end. And nights. Nights spent here in Athens, at his apartment. He didn't like to leave Lyn and Georgy at the beach house, but there had been no option. Now that he'd finally got the chairmanship of the whole Petranakos Corporation, with full executive powers, there was a huge amount to do, on far too many fronts, at the huge, complex organisation that would one day be Georgy's.

The deteriorating situation in Thessaloniki was the most pressing, but by no means the only one. For with Timon having been hospitalised until so recently, daily management had become lax in many quarters. Even so, the threatened strike was requiring the bulk of his attention. So much so that he knew he was going to be hard-pressed to find the time to do something even more vital.

Get out of Athens tonight and back to Lyn—to talk to her.

Talk to her as quickly and as urgently as possible. The day of their wedding was approaching fast, and he could hear the clock ticking. He was running out of time.

Tonight—tonight I'll sit her down and tell her.

Tell her what he *must* tell her without any further delay

He glanced at the document lying in its folder at the side of his desk. It had been delivered to him by courier only an hour before. It seemed to lie there like a heavy weight on the mahogany surface of Timon Petranakos's desk.

For a moment Anatole's face blanked. Had he done the right thing?

Yes! I didn't have a choice. I had to do it! It's the reason I undertook this whole business—right from the very moment of reading those sad, pleading letters to Marcos...

The phone rang on his desk, cutting dead his thoughts, and he snatched it up. Now what?

A moment later he knew—and his expression said it all. Face black, he pushed back Timon's huge leather chair, packed away his laptop in his briefcase and strode out of the office. Timon's PA looked up expectantly.

'Put the jet on standby. I'm flying up to Thessaloniki,' he barked.

Then he was gone.

Lyn was both pleased and surprised to receive a call from Anatole in the middle of the day. But she quickly realised that the call was serious rather than tender. He told her that he was calling from his car on the way to the airport, just to let her know what was happening.

'I'll keep this brief,' he went on crisply. 'I'm going to have to fly up to Thessaloniki right away. A strike has just been declared, there's a mass walk-out, and protests are building outside the factory gates. The riot police have been marshalled by the manager—just what I don't need!' He took a heavy breath. 'But at least—finally!—I've got the power to sort it out myself.' He paused. 'I don't know when I'm going to be able to get back, Lyn.' His voice changed suddenly. 'And I have to talk to you urgently the moment I do.'

'What is it?' Alarm filled her throat.

She heard him give a rasp of frustration at the other end of their connection. 'I need to explain to you face-to-face. But, listen, please—I hope you'll understand—'

He broke off. Lyn heard a staccato burst of conversation in Greek, then Anatole was audible again.

'I'm sorry! I have to go. I'm flying up with the chief finance director and he's just heard on his own phone that there's been a clash with police outside the factory—and that TV crews are arriving to film it! I've got to speak to the officer in charge and get the police to back off for the moment. This can't escalate any further!'

The connection went dead.

Dismay filled Lyn. Not just at the fracas that Anatole was going to have to deal with, but because of what he'd just said to her—that he needed to talk to her urgently.

He had sounded so sombre...

What's wrong?

The question burned in her head but she could find no answer. It went on burning even as she crossed to the TV and turned to the Greek news channel. Even without understanding much Greek she could see that the angry dispute at the Petranakos facility in Thessaloniki was making the headlines.

If you want to help Anatole let him get on with sorting it out without making any demands on him yourself! she told herself sternly.

She'd done her best to do that for the past few days. Yet the beach house felt lonely without him. Their bed empty...

Worse, when she set off for the main house later, with Georgy in his buggy, for his daily visit to his great-grandfather, she was intercepted by a uniformed woman who informed her that she was Georgy's new nanny.

'I will take Baby to Kyrios Petranakos,' she announced in accented English.

Lyn hesitated. She didn't want this to happen, but this was not the moment to make a fuss, she knew. Reluctantly, she let the nanny take Georgy from her.

'I will bring him home later,' the nanny said punctiliously, with a smile that Lyn made herself *not* think of as condescending.

She shook her head. 'No, that's all right. I'll wait.'

She went out into the gardens and settled herself on a little bench in the sunshine. Despite the warmth, she felt chilled. Clearly Timon, now that he was back home again, wanted to make his presence felt—and to arrange things the way he liked them.

Well, she would wait until after the wedding—when Anatole was not having to deal with a strike on his hands— to take issue over the nanny and agree just what her role and function would be, if any. For now she would be accommodating. Bothering Anatole with something so trivial when he was up to his eyes in trying to sort out a costly and disruptive strike was the last thing she wanted to do!

She clung to that resolve now, knowing that he had flown up to Thessaloniki to deal with the problem there first-hand. But another concern was plucking at her. Would Anatole even be back in time for the wedding? And, even if he were, would they be able to get away on honeymoon at all?

Well, like the nanny situation, there was nothing she could do about it right now. Their wedding was going to be small and private anyway, and only a civil one since both parties knew it was going to end in divorce at some point, so there would be no guests to unarrange. On top of that, because Timon and Anatole were still in mourning for Marcos, it would have been inappropriate to have a large wedding anyway. So, Lyn made herself reason, if the wedding had to be postponed for the time being, and the honeymoon too—well, that was that. Anatole would sort out the strike, find a resolution that kept everyone happy, then come back home again. Then they would marry, and everything would be all right.

While their marriage lasted…

That chill formed again around her heart. She didn't want to think about the terms of their marriage—didn't want to think how it was supposed to end once Timon was no more. Didn't want to think about how, at some point, Anatole would divorce her and they would make suitable, civilised arrangements to share custody of Georgy…

Suitable. Civilised.

Such cold-blooded words—nothing like the passion that flared between her and Anatole! Nothing like the emotion that swept through her as he swept her into his arms…

She closed her eyes a moment, swaying slightly.

If only…

Words formed in her head—tantalising, yearning.

If only this marriage were not just for Georgy's sake…

She made herself breathe out sharply. She must not think such thoughts! This marriage *was* for Georgy's sake— that was the truth of it. And anything else—anything that had happened between her and Anatole—could not last any longer than their marriage…

It could not.

However much she yearned for it to do so…

CHAPTER TEN

SHE WOKE THE next day in low spirits to the sound of Georgy grizzling in his cot. His grumpy mood seemed to echo her own lowness, and nothing could divert him. She got through most of the morning somehow, restricting her urge to phone Anatole and merely sending him an upbeat e-mail, assuring him that everything was fine on her end and refraining from expressing her own down mood or mentioning Georgy's tetchiness. By early afternoon she was glad to be able to set off with Georgy to the big house, for at least it gave him something to think about other than his grouchiness. Maybe he was starting to teethe, she thought. Whatever it was, he was not a happy bunny—and nor was she.

She eked out their expedition to the big house, first wheeling Georgy along the shoreline and pointing out things that might cheer him up, and then, giving up on that, heading into the gardens towards the house. She took a meandering route, not caring if she were running late.

When she duly presented herself the new nanny did not come forward to remove Georgy from his buggy. Instead she gave Lyn a tight smile and informed her that she would take Baby for a stroll in the gardens.

'Kyrios Petranakos wishes to see you without Baby,' she announced loftily, and took the buggy handles from Lyn.

'Oh,' said Lyn, feeling mildly surprised and mildly apprehensive.

What could Timon Petranakos want? she thought. She reasoned it must be something to do with the forthcoming wedding.

Oh, please don't say it's going to have to be postponed because of all that's going on in Thessaloniki!

She took a breath. Well, if it had to be postponed, so be it. Anatole was under quite enough pressure as it was.

She let the nanny wheel Georgy away, warning her that he was a bit grouchy today and getting a condescending smile in return, and then set off after the manservant who was conducting her to Timon's quarters. When she was shown in he was in his day room, next door to his bedchamber—a huge room with the same ornate, opulent decor as the dining room that Lyn found a tad oppressive and overdone, but she appreciated it was a bygone style suitable for a man of his age and position in society.

When she was shown in his wheelchair was in front of his desk and he was clearly studying the documents laid out on it. He wheeled the motorised chair around to face her as the manservant backed out of the room, leaving Lyn facing Georgy's great-grandfather.

There was something different about him. At first she thought it was something to do with his state of health, but then she realised it was his expression.

Especially his eyes.

They were resting on her, but the brief, penetrating glance she'd got used to was now a more focused stare. She stood still, letting him look her over. Somewhere deep inside her, unease was forming.

What was going on?

With a hideous plunging of her heart, she heard her voice blurting out, 'Has something happened to Anatole?'

Dear God, was *that* what this was about? Had something happened to him? Something to do with the protest, violent clashes?

Please don't let him be injured! Or worse...

Fear pooled like acid in her stomach.

'Yes—something has happened to Anatole.'

She heard Timon's words and faintness drummed through her. Then, at his next words, her head cleared.

Brutally.

As brutally as the harsh words came from Timon Petranakos in his hoarse voice.

'Anatole is free—finally free. Of *you*!'

She stared. 'What do you mean?' she said, a confused expression filling her face.

A rasp came from him, and she could see his clawed hand clench the arm of his wheelchair.

'I mean what I say!' he ground out. 'My grandson is free of *you*!' His expression changed, his eyes hardening like flint. '*Hah!* You stare at me as if you cannot believe me! Well, believe me!' The dark eyes pinioned her. 'Did you really think,' he ground out, his accent becoming stronger with the emotion that was so clearly visible in his lined face, 'that I would permit him to be trapped by *you*?'

Lyn's face worked, her senses reeling.

'I...I...don't understand,' she said again. It sounded limp, but it was all she could think right now. What was happening? Dear God, what was *happening*? It was like being hit by a tsunami—a wall of denunciation that she had never expected! Never thought to receive! Her mind recoiled and she clutched at flying words and thoughts to try desperately, urgently, to make some kind of sense of them! Find some kind of reason for what was going on here.

Timon's jaw set. The flint in his eyes, sunken as they were with age and illness, hardened.

'Then understand *this*, if you please! Your dreams of being Kyria Telonidis are over! *Over!*'

A little cry came from her throat, tearing it like a raw
wound. She wanted to speak, shout, yell, but she couldn't—
not a single word. She was silenced. Helpless to make sense
of any of this—anything at all!

Timon was speaking again, his voice harsh and accusing. His words cut at her, slashing into her.

'You thought to trap him. You took one look at him and
thought you had it made. Thought you could use *my* grandson's boy to trap my other grandson! To land yourself a life
of ease and luxury that you have *no* right to! None! You
saw your opportunity to make a wealthy marriage and a
lucrative divorce and you took it!'

The bitter eyes flashed like knives, stabbing into her.

Shock spiked her riposte. 'Anatole *offered* to marry
me—it was *his* idea, not mine! He said it would make it
easier to adopt Georgy—I agreed for Georgy's sake!' Lyn
tried to fight back, tried to stand her ground in the face
of this onslaught.

Timon's face twisted in anger. 'For your *own* sake!'

'No!' she cried out desperately. 'It isn't like that! It's for
Georgy! It's all for Georgy!'

The lined face hardened. 'Then you will be overjoyed
to realise that you have achieved that! Marcos's boy is
here now—in the country where he belongs—and whatever those infernal, interfering, officious bureaucrats in
England say, no court in Greece will hand him back. No
court in Greece will take *my great-grandson* from me!
And as for you—know that for all your scheming you
have been well served in turn!' His expression twisted.
'Did you truly think that because Anatole took you to his
bed he would actually go through with *marrying* you? He
did it to keep you sweet—and it achieved his purpose—to
get Marcos's boy here the quickest way!'

'No! I don't believe it! *No!*' She covered her ears with

her hands, as if she could blot out the hateful, hideous words.

'Well, believe it!' Timon snarled at her. 'Believe it to be justice served upon you—justice for your scheming, for your lies!'

She froze, her hands falling inert to her sides. Her face paled. 'What do you mean—lies?'

His dark eyes glittered with venom. 'Ah—*now* she is caught! Yes—*lies*! The lies you've told Anatole…'

Her face paled. 'I…I don't understand…' Her voice faltered.

A claw-like hand lifted a piece of paper from his desk and held it up. Gimlet eyes bored into her. 'Did you think I would not have you investigated? The woman who stood between me and my great-grandson? Of course I did!' His voice changed, became chilled. 'And how very right I was to do so.'

As if weights were pulling at them her eyes dropped to the paper in his hand. She could read the letterhead, read the name of an investigative firm, read the brief opening paragraph with her name in it…

She felt sick, her stomach clenching.

'You don't understand…' she said. But her voice was like a thread.

'I understand *completely*!' Timon Petranakos threw back at her, dropping the paper to the desk.

Lyn's hands were clenching and unclenching. She forced herself to shift her gaze to the dark, unforgiving eyes upon her. The claws in her stomach worked.

'Have…have you told Anatole?'

It was the one question burning in her veins.

A rasp came from Timon. 'What do *you* think?' he exclaimed, and she could hear the bitterness in his voice, the anger.

'I can explain—' she started, but he cut her off with another harsh rasp of his voice.

'To what purpose? You lied to Anatole and now you are caught out! It is justice upon your head—nothing more than justice that all your schemes were always going to be in vain! That you were never going to achieve your ambition to marry my grandson, enrich yourself for life! And use *my* great-grandson to do it! Well...' He threw his head back, eyes raking her like talons. 'Your schemes are over now!' The claw-like hand reached for another paper on his desk, and thrust it at her. 'Look—*look!* And see how all your schemes have come to nothing!'

She felt her arm reach out, her fingers close nervelessly on the thick document that Timon was thrusting at her. It was typed in Greek, with a printed heading, and the unfamiliar characters blurred and resolved. It looked formal— legal—and she could not read a word of it. But at the base was a date—two days ago—and, above it a signature.

Anatole Telonidis.

Timon was speaking again. 'Here is a translation,' he said. 'I had it drawn up for you. For just this moment.' He lifted another piece of paper. The layout was exactly the same as the Greek document, but this was in English. Only the signature at its base was absent. With trembling hands she took the paper, held it up. Again the words blurred, would not resolve themselves.

'Keep it,' said Timon Petranokos. 'Keep them both. This document gives Anatole everything he wants—everything he's been asking for! He has taken over as chairman. Total control. Full executive power. I've given it to him. And all he had to do to get what he wanted,' he went on, the dark, sunken eyes glittering with animosity, 'was undertake not to marry you.' He paused. 'He signed it without hesitation,' he finished harshly, his mouth twisting.

He took another rasping, difficult breath, as if so much speaking had drained him of his scarce reserves of energy.

She should pity him, Lyn thought, but she could not.

She could only fear him.

But fear was no use to her now. It hadn't been when Lindy had died. It hadn't been when the social workers had sought to take Georgy for adoption. It hadn't been when Anatole Telonidis had turned up, dropping his bombshell into her life about Georgy's dead father and the vast fortune he would inherit one day from his dying great-grandfather—the fortune Anatole was now safeguarding for Georgy by agreeing to what his grandfather demanded: shedding the bride-to-be he did not want...

Had never wanted.

It was like a spear in her side, hearing those words in her head—a spear that pierced her to her very core! Her vision flickered and she felt her heart slamming in her chest, her lungs bereft of oxygen. She gasped to breathe.

Timon was speaking again, vituperation in his voice. 'So you see there is nothing here for you now. *Nothing!* All there is for you to do is pack your bags and go! Take yourself off!' His dark eyes were filled with loathing. 'Your lies have come to nothing! And nothing is all that you deserve! To get rid of you as fast as I can do so I will hand you this, to speed you on your way!'

He thrust yet one more piece of paper at her—a small one this time—the size of a cheque.

'Take it!' he rasped.

Lyn stared at it blindly, frozen. She couldn't think, couldn't function—could only feel. Feel blow after blow landing upon her. Hammering her with pain. But she must not feel pain. Must not allow herself to do so. Later she would feel it, but not now. Now, at this moment, pain was unimportant. Only her next words were important.

To buy time.

Time to *think*, to work out what she must do—whatever it took—to keep Georgy safe with her.

She took a breath, tortured and ragged, forced her features to become uncontorted. Forced herself to think, to do something—anything other than just stand there while she reeled with what was happening.

She lifted her head. Stared straight at Timon. She should pity him—old and dying as he was, with his beloved grandson Marcos dead and buried so short a time ago. But she could not—not now. All she could do was what she was forcing herself to do now. To reach her hand out jerkily, as if it were being forced by an alien power, and take the cheque he offered.

She was at the beach house, staring at her mobile on which sat an unread text from Anatole, which had arrived while she was out having her life smashed to pieces. Beside the laptop on the dining room table were the documents Timon had thrust upon her and her Greek dictionary open beside them. Her frail and desperate hope that the translation he had given her was a lie had died. As she had slowly, painfully forced herself to read the original version, with Anatole's signature on it, word by damning word her last hope had withered to nothing

Anatole had done exactly what Timon had told her he had done. He had taken control of the Petranakos Corporation with full powers, just as he had always aimed to do.

Lyn's insides hollowed with pain. And he had done what he had always intended to do with her too. *Always*—right from the start! It was obvious now—hideously, crucifyingly obvious!

Not marry me—

A choking breathlessness filled her. The air was sucked from her lungs, suffocating her with horror.

He was never going to marry me! Never! It was a lie—all along!

And now he did not need to lie any more. There was no need for it. No need for any more pretence, any more charade.

As she sat there staring at the damning evidence the phone rang. For a moment, with a jolt, she thought it was her mobile, then she realised it was the landline. Almost she ignored it, but it went on and on, so with nerveless fingers she picked it up.

It was not Anatole. It was a voice speaking to her in Greek and immediately changing to English when the speaker heard her halting reply. It was an official from the town hall, confirming that the wedding due to take place in four days' time was indeed, as requested by Kyrios Telonidis via e-mail the previous day, cancelled.

She set down the phone. There was no emotion left within her. None at all. She could not allow any—must not—dared not. She stared back at her mobile, at the unread text from Anatole. She pressed her finger down to open it. To read her fate. She stared as the words entered her brain.

Lyn, I'm cancelling the wedding. I need to talk to you. Urgently. Be there when I phone tonight. A

She went on staring. Numbness filled her the way it had filled her when she'd sat beside Lindy's dead body, all the life gone out of it. All hope gone. Then slowly she got to her feet, picking up the damning documents, looking around her at the place she had thought so *stupidly* was going to be her home…

The home she'd share with Anatole.

The man who had just cancelled their wedding.

Not just postponed—but cancelled…

There was a tapping at the French windows leading out

to the garden. She looked round. The nanny was there, smiling politely, with Georgy in his buggy. The nanny, Lyn now realised bleakly, Timon had hired to take her place.

How she got rid of her Lyn didn't know, but she did somehow. Somehow, too, she made herself go upstairs, walk into the bedroom she'd shared with Anatole and gaze down blindly at the bed where he'd taken her into his arms so often. She found her vision blurring, her throat burning.

She made herself look away, go to the closet, pick out the largest handbag she possessed. She put into it all the changes of clothes that she could cram in and, far more importantly, her passport, credit card and what little money she possessed. Then she went into Georgy's room and packed his bag with nappies and two changes of outfit, his favourite toys. Then, still with her vision blurred and her throat burning, she made herself go downstairs again, scoop him up and hug him tight, tight, *tight*...

With the shawl she had brought downstairs with her she made a makeshift sling and fitted him in the crook of her shoulder, awkwardly hefting the two bags onto her other shoulder. Her shoes were stout walking shoes and she needed them, for when she went outdoors she headed to the boundary of Timon Petranakos's property, scrambling over the rocky outcrop there precariously with her precious burden and then, on the other side, gaining the track that led up from the seashore to the main road, running east to west about a quarter of a kilometre inland. There, she knew, was a bus stop. From there she could take the bus to the nearby seaside town and then pick up a tram. The tram would take her where she so desperately, urgently needed to get to.

Piraeus, the port of Athens. Her gateway to escape...

It was crowded when she got there—crowded, busy and confusing. But she made herself decipher the notices, found the ferry she wanted—the one that was the safest—and bought a ticket with her precious store of euros. She would not risk a credit card. That could be traced...

She hurried aboard the ferry, head down, Georgy in her arms, trying not to look anxious lest she draw attention to herself. The ferry was bound for Crete. If she could lie low there for a while, and then somehow—anyhow!—get a flight back from Crete to the UK she could lie low again, consult a family lawyer...do something that might stop her losing Georgy.

Will I have any chance now even to be his foster-carer? What will happen now that Anatole isn't marrying me after all? What happens to the adoption application?

Questions, questions, questions—multiple and terrifying! Timon would make a move to claim Georgy, and surely Anatole would too? She had to get to a lawyer, find out what chance she had herself.

But, however puny her hopes, one thing was for sure—if she stayed here in Greece then the long, powerful arm of the Petranakos dynasty would easily overpower her! Georgy would be ripped from her and she would stand no chance—no chance at all—against what Timon and Anatole could throw at her, with all their wealth and influence behind them.

I have to get back to the UK! At least there I stand a chance, however frail...

Her mind raced on, churning and tumultuous, trying to think, think, *think*, trying to keep her terror at bay.

Trying to keep at bay something that was even worse than the terror.

It stabbed at her like a knife plunging deep into her.

Pain. Pain such as she had never known before. Pain that savaged her like a wolf with a lamb in its tearing jaws. That made her want to hunch over and rock with the agony of it.

She stumbled forward, gaining the seating area in the bow of the ferry, collapsing on one of the benches in the middle section, settling Georgy on her lap. He was staring about delightedly, fascinated by this new environment. She stared blindly out over the busy, crowded harbour, feeling a jolt as the ferry disengaged from the dock and started its journey. She willed it on faster, though she knew it would take until morning to reach Heraklion in Crete. She tried to think ahead, plan in detail what she would do once she arrived there, but her mind would not focus. The wind picked up as they reached the open sea, buffeting her where she sat exposed, feeling the savage jaws of pain tearing at her.

Anatole's name on the paper Timon had so triumphantly thrust at her.

Anatole's name betraying her.

His message to her confirming his betrayal.

His breaking of all the stupid trust she had put in him!

Her mind cried silently in anguish. *I trusted him! I trusted everything he said—everything he promised me!*

But it had meant nothing, that promise. Only one thing had mattered to him—getting Georgy to his grandfather and thereby getting control of the Petranakos Corporation.

And if that promise had meant nothing to him... Her eyes stared blindly, haunted, pained. Nor had anything else...

The stabbing pain came again. *Nothing about me mattered to him! Nothing!*

Like a film playing at high speed in her head all the time she had spent with Anatole flashed past her inner vision. Their time together with Georgy...

I thought we were making a family together! I thought he was happy to be with Georgy and me, happy for us to be together.

Being with her when Georgy slept...

Anatole's arms around her, his mouth seeking hers, his strong, passionate body covering hers, taking her to a paradise she had never known existed! Murmuring words to her, cradling her, caressing her...

But it had meant nothing at all—only as a means to lull her, to deceive her as to his true intentions. She heard his voice tolling in her head. Over and over again he'd said those words to her.

'Trust me—I need you to trust me...'

Bitter gall rose in her. Yes, he'd needed her to trust him! Needed her to gaze at him adoringly and put her trust in him, her faith in him.

Like a fool...

She heard his words again, mocking her from the depths of her being. She had meant nothing to him. Nothing more than a means to an end—to get Georgy out here the quickest and easiest way.

To get him here and keep him here.

Keep him here without her.

He lied to me...

But he had not been the only one to lie.

Like a crushing weight the accusation swung into her, forcing her to face it. She did not want to—she rebelled against it, resisted it—but it was impossible to deny, impossible to keep out of her head. It forced its way in, levering its way into her consciousness.

The brutal accusation cut at her. *You lied to him too— you lied to him and you knew that you were lying to him.*

And it was true—she *had* lied...lied right from the start...

Sickness filled her as she heard Timon's scathing denunciation of her—heard him telling her that she had got nothing but her just deserts...

A ragged breath razored through her as she stared out to

sea, the wind buffeting her face, whipping away her tears even as she shed them. But even as the wind sheared her tears away they fell faster yet. Unstoppable.

CHAPTER ELEVEN

ANATOLE RAISED A weary hand—a gesture of acknowledgement of what the union rep had just said. He was exhausted. His whole body was tired. He'd gone without sleep all night, going over and over figures and facts with the management team at the Thessaloniki plant, trying to find a viable alternative to the redundancies. Then he'd gone straight into meetings with the union representatives, trying to hammer out something that would preserve jobs.

At least he was making some kind of impact on the union. They were listening to him, even if they were still disputing with him. His approach was not that of the former manager, or his autocratic grandfather, issuing to the employees lofty diktats that had resulted in an instant demonstration outside the plant and ballots for full strike action. Instead he had disclosed the true finances of the division, pulled no punches, inviting them to try and find a way forward with him.

He sat back, weariness etched into his face. There was still muted discussion around the table. He wanted to close his eyes and sleep, but sleep could wait. It would have to. Would the deal he was offering swing it? He hoped so. Strike action would be costly and crippling, benefitting no one. Worse, in the terrifyingly volatile Greek economy it was likely to spread like wildfire through the rest of the

Petranakos organisation, possibly even beyond, to other companies as well, with disastrous consequences.

To his intense relief the union reps were looking thoughtful, and a couple of them were nodding. Had he swung it? He hoped to God he had—then maybe he could get some sleep finally.

But not before speaking to Lyn. It was imperative he do so! He'd managed to find the time to text her about the cancellation of the wedding, but that brief text was utterly inadequate. He had to see her, talk to her, explain to her…

Frustration knifed through him. He had to sleep, or he'd pass out, but he had to talk to her too. Had to get back to her…

'Kyrios Telonidis—'

The voice at the door of the meeting room was apologetic, but the note of urgency in it reached him. He looked enquiringly at the secretary who had intruded.

'It is Kyrios Petranakos…' she said.

He was on his feet immediately. 'Gentlemen—my apologies. My grandfather…' He left the sentence unfinished as he strode from the room. It was common knowledge how very gravely ill Timon was. In the outer office he seized the phone the secretary indicated. As he heard his grandfather's distinctive voice his tension diminished. He had feared the worst. But then, as he heard what his grandfather was saying, he froze.

'She's gone! She's gone—taken the boy! She's taken the boy!' It was all his grandfather could say, over and over again. Totally distraught.

'What did you say to her? Tell me what you said to her!'

Anatole's voice was harsh, but he needed to know what it was that had sent Lyn into a panic, making her flee as she had. Taking Georgy with her…

Since the call had come through to him in Thessaloniki life had turned into a nightmare. He had flown straight back to Athens, raced to Timon's villa, stormed into Timon's room.

His grandfather's face was ravaged.

'I told her what you'd done!'

Anatole's eyes flashed with fury. 'I told you to let *me* tell her! That I would find the right way to say it! I knew I needed to—urgently—but with that damn strike threatening I had to tell her to wait for me to talk to her! Why the hell did you go and do it?'

He wasn't being kind, he knew that, but it was Timon's fault! Timon's fault that Lyn had bolted. *Bolted with Georgy!* He felt fear clutch at him. Where were they? Where had Lyn gone? Where had she taken Georgy? They could be anywhere! Anywhere at all! She'd taken her passport, and Georgy's, but even with his instant alerting of the police at the airport there had been no reports of them. His face tightened. Athens Airport was not the only way out of Greece—there were a hundred ways she could have gone…a hundred ways she could have left Greece!

'Why?' Timon's rasping voice was as harsh as his. *'This* is why!' He seized a piece of paper from his desk, thrust it at Anatole.

Anatole snatched it, forcing his eyes to focus, to take in what he was reading. It was Latin script, in English.

As he read it he could feel ice congeal in his veins. He let the paper fall back on the desk, staring down at it with sightless eyes.

Beside him he could hear his grandfather's voice speaking. Coming from very far away.

'She lied to you—she lied to you and used you. Right from the start! So I told her—I told her exactly what you'd done.'

Lyn was pushing Georgy around a park. The buggy was not the swish, luxury item Anatole had bought. This one was third-hand from a jumble sale, with a wonky wheel, a stained cover and a folding mechanism that threatened to break every time she used it. But it was all she could afford now. She was living off her savings. Getting any kind of work was impossible, because it would never be enough to cover childcare.

She'd found a bedsit—the cheapest she could get—a single room with a kitchenette in a corner and a shared bathroom on the landing, so cramped and run down it made the flat she'd lived in while at college seem like a luxury penthouse! Whenever she stared round it, taking in every unlovely detail, a memory flashed into her head.

The beautiful colour photo from the estate agent that had come with the title deeds to the seaside house in the Witterings in Sussex…

Her expression darkened. She had thought in her criminal stupidity that it was a gesture of Anatole's generous sensitivity to her plea that Georgy should not lose his English heritage…

She knew now what it really was—had known from the moment Timon had destroyed all her stupid dreams.

It was my payoff.

Well, she wouldn't touch it! Wouldn't take it! Would take nothing at all from him! She'd left all her expensive new clothes in the wardrobe in Timon's beach house, leaving Greece in her own, original clothes. Clothes that were far more suited to the place she lived now.

Yet even taking the cheapest bedsit she'd been able to find was eating into her funds badly. She could not continue like this indefinitely. She knew with a grim, bleak inevitability that a time of reckoning was approaching—heading towards her like a steam train. The knowledge was like a boot kicking into her head. She could not go on like this…

And not just because she would eventually run out of money.

But because she'd run off with Georgy.

Run from the man who was trying to take him from her! The man she had trusted never to do that.

Pain knifed her. Pain that was so familiar now, so agonising, that she should surely be used to it? But it was still like a stab every time she felt it—every time she thought of Anatole. Every time she remembered him.

Being with him—being in his arms! Being with him by day and by night! All the time we spent together—all the weeks—all that precious, precious time...

She closed her eyes, pushing the buggy blindly around the little park that was not too far away from the shabby bedsit she'd taken here in Bristol, which had been the destination of the first flight out of Heraklion. As she walked, forcing one foot in front of the other, memories rushed into her head, tearing at her with talons of sharpest steel. Memories of Anatole walking beside her in another city park like this, in the cold north country spring, sitting down by the children's play area. She heard his voice speaking in her head.

'There is a way,' he'd said. 'There is a way that could solve the entire dilemma...'

Her hands spasmed over the buggy's push bar. Yes, there had been a way to solve it! A way that he'd had all worked out—in absolute detail. Totally foolproof detail...

He had known—dear God—a man like him must have known from the off that she would be putty in his hands! That he could persuade her, convince her into doing what he wanted her to do!

'I need you to trust me...'

The words that she had heard him say so often to her burned like fire in her head.

And what better way to win her trust, keep her doting and docile, than by the most foolproof method of all…?

He took me to bed to get me to trust him. Just to keep me sweet.

Until he did not need to any more.

Her heart convulsed and she gave a little cry, pausing in her pushing and hunkering down beside Georgy. He turned to look at her and patted her face, gazing at her. She felt her heart turn over and over.

I love you so much! I love you so much, my darling, darling Georgy!

Yet as she straightened again, went on pushing forward, she felt as if a stone inside was dragging at her. She could not go on like this.

The harsh, brutal truth was that, though she had panicked when Timon had smashed her life to pieces, had followed every primal instinct in her body and fled as fast and as far as she could with Georgy in her arms, she was now on the run.

Hiding not just from Anatole and Timon but from the authorities in whose ultimate charge her sister's son still was…

It could not go on. She knew it—feared it—must face it.

Face, too, against the resistance that had cost her so much to overcome, that she was also hiding from the truth. The truth of what *she'd* done…

I used him too.

That was what she had to face—what Timon had thrown at her. Her own lie—her own deceit to get from Anatole what she wanted so desperately.

But it had all fallen apart—everything—and now she was reduced to this. Fleeing with Georgy—on the run—with no future, no hope.

It could not go on. There was only one way forward now. Only one future for Georgy.

If you love him, you must do it. For his sake!

In her head she heard the words she had cried out so often.

I can't do it! I can't—I can't! Lindy gave him to me with her dying words...Georgy is mine—mine!

But as she plodded on through the scruffy urban park that was a million miles away from the Petranakos mansion, with its huge private grounds and pristine private beach, her eyes staring wildly ahead of her, her face stark, she could feel the thoughts forcing their way into her tormented mind as desperately as she tried to keep them out.

They would not be kept out.

You must not think of yourself—your own pain, your own feelings! What you must think of is Georgy! If you love him, then do what is best for him!

He could not go on living like this, in some run down bedsit, hand to mouth. Hiding and on the run. Being fought over like a bone between two dogs in a cruel, punishing tug-of-love.

Slowly, as if she had no strength left in her, she wheeled the buggy around and headed back out of the park.

She had a letter to write.

Anatole walked into the air-conditioned building that housed the London offices of his lawyers. It hardly needed air-conditioning, because the London summer was a lot cooler than the Greek summer, but the temperature was the last thing he was thinking of. He had only one thought in his mind—only one imperative. He gave his name at the desk and was shown in immediately.

'Is she here?' was his instant demand to the partner who handled his affairs as he greeted him in his office.

The man nodded. 'She's waiting for you in one of our meeting rooms,' he said.

'And the boy?'

'Yes.'

The single word was all Anatole needed to hear. Relief flooded through him. It flushed away the other emotion that was possessing him—the one he was trying to exorcise with all his powers, which had possessed him ever since that fateful call from Timon.

'Do you wish me to be present at the meeting?' his lawyer enquired tactfully.

Anatole gave a curt shake of his head. 'I'll call you when I need you. You've outlined my legal position clearly enough, so I know where I stand.' He paused, not quite meeting the man's eyes. 'Did she say anything to you?'

The lawyer shook his head.

Anatole felt another stab of emotion go through him. He tensed his shoulders. 'OK, show me in.'

He blanked his mind. Anything else right now was far too dangerous. He must focus on only one goal—Georgy.

Nothing else.

No one else.

Lyn was sitting in one of the leather tub chairs that were grouped around a low table on which were spread several of the day's broadsheet newspapers, a copy of a business magazine and a law magazine. Georgy was on her lap, and she was nuzzling him with a soft toy. It was one of the ones that she and Anatole had bought for him in London, at the very expensive department store and with Aladdin's Cave of a toy department. It seemed they had bought it a lifetime ago—in a different universe.

She wondered what she was feeling right now and realised it was nothing. Realised that it had to be nothing—because if it were anything else she could not go on sitting there.

Waiting for Anatole to walk in, as she knew he would at any moment now.

There was a clock on the wall and she glanced at it. Time was ticking by. In a few minutes she would see him again, and then she would say to him what she must say.

But she must not think about that. Must only go on sitting here, absently playing with Georgy, while the minutes between her and her endless empty future ticked past.

The door opened. Her head jerked up and he was there. Anatole.

Anatole.

Here—now—in the flesh. Real. Live.

Anatole.

As overwhelming and as overpowering to her senses as he always had been, right from the very first...

The nothing she had been feeling shattered into a million fragments...

Like a tidal wave emotion roared into her, the blood in her veins gushing like a hot fountain released from a cave of ice. Her sight dimmed and her eyes clung to him as he walked in.

On her lap, Georgy saw him too—saw him, recognised him, and held out his chubby arms to him with a gurgle of delight.

In two strides Anatole was there, scooping him up, wheeling him into the air, folding him to him and hugging him, a torrent of Greek coming from his lips. Then, as he nestled Georgy into his shoulder, he turned to Lyn.

For a moment—just a moment—there was a flash of emotion in his eyes. It seemed to sear her to the quick. Then it was gone.

He stood stock-still, Georgy clutched to him, his face like stone. But she could feel his anger coming off him. Feel it spearing her.

'So you brought him. I did not think you would.' His voice had no expression in it.

She made herself answer. 'I said in my letter I would.' Her voice was halting. As expressionless as his. It was the only way she could make herself speak. Say the words she had to say.

He frowned a moment, his eyes narrowing. 'So why did you? Why did you bring him here? What are you after, Lyn?'

She heard the leashed anger and knew that *she* had caused it. But his anger didn't matter. She gave a faint, frail shrug. 'What else could I do? I ran, Anatole, because I panicked. It was instinct—blind, raw instinct—but once I was back here I realised there had been no point in running. No point in fleeing.' She looked at him. Made herself look at him. Made herself silence the scream inside her head against what she was doing. What she was saying. What she was feeling…

What you feel doesn't matter. Seeing Anatole again doesn't matter. It doesn't matter because you never mattered to him—you were just an impediment, in his way, a stepping stone towards his goal. It wasn't real, what happened between you. You were nothing to him but a means to an end. An end he has now achieved.

She looked at him holding Georgy, the baby sitting content in Anatole's arms. She had seen them like that a hundred times—a thousand. She felt her heart crash.

You were nothing to him—Georgy is everything!

And that was what she must cling to now. That and that alone. It was the only way to survive what was happening. What was going to happen.

'I thought,' he bit out, 'you might have gone to the house.'

She frowned. 'House? What house?'

A strange look flitted across his face. 'The house by the sea—the house I gave you.'

She stared. 'Why would I have gone there?' Her voice was blank.

'Because it's yours,' he riposted flatly. But the flatness was the flatness of the blade of a knife...

'Of course it isn't mine! Nothing's mine, Anatole. Not even—' She closed her eyes, because the truth was too agonising to face, then forced them open again. 'Not even Georgy.'

There—she had said it. Said what she had to say. What she should have said right from the start.

If I had just admitted it—admitted the truth—then I would have been spared all this now! Spared the agony of standing here, seeing Anatole, knowing what he came to mean to me!

Dear God, how much heartache she would have saved herself!

She took another breath that cut at her lungs, her throat, like the edge of a razorblade.

'I'll sign whatever paperwork needs to be signed,' she said. 'I can do it now or later—whatever you want. I'll have an address at some point. Though I don't know where yet.'

As she spoke she made herself stand up. Forced her legs to straighten. She felt faint, dizzy, but she had to speak—had to say what she had come to say.

She took a breath. Forced herself to speak.

'I've brought his things—Georgy's. There isn't much. I didn't take much with me. And I've only bought a little more here in the UK. It's all in those bags.' She indicated the meagre collection on the floor by the chair. 'The buggy isn't very good—it's from a jumble sale—but it's just about useable until you get a new one. Unless you brought his old one with you... Be careful when you unfold it, it catches—' She pointed to where it was propped up against the wall.

She fumbled in her bag. Her fingers weren't working properly. Nothing about her was working properly.

'Here is his passport,' she said, and placed it on the little table. There was the slightest tremble in her voice, but she fought it down. She must not break—she *must* not… 'I hope—' she said. 'I hope you can take him back to Greece as quickly as possible. I am sure…' She swallowed. 'I'm sure Timon must want to see him again as soon as he can.'

Her voice trailed off. She picked up her bag, blinked a moment.

'I think that's everything,' she said.

She started to walk to the door. She must not look at Anatole. Must not look at Georgy. Must do absolutely nothing except keep walking to the door. Reach it, start to open it…

'What the *hell* are you doing?'

The demand was like a blow on the back of her neck. She turned. Swallowed. It was hard to swallow because there was a rock the size of Gibraltar in her throat. She blinked again.

'I'm going,' she said. 'What did you think I would do?'

He said something. Something she did not catch because she was looking at his face. Looking at his face for the very last time. Knowing that it was the very last time was like plunging her hand into boiling water. But even as she looked his expression changed.

'So he was right.' The words came low, with a lash that was like a whip across her skin. 'Timon was right all along.'

Slowly he set Georgy down on the thickly carpeted floor, pulling off his tie to keep him happy. Lyn found her eyes going to the strong column of his neck as he unfastened the top button of his shirt now that he was tieless. Felt the ripple in her stomach that was oh, so familiar— and now so eviscerating.

'Timon was right,' he said again. His voice was Arctic. 'He said you only wanted money out of all of this! I didn't believe him. I said you'd turned down cash from me to hand over Georgy. But he read you right all along!' His voice twisted. 'No wonder he set his private investigators on to you—and no wonder you took his money to clear out!'

She didn't answer. Only picked up Georgy's passport. Thrust it at him.

'Open it,' she said. Her voice was tight. As tight as the steel band around her throat, garrotting her.

She watched him do as she had demanded. Watched his expression change as he saw Timon's uncashed cheque within, torn into pieces.

'I took it from him to give me time to make my escape. Because I could think of nothing else to do.' She took a ragged shredded breath. 'I never wanted money, Anatole,' she told him. 'I never wanted anything except one thing— the one thing that was the most precious in my life.'

Her eyes dropped to Georgy, happily chewing on Anatole's silk tie.

She was lying, she knew. Lying because she'd come to want more than Georgy—to want something even more precious to her.

You! You, Anatole—I wanted you so much! And a family— you, and Georgy and me—I wanted that so much! So much!

That had been the dream that had taken shape in Greece—that had made her heart catch with yearning! Anatole and Georgy and her—a family together...

She lifted her eyes to Anatole again. To his blank, expressionless face.

'I kept telling you Georgy was mine,' she said. 'I said it over and over and over again. As if by saying it I might make it true.' She stopped. Took a razoring breath that cut at the soft tissue of her lungs. Then said what she had to say. *Had* to say.

'But he isn't mine. He never was.'

She looked at Anatole—looked straight at him. Met his hard, masked gaze unflinchingly as she made her damning confession.

'Not a drop of my blood runs in his veins.'

CHAPTER TWELVE

ANATOLE'S FACE WAS stark. Hearing Lyn say what he now knew...

'I know that now,' he said. His voice was strange, but he kept on speaking all the same. 'I know that Lindy wasn't your sister. She wasn't even your half-sister. She was nothing more than your stepsister. Timon showed me what his investigators found. She was the daughter of your mother's second husband, who left her with your mother and you when he abandoned the marriage—*and* his daughter.'

He shook his head as if he were shaking his thoughts into place—a new place they were unaccustomed to.

'When he told me it made such sense. Why Georgy doesn't look like you. Why your name is so similar to Lindy's—no parent would have done that deliberately—and why I sometimes caught that look of fear in your eyes. Like when you didn't want a DNA test done.' He paused. 'Why didn't you tell me, Lyn? You must have known I would find out at some point?'

She gave a laugh. A bitter, biting laugh.

'Because I wanted to be married to you before you did!' she cried. 'I was scheming to get your ring on my finger—the ring you never intended to put there!'

His expression changed. He opened his mouth to speak but she ploughed on. 'Timon told me! He told me that the whole damn thing had been nothing more than a ruse! All that stuff about getting married to strengthen our joint claim to adopt Georgy between us! All that was a fairy tale! You never meant a word of it!'

'*What?*' The word broke from him explosively.

She put her hands to her ears. 'Anatole—don't! Please—don't! Don't lie to me now—we're done with lies! We're done with them!' That brief, bitter laugh came again. It had no humour in it, only an ocean of pain, and she let her hands fall to her sides. 'Timon threw it at me that I deserved everything I was ending up with because I'd lied to you by not telling you that Lindy was only my stepsister. I knew perfectly well that your claim to Georgy would be stronger than mine ever could be! Because you were a blood relative and I wasn't! I was trying to trap you into a marriage you never needed to make!'

She threw her head back.

'When he tried to give me money to leave, told me he knew I only wanted to marry you because you were rich, I was angry! I've never wanted your money—*never*! I only wanted Georgy!'

She took a shuddering breath, shaking her head as if the knowledge of what she had done was too heavy a weight to carry. 'But none of it matters now. It's over. I know that—I've accepted it. I've accepted everything. And I've accepted most of all that I have to do what I am doing now.'

Her eyes went to Georgy again, so absolutely and utterly unaware of the agonising drama above his head.

'I called him mine,' she whispered. The words would hardly come, forced through a throat that was constricted with grief. 'But he never was. He was never mine. Only my stepsister's baby. Your cousin's son. Which is why…'

She lifted her eyes again, made them go to Anatole, who was standing like a statue, frozen. She felt her heart turn over. Turn over uselessly in her heart.

'Which is why,' she said again, and her voice was dead

now, 'I'm leaving him. He isn't a bone to be fought over, or a prize, or a bequest, or anything at all except himself. He needs a home, a family—*his* family. *Your* family. You'll look after him. I know you will. And you love him—I know you love him. And I know that Timon loves him too, in his own way.' She took a heavy razoring breath that cut into her lungs. 'I should have seen that from the start—that I had no claim to him. Not once you had found him. He's yours, Anatole—yours and Timon's. It's taken till now for me to accept that. To accept that I should never have put you through what I have. I see that now.'

She picked up her bag. It seemed as heavy as lead. As heavy as the millstone grinding her heart to chaff.

'I won't say goodbye to Georgy. He's happy with you. That's all that counts.' Her voice was odd, she noticed with a stray, inconsequential part of her brain.

She turned away, pulling open the door. Not looking back.

An iron band closed around her arm, halting her in her tracks. Anatole was there, pulling her back, slamming the door shut, holding her with both hands now, clamped around her upper arms.

'Are you insane?' he said. 'Are you completely insane? You cannot seriously imagine you are just going to walk out like that?'

She strained away from him, but it was like straining against steel bonds. He was too close. Far, far too close. It meant she could see everything about him. The strong wall of his chest, the breadth of his shoulders sheathed in the expensive material of his handmade suit, the line of his jaw, darkening already, see the sculpted mouth that could skim her body and reduce her to soft, helpless cries of passion.

She could see the eyes that burned with dark gold fire.

Catch the scent of his body.

See the black silk of his lashes.

She felt faint with it.

She shut her eyes to block the vision. Stop the memories. The memories that cut her like knives on softest flesh.

'What else is there to do?' she said. Her voice was low and strained. 'You don't want to marry me—you've never wanted to marry me—and Timon doesn't want you to marry me. He made that clear enough! And now you're not marrying me I can do what Timon told me to do—clear off and leave you alone. Leave Georgy alone, too. Because he doesn't need me. He's got you, he's got Timon, he's got everything he needs. The nanny will look after him while you're at work. She's very good, I'm sure. He doesn't need me and he won't remember me—he won't miss me.'

'And Georgy is the only person you're concerned about? Is that it?' There was still something odd about Anatole's voice, but she wouldn't think about that. Wouldn't think about anything. Wouldn't *feel* anything.

Dared not.

She opened her eyes again, made herself look at him. 'No,' she said. She stepped back and this time he let her go. She took another step, increasing the distance between them. The distance was more than physical—far, far more. 'There's you, too,' she said.

She made herself speak. 'I'm sorry I put you through so much anxiety—running away from Greece as I did—but at the time I was still...still in denial. Still thinking I had a right to Georgy. And that made me so...so angry with you.' She picked the word *angry* because it was the only safe one to use. Any of the other words—*anguished, agonised, distraught*—were all impossible to use. Quite impossible! 'Because I trusted you—just like you kept telling me to trust you—when you said you would make it all work out. That if we married we'd have a much better chance of adopting Georgy.'

She took another heaving breath, and now the words broke from her.

'But all along you were just telling me that in order to get me to agree to bring Georgy out to Greece. Because with me as his foster-carer it was the quickest way to get him there—me taking him—rather than going through the courts for permission on your own behalf. You knew I was fearful of bringing Georgy to Greece, so you spun me all that stuff about marrying and then divorcing. And to keep me sweet—'

She heard her voice choke but forced herself to speak, forced herself to say it all to voice every last agony.

'To keep me sweet you…you… Well, you did the obvious thing. And it worked—it worked totally. I actually believed you really were going to marry me—and I desperately wanted that to happen, because marrying you gave *me* my best chance to adopt Georgy!'

The words were pouring from her now, unstoppable.

'It's because I'm not a blood relation that that the authorities have always wanted him to be adopted by someone else! But then there was you—a close relation to his father—and being your wife would have been *my* best chance as well! That's why I did it, Anatole—that's why I agreed to marry you. And I've been well served. I have no claim to him and that's what I've finally accepted. Georgy isn't mine and never was—never will be!'

As her gaze clung to the man standing there—the man she had given herself to, the man who meant so much to her, who had caused her such anguish—she heard her mind whisper the words that burned within her head.

And nor are you mine! You aren't mine and never were—never will be! I'll never see you again after today—never! And my heart is breaking—breaking for Georgy… Breaking for you.

It *was* breaking. She knew it—could feel it—could feel

the fractures tearing it apart, tearing *her* apart as she spoke, as she looked upon him for the very last time in her life… The man she had fallen in love with so incredibly stupidly! So rashly and foolishly! She had fallen in love with him when to him she was only a means to an end—a way to get hold of the child he'd so desperately sought with the least fuss and the most speed!

She took another harrowing breath. 'So I can finally do what I know I have to do—walk away and leave Georgy to you. Because you love him and you will care for him all his life. He won't need me—I can see that clearly now… quite, quite clearly.'

'Can you?' Again he seemed only to echo her words.

She nodded. Her eyes were wide and anguished, but she made herself say the words she had to say. Say them to Anatole. The man who would be Georgy's father—she would never, *never* be his mother!

'Like I said, I accept now that he doesn't need me. He has you, Anatole, and that is enough. You'll be a wonderful father! You love him to pieces, and he adores you. *And* your silk ties,' she added.

But she mustn't attempt humour—not even as a safety valve. Emotion of any kind now was far too dangerous. Being here in this room, with Anatole and Georgy, was far too dangerous. She had to go now, while she still could…

'You can't see straight at *all*! You can't even see what's right in front of you!'

Anatole's harsh voice cut across her. Then it changed.

'But I can understand why.' He took a ragged breath. 'I can understand everything now.'

He reached forward, took her wrist. Drew her away from the door towards the group of chairs. He sat her down in one, and himself in the other. She went without resistance. Her limbs were not her own suddenly.

Georgy, still on the carpet, seeing her close by, started

to crawl towards her, a happy grin on his face. He reached her leg and clung to it with chubby arms. Her face worked.

'Pick him up, Lyn,' said Anatole.

She shook her head.

'I can't,' she said. 'I mustn't—he isn't mine.'

Her throat was aching, as if every tendon was stretched beyond bearing.

Anatole leant down, scooped up Georgy, put him on Lyn's lap.

'Hold him,' he told her.

There was something wrong with his voice again. It was harsh and hoarse.

'Hold him and look at me. Tell me again what you've just said. That you are going to walk out on Georgy. Abandon him.'

A vice closed over her heart, crushing it. 'I'm…I'm not abandoning him. I'm…I'm doing what is right. What has to be done. What I should have done from the moment you first found him. He isn't mine. He never was mine….'

Her throat closed again but she made herself go on, made herself lift her stricken gaze to the dark eyes that were boring into her like drills…

'I should have given him to you straight away—when you first came to me! Then you would never have had to go through that charade, that farce—the one your grandfather called time on. The one…' She swallowed. 'The one that you were just about to end yourself away.' She looked at him, her gaze heavy as lead. 'I got a phone call from the town hall after Timon had spoken to me—a phone call confirming that the wedding had been cancelled. And then…' She swallowed again. 'Then I got your text, telling me the same thing.'

'In that text I told you I would *explain everything* when I spoke to you later!'

Anatole's voice seared her.

'Timon had already made everything clear to me—and when I tried not to believe him he set me straight too. He showed me the document you'd signed—the one giving you the chairmanship of the Petranakos Corporation, the one affirming that you would not be marrying me. So what would have been the point, Anatole, in you telling me that yourself when I had it in writing already?'

Greek words spat from him.

Lyn's gaze slid away, down to the baby sitting on her lap, placidly chewing on Anatole's tie, content just to be on her knees. She wanted to put her arms around him but she must not. Not any more.

Anatole was speaking again and she made herself listen—though what could he say that she could want to hear?

'The *point*, Lyn,' he bit out, and each word was cut like a diamond from the air, 'was that *I* would have told you the truth!'

'I knew the truth,' she answered. 'Timon told me.'

'Timon,' said Anatole carefully—very carefully, 'lied.'

Lyn's eyes went to his. There was still that dull blankness in them. Why was he saying this? What for?

'I saw the document you signed,' she said. 'I saw it in the English translation and I saw the original—the one in Greek with your signature on it. I translated it myself. It said what Timon told me it said. You are the new chairman and you won't be marrying me.'

'And did it tell you *why*?'

There was still that strangeness in his voice. She heard it, but knew she must not...

'Timon told me why. Because you never intended to marry me. It was all a ruse, to get me to agree to bring Georgy out to Greece.'

'Well,' he said, speaking in the same clear, careful voice, as if she were hard of learning, 'in that case why didn't I just put you on the first flight back to London once Georgy was in Athens?'

She gave a shrug. 'I don't know. It doesn't matter.'

It didn't matter. Not now. Not now that everything she had hoped and dreamed was smashed to pieces. Not now when her heart was breaking—breaking twice over. For Georgy and for Anatole.

Georgy was looking up at her and absently she stroked his hair. It felt like silk beneath her fingers.

I'll never hold him again on my lap. Never hug him or kiss him. Never see him grow up...

Her eyes went to Anatole, standing there—so very dear to her, so very precious.

And she had never mattered to him at all...

Pain curdled around her heart. She wished he would stop talking to her, stop asking her things—things that did not matter that could not matter ever again. But he was talking again. Still talking at her—like some nightmare *post mortem*...

'Yes, Lyn—it *does* matter. Why would I want you to stay on in Greece, live with me in the beach house, sleep with me, if I'd already got what I wanted from you?'

Her brow furrowed. He was going on at her and there wasn't any point—*there wasn't any point!*

'Well, maybe it was because I might still have come in useful for some reason or other! You might have found it helpful to have me on side when you applied to adopt Georgy. I'd be kept sweet and not contest you.' Her voice changed. 'Only that wouldn't have been necessary, would it? Once you knew I was only Lindy's stepsister, it meant I wouldn't stand a chance of fighting you for Georgy. Then you could have—*would* have—done exactly what your grandfather did. Sent me packing!'

He looked at her. 'Do you know why he sent you packing, Lyn?'

It was clear to him now—crystal clear. But she couldn't see it yet. He had to show it to her.

She shook her head dully. Anatole's eyes—his dark sloe eyes that could melt her with a single glance—rested on her.

'He was frightened, Lyn. Once he knew that Lindy was only your stepsister he was frightened that you were using me—using me to strengthen your own claim to Georgy. By marrying me you'd become his adoptive mother if our claim went through, whether you were his aunt or only his step-aunt. It would have been too late then. He was scared, Lyn—scared you'd take Georgy back to England, divorce me there, go for custody. Hold Georgy to ransom.' He paused. 'It was fear, Lyn, that made him say what he said to you.'

She shut her eyes. Why was he saying these things? It was a torment to her! 'And did he fake your signature on that document?' she demanded, her eyes flying open again. '*Did* he?'

Anatole shook his head. 'No—I signed it.' He paused. 'I had to. He gave me no choice.' His voice was steady. Controlled. *Very* controlled. 'I need you to listen to me, Lyn. I need you to hear what I am telling you. I would have told you in Greece, had you not run away.'

He took a heavy breath, keeping his relentless gaze on her. She was as white as a sheet, as tense as stretched wire.

'I signed that document,' he said, 'because Timon was refusing to hand over the chairmanship unless I did. And you know what the situation was in Thessaloniki. But I did not want to sign it.' He took another breath. 'I understand now, as I did not then, that the reason he insisted on my signing it was because he already knew about you and Lindy! He already had that report from his investigators—an investigation I knew nothing about. That is what scared him—and that is why he used the only leverage he had: threatening not to give me the power I needed so urgently, that very day, so that I could end that disastrous strike, unless I undertook not to marry you. I only found out about you being Lindy's stepsister when I rushed back to him from Thessaloniki—*after* you'd fled with Georgy! He told me then—told me and denounced you for taking the cheque he offered you. And *that* is why I've doubted you—*that* is why I was angry when I came here!'

'You had a right to be angry, Anatole—knowing I'd hidden from you how weak my claim to Georgy was compared to yours.' Her voice was the same—dull, self-accusing.

He stared at her. 'You think I am angry at you for *that*?'

'Just as I was angry,' she countered. 'Angry that you said we would marry but you never meant it. That document was proof of that!'

His expression changed. 'I would *never*,' he bit out, his eyes flashing darkly, 'have signed such a document of my own free will! But,' he said, 'I signed it in the end because I didn't think it mattered. Not in the long term. I didn't have time to argue with my grandfather. I didn't have time to debate the issue—question why he was insisting on that condition. I had to focus on what was going on in Thessaloniki! Afterwards I would sort it out! I'd have had to postpone the wedding anyway—because of the strike threatening—and if you'd given me a chance, Lyn, when I got back I would have explained what my grandfather had made me do, why I agreed to it! I would have explained *everything* to you.' He took a razoring breath. 'If you'd trusted me enough not to run away back to England…' His face worked. 'If you'd only trusted me, Lyn.'

'Trust me—I need you to trust me…'

The words he had said so often to her. And he was saying them again!

Emotion speared within her—emotion she could not name. Dared not name.

'Trusted me as I need you to trust me now.'

His voice came through the teeming confusion in her head.

'As I trust *you*, Lyn—as I trust you.'

He stepped towards her and she could only gaze at him—gaze into his face, his eyes, which seemed to be pouring into hers.

He levered himself down beside her, hunkering on his haunches. 'You have proved to me that I can have trust in you now, in the most absolute way possible! There is no greater proof possible! *None!*'

He reached a hand forward. But not to her. To Georgy, who was contentedly sucking at his fingers now, clearly getting sleepy. Anatole stroked his head and cupped his cheek, smoothed his hand down his back. His face softened. Then his gaze went back to Lyn. Clear and unflinching.

'I trust you, Lyn—absolutely and unconditionally. I trust you to do the one thing that shines from you, that has shone from you like a beacon of purest light from the very first!' His expression changed. 'Your love for Georgy, Lyn. *That* is what I trust—and it is why I trust you. Why I will *always* trust you!'

There was a wealth of emotion in his voice, pouring from his eyes, from his whole being. She felt herself sway with the force of it.

'What does it matter, Lyn, whether Lindy was your sister—?' he began.

But she cut across him, her voice a cry. Anguished and trembling with emotion. 'She *was*! She *was* my sister! My sister in *everything*! I loved her as just as much! And when she died a piece of me died as well. But she gave me—' her voice broke '—she gave me her son, for me to look after, to love the way I'd loved her. And that's why... that's why...' She couldn't go on. But she had to—she *had* to. 'That's why I have to give him to you now, Anatole—because it's for *him*.'

Now it was Anatole who cut across her. 'And *that* is why I know how much you love him! *Because* you are willing to give him up!' His voice changed, grew husky. 'And there is only one kind of love that does that, Lyn—only one kind.' He looked at her. 'A mother's love.' He took a shaking breath and swallowed. '*You* are Georgy's mother! *You!* And it doesn't matter a single iota whether your blood runs in his veins! Your sister knew that—knew that when she entrusted Georgy to you! She knew you loved her and she knew you would love Georgy all his life, Lyn—*all his life!* With the love he needs to have—a mother's love… *your* love!'

He reached forward again, and now he was taking her hands with his, so warm and so strong, and he was placing her hands around Georgy's sturdy little body, pressing them around him, his own covering hers.

'And I love him too, Lyn,' he said. 'I love him with the love that Marcos was not able to love him with. I will always love him—all his life.' He paused and took another ragged breath. 'Just as I love you, Lyn.'

There was a sudden stillness. An absolute stillness. An immobility of all the world. All the universe.

She could not move. Could not move a muscle.

But she could feel Anatole lifting her hands—lifting them away from Georgy, who slumped his slumberous body back against her, his eyelids closing. Anatole lifted her hands to his lips, kissing first one and then the other. The softest, sweetest kisses…

'How could you think I didn't?' he whispered. His voice was cracking—cracking and husky. 'How could you possibly think I didn't love you? How did you think I could hold you in my arms night after night, be with you, at your side day after day, and not come to love you as I do?'

Her eyes clung to his. Was this true? Oh, was this true? These words he was telling her? Those sweet kisses he had blessed her hands with? Was it true? Her heart swelled with hope—with yearning that it might be so—that she was really hearing him say those wonderful words she had so longed to hear and had thought could never be said by him.

But she *was* hearing them—hearing him say them— and feeling the blissful brush of his lips on hers, the glowing warmth of his gaze, his fingers winding into hers…

He was speaking still, saying what was bliss for her to hear. 'And I know—I *know*—you love me too! I can see it now—in your face, your eyes, your tears, Lyn, which are pouring down your face. You love Georgy and you love me—and I love Georgy and I love you. And that's all we need, my darling, darling Lyn—all that we will ever need!'

He reached with his mouth for hers and found it, kissed it, tasting the salt of her tears.

'All we'll ever need,' he said again, drawing away. He looked at her. 'You must never, never doubt me again. *Never!* To think that you thought so ill of me that you fled back here—that you felt you had to give up Georgy to me. To think that is like a sword in my side!' He kissed her again—fiercely, possessively. 'We are *family*, Lyn! Family. You and me and Georgy—and we always will be! *Always!*'

She swallowed, fighting back the longing to believe everything he was telling her. 'Our plan was to marry and then divorce,' she said. Her voice sounded wonky to her, the words coming out weirdly. It must be because there wasn't any room for them, she thought. There was only room for the tidal wave of emotion coursing through her— filling her being.

'That,' he answered her roundly, 'was the stupidest plan in the universe! What we are going to do is just marry. And stay married! For *ever*!'

'That document you signed…'

'Timon will tear it up—or I will do it for him!' He gave a ragged laugh. 'Timon will only have to take one look at us to know his fears are groundless—pointless.' His expression changed, and so did his voice, becoming sombre, worried. 'Can you forgive him, Lyn? For lying to you and saying that I never intended to marry you so that he could drive you away? It was fear that made him do what he did. I can see that now. The fear of losing Georgy.'

Her eyes shadowed. She knew what fear was. Knew it in her bones—knew the fear of losing Georgy…knew just what that fear could make one do…

She took a breath, looked at Anatole straight. 'I lied to you because I was so frightened I might lose Georgy,' she said, swallowing. 'I understand why Timon lied to me for the same reason.'

His hands tightened on hers. 'Thank you,' he said. His eyes were expressive. 'And I can tell you with absolute certainty that when he knows that we are to be a real family now he will be overjoyed!'

A little choke escaped her. 'Oh, God, Anatole—is it true? Is *any* of this true? I walked in here and my heart was breaking—breaking in two. Breaking at giving up Georgy, breaking because I love you so much and I thought you'd only used me and thrown me away! I can't believe this now—I can't believe this happiness I'm feeling! I can't *believe* it!'

Did she dare? Did she *dare* believe what Anatole was saying to her? Did she dare believe in the love pouring from his eyes…?

Believe in the love pouring from her heart…

There was only one answer he could give her. Only one answer, and she heard him say the words she had heard him speak so often.

'Lyn, I need you to trust me on this!' He took a ragged

breath. 'I need you to trust that I will love you for the rest of my days! Just—I *beg* you!—trust me!'

As he spoke, with his love for her pouring from his eyes, she felt the dam of her fears break—and all those hideous, nightmare fears that had convulsed and crucified her flowed away, emptying out of her, never to return.

And in their place blossomed the sweet and glorious flower of her love for Anatole—love given and received, each to the other.

Anatole! *Her* Anatole. And she was his—*his*! And she always would be. She would trust him now—for ever, in everything!

He kissed her again, sealing that love in tenderness and passion, with Georgy cradled in her lap, their arms around him. It was an endless kiss…interrupted by the sound of someone clearing his throat from the doorway. She and Anatole sprang apart.

'Oh,' said a surprised voice. 'Ah…' It fell silent.

Lyn bit her lip, looking down at Georgy, unable to look anywhere else. But Anatole got to his feet, slipping Lyn's hand from his but standing beside her, his hand resting on her shoulder warmly. Possessively.

The room was bathed in sunlight—which was odd. Because outside he could see that it was mizzling with the doleful rain of an English summer. Yet the air inside the room seemed golden with the sun…as golden as the happiness flooding through him.

He looked across at his lawyer. 'I think,' he said, 'we've just reached an out of court settlement.' His voice was very dry.

His lawyer's was even dryer. 'Well, I'll just leave you, then, to…ah…hammer out the details, shall I?'

'That,' said Anatole, and his hand pressed down on Lyn's shoulder, 'might take some time.'

He glanced at Lyn and his gaze was as warm as the love he felt for her. Her answering gaze was just as warm.

'It might take a lifetime,' he said.

EPILOGUE

LYN SETTLED BACK into the padded beach chair beneath a striped parasol. Beside her Timon, resplendent in a very grand wheelchair, sat smiling benevolently. A little way in front of both of them, on the beach in front of Timon's villa, was Anatole, in shorts and T-shirt in the late summer heat, sprawled on the sand with Georgy, showing him how to use a bucket and spade. Georgy, recklessly waving his own plastic spade in a manner likely to engage hard with Anatole's tousled head, was happily thumping at his upturned plastic bucket with enthusiastic dedication and muscular vigour.

'I thought you were supposed to be building a sand-castle,' Lyn called out, laughing.

It was good to see Anatole relaxing, having more time to do so. His dedicated attentions to the Petranokos empire had been successful, and it was on a much surer footing now, with all the employees' jobs secure, which allowed him to ease back significantly on his work schedule. Giving him far more time with his family.

With his adored Georgy.

And his adored bride.

They had married as soon as they had returned to Greece. Timon, enthroned in his wheelchair, had proved a benign and approving host for a wedding followed by a luxurious and leisurely honeymoon—with Georgy!—on a tour of the Aegean in the Petranakos yacht.

The honeymoon had been followed by a journey back to England to take possession of the seaside house in Sussex that Anatole had bought for Lyn. It would be their UK base for future visits and holidays. And they had attended, hand in in hand, their closeness and unity and their devotion to Georgy visible to the family court judge, the hearing of their application to adopt the baby they both loved as much as they loved each other. Their application had been approved, and now Georgy was theirs for ever.

Every day Lyn spent a considerable amount of time with Georgy and his great-grandfather—a lot of it here, on the beach that Georgy loved, with Timon's wheelchair shaded by an awning.

'We'll start on the sandcastle any minute now,' Anatole riposted. 'Once Georgy's got bored with hitting things!'

A low rumble of laughter came from Timon. Lyn glanced at him. He was looking healthy, considering… He was still doing well on the drugs, and it was buying him some time. The precious time he so desperately wanted.

As if he could sense her looking at him, Timon reached to take Lyn's hand and pat it affectionately with his own gnarled one. He turned his head to smile at her.

Though she had had some trepidation, they had made their peace.

'I wronged you,' he had told her. 'And from the bottom of my heart I apologise to you. It was fear that made me harsh—fear that you would take Marcos's son from us. But I know now that you would never do such a thing. For you love him as much as we do.' His voice had softened. 'And you love my grandson too. You will both, I know, be the parents that Marcos and your sister could not be. I know now,' he'd said, 'that Marcos's son is safe with you and always will be.'

It had been all she'd needed to hear. Just as now all she needed in the world was to be here, with her husband and their son, a family united in love. Tragedy had reached its dark shadows across them all, but now sunlight was strong and bright and warm in their lives.

Timon turned back to look at his grandson and Georgy. 'The years pass so swiftly,' he said. 'How short a time it seems since it was Anatole and Marcos playing on the beach. But I am blessed—so very blessed—to have been granted this, now.'

She squeezed his hand comfortingly. 'We are all blessed,' she said.

Unconsciously she slid a hand across her still-flat stomach. Timon caught the gesture. They had told him as soon as they had known themselves of Lyn's pregnancy. Timon needed all the reasons they could find to keep on fighting for his life. Another great-grandchild could only help that.

'A brother for Georgy,' he said approvingly.

'It might be a sister,' Lyn pointed out.

Timon shook his head decisively. 'He needs a younger brother,' he said. 'Someone he can look out for, just as Anatole looked out for Marcos. Someone to encourage him to be sensible and wise.'

She smiled peaceably—she was not about to argue. Whether girl or boy, the new baby would be adored, just as Georgy was, and that was all that mattered.

As if sensing he was being discussed, and in complimentary terms, Georgy ceased his thumping and grinned at all of them.

'Right, then, Georgy,' said Anatole briskly, '*this* is how we build a sandcastle.'

Georgy turned his eyes to his new father, gazed at him with grave attention and considerable respect—then hit him smartly on the head with his plastic spade, chortling gleefully as he did so.

'Oh, Georgy!' exclaimed Lyn ruefully. 'You little monster!'

* * * * *